THE YOUTH OF OUR TIME

E.J. BURGESS

THE YOUTH OF OUR TIME

First Edition Published 2022 by
Midas Tomes | Great Britain

This is a work of fiction. Names, characters, places, and incidents either are the product of the author's imagination or are used fictitiously. Any resemblance to actual persons, living or dead, businesses, events, or locales is entirely coincidental.

Although every precaution has been taken in the preparation of this book, the publisher and author assume no responsibility for errors or omissions.

The Youth of Our Time text copyright © E.J. Burgess 2022

The right of E.J. Burgess to be identified as the author of this work has been asserted by her in accordance with the Copyright, Designs and Patents Act 1988.

All rights reserved. No part of this publication may be reproduced, stored in a retrieval system, or transmitted in any form, whether through electronic, photocopying, recording or otherwise without prior written permission from the publisher.

01

Cover Design by Andrew Urquhart © Midas Tomes 2022
Cover illustration © Canva

Edited by Benjamin Humphreys

ISBN 978-1-7397058-0-0 (Paperback)
ISBN 978-1-7397058-1-7 (Ebook)

www.MidasTomes.com

In dedication to those who encouraged me when
I struggled to encourage myself.

1941

THE LIGHTNING WAR

THE SIRENS WAILED, haunting and hideous, alerting the people to seek refuge anywhere they could. Families crammed into Anderson Shelters with fearful embraces while others fled to the Underground in hopes of finding an empty comfort. The streets were left abandoned, vulnerable to the formations of bombers that hid above the clouds.

Bombs hurtled through the night sky with unrelenting ferocity. The distant combustions could be heard from within the Underground. Children were rocked to sleep in makeshift hammocks hung across the tracks. Games and singing eased some people, but they could not ignore the commotion above and the sirens that screeched amongst the carnage.

A boy grasped a picture of his father who was clad in a khaki green uniform. He was approaching his mid-teenage years, and his innocence was to be taken by the conscription biting at his heels. His watery gaze lifted from the photograph, yet he held it tightly, keeping it close to his chest. Meeting the eyes of a young girl, he found comfort in her glance. With an empathetic smile, she lifted a locket from around her neck and opened it with shaking hands; trying to provide consolation while she, herself, felt none. A picture of her brother was held safely inside. The boy looked to it, that little reassurance that he was not alone. There was a longing to remain within the Underground, to not have to face the outside world, but the Blitz could not be ignored.

Leaving the safety of Mile End Tube Station, the girl's eyes met the morning sky with a squint. Mangled metal structures were ablaze, broken glass lining the pavements. Smoke followed the city streets, navigating its way into the sky in a swirling grey mass. Buildings had fallen to the ground in a circulated fashion as London staggered to its feet once again.

It was a sight of destruction and abandonment like the forgotten battlefields of the Great War before, yet this was not the war prior, but the war of the present. With every blackout came a body divulged and wounded. The bombardment had created damaged pathways, cracking and crumbling their way into the depths of the city's anatomy. Emergency vehicles pursued the concrete until a build-up of debris blocked the way like a clot in an artery, killing off the possibility of continuing deeper into the heart of the city.

CHAPTER 1

THERE WAS A peaceful persuasion to this particular Sunday morning. The final frost melted amidst the repetitive roof tiles as blue tits fluttered in and out of the rows of red brick chimneys, singing a joyful tune. Sitting on a half-broken branch, one of the little creatures looked through the window of a not so peaceful East London home. It was occupied by three completely different women despite their blood relation.

'Fran, please help your grandmother to church, you don't want to be late,' Stephanie fretted, looking at her thin wristwatch. She had a floral pinnie tightly fastened around her waist. Gripping a wooden spoon in one hand, and a mixing bowl in the other, she tended to a thick batter.

Francesca bundled down the stairs. She hurried to plait her brown hair to one side as she met her mother's troubled eyesight. The strands fought against her, tangling around her fingers causing her to wince, her face contorting as she attempted to speak. 'You've got till this afternoon to get the scones ready, there's plenty of time.'

'Oh, pop to the shops after, will you? We've run out of tea,' her mother spoke with strained enthusiasm as her flour-covered hands met her daughter's cheeks, planting a kiss on her forehead. Francesca could feel the stress radiating from her. She peered at Vera who was sitting on the end of their vibrantly printed sofa.

'Your mother is going senile,' Vera said bluntly.

With a sigh, Francesca helped her to the door. 'This afternoon is a big deal for mum, the Priest is coming for tea and a chat.'

'Yet she won't step into a church,' Vera muttered as she gripped her granddaughter's slim arm, allowing her to guide the way out onto Coborn Road.

The long, looming narrow road was met by the rays of springtime sunshine that flashed and filtered in and out the tightly compacted semi-detached houses. The rows of red brick buildings stood to attention as they trailed the familiar territory at a slow and steady pace.

'Good morning, Mrs Peters,' a boy called out. He was lobbing a newspaper onto every doorstep with a large stack attached to the front of his bicycle.

'And to you,' Vera replied. 'Are you ready for your interview, Fran?' she asked, looking up to her granddaughter who was considerably taller.

Distracted by the blue tits above that were singing a beautiful duet, Francesca was suddenly pulled back down to earth. 'As ready as I'll ever be,' she said nervously. 'Mum's trying to set me up with the Priest's son,' she added quickly, trying to change the subject as even talking about the interview made her stomach turn.

Lifting an eyebrow Vera mumbled, 'The last thing you want

is a pencil pusher parish Priest's son. Trust your mother to pick someone so boring, she doesn't make the effort to attend a service but will play matchmaker with the congregation like some Cockney Cupid.'

'Grandma!' Francesca exclaimed, embarrassed by her relative's bluntness on the matter. She was not necessarily opposed to the idea, the Priest's son seemed nice enough considering their minimal interactions at church.

'Oh, I'm sure he's lovely, dear, but you need to explore your options,' Vera clarified.

'Options huh, any suggestions?' She chuckled.

'I heard the Italians are quite a catch, impressive in certain areas if you know what I mean. Judy down the road has met a man from Naples, says he's—'

'Too much information!' Francesca squirmed at the idea of Judy, resident of house number 27, and her Italian companion.

As they turned left down Morgan Street, they passed the same repetitive funnel of houses that seemed to continue down every road within the district. For a native, it was easy to navigate, but for a newcomer, the prospect of remembering the correct route was an intimidating task. There were, however, a few saving graces in the memorable buildings that could guide a weary traveller. These normally came in the form of a stagnant pub like the Morgan Arms or one of the many prominent chimneys that had polluted the skyline since the Victorians and their obsessive industrialisation. Then there were the defaced buildings that stood bleak and broken. The ruins, although dangerous, were a makeshift playground for the young daredevils of the area who would test their climbing skills on the blocks of charred concrete. Watching the children dressed in their Sunday best, Francesca recognised their mischievous grins, and obvious desire to return to their dusty utopia.

'I wanna go play,' a little girl cried. She was being pulled along the pavement by her mother.

'Later, I will not have you lookin' a mess at church,' she scolded.

Francesca tried her hardest not to laugh as the little girl began to screech like a Banshee.

Passing a pleasant set of boarding houses with enormous bay windows lined with white netting, a cardboard sign sat visibly behind the glass with large black lettering. It read *No Irish, No Blacks, No Dogs.* This seemed rather preposterous in the eyes of Francesca and her irritated grandmother who scowled at the sign.

'I'd rip that down myself if I got the chance,' Vera grumbled.

'I think many people would.' Francesca frowned.

'Signs like that give this place a bad name, there is no difference between any of us. That man has no right to deny housing, and especially to those who fought alongside this bloody country,' her grandmother lectured whilst thinking of a few choice words she'd like to use if she ever bumped into the landlord.

'Some people are ignorant.'

'Ignorance can be dangerous, Fran,' she sighed.

Reaching an open patch of green, the sun seeped onto them. No longer confined to the red brick passageways, they met the church gardens as a welcome refuge. The large white building sat prominently with its recognisable spire rising high into the air. Flowerpots sat stiffly around the church walls as the blades of grass defrosted, bathing in the sudden sunlight. The flowerpots comprised of clusters of newly flourishing white, pink, and red geraniums whose odour tickled Francesca's nostrils and induced a repetition of sneezes. Wiping her nose with the back of her hand, Francesca recognised the Priest's son out of the corner of her eye. As she removed her hand, a thin trail of snot trickled down to her upper lip, her cheeks turning pink from embarrassment. Vera swiftly passed her a handkerchief, but the damage was done, and he watched her with amusement.

Greeting the Priest with a somewhat fearful smile, Francesca guided her relative down the aisle to a precise position; the second pew back, three spaces from the left. This allowed her grandmother to be close enough to hear the sermon yet sheltered enough for her to hide behind her hymn book upon forgetting the verses—as she always did.

As the service began, Francesca concentrated on the stained-glass. The bright panels presented different images, one depicted Saint George on a white horse. He appeared as though he was watching her, judging her every movement just as the Priest did from the main altar. Catching sight of her best friend, Elaine, they exchanged a variety of facial expressions. They were complete opposites, and Elaine sat with her hair in bouncy dark blonde curls.

Turning back to the service they were met with the stern-looking Priest who had acknowledged their attempted interaction but continued reading despite his annoyance. He directed everyone to the relevant page as *abide with me* jolted out of the organ.

Judy, yes Judy resident of house number 27, played as the Priest studied his congregation. Awkwardly lip-syncing, Francesca caught his eye once again sending her to duck behind her hymn book. She couldn't help but wonder why the Church of England had such a monstrous number of hymns embedded within every service. This brought her to question God's desire to hear a load of shrieking Cockneys first thing on a Sunday morning. She imagined he'd much rather listen to the blue tits outside. At least they could sing in tune.

Vera sang with such grace, the same could not be said for her granddaughter who painfully waded through verse after verse. At the end of the service, a collection basket was passed around. Vera placed a generous number of shillings in it as she shifted from the pew. Greeting Judy, they nattered as Francesca and Elaine tried to make a run for it out the back of the church.

'Was there something distracting you today?' the Priest asked sharply as he appeared at their side, manifesting as though he was an apparition which gave both girls a fright. He wore long black robes that hovered just above the ground, a white collar sitting tightly around his neck. He stood in the doorway, not letting the two escape so easily.

'No, nothing,' Francesca said awkwardly, looking to Elaine for assistance.

'Fran has an interview on Wednesday for a secretary position and she's been thinking about that a lot lately—'

'Please be quiet.' Francesca cut her off.

'What, you do!' Elaine said as they began to bicker like squabbling siblings.

'Good luck, Francesca,' he uttered, moving from the doorway.

With a grateful glance they hurried past, but they both knew he was far from pleased.

Francesca looked at her friend in reminiscence. Elaine Anderson had lived in Mile End her entire life, just as she had. Living a short distance apart meant they were rarely separated, like sisters almost. That short distance meaning opposite the road from one another, allowing them to get up to all sorts of mischief.

'Come on Fran, it'll be fun,' Elaine encouraged as they bundled down the street, taking in the smell of freshly baked goods that created a delightfully distracting aroma.

Rushing down the road at a rate of knots with tea in hand, Francesca met the doorstep with a halt. She panted and held the side of her abdomen, hoping to relieve the pain of her acquired stitch. Taking a deep breath, she stepped inside and confronted her mother's fluster.

'Just in time, make some tea will you, he'll be here any minute.' She whizzed past her daughter, nearly knocking her off her feet.

'Mum, please calm down, you're going to give yourself a heart attack,' Francesca pleaded as she poured the boiling water into a teapot.

'Oh, don't be dramatic dear, your mother is simply having a midlife crisis.' Vera observed as a knock sent everyone's attention to the door.

'The tea!' her mother demanded, flinging her pinnie over the wooden banister.

As the Priest entered, he caught sight of Francesca scoffing a piece of shortbread. She had nicked it from a ceramic bulldog shaped biscuit jar that she and Elaine referred to as Winston. With a smile, he sat down and was fussed over by her mother.

'Scone?' she asked as she thrust the plate into his face, barely giving him the room to breathe. Graciously he accepted as Francesca waddled in, tray in hand, attempting not to drop the teapot, cups and saucers. Laying them down she poured the tea, scolding her hand in the process making her jolt backwards.

'Jesus bloody Christ,' she blurted out, cheeks reddening with every word until she held herself to silence. Flustered with embarrassment, she hurried into the kitchen to run her hand under the cold tap. This was only to turn back to see Vera's amusement and her mother's annoyance.

'I apologise for my daughter's blasphemy,' she said, her fixed glare aimed in her direction.

'No apology necessary, you should hear the things the kids say where I'm from.' He grinned, bringing the cup to his lips.

'I'll be in my room if you need me.' Francesca darted up the stairs.

The Priest turned his attention to Vera who was sitting firmly in her armchair. 'Did you enjoy this morning's service?'

'It was a bit bland,' she answered. Meeting her daughter's irritated glance, she quickly clarified, 'The communion bread I mean.'

'I'll see what I can do about that.' He smiled, taking another sip from the teacup.

There was an uncomfortable silence that filled the room. Stephanie sat on the edge of her seat in a rigid posture, clearly unnerved. In contrast, Vera was perfectly relaxed and twisted her teaspoon gently around her china cup.

'So, Stephanie, I hear Francesca has got an interview on Wednesday?' the Priest asked, attempting to make conversation.

'Yes, for a secretary position, it should go well,' she answered, nervously taking a bite from a scone.

'She's ever such a smart girl,' Vera quickly contributed.

'Intelligence is worth more than anything nowadays,' he preached.

'Was Belfast heavily bombed during the war?' Stephanie asked suddenly, catching him off guard.

'Unfortunately, yes, but we moved to the west midlands for a while, to avoid the bombings,' he replied, slightly saddened. 'But there are better opportunities for Colin in London, hence the permanent move here after the war was done and dusted,' he continued.

'Was that the only reason?' Vera asked.

'One of the reasons,' the Priest replied cagily.

'What of his mother, you don't wear a wedding ring?'

'Passed away and is now watching over us, I admit I was never married to Colin's mother.'

'It's unusual for a Priest to have a child out of wedlock,' Vera stated.

'No more unusual than any other human being,' he said, putting his cup and saucer back in the tray.

'That you are right,' Vera said in sudden agreement, her nosy intentions satisfied for the moment. She pulled herself from the chair with a struggle. Making her way to the stairs, she called to her granddaughter for assistance. 'Last of the cold weather has got my joints playing up left, right and centre,' she sighed.

Looking out the window as the sunlight flickered in and out of cloud cover, Stephanie tried to distract herself. The Priest watched her, aware of how painful the pending conversation would be.

'So, Stephanie, how have you been coping with the loss of your husband and son?' he asked, straight to the point now that they were finally alone.

Her heart dropped at the question. 'I'm getting there.'

'No, you're not. Truth is a wonderful thing, speak it, God is listening, as am I,' the Priest encouraged.

With a pause, she readjusted her gaze, staring firmly at the ground. 'My son's death hurts the most, my husband's not so much, sickness is natural, and he'd been ill for a while. But my son, there was nothing natural about his passing, he shouldn't have been taken so cruelly.'

'Is that why you won't come to church anymore because you're angry at God for taking your son?'

'I-I don't know. I think I've lost faith,' she admitted. Her eyes grew watery, her vision blurring.

'Have you prayed?'

Shaking her head, her stare became immovable.

'Then that's the first step to regaining your faith,' the Priest said.

Shutting her eyes, she spoke quietly, attempting to hold her voice from shaking, 'You know, every night during the war I'd pray for him to come home, even when I could hear the bombs in the distance. They'd get closer and closer with every word. I could tell his time was running out. And by the end of it, I didn't even get his body back.'

The Priest placed a hand on her shoulder. 'He died valiantly and is now at peace.'

'How do you know that?'

'Because I have faith,' the Priest answered simply.

'It shouldn't have happened, he was too young.'

Removing his grip from her shoulder, he placed his hand on hers. 'The Lord has plans for all of us, and there is nothing we can do to stop it.'

'I just don't think I'm ready to accept that,' she whispered as tears rolled down her cheeks.

'God is with you always, as he is with your son and husband. Know they both look upon you, all you must do is look to them. Then, in time, you will regain your faith.' The Priest stood, releasing her hand as she wiped away the tears.

Sitting at the end of her friend's lilac coated bed, Francesca fiddled with the gold chain that sat around her neck, manipulating it between her fingers. Opening the oval locket, she looked to the image within and met the glance of her brother. That glance she remembered at the start of the war was far different from his military portrait that was framed within the intricate locket. He looked stern and patriotic with his head held high, but she knew that there was fear behind his gaze. She remembered when he would play with her in the garden or take her down to Victoria Park to pet the reindeers at Christmas. Those little things that she could remember him by. She certainly didn't want to remember the war or the way he met his end.

Elaine wandered into the room with two glasses of Robinsons Lemon Squash and a couple of Dairy Milk Bars nestled in her pocket. Passing one of each to her friend, she propped herself up with a cushion at the head of her bed. Francesca attempted to unwrap the chocolate, her fingers fiddling to undo the shiny purple packaging. Upon opening the bar with delayed success, she took a bite.

'What do you even do at a dance hall?' she asked with her mouth half-full.

'Dancing.' Elaine smirked as she opened her Dairy Milk Bar with ease.

Francesca's cheeks reddened. 'No, I know that, I mean, what's it like?'

Biting into the sickly chocolate, Elaine enlightened her friend. 'So, it's kinda like a jubilee, but just for young people. You get together, enjoy the music, and throw everything our parents have ever taught us out the window.'

'What do you mean by that?' she asked, taking a gulp from her glass.

'Well, let's put it this way, your mum wouldn't approve of the people there,' Elaine said as she licked her fingers, making sure she was getting her money's worth.

'Why? Are they rough?'

'A little rough around the edges I suppose, but they're just different really, like nothing you've ever seen. Some of them dress strange, and some of the girls wear manly-lookin' clothes,' Elaine informed Francesca who sat with an uneasy expression.

'How odd... What else?'

'Oh, the dancing, wait until you see how they dance.' She shuffled off the bed and attempted to mimic the swinging movements she had witnessed.

Francesca cringed at the thought of it. 'I can't dance, Elaine, I have trouble with movement in general.'

'Well, if that's the case, then maybe you need to see a doctor.' Elaine grinned.

'It's not funny, I just have two left feet,' she said as she pulled at her cardigan, hoping the fabric would swallow her up.

'Two left hands as well, considering that burn. We might have to remove that, it's not a good look,' Elaine added, recognising the makeshift bandage around Francesca's right hand that consisted of a piece of kitchen towel fastened with leftover gauze found in her mother's first aid box. 'More importantly, let's see if we can find shoes for those two left feet.' She leapt to her wardrobe, pulling out a pair; luckily, she and Francesca were the same size. Enthusiastically, she threw the black heels onto the bed whilst eyeing her up. This resulted in her picking out a navy-blue check circle skirt. Calculating the possible combinations, Elaine eliminated a series of tops by flinging them back into the wardrobe. This left one in her hand which had a low-cut neckline. Francesca grumbled at the decision, thinking of how ridiculous it would look on her.

'That'll do you.' She examined the chosen garments, pleased with her decision even though Francesca's face proved otherwise.

'I don't really feel up to this tonight,' she said, reluctantly pulling on the outfit.

Elaine sat at her vanity and allowed her dark blonde ringlets to be pulled and yanked at the end of a hairbrush. Pushing the strands into position with a few clips, Francesca assisted her by sliding a few in at the back; causing a half up, half down effect.

She reassured her friend's reflection. 'You're just nervous, come on, live a little, it's 1955 for goodness' sake, there is no better time to be young. It's not like we have to fight a bloody war.'

Francesca admired her carefree attitude, yet she remained unconvinced.

'Your brother would want you to enjoy yourself for a change. If you don't like it, then you don't have to go again.' She pulled Francesca onto the vanity stool beside her, proceeding to undo her long plait.

As they entered the dance hall, Elaine immediately blended in, leaving Francesca to face the commotion alone. Every Tuesday evening the local dance hall would open its doors. Francesca had never bothered to step inside. She met eyes with bodies tumbling and turning to every beat, twisting and sliding to every rhythm. The room had a faint aroma of sweat and the air was intoxicated with the smell of alcohol and cigarette smoke. The smoke curved around everybody, taking on a life of its own, curling and manifesting with the movement.

A new type of sound bellowed around the hall, off the walls, and down to the floor below, pulsing under the foundations. It was a type of music that Francesca was not familiar with, and the movement surrounding it made her curious. Smiles and seductive glances were passed from youthful faces as they sat in tight groupings. The more Francesca watched these groupings, the more she realised their sense of belonging, their confidence and ability to dress immaculately despite their working-class budgets. There was an oddness to the situation as she found herself utterly isolated in a room full of so many people. Sitting to attention, she absorbed the surrounding commotion as best she could. It was like nothing she had ever seen before, let alone experienced. Even though she was tucked away to the side of the room, she sat exposed. That's when he saw her.

'I take it this is your first time to a dance hall then?' a young man questioned. His voice was calm and sturdy in opposition to the screams and shouts expelled from excitable lungs. Startled from her trance-like state, Francesca looked to the young man who was now kneeling at her side.

'Um, yes, it's quite something,' she replied, the room intimidating her into speaking few words.

'You'll get used to it.' He smiled.

'I don't even know how to move to this kind of music,' she admitted, feeling inadequate as she met his inquisitive blue eyes. He appeared smart and wore a three-piece dark grey suit that fitted him like a glove. She imagined him to be wealthy from the quality of his clothes, yet his accent was Cockney through and through.

'I can show you,' he suggested, putting out his hand.

'I'd rather not,' she said, her cheeks reddening at the thought.

'Oh, come on, you'll enjoy it,' he encouraged.

'I'll just embarrass myself.'

'There's no harm in that, trust me.'

'Trust a stranger I just met? I don't even know your name.'

'This stranger knows what he's doing, and his name is Oliver. You're in good hands, I promise.' Grinning, his hand remained outstretched.

'You're very persistent.' She smiled, placing her hand in his.

'I've been told.'

Leading Francesca into the chaos, Oliver guided her to the beat slowly. He placed his hand on her back, feeling her long hair meet his fingertips. She looked up at him as he cradled her.

They danced until midnight, and she felt as though they were the only two in the room.

CHAPTER 2

RUBBING HER EYES to greet the bright spring morning, Francesca felt a wave of dread consume her as she bolted upright, recognising that it was, in fact, a Wednesday, but not just any Wednesday for it was the day of the interview that according to the ticking clock that sat on her bedside table, was in approximately forty five minutes.

She leapt into the bath, pulling the shower curtain around herself as she embraced the cold water with chattering teeth, there was no time to wait for the change of temperature. The liquid petrified her skin as the remaining makeup from the night prior slipped reluctantly down the drain.

She ran around the room with a towel clinging onto her body for dear life. Pulling on a smart but dull grey business dress and somewhat clumpy leather shoes, she greeted her image in the mirror.

Yanking her hair into a tight and headache-inducing plait,

she bundled down the stairs in a fluster, taking no appreciation for her sleeping relatives who awoke to the commotion.

'You're cutting it fine, Fran,' Vera called out from her room, making Francesca wince.

'I know, I'll make it if the traffic is clear,' she said hopefully. But she couldn't help but feel annoyed at herself for going to the dance hall, if she hadn't gone, she wouldn't be running late. She scowled as she thought of Elaine and her persuasive ways, but her expression softened as she thought of Oliver. *Enough of that, Francesca, focus, you'll probably never see him again,* she disciplined herself, throwing the thought of him from her mind.

Closing the front door, she read a piece of paper containing the details of the interview, *10:30, 144 Fenchurch Street.*

The compact houses loomed over her as she hurried along the pavement, her heavy shoes dragging across the concrete. She quickly met the hustle and bustle of Mile End Road. The bus stop was only a short distance from her, but she had to battle through the many people trapesing their way along the busy street. Most people were funnelling into the Underground, however, Francesca preferred to remain on the city's surface, the Underground reminded her of the bombings, a time she'd rather not recall. Meeting the stop, she sighed with relief yet winced at the developing blisters that her clunky leather shoes had created. The bus was only a few minutes away according to her wristwatch. She impatiently stared at its hands, hoping that a double-decker would appear when she readjusted her gaze.

In a method of distraction, she watched the different people tending to their business. Some were buying vegetables from the greengrocers while others left the nearby telephone exchange. A lucky few turned down Aberavon Road that was home to a large Odeon Cinema. It was only early, but people were already queuing to get inside. Francesca and Elaine would go on day trips to the cinema during the winter months. It was always warm inside and cost less than heating the house, so her mother encouraged it. There she could drift off into different worlds and imagine a life outside of her own. Thinking of the various feature films and the glamour of the silver screen, she was pulled back to reality as a red double-decker met the kerb.

Boarding the vehicle, she held the metal bar above her head, too irritable to sit down. She opened the locket and looked at her brother's image, if he were there, he'd know exactly what to say to make it all seem a little less intimidating.

Her feet met the miserable grey pavement. The sun attempted to cast its rays upon the concrete, but even the light grey streaks portrayed a miserable presence. The area was a strange mixture of official-looking buildings, ruins, and the odd pub.

Francesca's thick leather shoes hastily swerved around the experienced businessmen who navigated the pavements with precision. Removing her eyesight from the small piece of paper, she looked up to meet the impressive structure that occupied *144 Fenchurch Street*. The building was a large bank spewing people out in every direction. She fought against them to meet the entryway.

It was funny considering she hated mathematics, but she completed a college course in typing and was more than capable of noting down a few digits. Her mother had pulled a few strings with a friend who worked in the large establishment, granting Francesca an opportunity that rarely came the way of a working-class girl.

Taking a deep breath, she stepped inside.

A bubbly character behind the desk was busy whizzing which and every way, balancing a phone in one hand and a pen in the other.

'How can I help?' the lady asked whilst multi-tasking at an expert level.

'I-I'm here for an interview,' Francesca stuttered, trying to force out the correct words before giving up and simply revealing the note.

'Oh Francesca, I've been expecting you, I'm ever so sorry we've been extremely busy, and your arrival slipped my mind. Follow me and don't be nervous, I know that's easier said than done.' She smiled, ushering her into a large room.

The space had rows upon rows of desks illuminated by enormous lights suspended from the high ceiling. There was a repetition of telephones on each desk, and a magnitude of paperwork and stationery that sat on every table; it was a busy place indeed. The vast walls were made of red marble and contrasted the broad oak window frames. Francesca considered the possibility of escaping out of one as she nervously fiddled with her locket. All the people that occupied the area were men, and they looked at her judgingly as she invaded their space.

Francesca hurried to keep to the pace of her guide. She was a little plump woman with short ginger hair and a love for flamboyantly printed dresses.

'My name is Penny by the way, I know exactly how you feel, I've been here less than a year and I remember my interview like it was yesterday.' Her voice was more pronounced than the accents Francesca was used to.

'Nice to meet you,' she said politely whilst following the little woman to a large wooden door. This was the point where Penny could go no further.

'I've got another one for you, Mr Montgomery,' she informed as she poked her head around the doorframe.

'Let her in,' he said sternly. His gaze remained fixed on the paperwork before him while his fingers tapped in sequence on top of the desk. A few were adorned with gold rings intricately engraved with initials.

'Go on then, you'll be fine,' Penny said, coaxing her into the room.

Cautiously entering the office, she noticed it was filled with antiques from what looked like the early 1900s, including a large aeroplane propeller that dominated the left-hand wall.

'Take a seat. What's your name?' he asked.

She quickly sat down on the dark green leather chair adjacent to him. 'Francesca Parmenter,' she answered, noticing that he hadn't yet made eye contact with her.

'My nan was called Francesca, ugly cow. I can't say the same for you.' He grinned as he finally looked at her.

'Thank you?' she questioned with confused flattery at the backhanded compliment. The man's strong Cockney accent baffled her since it was the opposite of what she expected. A man of his fifties, greying hair, with an influential position in a bank, and a quite frankly posh sounding surname led her to believe her possible boss was from a more privileged background; not to mention his expensive dark blue Burton suit that Francesca recognised from an advertisement in a past magazine.

'You're from Mile End, yes?' Mr Montgomery asked as he continued his paperwork.

'Yes.'

'I'm from Bethnal Green. Ok, Francesca, I'll give you the job on one condition—'

'But you haven't asked me any proper questions yet?' she

interjected.

'One condition,' he emphasised, disregarding her latter response. 'As my personal secretary, I expect you to do what I've asked of you and to keep the questions to a minimum, understood? I bloody hate questions, it shows that people have no initiative to work out the answer for themselves.'

'Understood,' she repeated.

'Well then, we seem to have come to an understanding, you can start on Monday at nine. Now off you go, I've got business to attend to,' he dismissed.

Taken aback, Francesca pulled herself from the chair. 'Thank you for the opportunity, Sir,' she gulped, leaving the office.

She felt a huge weight lift from her shoulders. Her hands were still trembling, and her stomach tumbled and turned, but her mind was at ease. Penny caught sight of her as she tended to her duties, sending a relief-filled smile in her direction, most girls walked out of that office in tears.

As soon as she left the bank, Francesca bundled towards the nearest telephone box. Her fingers fumbled for a few coins, jamming them in whilst pulling at the dial. She fidgeted as she waited for a response.

'I got it!' she exclaimed. Met with ecstatic responses from her relatives, she put the phone down and hurried home.

Francesca left the double-decker with an enthusiastic prance despite the painful blisters that bit at her skin. The concrete was decorated in chalk which was the handiwork of bright-eyed school children. As she fought the desire to jump through a depiction of hopscotch, her eyes latched onto the old sweetshop.

Multi-coloured gems glistened from their glass containers, resembling treasure kept safely in secure chests. They were organised perfectly in stacks that reached the ceiling. It was only a small shop, but it contained enough sugar to turn the whole of London hyper. Peering at the assortment, she couldn't help but consider picking up a bag of celebratory sweets. There was a varied mix of colours, sizes and textures. Liquorice was positioned next to the Dolly Mixtures, and a mass of Treacle Toffee stood on the front counter where a friendly man greeted her as she entered. The hard-boiled sweets were presented at the other side of the room, Pear Drops, Rosey Apples, Peppermint Humbugs and Sherbet Lemons to name a few.

Being in the shop made her feel like a child again. It brought back memories. Grandma Vera would let her pick out a few sweets every Wednesday after school if she'd been good. Smiling as she recognised a stack of Barratt's Sweet Cigarettes, Francesca remembered the time when she and Elaine would pretend to smoke, imitating their fathers with the sugary substance hanging from their lips. There were all sorts of chocolate there too, including Mars Bars which Francesca recalled her, Elaine, and their brothers buying one for thruppence, splitting the spoils between them, leaving about an inch of the gooey goodness to each of them. Her large brown eyes devoured the different sweet treats as she decided. Paying the man, she happily wandered back onto the street with a little striped pink and white paper bag in her clutches.

'Hello treacle,' a familiar voice said from behind her.

She turned to meet the glistening blue eyes of Oliver. They looked as though they were opals, glinting with every reflection of sunlight. He stood dressed in a classic Edwardian grey suit that was coated in a long black drape jacket. She stared at him. She had already cast him from her mind, and now he was standing before her, again. Her heart fluttered with excitement.

'What you got there then?' he questioned.

'Just treated myself, you want one?' she asked, lifting the bag so he could peer at the assortment.

'Don't mind if I do.' He placed a Pear Drop in his mouth. 'I never caught your name,' he said, watching carefully, looking more interested in her than the sweet that he crunched between his teeth.

'You never asked, my name's Francesca.' She smiled as she ate a Dolly Mixture. 'Aren't you hot wearing that coat?' she questioned, acknowledging his thick drape jacket that fought against the sudden springtime heat.

'Why? Are you concerned for me, Frankie?' he teased.

'More amused by your unpractical choice of clothing, and I prefer Fran,' she uttered. Nicknames were for people who knew each other well, and she didn't know him very well at all. Fran was her assigned name due to its simplicity unlike Francesca, which appeared to be a mouthful to most people; but Frankie, nobody had ever called her Frankie.

He grinned as he studied her outfit. 'I can say the same for you.'

'I had an interview this morning, thank you very much.'

'Ah I see, so you're a working woman. Where was the interview?'

'I am now, and it was at a bank in Fenchurch Street,' she answered as she ate another Dolly Mixture, the sugar coating her lips.

'Moving up in the world then, that does explain the dull dress,' Oliver said as he spun her around, taking in her attire. He found her bulky leather shoes to be particularly amusing.

'I wasn't going to wear what I wore last night to an interview,' she joked.

'I think you should have, would've made a lasting impression, just like you did with me.' He smiled.

'I borrowed those clothes, and that style from my friend.'

'Your friend did a good job,' he commended.

'That's not who I am,' she said confidently, however, she hoped not to burst his bubble.

'Well, I'm interested in getting to know who you are.' He recognised his friends who were lingering on the street corner. 'I'll see you around, Frankie,' he said as he left her to her business.

Oliver wandered towards them, acknowledging their intrigued glances as Francesca disappeared in the opposite direction.

'Is that the girl from last night then?' Jack pressed as he connected the dots. He cracked his knuckles, leading them to make an unpleasant sound.

'What girl?' Oliver replied, intent on keeping Francesca to himself.

'Don't play stupid, Oli, we have eyes if you haven't noticed,' Harry said bluntly. He was a big lad, larger than the others and matched in image, sporting a drape jacket that coated his broad shoulders.

'That's Francesca Parmenter, she goes to my church,' Colin informed the two of them.

'Oh, so she's a little God botherer like you then,' Jack said with a smirk.

'Piss off,' Colin snapped.

'Both of you knock it off. I don't want any of you approaching her,' Oliver said sternly, looking at the three of them with his now sharp blue eyes.

'I wouldn't dream of it,' Jack said with an unnerving grin, running a hand through his messy greased hair.

'I see you're marking your territory already then,' Harry said.

'No, I'm just protecting her from you tossers,' Oliver mumbled, growing tired of the conversation.

Colin turned to him with unease. 'It's not us you should be worried about, if the girls get hold of her—'

'Yeah, well, that's why you're not going to say anything to the girls.'

'Kerry would tear her in half,' Jack said.

'Kerry would tear us all in half,' Colin added.

'Just keep quiet about it, act like you haven't seen her,' Oliver pleaded as he caught sight of the approaching women.

'Our lips are sealed,' Harry assured him.

Stephanie stood in her pinnie wielding a large rolling pin. She was tending to her pastry, focusing to follow the recipe precisely. Francesca stood at her side, a borrowed pinnie loosely gripping her waist. With a teaspoon plunged in the jam jar, she feasted on the sweet jelly.

'You're not being very helpful,' her mother said with annoyance.

'You look like you've got it under control,' Francesca said cheekily, shoving another spoonful into her mouth.

'Sit with your grandmother, and leave the jam, I want some left for the tarts,' she muttered as her daughter licked the sticky spoon.

'How was the dance hall, Fran? Did you enjoy it?' Vera

asked, a cup of tea in her grasp.

Francesca sat before her. 'Yes, I did. At first I didn't,' she admitted.

'Why's that dear?'

'Elaine buggered off and left me on my own, so I didn't really know what to do with myself.'

'Language,' Stephanie disciplined.

'Sorry, mum.'

'And then what happened?' Vera questioned nosily, taking a sip from her cup.

'I danced with someone,' she confessed, unable to contain the smile that was developing on her face.

'A boy?' Stephanie asked, quickly stopping what she was doing to join the conversation. Perching herself on the end of the sofa, she listened intently.

'Yes, he was very kind and tended to me all night. He was dressed smartly, much nicer than most of the boys in this area.'

'It sounds like you had a wonderful evening.' Vera grinned.

'I saw him again down Mile End Road, I gave him a few of my sweets.'

'Well, he must be special if you were willing to give up some of your sweets,' her mother teased.

'I'm pleased you are getting to know some new people, it's about time. I know it's been difficult for you,' Vera said.

'It's been difficult for all of us,' she said as her mother held her hand tightly.

'You are allowed to act your age, Fran. I know you feel responsible for us, but your grandmother and I can look after ourselves. We want you to put yourself out there, to explore the world,' Stephanie encouraged.

Sitting on a pile of brown hessian sacks, Francesca was careful not to dirty her skirt as she avoided the grimy nature of the docks. Ship horns could be heard in the distance while rigging swayed lightly with the afternoon breeze. Men hurried about the area, lugging heavy shipments inland. Boats were leashed to the wooden landing stage with thick ropes. Content on pulling against the lines, they bobbed up and down with the current flowing through the Thames River. St Katharine Docks sat perfectly at the centre of London's trade. The hustle and bustle was a 24/7 occurrence and Francesca would often sit amongst the commotion in that exact spot on the corner of the Western Basin, hoping to meet Charley, Elaine's older brother of whom she considered family.

'Hello, kid.' He smiled as he caught sight of her.

'That looks heavy,' she said, recognising the large sack swung over his shoulder.

'No heavier than usual.' He tossed it onto the pile with ease.

'They're making progress I see,' Francesca said, watching the large metal cranes that were tending to the bomb-damaged wood. They were now constructing modern storage sheds where crippled warehouses had previously sat.

'It's only taken them ten years,' Charley muttered.

'I'm sure it will return to its former glory.' She smiled.

'I can only hope, otherwise I'll be out of a job. How's Steph and Vera?' Charley asked as he removed his gloves, revealing the rough layers of calluses that had developed on the palms of his hands. He was dirty and sweat-ridden due to the influx of sudden heat that latched onto his linen shirt.

'They're bickering as usual,' Francesca said, rolling her eyes.

'Oh, is this the whole church issue?'

'Yeah, the church issue.'

'Your mum has been through a lot, it takes time,' he said as he plonked himself down beside her.

'We had the Priest round.'

'Murphy? That man has suffered a lot in his time as well.'

'How so?'

He turned to her and informed. 'From what I heard, his lady was killed in Belfast, crushed by a building during the bombings. Him and his son moved down south for a new start, as well as the fact that it's going tits up in Northern Ireland, Protestant and Catholic tensions and what not. Not many people know about Colin's mother, he rarely speaks about her. I only heard about it through whispers.'

'That's awful. It explains why he's so cold,' she said.

'He may be cold, but don't think for a second that that man doesn't have a heart of gold.' He wasn't a religious man, but he had respect for it entirely. Charley acknowledged the power of faith, and that it gave comfort to men in crisis.

Francesca took in his words. 'I'll keep that in mind. Oh! I brought you sandwiches.' Remembering, she passed him an ammo pouch that contained his lunch. After the war, Charley used his old ammo pouch as a lunch box, hoping that the idea of fresh sandwiches would remove the image of bullets and grenades from his head.

'Aren't you a sweetheart, cheese and pickle?' he questioned with a grin.

'Of course, they are your favourite, and I brought you some of mum's tarts,' she said as he tore at the tinfoil.

'You can't beat Steph's baking. I heard you got that job, I'm proud of you, kid.'

'Thanks, Charley, I swear you hear everything.' She laughed.

'You'd be surprised how loose-lipped East Londoners are, especially the dockworkers after a few drinks down the pub,' he informed as he munched.

'I can only imagine,' Francesca said as she watched them hurrying up and down the landing stage.

'You'd know better than anyone, my sister loves a gossip. Hold your cards close to your chest with that one I tell ya,' he said humorously, finishing the crusts.

'Can I ask you something?'

'Of course, fire away.'

She watched the tranquil water that filled the Basin, distracting herself just like her mother did whenever she had to speak about difficult things. 'How long did it take you to let go?'

He smiled slightly. 'The truth is, I haven't, Fran, it's difficult. Your brother meant a lot to me. But I am trying, and it's important that you try too. You spend every waking moment of your life looking after the people that he cared about, me, your mother, your grandmother, but you need to start living for yourself.'

'Your words of wisdom always come in handy,' she said.

'I'm not sure how wise I am, but I'm always truthful. Now on you go before it gets dark,' Charley ordered, recognising the afternoon sun that was residing behind cloud cover. Obeying his command, she scurried along the dock, weaving in and out of the busy workers.

As the night drew closer, Vallance Road developed a sombre atmosphere, the dark clouds dragging across the sky. The many warehouses in the area stood stiffly with their large grey exteriors tarnishing the district as though they were tumours upon the landscape. A mass of tired workers flooded out of a nearby fish curing factory. The unpleasant smell followed them as they invaded the neighbouring roads and alleyways. The violent scent of raw fish bullied its way down onto the recreational ground where a few boys were playing football. Upon recognising the stench, they ran into retreat.

Susan shut the windows quickly, trying not to gag.

'Fuckin' stupid place to put a fish factory,' Kerry tutted as she caught a potent whiff.

'Well, it made this place considerably cheaper for Oliver and I,' Susan sighed.

'Have you heard from your dad?' she asked, leaning against the kitchen worktop.

'Not in years, he's as good as dead in my eyes, left us to fend for ourselves,' Susan said, growing angry at the thought of him.

'It's probably for the best, I wish I could get rid of my uncle.'

'Is he still using your mum as a slave?'

'Yeah, she sits and takes it, just like she's always done,' Kerry muttered, looking out the window, watching the darkening sky.

'His time will come,' Susan assured. She flicked through the post that had accumulated at the front door, dreading the sight of overdue bills. Sitting at the old wooden table, she reached for the letter opener.

'You're the spitting image of your brother, you know that?' Kerry observed.

'If it wasn't for the three-year age gap, people would think we were twins.' She grinned. Her image was traditional but bold, just like her older sibling. She mirrored him with bright blue eyes and black hair, but hers was long and reached the middle of her back. She wore a pencil skirt that encased her thin waist, a tailored blazer covering her shoulders. The blazer was adorned with a rose-shaped brooch she had inherited from her mother. Its pale pink crystals shimmered under the dimming light.

'Speaking of your brother, he's hiding something from us, I can tell,' Kerry said irritably.

'My brother hides a lot of things.'

'Don't you want to find out what?' she pressed.

'Not particularly,' Susan said, slitting open the envelopes with the silver letter opener. It had a chunky moulded duck's head as the handle and was more for show than it was for being used, clear with the awkward slashes it made in the paper.

'He'll get himself into a pickle.'

'He always does, Kerry, there's no difference there.'

'Tea?' she asked, holding up the kettle.

'I'll never say no to a cuppa.' Susan smiled as she retired her gaze from the paper littered table.

'I'm just saying, he's being too secretive, it's setting off my intuition,' Kerry insisted as she searched the cupboard for two mugs.

'If my brother wants to tell us, he'll tell us,' Susan said. Her sibling was the least of her worries considering the bills that laid on the surface in front of her.

Kerry respected Susan, so she let the topic lie, but not before getting the last word. 'Sooner better than later,' she grumbled as she passed her a cup of steaming tea. 'Where's Lottie?' she asked, running a hand through her short platinum blonde hair.

'Working in the factory, till late I imagine,' Susan answered, taking a sip.

'And Isla?'

'It's probably best not to ask after Isla's antics,' she muttered.

The night sky covered the city and bright lamplights illuminated the streets in a persistent glare. Foxes scurried along the back alleys while a dubious character or two hid in the darkness. The streets were as quiet as they could be for a capital city that never slept.

Jack sat in a dishevelled state as Isla took in his bloody knuckles and slurred demeanour. The room was silent, and the two stared at each other with longing glances. She stood with her auburn hair meeting her shoulders, her green eyes passionately focused on the young man before her.

'You're absolutely plastered,' she said, passing Jack a glass of water, hoping to dilute his current state.

'Maybe.' He pondered with a pause, taking another swig of the whiskey beside him. 'So, what are you waiting for?' he questioned, watching her as he dragged a hand through his greased hair.

'Patience is a virtue,' Isla teased as she met his intensity with her lustful eyes.

'Not a virtue of mine,' he said, pushing her up against the wall, pressing his body to hers.

CHAPTER 3

FRANCESCA WOKE IN a fluster, her heart pounding as she acknowledged the time. *You've got to be kidding me.* Today she didn't have Elaine or a dance hall to blame her lateness on. Pulling on the grey business dress, she battled with the rough and unruly fabric. Throwing herself down the stairs, she pulled her hair into a firm plait.

Vera sat on her armchair filling out a crossword puzzle. 'You really should go to bed earlier,' she muttered, peering at her scatty granddaughter through the strong-lensed reading glasses that perched on the end of her nose.

'It's a work in progress,' Francesca said as she hunted for loose change.

'Your mother has made you lunch, it's on the side in some tin foil, ham I believe. Here take this,' Vera insisted as she extended her hand, revealing a few coins.

Francesca jammed them into her purse gratefully.

'Oh, and on Sunday afternoon we're going to the Ladies' Market, you can't be wearing your mother's dress and shoes forever,' Vera added as her granddaughter gave a hasty nod in agreement.

The days were getting longer, and the mornings appeared brighter. She squinted as she waddled along the cobbles. Coborn Road was lengthy and took its toll on her delicate feet, not to mention the clumpy shoes that aggravated her healing blisters from the previous week. The repetitive houses proved an illusion, the end of the pavement seeming impossible to reach. The challenge proved even greater upon meeting Mile End Road where her sore ankles had to swerve around busy commuters intermixed with giddy school children. She arrived at the bus stop just in time as a double-decker met the kerb.

The journey was plagued with rush hour traffic and Francesca feared she had lost her job before she had even started it. With flushed cheeks, she leapt onto the pavement and started running. Meeting the outside of the bank, she winced as she felt a new set of blisters develop. Straightening up, she approached her co-worker who was busy darting about behind the front desk.

'Just in time,' Penny said with considerable relief. 'It's good to see you again, Francesca, follow me.' She smiled as she guided her to Mr Montgomery's office. 'A word of advice, follow his instructions precisely, do that and you'll last longer than the others,' she advised as they met the large oak doors.

Francesca nodded at her before entering the office. 'Hello, Sir,' she said politely.

'Francesca, take a seat, that's your desk, I expect you to type up exactly what I say,' he ordered.

'Is this all mine?' she asked in awe. The little desk had its own state-of-the-art typewriter, paper, and fountain pens. Even at college she did not experience such resources.

'Well, it wouldn't be for anyone else now would it. Hurry up, I haven't got all day,' he said impatiently.

'Sorry, Sir.' Nervously she placed herself in position, setting up the typewriter as quickly as she could.

Fingers aching and eyes growing tired, Charlotte sat at her sewing machine, wading her way through piece after piece. She looked to the clock with worry; if she didn't stitch her quota of car interiors for the day, she wouldn't get paid. Her hair was wrapped back, and she could feel bags forming underneath her eyes.

The factory floor was wide and grim, with metal walls and horrid luminescent lights that would induce a migraine if stared at for too long. Rows of women sat with their feet anxiously hovering over the pedal, their fingers locked in a constant cycle around the needle of the machine. The noise was unbearable, and some girls plugged their ears with spare bits of cotton. No natural light made its way into the factory, and the female staff remained isolated from the male workers.

'Charlotte Lovett,' a sharp voice hissed from above.

She turned, dreading the sight of her boss who glared down at her from the steel walkway.

'My office, now,' he said firmly.

Nervously, she ascended the metal railings. Peering back at the other women, they gave her a nod of encouragement as she entered the office.

As the owner of the factory, Mr Talbot liked to throw his weight around. More specifically, he liked to use the women as his personal punching bag. He sat in an agitated state, his hefty limbs barely clinging onto his desk chair as he rubbed his fierce moustache.

'You sound awfully mad, Sir.' Charlotte looked at the floor timidly like a child who had been called to the headmaster's office.

'And you wonder why that is?' he spat.

'I haven't the foggiest.'

'Well, let me clear your vision. You are behind on production by three pieces an hour.'

'With all due respect, Sir, it's a bit overwhelming, you know, with the new requirements.'

'Do you wish to make a complaint about the increased workload? You should be grateful,' he said.

'I am, believe me. It's just by the time I'm done each day I feel like my fingers are gonna fall off,' she said, looking down at her pierced and punctured hands.

'If you're going to complain you might as well find work elsewhere, that's if anyone will take you on after I pass on the information about your sudden laziness,' he threatened.

'No please, I need this job,' she said, anxiously wringing her hands, feeling the scabs that had formed on top of her freckled skin.

He leant over the desk and pointed a finger. 'Then stop whinging, get the rest of those car interiors stitched before you leave, or I'm docking your pay.'

'I'll try.'

'You'll do more than try, get it done, what did I employ you for? Oh, wait.' He looked her up and down, clearly feasting on her features. 'Now I remember what I employed you for,' he said with a satisfied grin. 'Oh, and shut the door behind you,' he bellowed as she escaped his grasp.

As Francesca walked the route home from the bus stop, her tired arms struggled to hold onto her heavy handbag that was overflowing with paperwork. Her shoes were scuffed due to her sore legs that slowly dragged her feet across the pavement. Her eyes ached as she looked up to the mellowing sky. Pale orange mixed with fading blues while the clouds gently continued their journey across the horizon.

'Hello, Frankie,' Oliver said as he left a nearby corner shop, a packet of cigarettes lodged firmly in one hand.

'We really need to stop bumping into each other like this,' she said, grinning. Her arms buckled with the weight of the bag so she placed it on the floor for a moment.

'You on your way home?' Oliver asked as he studied her shattered expression.

'Yeah, on my way home from work.'

'Here, I'll give you a hand.' He offered to carry her bag. With a thankful smile, she allowed his assistance as they proceeded down the street.

'Busy day then?' he questioned.

'You have no idea. I've been typing all day and both my hands are killing me. Also, my boss is a bit of a dictator, barking commands every two seconds.'

'Just a bit of a dictator?' he asked, amused.

Francesca looked at him. 'Well, I haven't worked their long enough to assess him fully.'

'I've never been one for being told what to do,' Oliver said defiantly, running his fingers through his black hair.

'I can tell.' She laughed, sensing his prideful nature.

'Is it that obvious?'

'Well, you're not exactly conforming,' she stated with reference to his attire and the way older generations looked at him as he walked down the street, almost fearful of his image and demeanour.

'And that's why you're attracted to me,' he spoke boldly.

'Don't flatter yourself, we're complete opposites.'

Oliver, confident in his statement, continued his point. 'You know what they say, opposites attract. I think that's why you look at me the way you do.'

'Oh, and how do I look at you?' she questioned with folded arms.

'With fascination, the same way I'm fascinated by you with those big brown eyes of yours, you're like Bambi.'

She blushed and he grinned. 'Why do I get the feeling it's no coincidence that we've come across each other again?'

He shrugged. 'Maybe it's just fate. Are you peckish?'

'Starving, but I really should be getting home,' Francesca said, looking to her wristwatch that had just turned half five.

'Come on, live a little. You like pie and mash? There's a shop down the end of Grove Road that does the best in the entire district, also it's near Victoria Park if you fancy a stroll,' he said persuasively.

She stared at him, making her mind up. 'That sounds like a lovely idea. Who doesn't like pie and mash? It's practically treason to be from the East End and not like it.'

'My kind of girl.'

They sat on a bench in Victoria Park. The atmosphere was like a premature summer, shielding them both in a golden Ombré; yet it was chilly, and the crisp breeze caused Francesca to shudder. Oliver offered her his drape jacket, which swamped her in black fabric.

'Not so impractical now, is it?' Oliver smirked.

'Fine, I take it back, it has its uses,' Francesca admitted as she pulled at the jacket, looking as though she was wrapped in a blanket. She sat with her legs crossed facing Oliver who was perched sideways with one arm resting on the old oak frame. Admiring his white poplin shirt and black waistcoat, a silver pocket watch caught her eye.

'That looks vintage,' she said as she munched on a freshly baked pie drenched in liquor. The pierced pastry sent steam into her face, warming her cold skin.

As Oliver helped himself to some of the spoils, he explained, 'My dad gave it to me, it's been passed down through generations of male family members.'

'It's got quite some sentiment then, did your dad not want it anymore?' Francesca asked, shoving a forkful of pastry into her mouth.

'It's complicated, my sister Susan and I don't have a great relationship with him, he's an alcoholic and drinks himself silly, we haven't seen him in years,' he admitted.

'I'm sorry, if you don't mind me asking, why do you wear it?'

'It's a matter of principle, I suppose, it resembles many other family members. Think of it this way, I can't throw out a bunch of flowers if only one has failed to flourish,' he explained.

'That makes sense, I didn't mean to bring up a sensitive topic.'

'It's no bother. Your turn, what's up with the locket?' he questioned, looking to the gold pendant that sat around her neck. Its delicate design featured floral patterns that covered the front and back.

'It belonged to my grandma, she gave it to me. Nothing massively prestigious,' she informed him, holding the necklace in her hand.

'If it means something to you, then that's the most important thing. Who's inside?' he asked.

'My brother.'

'How old is he?'

'He's not with us anymore,' she spoke quietly as she opened the locket to reveal his military portrait.

'How did he pass?'

Fighting to decipher the facts, she stated what she knew. 'He was shot down over the English Channel, body was never recovered, he was young too. The funny thing is, he was so excited to sign up to the armed forces, to do his bit. I remember it as clear as day, I was only little, he said he was doing it for a cause and what have you. Now he's just a name engraved on a memorial.'

'He died out of love for you, not out of hate for those who shot him down, remember that. I know it doesn't help much, but I lost two cousins,' Oliver said empathetically.

'I'm sorry to hear that, it's difficult losing family. I enjoyed the dance hall, I never thanked you for dancing with me,' she said, trying to change the conversation onto something a bit more cheerful.

'It was my pleasure. You weren't bad considering it was your first time. Rock 'n' Roll ain't easy to dance to,' he complimented.

'No, it certainly wasn't.' She laughed, hoping her two left feet hadn't embarrassed her that badly. 'And your friends were there too?'

'At the dance hall?'

'Yes, the same ones that were waiting on the corner last Wednesday by the sweetshop.' She recalled.

'Bloody hell, you're observant, you should be a detective,' Oliver said, impressed.

'I just take things in that's all,' Francesca said awkwardly.

'I can introduce you if you really want, we're meeting down the Tredegar Square ruins on Saturday,' he invited, yet his tone was reluctant.

'I'd like that,' she accepted as she munched on the remaining pie crusts. The idea of meeting new people made her nervous, but she remembered her mother's advice.

'You can bring your friend from the other night to make it a little less intimidating.'

'Should I be worried?' she asked, slightly concerned.

'No, it's just they can be a little bit prickly to newcomers. You can meet my sister too,' he said, helping himself to a forkful of mash.

Tredegar Square was an almost apocalyptic sight. Decaying buildings stood like rotting teeth. Fragmented grey stone presented the cracks and crevices embedded from past destructions. A time of war was encapsulated among the ruins, with every blast and burn marked onto the scarred surfaces. It showed the injuries of conflict, cut into the skin, the city's body permanently fractured. The walls, although crippled, stood firm and allowed the area of abandonment to become a meeting place for the group.

The thick concrete followed them as they walked. Guided by Oliver, Elaine and Francesca turned the corner to meet eyes with all ten of them. It was an intimidating sight, one of which neither of them was accustomed to. Acknowledging them one by one, Francesca realised that they all shared the same identity, but with their own originality. She recognised the three boys from the other week, and was presented with seven unfamiliar faces, some welcoming, some reluctant.

'So, this is the girl you've been hiding from us,' Jack said with a grin, sussing her out.

'Yeah, this is Fran and her friend Elaine,' Oliver introduced.

'Hiding in plain sight,' Finn uttered under his breath. He sat on a carved piece of concrete and was careful not to damage his well-kept suit. The Savile Row approach was evident regarding all of them, however, they were all a working-class breed. Pricey footwear such as oxfords and chunky creepers appeared polished and peeped out from under their trousers.

'Pleasure to meet ya poppet, the names Albie,' he said, jumping to his feet with a prance. Albie had an almost gaudy appearance sporting a vibrant brocade waistcoat. His ginger hair sat in a quiff that twisted out at the end.

'Pleased to meet you,' Francesca said politely.

'So, what are you doing here then?' Kerry asked coldly, leaning against one of the decrepit walls.

'Try to be nice, Kerry,' Oliver said, irritated.

'I'm just surprised that's all.'

'What do you mean?' Oliver pressed as he looked at her now angered golden-brown eyes. Kerry was a new breed entirely, her presence fierce and intimidating. Francesca had noticed it instantly and was trying her hardest not to stare at her as she stood in her thick creepers and drape jacket.

'She's clearly not one of us,' Finn butted in.

'No, she certainly is not. Pretty though, I can see exactly why you chose her.' Lewis grinned. He sat with a comb in his hand, tending to his strongly moulded, carefully kept strands of blonde hair.

'Right, stop it now, it's impolite,' Susan ordered.

'What do you do then, Fran?' Harry asked as he kicked around a piece of rubble.

Francesca remembered him as soon as she met his glance, the tallest of the boys. 'I have a job, as a secretary in a bank,' she spoke shyly.

'Yeah, but you've only had that for a week. And she goes to church. The same one as Colin. She spends most of her time with her grandma and mum. Apart from that, she doesn't get up to much,' Elaine stated in an outburst.

Francesca glared at her but said nothing.

'What an interesting existence you have.' Harry observed.

'Church is the most pointless thing. Just higher thinking bastards that tell you how to live, and how to be,' Jack preached as he waltzed around the bombsite.

'Don't be a twat, some people have faith unlike you,' Colin said, taking the statement to heart.

'Let's face it, if it wasn't for your dad being a Priest, Colin, you'd have no faith,' he said, pushing his buttons.

'You clearly don't understand how faith works,' Colin dismissed.

'I think it's commendable that you both go to church,' Isla said with a smile.

'And when was the last time you went to church, Isla? Considering you're the opposite of the Virgin Mary,' Lewis questioned cruelly.

She peered at Oliver awkwardly before Jack grabbed her attention, looping an arm around her waist, pulling her close to him. 'You want me to make him apologise?' he asked, a sharpened glance aimed in his direction.

'He wouldn't mean it,' she said, frowning.

Oliver stared at her, saddened by her now dulled jade-green eyes. 'You need to be taken down a peg,' he snapped, causing Lewis to grin.

'Oh yeah, and who's gonna do that then?' he said cockily, looking to them all individually. 'That's what I thought, none of you have the bollocks to,' he added with self-assurance as the bombsite fell silent.

'You really are a piece of work,' Susan said under her breath.

'And you've only just figured that out, sweetheart?' he bit back.

'Don't talk to my sister like that,' Oliver warned.

'Oh yeah, I forgot who I was talking to for a second, the prince and princess of Vallance Road,' he agitated. This was met by angered glances, but both siblings held their tongues; showing how volatile they could really be would scare Francesca off entirely.

'You ever smoked?' Harry turned his attention to her once again. He pulled out a packet of cigarettes and passed them around.

'Of course she hasn't, look at her,' Jack answered for her as he lit one, letting it hang from the corner of his mouth.

'No, I haven't,' she admitted with reddening cheeks.

'Don't worry love, we'll spice up ya life.' Albie grinned.

The ruins sat quietly as smoke curled into the air.

'What do you do for fun?' Isla asked, trying to provide Francesca with an opportunity to speak.

'I like sewing.'

'I love sewing too! I know we are going to get on just fine,'

Charlotte blurted out with happiness. She wore a blazer that she had embroidered herself, evident with stitching on both shoulders.

'Well, that's decided then, if Lottie approves,' Jack confirmed, exhaling his smoke-filled lungs.

'Lottie approves of everyone,' Kerry interjected.

'I'm just being friendly, maybe you should try it,' she said snarkily.

'Oh, my heart, that almost offended me,' Kerry said, staring.

'Right, as lovely as this little gathering is, I have places to go, people to see, you get my drift,' Albie said, bolting out of the situation as quickly as he could.

As the others began to leave, Susan reassured the despondent girl before her. 'Don't worry, Fran, they take a while to get used to new people. Beautiful necklace by the way.' She smiled as she abandoned the ruins alongside the others.

'I'm sorry about that, as my sister said, it'll take a bit of time,' Oliver explained.

'I'm sure I'll manage,' Francesca said, looking up at him with a hopeful glance.

Elaine and Francesca walked their way back through the cremated concrete of the bombsite. They met the busy high street that mingled them in with fellow Londoners going about their business. Even though the surrounding area was noisy with the shouts of market stall owners, both girls continued along the pavement in silence.

'Is there something wrong?' Elaine questioned, sensing her friend's dismay.

'Why did you say that to them? It was like you were trying

to embarrass me,' Francesca said.

'I only told them the truth, you hardly ever go out, and if you do it's because you're working, going to church, or following your relatives about.'

'What are you trying to say?'

'Look, nobody is going to want to hang around you if you're boring, especially those types of people,' Elaine explained.

'So why did you say it?'

'Well, maybe I hoped it would make you live a bit, to make you realise how difficult it is for me having to deal with someone—'

'Someone?'

'Who can't let go of the past and enjoy the here and now.'

'You know exactly why I can't do that,' Francesca said, her cheeks flushed.

'What? Because you lost your brother and your dad? Everyone's lost somebody, Fran, you're just using it as an excuse,' she spoke spitefully.

'That's easy for you to say, you didn't lose anybody,' Francesca snapped as they parted down different streets, leaving the tension to engulf the space between them.

CHAPTER 4

THE RUINS WERE only a short distance from Coborn Road, yet at the slow pace Elaine was walking it seemed like it would take her the rest of the day to get home. She passed the normally neglected Morgan Arms Pub that was now lively. This was due to the accumulation of drunk Cockneys who were drinking away their sorrows after a hard week's work.

'Your name's Elaine, right?' the girl with the embroidered blazer asked as she walked towards her.

Startled, Elaine stopped dead in her tracks. 'Yes, and your name is—' She tried to remember.

'Charlotte, Lottie, my friends and family call me Lottie, you can call me Lottie too if you'd like?'

'Sure, it's nice to meet you properly, Lottie,' she said with a forced smile, the truth was she wasn't in the mood to chat.

'Sorry about my friends, they bicker a lot,' she mumbled as they continued down the road, the sound of drunken voices becoming a faint whisper.

'It's ok,' Elaine said, looking to the girl at her side. Charlotte was much shorter than her and her golden blonde hair was gripped in tight victory rolls on the top of her head, adding a few inches to her small height.

'So, you and Fran seem nice.' She smiled.

'Thanks, you and your friends seem… Interesting.'

'I hope we didn't come off in a bad way. I'd like you and Fran to meet the girls on their own. The boys can be a bit overpowering,' she suggested.

'I'm not sure,' Elaine said warily. She was overcome with guilt as she thought of her spiteful words towards her friend.

'Well, if you decide you want to, we'll be about the ruins tomorrow late-morning,' Charlotte invited before speeding ahead.

Francesca recognised the heavy-set clouds latching onto the dark sky. It would tip it down at any moment by the looks of things. She felt relieved as she entered the house but was met with quite the commotion.

'What the hell?' she blurted out, ducking as a budgie swooped around the ceiling.

'Less of the blasphemy,' her mother disciplined as she quickly turned her attention back to Vera. They'd clearly been arguing, and chaos had erupted. Shouting filled the room as the bird flew around the air space like a Spitfire over the cliffs of Dover.

'Shut the door before Twinkle escapes,' Vera ordered as her granddaughter quickly obeyed.

'I can't believe you bought a bird, a bloody bird,' Stephanie shouted.

'I thought he might liven up the place considering you're such a bore,' Vera snapped as the bird's green and yellow feathers soared above their heads.

'Twinkle, did I hear that correctly, you honestly named the bird Twinkle?' Francesca asked, amused.

'I wasn't going to call him Lancaster Bomber now was I,' Vera muttered.

'It might be fitting considering the bombs it's dropped.' Francesca laughed as she acknowledged the poo ridden floor.

'Not funny, have you seen the mess this creature has made,' Stephanie said, her face twisted in anguish.

'I think it's hard not to see, mum.'

'Just get it back in the bloody cage,' her mother said sternly, retreating to the kitchen.

'How did he even get out of the cage?'

'That, my dear, is an excellent question,' Vera said, studying the bird's movements with her hands firmly placed on her hips.

'We should call him Houdini,' Francesca suggested.

'That seems fitting, Houdini it is,' Vera agreed.

Charley looked exhausted. He appeared drained with dark circles around his eyes. Every movement gave way to a sharp pain in his muscles, yet this was not new to him. Even though he was a muscular man who made light work of hard labour, the long shifts down the docks took their toll. He rubbed his shoulder, feeling the scarred skin hidden underneath his linen shirt. Entering the house, he was met by his mother who, by the smell coming from the kitchen, was preparing a dinner consisting of corned beef, potatoes and peas.

'Charley, darling, can you check on Elaine? She's been in a foul mood all afternoon and won't speak to me,' she said, tending to the potatoes.

'Of course I will,' he said, ascending the staircase, leading him to his little sister's room. 'What's up then? Mum said you've been a grumpy git.' He sat on the end of her bed.

'I don't want to talk about it, Charley,' she said stubbornly. Elaine was perched at her vanity, brushing her curls.

'Well, I do, so spill the beans,' he persisted.

'I went with Fran to meet the boy she met at the dance hall, and his friends. I made some comments, and she said I embarrassed her,' Elaine explained.

'What did you say exactly?' he asked, watching his sister's reflection.

'Only the truth. They asked what she did, and I said that she doesn't get up to much, and that if she does it's because she's going to church, work, or running after family.'

'So, you implied she was boring,' he said, rolling his eyes.

'Yeah, but we got in an argument, and I said some things I shouldn't have,' she admitted.

'Like what?'

'I said she was using her dad and brother's deaths as an excuse not to have fun and enjoy herself.'

'For goodness' sake, Elaine, what were you thinking saying something like that?' he said sharply.

'I know, thinking about it now, I shouldn't have said it,' she said regretfully, turning to meet his irritated glance.

'You need to go over there and apologise.'

'But I'm in my pyjamas,' she protested.

'That's never stopped you before,' he muttered, standing from the bed.

'You know you smell really damp,' Elaine commented as she walked past him.

'Funny that. I work down the docks, you know, near the water?' Charley teased.

She glared at him before bundling down the stairs.

Saying goodnight to her grandmother who was sitting comfortably in her armchair, Francesca looked at Houdini who sat patiently in his cage. However, this was ever so slightly disconcerting as the bird's calmness gave way to the idea that he was plotting his next great escape.

She had a hot chocolate in her hands. Specifically, it was Charbonnel hot chocolate that she had received a tub of as a Christmas present and had preserved its use for especially strenuous days. As the Queen's favourite hot chocolate, it made Francesca feel regal as she proceeded up the stairs in her nightgown. Meeting her mother's glance, she continued to her room whilst blowing on the steaming mug.

'Fran, come here for a minute.' In a fetching pair of slippers and a dressing gown, Stephanie beckoned her in. She was sat on her double bed, covered by a large patchwork quilt made of varying shapes and colours. It resembled the stained-glass that decorated the church windows. A pile of past Women's Weekly and Stitch Craft magazines laid open on the bedside cabinet.

'What's the matter?' Francesca asked as she poked her head around the doorframe.

'Oh, I'm quite alright, I'm more concerned with what's bothering you.'

'Nothing's wrong,' she said.

'Don't take me for a fool, I can tell when you're fibbing.'

Her mother persisted, patting the space beside her.

'I just had a falling out with Elaine, that's all.' She sat on the bed, careful not to spill her hot chocolate.

'Well thank goodness, I thought it could be something more serious. I always know you've had a troubling day when you whip out the hot chocolate,' Stephanie said with relief.

'But it is serious, mum.' Francesca tapped her fingernails on the mug's ceramic edge.

'You've had many fallings-out before, and they've always been resolved, this one is no different,' her mother assured.

'How do you know that?'

'Because I know you both, you've been in each other's lives since birth. That connection can't be broken with one stupid argument now can it.'

'I suppose, but she hurt my feelings,' Francesca said, taking a sip, chocolate lining her top lip.

'If that's the case, I'm sure she'll apologise, and anyway, you're made from tougher stuff than to be so affected by words.'

'It's not the words that bother me, it's the person who said them.'

'People say the obscenest things when they're angry. I mean, look at me and your grandmother. We may argue, but it doesn't mean we love each other any less,' she said.

Francesca sat, contemplating. 'I'll make things right with her.'

Stephanie planted a kiss on her forehead. 'Not before getting some sleep.'

Hopping off the bed, Francesca wandered to the doorway. Stopping, the lacy hem of her nighty brushed her knees. 'You know, I think it's time for you to come back to church, everyone always asks after you,' she said before leaving her mother to her thoughts.

Retiring to her room, Francesca sat at her vanity. It displayed a set of old school silver brushes and perfume bottles. Her hair clips and ribbons sat in a little silver box, while a few lipsticks and other bits of makeup hid in the drawer below. Taking down her hair, she greeted her reflection whilst sipping the rest of her hot chocolate.

Yanking off the frilly cushions that decorated her small double bed, she pulled back her champagne pink covers and laid herself down. Turning off the bedside lamp, she felt an appreciation for the darkness for it allowed her to be at peace. This was quite a change from when she was younger and feared the dark, or more specifically what lurked in the dark. The darkness was merely a space for entities to hide until they decided to show themselves. The nights spent in the Underground were the most frightful times, and she could recall the sound of every explosion as though it was yesterday. Flammable entities raged havoc on the city streets, traumatising those unfortunate souls who were caught in the blackness. She remembered the shaking walls, the scared faces, fearful embraces, bangs, crashes, noises that made it seem as though the world had been turned upside down, and hell itself had been unleashed on the earth's surface.

She heard a whack, but this wasn't a memory from the past. Whack again, and once more. She opened her eyes and reached for the light. Hurrying to the window, she opened it up to see a soppy looking Elaine who stood in her pyjamas with a handful of pebbles.

'I, um, I just thought I'd come to apologise, I didn't mean what I said.'

'Did your brother put you up to this?' Francesca questioned, sussing out her change of heart.

'Of course he did, but that doesn't mean I'm not sorry,' she admitted as she shivered, the night-time air biting at her exposed ankles.

'It's ok, I'm made of tougher stuff,' Francesca said proudly as her long hair dangled out the window.

'So, you forgive me?' Elaine asked, performing a few jumping jacks, attempting to keep warm.

'Yes, I forgive you, now get off the pavement, you're in your bloody pyjamas!' she exclaimed.

Elaine jogged on the spot. 'Oh, before I go, I bumped into one of Oliver's friends, Lottie I think, she invited us to hang out with her and the girls tomorrow morning, I thought we could pop along after church,' she informed.

'Sounds like a plan, as long as I'm back in time to go shopping with grandma, now go before someone sees you.' She laughed.

Returning to the bombsite, the girls greeted them. The ruins masked them in shadows as the sun attempted to filter through the cracks of the defaced buildings. The morning air pushed its way around the rubble, swirls of dust decorating the floor in an elaborate display. Francesca perched delicately on top of a chipped and charred concrete block, her long legs swinging to-and-fro.

'I take it Oli has lured you in with some sort of gentleman act,' Kerry stated, straight to the point. Her thick creepers poked from under her tailored trousers, and her hands were balled fists in the pockets of her drape jacket.

'He seems nice enough,' Francesca said, looking to the others for reassurance.

'You don't know him like we do.'

'Don't scare her off, she's our new friend.' Charlotte stared angrily at her.

'Oh, is she now,' Kerry retorted, unconvinced.

'Why don't you go and iron your trousers or somethin',' she said, the group sniggering.

'You're brave considering you're five-foot fuck all, Lottie, be careful, I might step on you by accident.'

'Better to be five-foot fuck all than built like a brick shithouse.'

Kerry's scowl turned into an amused grin, and Charlotte started to giggle. Francesca sat awkwardly, confused by the verbal back-and-forth until she was pulled back into the conversation.

'Don't worry about Oli, he'll treat you like a princess,' Isla said kindly.

'Isla knows from personal experience, she can tell you about all their 'adventures'.' Kerry smirked as she lit a cigarette, offering one to Elaine who politely declined.

'That was a long time ago,' Isla said, her green eyes awkwardly meeting Francesca's.

'This is my brother you are talking about,' Susan interrupted.

'Did he...' Kerry continued.

Francesca fiddled with the buttons on her cardigan. 'What?' she panicked.

'You know...' she pressed.

'I really don't know.'

'Stop being so bloody nosy, Fran, you don't have to tell us anything,' Susan said, looking at Kerry with annoyance at her sudden personal interrogation.

'Oliver has been very secretive lately,' Charlotte added.

'My brother's business is my brother's business, and I intend on keepin' out of it,' Susan said bluntly.

'It's a bit difficult when his business is sittin' right in front of us,' Kerry continued. 'So, have you, you know, slept with him?'

'What, no!' Francesca exclaimed.

'Come on, it's not very polite asking that,' Isla muttered.

'I, um, haven't really done anything with anyone at all,' Francesca admitted, looking at them timidly.

'I bloody told you she was a virgin,' Kerry blurted out, turning to Susan with a smug grin.

'I think we all knew that, and we were all one once,' Susan said as she lit a cigarette, hoping she could use it as an excuse not to contribute to the conversation.

'Is it that obvious?' Francesca asked anxiously.

'Of course not,' Charlotte said sincerely as she played with a piece of rubble, passing it from one foot to the other.

'Don't worry, Fran, it'll happen when you're good and ready,' Isla assured.

Vera was in pursuit of the latest bargains as she caught sight of the distant market. She rarely moved for anything, her short heavy frame only hurried for two things, church and the Ladies' Market that occurred every Sunday. Francesca followed behind as she carried her grandmother's bulky handbag. It was heavy and appeared to be containing everything but the kitchen sink.

'Do come along, dear, it'll be the evening by the time we get there if you keep walking at that pace. Shoulders back and chin up, the way you are walking would never have been accepted in the Air Force.'

'Well, it's a good thing I'm not thinking of joining the Air Force any time soon,' Francesca muttered, falling behind.

'Oh, it was a wonderful experience, I got to travel all over the place, even persuaded one lad to take me up in a Bristol Fighter,' Vera said, blissfully unaware of her granddaughter's struggle.

'I don't speak military.'

'An aeroplane, a very exciting one at that, they used them during the Great War.'

'Fascinating, but I'd rather keep my feet firmly on the ground,' she said.

'Is that why you slouch, so you can get closer to the ground?' Vera asked, turning back to Francesca in one surprisingly swift motion.

'You're making it sound like I'm the Hunchback of Notre Dame,' she spoke despondently.

'Don't be silly, you couldn't be further from it, I just have high standards for you. But what more could I ask for, I've already got a perfect granddaughter.'

Francesca blushed, whether it was due to the compliment or the strain of the weighty bag in her arms she wasn't quite sure.

'Not all jobs in the Air Force involve flying, Fran, I was a mechanic, I did technical work, but mostly welding and fitting, it was a bonus when the airmen would take me up.'

'When did you join?'

'A very long time ago, but I remember it like it was yesterday. That was the making of me.' She reminisced.

'Wasn't having mum the making of you?' Francesca questioned.

'Not when you're unwed and with child at seventeen, it was nearly the breaking of me, if it wasn't for your grandfather,

God rest his soul. I was a child myself, with a child,' Vera admitted, slowing her pace.

'I never knew that. Why do you never talk about it?' Francesca asked.

'Few people will speak of their most vulnerable times unless it's to someone they really trust. You're old enough to understand that people make mistakes.'

'Was mum a mistake?'

Stopping in her tracks, Vera answered, 'I'm not going to sugar-coat it, it was the biggest mistake I could have ever made at such a young age. But you know what, I wouldn't change a thing, because here, now, in 1955, I have both my girls beside me, and I love you more than anything. Everyone makes mistakes, the most important thing is that we learn from them and pick ourselves back up.'

'So, you recommend a few mistakes here and there.' Francesca grinned as they reached the market.

'Yes, for that is what life itself is made of, mistakes and lessons, you'll always get something out of them whether you like it or not. Now, less of the sentimentalism, it's time to find you some clothes,' she declared.

Market-goers flocked to the area while the shouts of stall owners penetrated the air, speaking of the best prices they could offer. The market presented a huge array of garments. Traditional dresses sat alongside modern three-quarter-length denim jeans. Clothing lined the pavements on mannequins and hangers; the pieces incorporating textures from velvet and satin to cotton. The natural and synthetic structures allowed an endless presentation of designs. As the gentle breeze followed through the carved fabric pathways, organza materials fluttered in the wind, creating an almost otherworldly looking location.

This 'Ladies' Market', which acquired its name because of the mass of fabric on display, attracted all sorts of people, especially the youth. Spending their weekly wages, they were quick to gobble up the latest trends at their expense. This could be seen as stalls were dedicated to new American fashions with bolo ties and hair grease.

Accessories were also on display. Beads and costume jewellery lined tables while more delicate pieces laid within glass boxes. Gold and silver gleamed and glistened with every jolt of sunlight, attracting people to the stalls like treasure hunting magpies. Shoes sat in rows, they were made of leather and suede, and their buckles shone brightly as though they too were adorned with jewellery.

Vera was on a mission that led her straight to a stall that presented skirts of all descriptions. Turning to her granddaughter with a grin, she held up two pencil skirts, one black and one grey. Sizing up her waist, she deliberated. 'Now this will have you looking like a real businesswoman.' She smiled.

'Don't you think it'll be a bit tight?'

'It's never too tight, my dear, women used to wear corsets back in the day remember, I'm sure you can manage.'

'If you insist,' Francesca said as she held the skirt to her waist.

'I'm not sure about the colour,' she said with a judgemental squint.

''Ello Vera, is this your Fran?' A little lady asked as she appeared from the back of the stall. She was wrinkly and her grey hair was thinning.

'Yes, this is,' Vera answered proudly as she looped her arm around Francesca's waist, hugging her tightly.

The lady smiled at her with an almost toothless grin. 'She

speaks ever so highly of you. I take it you're shopping for a work outfit like she told me. We have got a burgundy one if you'd like, it's the last one in stock.'

'Well, if it's the last one,' Vera said, taking out her purse, retracting a few coins.

'I'll knock a few bob off for ya, Vera, as you're a regular.'

'Thank you very much.' She grinned.

The group sat around a table at one of their regular haunts, a café on the corner of Brady Street. It allowed a wide view in four directions so they could watch people going about their business. Some funnelled into the Underground, while others walked the long pavements that lined Whitechapel Road. London Hospital was large and loomed over the busy traffic. It had a huge red brick exterior, and a faded green clock tower that sat at its centre, the hands relentlessly ticking the minutes by.

The Tube could be heard trapesing its way through London's underbelly. It was a homely sound, one of which Oliver remembered from when he was very young. He sat contently, taking in the area. He listened as the nearby Blind Beggar Pub sign swung gently, creating a repetitive creak. The boys would go in there to catch a rumour or two, or perhaps a fist if one of them got particularly rowdy. This was normally Jack who was naturally aggressive without alcohol and was always bruised or battered in one way or another. Spending his days working in his father's butcher shop, he was never far from blood and guts.

'So, is this Fran girl a passing phase, or is she gonna stick around?' Jack pressed as he scraped a bit of dried blood from his wrist.

Oliver's jaw clenched. 'She's lovely.'

'So, I take that as a yes.' Colin analysed, sitting poised in his three-piece bottle-green suit.

'She looked like she'd be as tight as a duck's arse, be careful, she might make you wait till marriage,' Jack mocked as the boys cracked up at the thought. The sun melted onto their black drape jackets as the morning sunshine transpired into mid-day heat.

'Watch your mouth,' Oliver said through gritted teeth.

'Oh, come on, Oli, it was just a shock to us all,' Colin said.

'What was a shock?' he snapped.

'Well, you know…' Cautiously he looked to the others for back up.

'Go on, spit it out,' Oliver ordered with increasing frustration.

'She's delicate, you'll probably break her in half,' Harry answered bluntly as he sipped his tea.

'Physically speaking,' Jack said with a grin.

'And mentally,' Colin said, concerned.

'I can be gentle,' he stated, trying to reassure them.

'Yeah right, that's not what Isla said,' Albie uttered, spilling the beans as he munched on his full English breakfast.

'And why should I care for what Isla said?' Oliver asked sharply as his friend touched a sensitive nerve.

'Because she gave us a first-hand account,' Harry informed him as he reached for the teapot.

'Leave Isla out of this, her and Oli are old news,' Jack huffed.

'Sorry, Jack, I keep forgetting you're an item,' Harry said, realising his mistake.

Colin looked worryingly at his friend. 'Fran will be a challenge, you know you'll have to chase her. What I'm trying to say is that she's trouble, you'll get too emotionally invested.'

'Yeah, traditional girls want someone who will treat them right, a gentleman of sorts,' Albie said as he wiped his mouth with a napkin.

'You lot just don't want change, it scares you,' Oliver said, looking at them all.

'Not as much as the prospect of you becoming civil,' Albie proclaimed.

'And we all know there is no fun in being civil,' Jack added as he brought a cigarette to his lips.

As Lewis joined them, Finn shortly followed and made himself comfortable.

'Tea?' Harry offered as he held up the pot.

'I'm more of a coffee person,' Lewis said, beckoning the waitress over. Jack handed a cigarette to Finn who exhaled smoke into the air.

'So, Oliver, quite the catch you've reeled in,' Lewis squeezed, running the comb through his blonde hair.

'It is what it is,' he said cautiously.

'Well, if it goes tits up between you two, I'll happily take her off your hands,' he said as the waitress brought over a pot of steaming coffee. The boys stared each other down, a smile creeping over Lewis's face.

The van provided hot food and condiments from punnets of chips to steaming bacon butties. Francesca fought against the dripping oil as the bacon fat seeped into the white bread roll. It was a messy ordeal and her grandmother quickly passed her a handkerchief to wipe off her sticky fingers.

She rummaged through the items that had been bought for

her. There was the burgundy pencil skirt and a matching velvet blazer. A plain blouse accompanied by flat pumps finished off the outfit.

'I want to pick up a scarf, my one is getting tatty.' Vera decided as she looked down at the dishevelled piece of fabric that sat around her neck.

'I'm sure I saw a stall selling a whole load of scarfs,' Francesca said, pointing.

As they proceeded to a table littered with material, Vera contemplated the printed and patterned designs. As she nattered with the stall owner, Francesca looked around impatiently. She loved her grandmother, but she knew everybody and could talk the hind legs off a donkey. As she peered at the different pieces, a shadowy figure appeared behind her.

'Boo!' a female voice said mischievously, grabbing her ribs.

Francesca turned quickly. 'Oh, hello Lottie, you startled me for a second.' She laughed.

Charlotte stood in a circle skirt and an embroidered top while two victory rolls sculpted her golden blonde hair into position. She looked exactly as she had done that morning, however, her pumps were now dusty from the ruins.

'You fancy a walkabout?' she asked with a grin.

'I'm here with my grandma,' Francesca said.

'Oh, don't worry about me, go and enjoy yourself,' Vera insisted as she turned her attention back to the stall owner.

Walking through winding alleyways, Francesca followed her guide as she was led further into the city.

'So, is Lottie your proper name, or just a nickname?' Francesca asked, trying to keep to the pace of the girl before her.

She was shorter, faster and more agile at navigating London's hidden paths.

'It's my nickname, my proper name is Charlotte Lovett, and I'm eighteen-years-old. I work in one of those big factories, you know, those car ones. I sew interiors and stuff, but I prefer making dresses. I like the colour purple, I heard it's a royal colour, I would love to be a royal, wouldn't you?' Francesca had asked one simple question, yet the response left her with a life story and her acquaintance's regal ambitions.

'Well, I'm nineteen and my name is Francesca Parmenter.' Acknowledging the scabs that lined her freckled skin, she couldn't help but ask, 'What happened to your hands?'

'Oh, my hands always look like that,' Charlotte said dismissively.

'Why?'

'Because I work them to the bone every time I step into that factory. It's quantity over quality in there. If I don't get enough done I don't get paid. I have to rush, and my hands end up looking like pin cushions by the time I leave.'

'That's awful. My hands are in pain after typing all day at work, but they never look like that.' She looked down at her delicate piano player fingers—as her grandmother called them.

'I'll live, so where do you work?' Charlotte asked. Her gaze remained fixed on the cobbles ahead as they swerved in and out of the red brick maze, under washing lines and over manhole covers.

'A bank.'

'Oh, I wouldn't be able to do that, I'm no good with numbers.'

'Luckily I only have to deal with words as I'm a personal secretary, a few digits here and there, but it's nothing too challenging. What's your boss like?' Francesca asked.

'A fat prick with a habit for making my life difficult,' she muttered.

'Can't you leave?'

'It's not that simple, I have no college education, opportunities around here are pretty limited, and I can't risk being unemployed, I have to support my family,' Charlotte answered as they spilled out onto a busy street.

'I'm sure you could find a job as a seamstress, you sound like you'd enjoy that kind of work,' Francesca suggested as she caught up with her, positioning herself at her side.

Daydream-like, Charlotte rambled, 'Anything is better than making car interiors. I like the sound the machine makes, you know, when you stitch into the fabric. Bright fabrics, dark fabrics, I can do anything really.'

'If it makes you feel any better, I sit at a desk typing away my days taking orders from my boss who smokes twenty cigarettes a minute.'

Charlotte sniggered as they entered a courtyard. Francesca had been to Stepney before, but her guide's winding twenty-minute route comprising of back alleys and dodgy diversions had confused her entirely; not to mention her difficulty in recognising the district after being partially destroyed by the Blitz.

'Where are we?' she asked.

'Home, I thought you'd like a cuppa.' Charlotte smiled as they met eyes with a block of flats.

'That would be nice, I've not really been here, ever since the bombings that is,' Francesca said, following her up a steep set of stairs to the first floor.

'Yeah, the government made these apartments after the war.

A more modern touch, I guess.' Reaching the front door, she welcomed her in.

The interior was a small space complete with a shaggy rug, a tiny metal fireplace and a printed sofa. An arch led to the kitchen that revealed a little pine wood table with a small vase of roses at the centre which appeared to be reaching the end of their life span. Popping the kettle on, Charlotte reached for some custard cream biscuits that she laid on a Denby plate. Taking a seat on the weathered sofa, Francesca acknowledged the pairs of shoes that carefully lined the entrance.

'Who lives here with you?'

'My dad and younger sister. My mum died in the smog. She always had breathing problems and they got the better of her,' Charlotte explained.

'I'm sorry. It must be difficult for you. I remember the smog, it covered the whole of London,' Francesca said with dismay.

'Yeah, who doesn't remember the smog.' She frowned as the kettle bubbled and boiled, sending steam into the surrounding air.

1952

THE BIG SMOKE

THE CAPITAL WAS laced in an unbreakable fog. Toxic fumes navigated the entrails of London, finding its way into the lungs of its inhabitants. The city came to a standstill, and panic thrived as days turned to nights. London stood in a stagnant state as people resided inside like rats to the gutter. Even the Underground was invaded by the havoc-wreaking fog, and those who braved the streets shuffled cautiously along the walls.

'The hospital is only a little way ahead,' Charlotte said hopefully as she navigated the brick wall beside her. She was leading the way to a woman in her early forties.

Her mother.

She was coughing and spluttering as she battled against the thick air. She removed a handkerchief from her mouth.

'I don't think I'm going to make it,' she said as she felt her lungs groan with every exasperated breath.

'Don't be silly, I can see the hospital, we're nearly there.'

'I'm not talking about the hospital, Lottie,' her mother said as she collapsed against the wall, suffocating on the inescapable fumes.

As she cried out for help, her mother's heart slowly stopped beating. Charlotte's screams failed to break through the thick layers of dense gas that had rendered the city unconscious.

CHAPTER 5

THE SUNDAY MORNING presented a mild environment, not too hot, not too cold. People wandered around in a docile state. London resembled that of a clock, winding down as the seven days ended. The mixture of unmoving clouds and the blue sky created a diluted presence as both blended in harmony. The sun's gentle rays glimmered onto the bright white church and Francesca squinted as she stared at it, her eyes tired from a week of typewriting.

Her grandmother held her arm as they proceeded to the large wooden doors. Despite feeling incredibly exhausted, she was well put together and wore a petal pink dress and a red cardigan. She fiddled with her plaited hair, making sure it was in perfect placement.

'Good to see you both this morning,' the Priest said, meeting eyes with them.

'And you,' Vera replied.

'No Stephanie today?' he questioned.

'Mum wasn't up to it,' Francesca said timidly.

'She's never up to it,' Vera muttered.

'I'm sure she'll come back when she's good and ready, sooner, however, is better than later,' the Priest said as he guided them down the aisle.

Catching sight of Elaine, they bolted to each other's side. As Vera nattered to Judy, the Priest approached both girls.

'Congratulations on getting the job, Francesca, I didn't get the opportunity to tell you last Sunday as you rushed off so quickly,' he said. It seemed almost contradictory, his praise was delivered with such a firm tone that it sounded as though she was being told off.

'Thank you. We were meeting with some friends after the service, so we had to hurry,' she said politely. There was an element of awkwardness to the interactions between them. Maybe it was down to the unsettling presence of an authority figure, or possibly the fact that she could never seem to behave as she was supposed to in his presence.

'How is your brother, Elaine? He's been absent from church for quite some time,' the Priest interrogated.

'He's just been really busy recently, and uh—'

Saving her friend's skin, Francesca was quick to answer. 'He has trouble making the time, it's very hectic down the docks.' They looked to each other guiltily, they both knew that Charley was lacking in the faith department.

'That's a shame. Faith is a very important part of life, one that people should make time for,' the Priest lectured.

'But is reading stories out of a book and chanting the same thing over and over really showing your faith?' Elaine asked, unconvinced.

'No, it's enforcing it, both of you better take a seat,' the Priest said, recognising his full congregation, leading him to proceed to the main altar.

'Do you think we pissed him off?' Francesca questioned as they shuffled in between the wooden pews. Plonking themselves down, they grabbed their bibles and flicked through the service books.

'Nah, he's just a grumpy git,' Elaine said carelessly.

'Watch your mouth, Elaine. He may be a 'grumpy git' but that is my dad you're talking about,' Colin teased. He sat on the pew behind them wearing a structured brown three-piece suit and a visible gold crucifix that hung loosely around his neck. With his dark hair slicked back, he sat comfortably on the hard bench.

'Sorry, Colin, I didn't realise you were behind us,' Elaine apologised in a fluster.

'No harm done, just be careful who you slag off,' he said, smiling. His accent was Northern Irish, but not as fierce as his father's due to the slight dilution of British phrases. This was accountable to his time spent in the west midlands when he was a child and the influence of the company he now kept in Mile End.

As the service progressed, Francesca lost interest and she looked at the stained-glass around her for an escape. The Priest acknowledged her distraction, his eyes narrowing in her direction. Elaine nudged her back to concentration as she repositioned her gaze on the leather-bound Bible in her hands.

Kneeling at the front of the church, the girls received communion as they did every Sunday. Colin knelt beside Francesca as the wine and bread were ceremoniously dispersed. Elaine left after receiving her weekly intake of wafer. It stuck to the roof of her mouth like glue. Francesca too rose from her place only to be pulled back down by Colin who gently gripped her arm.

'I know we haven't spoken much, and I don't know you very well, Fran, which is embarrassing as we attend the same church but anyway, I'll keep this short and snappy, for your sake please be careful with Oliver.'

'What do you mean?' she asked, caught off guard. It wasn't exactly the most appropriate conversation to have while receiving communion.

'Nothin' bad, but you have to look after him. His ego is fragile and his temper is fierce. I'm not trying to scare you off, that's the last thing I wanna do.'

'So, what are you suggesting?' Francesca asked.

'That you don't enter into something without being 100%,' he said as he placed the polystyrene-like communion wafer into his mouth.

'I've known him less than a month Colin, I can only confirm about 65%,' she answered with unintentional wit.

Almost choking on the wine-filled chalice, he turned to her, amused. 'You got me there, I'm just saying first-timers fall hard.'

Rising from her place, she returned to the pew. As he sat down behind them, she turned and assured him. 'I may be a 'first-timer', but I am not naive in terms of my emotions. He'll have to work for that remaining 35% I promise you that.'

'Well, that told me,' he sighed as he leant back in his seat.

Sitting stiffly, Francesca slowly navigated the words that laid before her on a very pompous letter. Following it with her finger, she slowly replicated the precise lettering with her poised and polished typewriter.

'Less haste, more speed, Francesca,' Mr Montgomery ordered from over his large desk. A few antiques glistened on top of the wooden surface, and his slicked-back silver hair shone slightly as the bright Monday morning sky forced its way through the large glass window behind him.

'Sorry, Sir,' Francesca stated automatically as she processed the text as quickly as she could. She'd got used to apologising for the littlest things, whether for staring out the window, watching the clock, or fiddling with her locket. She never seemed to be able to do anything right in the eyes of her grumbling employer.

'Stop apologising, it's a waste of both our time,' he said sharply, flicking through the files in front of him. 'Has Penny mentioned to you how many people have failed at this position?' he questioned, lifting his gaze to meet hers.

'She's hinted at it,' Francesca answered, nervously fiddling with the hem of her pencil skirt.

'Well then stop bloody apologising, just get on with it. I want you to do as you're told, but I want you to have a backbone, to talk to me honestly. Ever since you started here you've sat there silently, not uttering a word unless it's to apologise. Telling you the truth, the amount of North and West End girls who have tried and failed at this position is astounding, I need someone that's able to do more than just sit and look pretty. I know from experience, women from our neck of the woods will get shit done and they speak their mind, that's why I hired you, do you understand?' he said, discarding file after file back into the cabinet.

'I understand, Sir, and I'm grateful for the opportunity, I really am. I'm just not used to it yet, all the marble and fancy equipment, big offices, and important looking people. It's just a bit intimidating.'

'You'll get used to it, and it does get easier. I started here ten years ago, and it was only by the skin of my teeth that I managed to work my way up to this position. I could have never dreamed of such a job as a young boy from Bethnal Green, but times are changing. You need to take advantage of the times, make the most of your opportunities,' he said with a grin as he lit a cigarette, his third that morning.

'I'll try and do that, Sir.' She nodded appreciatively.

'Now chop chop, get on with it,' he bellowed whilst exhaling a cloud of grey smoke, camouflaging his silver locks of hair.

'Good morning you,' Colin said as the outside brightness invaded the bedroom, under and over the breeze blown curtains. The wooden bed concealed the two of them and allowed a comfortable refuge of magnolia cream sheets and scattered pillows.

'Good morning,' she said, turning into his arms.

'And to think people hate Mondays,' Colin said as he hugged her.

As Susan's messy black hair tickled his chin, she looked up at him. 'Well, I can imagine the prospect of rising early to face five days of labour to be an experience justifiably hated.'

'I love the way you use big words to prove a point.' He laughed.

'It normally confuses people into agreement, it's what the politicians do. Maybe you will have to use a few big words when you tell my brother about us,' she implied.

'That's if I can even get any words out without gettin' my

jaw broken,' Colin said pessimistically.

'That won't happen, you're his best friend,' Susan assured him.

'That's exactly why it will happen,' Colin said, reluctant to face the harsh reality that he had been sleeping with his best friend's sister behind his back for the past six months, which probably wouldn't result in his understanding.

'You have to tell him, Colin. We can't keep sneaking around in each other's bed sheets. Someone will see, and God help us if my brother finds out through someone else.'

'I know. I'll tell him when it's the right time.'

'Good, you do realise you're gonna be late for work,' she said, concerned as she looked to the old clock on his bedside table.

'I'll just tell them I was a little pre-occupied,' Colin dismissed, looking down at her.

'A little pre-occupied?' She smiled with devilish eyes.

'Yeah.' He grinned.

'Well let me help with that pre-occupation.' Susan navigated her hand below the bed sheets.

'I fuckin' love Mondays,' he said under his breath.

The streets were calm. People wandered along the cobbles as the late spring breeze brushed by them. A florist sat along the road. The wind caused the assortments of displayed flowers to sway gently. Elaine, who was picking a few freshly bloomed tulips, met eyes with Oliver's reflection in the glass.

'What would you recommend?' he asked as he met her side.

'I'm not an expert, but daisies are always a good bet.' She smiled.

'Daisies it is then.'

'I take it they're for Fran?' Elaine questioned as she picked out a few more tulips, their red and yellow petals bright and beautiful.

'Yeah, I'm going to ask her out,' he informed.

'Flowers are a good start. You better treat her right.' She turned to him, looking into his bright blue eyes.

'You think I won't?' he questioned, surprised by her boldness.

'I don't know what you'll do. Why did you choose her?' Elaine asked suspiciously.

'She's a pretty girl, why wouldn't I?' he justified.

'She's just not the type I'd imagine you'd go for judging from the girls you hang around with.' She observed.

'You shouldn't be so quick to judge, and you have nothing to worry about, I promise,' he assured as he grabbed a handful of daisies. 'You wouldn't happen to know how I can get these to her? I don't know where she lives.'

'15 Coborn Road. Grab some pebbles from one of the flowerpots and aim for the top window, it'll save you from being interrogated by Vera, her grandmother.'

'Thanks for the heads up.' Oliver grinned.

The garage was only small, but it had enough clutter in it to fix up every vehicle in the city. A couple of cars sat patiently inside, being worked on by men in sweaty and oily shirts.

'What flavour is that then?' Harry questioned as his head appeared from under the synched-up car.

'Apple, you want a lick?' Charlotte asked as she took the lollypop from her mouth, passing it down to his greasy grasp. She sat in a prim and proper state with her hair fastened back with a blue bow. Perched on the car bonnet, she fiddled with the red toolbox beside her. 'What's this?' she asked, pulling out a wrench.

'Somethin' you shouldn't be playing with,' he said as he ducked back under the vehicle, fiddling with the car's underbelly as the lolly hung from his mouth.

'What are you doing?' she questioned, swinging her legs back-and-forth.

'My job,' Harry answered bluntly, trying to concentrate.

'Do you like your job?' she asked again, forcing the conversation from him.

'I wouldn't be here if I didn't,' he said as he appeared from under the metal structure. Harry passed the lolly back to Charlotte as he sat upright.

'I wish I could leave mine,' she said despondently, feeling the inflamed freckled skin that was concealed by her blazer. She quickly shoved the lollypop back into her mouth.

'Why's that? Is that bastard still giving you trouble?' Harry asked, wiping his dirt ridden hands with a cloth as she lifted her blazer sleeve. 'I'll take his head off.' He scowled as Charlotte revealed a set of bruises that lined her lower and upper arm.

'I need this job, I can't keep it if my boss has no head.'

'We'll see about that,' he said stubbornly.

'Harry, please don't do anything, it'll just make it worse.'

'This can't keep happening, Lottie.' He rose from the ground, studying her injuries, his huge frame casting a shadow over her.

'Yeah, well nobody's gonna believe me,' she dismissed, rolling the blazer sleeve back down, concealing her skin.

'You leave Talbot with me, he will never touch you again.'

He lifted her chin, so her gaze met his.

'You're too good to me, Harry.'

'We've gotta look out for each other,' he said protectively. 'Now pass me that spanner,' he uttered before ducking back under the metal carcase.

'I'd love a car like this,' she said as she passed him the tool.

'Can you even drive?'

'No, but you could teach me,' she implied.

'Maybe one day.' Harry chuckled, wriggling his broad shoulders further under the vehicle.

Francesca let the warm water trickle down her body. Careful not to get shampoo in her eyes, she lifted her head back to allow the soap suds to cascade from her hair. Like a foamy waterfall, the suds plummeted down to the plughole. Reaching for a flannel she wiped her eyes, saving them from irritation.

'Fran, dear, are you going to be long? I could do with using the facilities.'

Quickly yanking on a mustard-coloured towel, Francesca opened the door to greet her fidgeting grandmother. 'All yours,' she said with a smile as she waddled quickly into her room, careful not to leave a trail of water on the carpet. Wiping herself down, she pulled on her dressing gown and plonked herself at her vanity. Combing the stubborn strands of hair, she battled with the knots and tangles.

Hearing a sudden bang on the glass, she leapt to her feet. Hurrying to the window, she expected to see Elaine, but Elaine never threw the pebbles that hard. Opening the wooden frame, she was met by the blinding sky.

'Oliver? What are you doing down there?' She laughed,

squinting as she looked down at him.

'Elaine said this was a way to get your attention,' Oliver stated, fiddling with a few pebbles in his right hand.

'By breaking my bloody window? And how do you suppose you're gonna get up here?' she asked with amusement. Her wet hair dangled from the frame.

'I didn't really think it through, just wanted a chat, Frankie. You look like a brown-haired Rapunzel!' Oliver shouted up at her.

'Yeah, if Rapunzel got caught in a storm, and please try to be quiet, my grandma is in the other room,' she fretted.

'I think you look very stylish, especially the dressing gown at four thirty in the afternoon,' he said cheekily, looking at his pocket watch.

'Montgomery let me go home early. Hang on, I'll come down to you,' she said, shutting her window. Navigating her way past Vera who was occupied in the bathroom, she greeted Oliver in the doorway. 'So, what can I do for you? There better be a good reason for me to open the door in this state.'

'I wanted to give you these,' Oliver said happily as he passed her a bouquet of daisies that he'd been hiding behind his back. 'And to ask when you're next free for dinner, I was thinking Friday after you finish work?' he suggested as she hugged the bunch, giving them a sniff.

'That would be lovely,' she replied, trying to conceal her Cheshire cat-like grin.

'Oi Oli, get your arse over here,' Jack called out from behind them. He stood with the other boys who were kicking their feet in frustration on the opposite side of the road.

'Lovely thing, shame it won't last long,' Lewis said, watching Francesca as she lingered in the doorway.

'I'll give it two months at the most.' Finn smirked, leaning against the wall with crossed arms.

'Both of you pack it in,' Harry muttered. Francesca caught sight of the boys staring; they quickly diverted their eyes.

'I love what you've done with your hair, it's very rough and ready, wartime chic,' Albie added humorously as he sauntered up to the doorway.

'I'm glad you like it.' Francesca laughed as she met eyes with him, his ginger hair was sculpted meticulously. 'Friday then?' she asked.

'Yeah, Friday,' Oliver confirmed. His gaze remained fixed on her until she shut the door.

'I love a Friday,' Albie exclaimed as they wandered along the road.

'I'm more keen on a Monday,' Colin said, smiling.

'You're mental, nobody likes a Monday,' Jack said as he lit a cigarette, holding it between two fingers.

'So, Oliver, we have a little situation,' Harry informed as the group navigated the pavement in their Edwardian style suits.

'A situation? We better stop off for Kerry then,' Oliver said.

'So, who was that boy?' Vera interrogated as she plonked herself into her armchair. Houdini sat intently in his cage, watching Francesca from behind the bars.

'Nobody, grandma, just a friend,' she said reluctantly.

'So, he's gone from nobody to a friend in one sentence,' she persisted.

'It's nothing.'

'Judging by the bunch of flowers in your hand, the state that you were willing to open the door in, and the grin on your face, it doesn't look like nothing. I was in the military, dear, I've picked up a few things in my time, one being able to detect when my granddaughter is telling porkies.'

'He's lovely, he's the one from the dance hall,' Francesca said as a smile crept over her face.

'So, what is this lovely boy's name?'

'Oliver Thomas.'

'Oh, I know of the Thomas' reputation,' Vera muttered as she popped on her reading glasses.

'Reputation?'

'Yes, his father is a violent man, constantly in and out of prison from what I've heard. And if the rumours are true, Oliver is hardly a saint himself, he leads a gang of antique clad hooligans and is partial to the odd scrap. The newspapers refer to his type as 'Teddy Boys', not very nice characters by the sounds of things. I don't care for the opinions others have of him, but know this, Fran, that reputation won't save him if he hurts you.'

'Well, at least he isn't a pencil pusher. Please don't tell mum, it's still early days,' she said nervously, looking down at the bouquet of blooming daisies that sat in her arms.

'Your secret is safe with me, now put those in a vase, we'll say Judy brought them over.'

The factory was a dingy structure. Quarter past nine and blackness was grasping the sky, the building looking even more uninviting. Entering, they studied the interior. Shadows crept into the dimly lit spaces, dancing along the vast, cold metal walls. The metal railings trailed about the ceiling while a mass of sewing machines lined the factory floor on wooden tables. Only a couple of women remained. They sat with glasses and headbands on.

The material around their heads attempted to keep their hair out of the machine's path while their ears were plugged with pieces of excess cotton. As the distinguishable group passed by, Lewis looked at them, bringing a finger to his lips. The women watched as the eight youths ascended the metal staircase. They turned to each other with confusion as they noticed the bicycle chain that dangled out the big lad's back pocket. Kicking the door open, the group entered the office.

Kerry circled Talbot, her angered golden-brown eyes latching onto him. 'Now listen to me you prick, you are gonna leave Charlotte alone and give her what she deserves, some fuckin' respect. That means you will not lay a finger on her. Is that understood?'

Harry and Oliver loomed over him as Kerry continued her verbal attack. Lewis and Finn sat on a nearby cabinet that stowed whiskey and brandy. Jack helped himself while Colin stood at the back of the room with Albie, making sure they were not interrupted.

'Fuck off bitch. Wait until the police hear about this, a group of wannabe gangsters thinking they can intimidate me, well you won't be so tough when you're bent over in a prison cell, especially you,' he said, pointing at Albie whose flamboyant style stuck out from the rest.

'Is this bloke deaf or somethin'?' Jack questioned as he gulped the whiskey, passing a glass to Oliver who stood beside a gradually more pissed off Kerry.

'Or suicidal,' Finn uttered as he grasped the flick knife in his pocket. It was his favourite, and he always found himself playing with it without realising.

Lewis turned to Talbot with a grin as he lit a cigarette. 'I wouldn't try and rat us out if I were you, because we will get to you first, and judging by the size of you, you wouldn't get very far.'

'You little wankers,' he spat.

'I see our point isn't getting across. Maybe our friend here needs a little persuasion,' Oliver insisted as Harry wrapped the chain around his knuckles.

'About bloody time.' Finn smiled sadistically as a couple of blows left a bruised and battered man before them.

The two women on the factory floor acknowledged the struggle but continued working. There was a certain satisfaction to their expressions.

Talbot lifted his hands in a pathetic attempt to protect himself. Harry quickly sent the chain into his open palms, making him screech.

'You leave Charlotte alone or we will cut your tits off. Am I understood?' Oliver threatened. Catching sight of Finn taunting him with the knife, the bloodied man realised that that statement could easily be made into a reality.

'Y-yes,' Talbot stuttered, his fearful gaze focused on Harry.

'Yes, what?' Oliver questioned.

'You're understood, what else can I say,' he panicked as Oliver pulled a hefty knuckle duster from his pocket.

'A little pay increase may help ease the situation,' Harry suggested.

'Whatever you want.'

'Now apologise to my friend here before she tears you a new one,' Oliver demanded as Kerry thrummed with anger. Her slick, short platinum blonde hair contrasted her red cheeks like strawberries and cream, however, she had a bad taste in her mouth.

'I'm sorry,' Talbot said insincerely. He clearly didn't fear

Kerry like he did the others, and this was the biggest mistake he could have made.

'I don't believe you, say it like you fuckin' mean it,' she sneered. Yanking the knuckle duster from Oliver's grasp, Kerry entered into a fury, driving her fist into his face.

'I'm sorry, I'm sorry, just stop her!' Talbot pleaded as his jaw cracked and slanted to one side. Harry pulled her from her victim upon Oliver's command.

Kerry, still furious, was intent on having the final word as blood spurted from Talbot's mouth. 'The next time your vile mouth decides to open, I will close it permanently. It's my favourite hobby silencing men like you.'

'She's not kidding, ask the last man that crossed her,' Colin stated from behind them.

'It's funny because he can't ask as his jaw's broken.' Jack laughed drunkenly as he helped himself to more whiskey.

As the group left the bloody mess that was Talbot behind, Albie leant down to the man who looked as though he had fallen into one of the factory machines. 'It's highly advisable that you make up a creative little story to explain your facial region. For example, you tripped over one of your porky limbs which sent you tumbling down those stairs.' Patting him on the shoulder, Albie followed the others.

'I'd go home early if I were you ladies,' Oliver advised both women. Kerry was wiping the blood from her face with a handkerchief that Lewis had given her. Jack stumbled along the aisle after consuming almost all of Talbot's alcohol.

They stared at one another. Darkness flooded under the curtains as they sat at the kitchen table, a deck of playing cards placed between them. Shuffling them, Susan was quick to notice her brother's icy glance.

'You've got that look in your eyes.' She observed, dealing the cards.

'And what look would that be?'

'I'm not thick, Oliver, what have you done this time?'

'Harry told us that Talbot put hands on Lottie, so we put hands on him. An eye for an eye as they say,' he explained as he studied the assortment that now sat in his hand.

'It's very hypocritical for somebody so godless to be quoting God's law.'

'It's a principle to live by,' he said.

'Just be careful, one day you will hurt the wrong person,' she said, laying down a card. The queen of hearts looked up at him, waiting for his move.

'I'll be fine. How are you? You look knackered,' Oliver asked as he placed a king of hearts on top of the queen.

'I'm just tired. I'm sure I'll feel better soon. I went to the pharmacy and got some iron tablets.' Susan rose from the table to check the frying pan. It contained a few sizzling sausages and tomatoes.

'Do you need money for the prescription?' he asked as the smell of smoking fat invaded his nostrils.

'No, I sorted it. Fran is lovely.' Susan smiled.

'She is,' he agreed.

'I like her, I'm pleased for you.' She shoved a few sausages and fried tomatoes into bread rolls. Placing them on the table, Oliver helped himself, the grease coating his fingers.

'I'm glad you approve for a change,' Oliver mumbled.

'Well, considering your past relationships—'

'I don't want to talk about that,' he snapped.

'I'm just glad you've found someone new,' Susan said, watching him intently.

The water was hot and sent steam into the air, fogging up the nearby mirror. Kerry slipped down a little, letting the water meet her broad shoulders. She pulled a hand through her hair, allowing the water to trickle from her fingertips down the back of her neck.

'Enjoying my bath?' Lewis asked as he strolled into the room.

'Yes, it's peaceful here, unlike my house. I can't get a word in edgeways without being moaned at by my uncle. Not to mention mum would lose the plot if she saw my hands,' she said, looking to her fists that were coated in congealed blood.

'You know you're always welcome.' He grinned as he sat on the side of the tub. 'Here, give me your hands,' he said, grabbing a flannel.

As Kerry offered her knuckles, she winced slightly as he cleaned them. A trail of blood slipped into the bathtub, a diluted pool of red twisting around her body. Her hands were raw and bruised with patches of purple developing on her bones.

'You got him good, didn't you?' He smirked as he tended to her injuries.

'You know there is nothing I hate more in this world than people like Talbot who sit on their arse and use their position to pick on people less powerful than them,' she sighed.

Flinging the bloody flannel into the sink, Lewis watched her, transfixed. 'There you go, good as new,' he said as her amber eyes peered up at him. They were normally in a constant state of sharpness, but around him, they appeared wide and expressive.

'You put on quite the performance the other week, you nearly scared that Fran girl half to death.'

'And you didn't?' he asked, raising an eyebrow.

Kerry flashed a grin.

'What do you think of her?'

'A little different to Oli's usual victims. They haven't slept together, which is unusual for him, and he sure as hell wouldn't introduce her to us if he didn't see somethin' with her down the line,' she said.

'Yeah, well, she may be a pretty little distraction, but I don't want her gettin' in the way. I like things the way they are,' he said coldly.

'Don't mess around with her, I know what you're like. Especially with Finn, you have the habit of becoming quite cruel to newcomers.'

He smirked. 'And you're not cruel?'

'I'm realistic, you're sadistic. I know you get a kick out of it.'

'I wouldn't do such a thing. Remember, I was never cruel to you,' he said, laying a hand on her cheek.

CHAPTER 6

CHARLOTTE ENTERED THE office to see the most pleasing sight. It made her Tuesday, to say the least.

'One of the girls said you wanted to see me, Sir?' she questioned.

A fumbling Talbot pointed to an envelope on the table. His jaw was wired shut and he winced, his hands grotesquely puffy and bruised.

'This?' she asked as she followed his direction. Opening the little brown envelope, she met eyes with a wodge of pound notes. 'A pay rise, how generous of you,' she said, grinning.

As her boss grimaced with pain, she couldn't help but think of the events of the night prior and the actions that had been carried out by her not so merciful guardian angels.

'What a lovely surprise. Will there be anything else? No? I'll be off then,' she said smugly. Reaching the doorway, she turned back to him. 'Staircases are ever such dangerous things, you should be more careful next time,' she warned with a victorious smile, leaving the door wide open behind her.

As Friday's sunset faded over Victoria Park, they sat on the old wooden bench. Munching on battered fish and chips wrapped in newspaper, Francesca happily devoured the food before her. Oliver helped himself as he studied the gold-tinted park. He looked at the ducks and fluffy ducklings that were bobbing along the surface of the lake; he watched the blue tits dance in and out of the branches of the flourishing oak trees. A large fountain sat at the centre of the park, its octagonal roof sheltered an intricate set of statues, and the arches presented complex patterns developed onto the stone. Oliver had pleasant memories of the fountain, remembering the times he would play in the water with his sister when they were little.

'I wonder how they invented these?' Francesca asked as she fiddled with the little wooden fish and chip fork.

'I don't know, probably someone who was fed up with eating with their hands,' Oliver said as he popped a few chips into his mouth, taking his eyes off the fountain. His knuckles were slightly bruised. Francesca stared at them.

'Fighting, I've been doing it for God knows how long down at Repton Boxing Club. It's also how I acquired these beauties,' he said, feeling the rough cartilage that covered his ears.

'I think they suit you. It's a good conversation starter,' she said, smiling widely.

'Jack's are worse, like rank fleshy earmuffs,' he said, making Francesca laugh.

'I've heard some of the best come from that club. Do you fight for medals?'

He smiled at her naivety. 'No, belts, but I'm nowhere near good enough for that.'

'Is that what you want to do?' she asked.

'Probably not, I don't want to end up having a face like the Elephant Man, but it's something to do, I spend most of my time there. I do compete, much to Susan's annoyance as she's always the one that has to patch me up.'

'How is your sister?' Francesca questioned.

'She hasn't been too well but seems in good spirits. She likes you by the way, thinks you're a breath of fresh air,' he informed her.

'I'm glad, I don't think you can say that for the blonde one.' Francesca laughed.

'Oh, what Kerry? She's just protective,' Oliver said.

'Or territorial,' she muttered.

'Look, Frankie, it's not a good idea to ruffle her feathers,' he warned as he dunked a bit of fish into a blob of tartar sauce.

'I wouldn't dream of it. My grandma recognised you, said you have quite the reputation,' she said, catching sight of a swallow tattoo that sat on the back of his hand, its deep black ink contrasting his bruised skin.

'Oh yeah? And what reputation would that be?' he asked as a mischievous grin covered his face.

'That's where I was hoping you could elaborate. She said you and your friends are 'Teddy Boys'?'

'Ah yeah, clearly your grandmother reads the papers, they're out to make us look bad, Frankie, and give young people who dress different stupid nicknames. I just don't want to follow the path that older generations have, and they don't like that.'

'She didn't say that she didn't like you, only that you could be trouble,' Francesca clarified as she shoved a few chips into her mouth.

'My friends said the same about you.'

'Really, and how am I trouble?' she asked with her mouth half-full.

'They say I'm going to fall for you,' Oliver said, licking the salt from his fingers.

'Colin suggested the same to me in church of all places,' Francesca muttered, letting the conversation slip.

'I told him not to talk to you,' he said irritably.

'Hey, no harm done, I think he was just looking out for you,' she said, the potent scent of vinegar causing her nose to scrunch.

'The truth is I am falling for you, and they're going to have to get over it… And you've got tartar sauce on your face.'

'Where?' she asked, feeling her cheeks for the runaway sauce.

'There,' he said as he leant in. Francesca's cheeks burned as he placed a finger under her chin, guiding her lips onto his. He kissed her softly and, in that moment, desire shot through her. He pulled away but kept his finger under her chin, gently caressing her lower jaw. She gulped and he watched her with a grin, as though he knew exactly what she was thinking.

As Francesca entered the house, her mother locked onto her with hawk-like vision. She was hurrying around in her pinnie with a large pink feather duster in her hand. Her brown hair was tied back in a bun, a few strands had escaped and gently swept her cheeks.

'You seem chirpy, Fran.' Her mother observed whilst dusting the lampshades meticulously. Houdini squawked as he watched them both.

'I've had a good day,' she said, trying to contain her grin.

'And this good day doesn't happen to have anything to do with that boy from the dance hall, does it?' her mother pressed as she continued her housework.

'No, mum, you're imagining things,' Francesca dismissed as she attempted to escape.

'I'm not imagining those flowers, am I?' Stephanie questioned as her daughter froze in position halfway up the stairs.

'No, Judy got them for grandma,' she replied.

'Oh, did she now? I spoke to Judy today, and it just so happens that she is allergic to daisies, so that was an interesting choice of bouquet,' she interrogated further.

'Ok, it was a boy, the lovely one from the dance hall,' she admitted, turning back to her.

'So, things are progressing then?' her mother questioned with a smile.

'You could say that.' Francesca grinned to herself.

Stephanie dusted the table. It was covered in a white tablecloth and played host to a variety of ornaments, including a fake silver candelabra and a Royal Doulton figure named Grace. Her fine china was crafted into a beautiful eighteenth-century light blue gown adorned with pale pink flowers. Her firm pouf hairstyle could have rivalled Marie Antoinette herself. As a child, Francesca always wanted to play with her, yet her mother would never allow it due to the figure's delicate nature.

'How did you know?' Francesca asked, watching her mother tend to the ornament.

'I was young once, I know the signs, the sudden giddiness. It goes hand in hand with love.'

'I'm not in love yet,' she stated firmly.

'But you're falling in love, and that's the best part,' her mother said, wandering into the kitchen.

The cold gym was filled with the smell of sweat. Old men with faces resembling beat leather watched their protégés. Taking in their every move, they sent cigar smoke into the high ceiling. The raised canvas at the centre was a stage, and the boys danced upon it.

Oliver stood in the middle of the ring as Jack swung at him. Missing his chaotic fists by inches, he sent a punch into his abdomen, ending the sparring match.

'Fuck, Oli, I think you nearly burst my kidney,' he winced as he retreated to the corner.

'It's ok, you've got another one,' Oliver said unsympathetically, catching sight of Colin as he met the side of the ring.

'Looks like training's going well then.' He observed, recognising Jack's skin that was bruising by the second.

'It's getting there,' Oliver said, leaning over the top rope, his leather-bound hands dangling in the air.

'You up for a fight, Colin? If your God will allow it,' Jack quipped.

'Judging from your technique you'd lose a fight against a fly,' Colin critiqued. Jack scowled at him.

'Easy boys, enough of that,' Oliver said. 'I heard you had a chat with Fran,' he mentioned, looking down at him.

'Yeah, but nothing was meant by it,' he said.

'Well, I'd rather you didn't say anything at all, I don't want you frightening her off,' Oliver said sternly.

'I think we all know you're the only one capable of scaring

her off.' Jack smirked.

Sunday seemed to take a particularly long time to tick over due to a christening that required the attention of the entire congregation. As the titchy baby girl was passed around in her little frilly off-white dress, Francesca looked around for Elaine. Judy bobbed the baby up and down as Vera distracted her from crying. Trying to avoid an awkward encounter with the Priest, Francesca ducked behind a pillar where she bumped into Colin.

'I think the baby's a bit young to be playing hide and seek.' He glanced down at her, grinning.

'I wasn't hiding,' she said, trying to spot her best friend.

'If you say so. I just wanted to say sorry for the other day, I shouldn't have involved myself.'

'It's ok, Oliver had a word with you, didn't he?' she asked, frowning.

'Yeah. It wasn't my place,' Colin said regretfully.

'I'm sorry, I shouldn't have told him you spoke to me.'

'Why are you apologising? You've done nothing wrong,' he assured her.

'I got you into trouble when all you were doing was looking out for your friend,' she said with equal regret.

'As I said, it wasn't my place.'

'There you are, I've been looking for you everywhere!' Elaine exclaimed as she bundled towards them.

'I'll see you around,' Colin said, catching sight of his father who waved him over.

'The baby is so cute, Fran, have you held her yet?' she asked enthusiastically.

'Not yet, I'll get the chance once Judy's stopped baby

hogging,' Francesca muttered, looking at the nattering congregation.

'What did Colin have to say?' she asked nosily.

'Just apologised for the other day.'

'Have you seen Colin?' a voice said quietly from around the door. As Susan stood looking a little worse for wear, she scanned the church's bright white interior.

'He's a little pre-occupied,' Elaine said, pointing at Colin, the baby girl sitting contently in his arms.

'Oh, don't worry then,' she said, catching sight of the Priest who sent a menacing glance in her direction.

'She's taken a liking to you, Colin,' Judy said as the baby looked up at him with a happy little toothless grin.

'You have a gentle touch.' Vera smiled.

'She's just behaving well, nothing to do with me is it little one,' he insisted, pulling out his crucifix necklace so she could play with it.

'Are you ok, Susan?' Francesca asked as she followed her out of the church.

'Yeah, just forget I even came here,' she dismissed, trailing the old stone wall.

'Well, are you sure?' Francesca grew increasingly worried as she recognised the paleness of Susan's face.

'I'm sure. I just wanted to talk to him about something. I don't feel very well,' she said, grabbing her stomach. Leaning, she paused as her insides turned and tumbled. As Francesca approached, she vomited over the church wall.

'Oh my gosh, we need to get you home,' Francesca stated, grabbing hold of Susan's arm.

'It's ok, honestly,' she refused, her face turning as white as a sheet.

'It's clearly not ok, Susan, for goodness' sake let me help you,' she insisted.

'I've been feeling rough all morning, must have ate something dodgy,' Susan said as Francesca guided her onto the pavement.

'Sometimes things just don't agree,' she sighed, helping her down the road.

As people dispersed from the building, the Priest watched his congregation from the main altar. Colin gathered up the Holy Bibles and placed them neatly on a shelf. Turning his attention to the Church of England service books, he was confronted by his father who was wearing a sour expression.

'That Catholic girl will do you no good, Colin,' he preached from the altar.

'I know, we've had this conversation before,' Colin dismissed.

'Then why was she in my church?' his father muttered as he walked down the centre aisle.

Colin shrugged. 'She knows Fran and Elaine, probably came to see them.' Distracting himself from his father's angered glance, he passed through the pews, collecting the service books in one hand.

'I'm not stupid, I see how that girl looks at you,' he snapped.

'You just have a problem with Susan because of her religion,' Colin bit back, shoving a few service books onto the shelf.

'No, I have a problem with her because of her morals, her whole family's morals.'

Colin turned to him with clenched fists. 'Oliver is a good

person and so is his sister, it's only their dad that let the side down. And it's not like you can talk with your generational sin.'

'I've warned you against being around those types of people,' he uttered sharply.

'Those 'people' are my family, more family than you'll ever be,' Colin spat, throwing down the remaining service books. Leaving the church, he met the boys who were lingering on the street corner.

'Do I sense a domestic?' Jack teased as Colin approached them.

'Shut up, Jack,' he sneered, walking past.

Oliver stared at Colin, concerned as he met his pace.

'Are we going out later?' he asked angrily.

'I guess we are now, might help you let off some steam,' Oliver decided.

Charlotte's small room was consumed by a double bed that was decorated in a multi-coloured floral bed sheet. A floor-length mirror clung to the wall, while an old wooden wardrobe was squished in the corner. A dated black wind-up gramophone sat proudly on a chest of drawers and blurted out a sequence of songs that sounded optimistic in tone, mentioning first loves and a general lust for life. They played loudly as the ancient thing had no volume control.

The little walkway between the wall and bed led to a small bathroom. A white shower curtain shielded Charlotte as she whistled along to the music. As the afternoon peaked, Francesca sat, poised at the end of the colourful bed, its tired metal frame creaking with every shift of movement. Items of clothing laid around her in a calculated assortment.

She fumbled through a few magazines left scattered on the bed. One weekly comic magazine featured a group of women controlling a monstrous aircraft. Titled *Kitty Hawke and her All-Girl Air Crew*, the magazine captured Francesca's imagination. She looked at the characters and their spotless military uniforms; it reminded her of her grandmother. Only Vera would be fearless enough to go up in an aircraft like that, and for a moment, Francesca wondered what it would be like to soar above the clouds.

'So, what did you want me to come around for, Lottie?' she asked, placing the comic down beside her.

'Something very important!' Charlotte exclaimed.

With a sudden mute of cascading water and a few shuffles, she wandered into the room butt naked, her coral-coloured towel used to contain and hold up her wet hair. Francesca quickly covered her eyes, much to Charlotte's amusement.

'You could have given me warning,' she said as her friend pulled on her chosen clothes.

'What? There was only one towel.' She sniggered to herself.

'Tell me when you're decent,' Francesca said as her eyes were subjected to the darkness of her palm.

'Calm down, I'm nearly there,' she assured. 'Ok, you can look now.'

'I did not intend on seeing that today,' Francesca muttered.

'Hey, we're friends, so what's the problem? Anyway, more importantly, you are here for a lesson,' Charlotte said as she took down her sodden wet hair, the golden strands meeting her freckled cheeks.

'A lesson in what?' Francesca questioned, watching her as she towel-dried the soggy ends.

'Outfits, so you can be a part of the group,' she replied,

flipping her messy hair behind her shoulders.

'Oh, I'm fine with the clothes I've got, and I don't think I'm a part of the group,' Francesca said reluctantly, standing from the bed.

'You are to me, whether you like it or not, so sit your bum down.'

Francesca sat as Charlotte showed her different fashion items, educating her in the art of the 'Teddy Girl' or 'Judies' as she preferred. The tailor-made image was explained to her as each item contributed to the lesson. Using a few magazines, she pointed out the different outfits and fashion necessities. Drainpipe trousers and beetle-crusher shoes were among them.

'You don't have to look like Kerry, all manly and stuff, there are lots of different ways to make it work, that's why it's so much fun,' she said as she rummaged through her wardrobe. 'And this is my favourite.' She pulled out a blazer. It had a firm silhouette with delicate detailing in pink embroidery thread.

'Go on, try it,' she insisted, passing the garment to Francesca.

The bulky material enclosed her thin frame as she tried it on. 'I'm not sure this suits me.'

'Don't be silly, it looks perfect, it's just a bit big for you.'

'If you say so.' Francesca laughed, unconvinced. 'I do like the patterns though.' Admiring the fine needlework, she felt the pink thread between her fingers.

'I did that myself, took me a little while I have to say, embroidery can be really pickily,' she said proudly as the navy-blue blazer was passed back to her.

'I can agree with you on that. My mum made me decorate some of her patchwork quilt. It's on her bed.'

'Oh, that sounds wonderful, I love patchwork quilts. I bet

it has all sorts of colours and textures, patterns and shapes,' Charlotte sighed, drifting off into the world of fashion and fabrics.

'Yeah, it's quite abstract really,' she said.

'Oh, Albie would like that then.'

'Does he like designing things?'

'Loves art, not so good at it himself, but of course don't tell him I said that.' Charlotte grinned as she fumbled through her wardrobe. 'This should get you started, to ease you into the style,' she said, passing Francesca a polka dot printed neck scarf.

'I can't take that, Lottie, it's yours,' she said, refusing the delicate accessory.

'I don't mind, I've got plenty of others.' Charlotte smiled happily, popping it around her friend's neck, setting it perfectly into place.

Francesca pulled her cardigan tightly around herself as she walked through the alleyways. Recognising that the sun was fading faster than she expected, she decided to cut through Tower Hamlets Cemetery. With a quickening pace and a chilling shudder, she hurried across the grass. Decaying tombstones poked from the ground like old bones. The mortuary chapel sat isolated against the backdrop of heavy-set trees. She always found it creepy, remembering the time Elaine dared her to enter the woods alone. She got lost, and, in a panic, Elaine confessed her wrongdoing to her brother who ran swiftly to Francesca's aid. He found her amongst the shrubbery in tears and made her vow never to enter the cemetery alone again. She was older now and could manage on her own, despite feeling incredibly uneasy about the grizzly stone statues that stalked her amongst the trees.

'Fran, ain't it?' Lewis asked, startling her as he appeared at her side.

'Yes, and you're Lewis?' she spoke uneasily, remembering him from the ruins. His blonde hair and sharp suit were hard to forget, alongside his attitude.

'What are you doing out here all alone then?'

'I'm just passing through, I went to see Lottie,' she explained timidly.

'I assume she gave you that scarf, it looks very pretty,' he said.

'Thank you.' She quickened her pace.

Lighting a cigarette, Lewis smirked as he exhaled, the smoke creeping over his cheeks. 'You don't have to be frightened of me.'

'In all honesty, you do frighten me a bit, you don't seem like you have good intentions,' she admitted.

'It seems you're not as gullible as I thought,' he muttered. 'I don't like new people coming into the group unless they've got something to offer. You seem like a sweet enough girl, but you have nothing to offer, you don't belong with us, and you don't belong with him. You're just a passing phase.'

'That's not up to you to decide,' she said, unnerved.

'I guess not, but remember when Oliver's done with you, I can always show you a good time,' he said, grinning.

'I think I'll pass on that,' she spoke angrily.

Lewis whistled as he disappeared into the darkness.

Meeting the concrete sanctuary of Southern Grove, Francesca proceeded along the pavement, intending on returning home. However, her eyes caught sight of the corner shop. Grabbing a can of Heinz Tomato Soup, she trailed her way back, remembering the route Susan had instructed her earlier that day.

Passing phase, she thought to herself, irritated by his rudeness. Now she was determined to make an impression.

Meeting the doorstep, she paused. A disjointed tune consisting of mismatched dings and dongs greeted her as she pressed the doorbell. Much to her surprise, she was met with Kerry's glimmering golden-brown glare.

'Oliver's not in if that's why you're here,' Kerry said bluntly as she stepped out onto the concrete, forcing Francesca to take a step back.

'I'm not here for Oliver, just wanted to see if Susan's any better,' she explained.

'She's alive and kicking,' Kerry said, studying the girl before her with folded arms. Her eyes narrowed as she recognised the polka dot scarf around her neck.

'Can I see her?' she asked shyly.

'No.'

'Oh, well, I got her some soup, thought it would make her feel better,' Francesca said, revealing the tin.

'Thanks, I'll pass it on to her.' She accepted the can into her firm grasp.

Francesca stared up at her, realising she was getting nowhere. 'I'll be off then, give her my best,' she said quickly as she retreated down the pavement.

'Fran, wait, it was a nice thing that you did earlier,' Kerry said approvingly.

'I was always taught to treat people how I would like to be treated,' she said, looking back at her with a smile.

'Words to live by,' Kerry agreed, peering down at her bruised knuckles. Closing the door, she wandered back into the kitchen.

'Who was that?' Susan asked. She sat with her knees up,

studying that morning's newspaper as a cigarette slowly burnt between her fingers.

'Your brother's business. And she brought soup,' Kerry informed, tossing the can from one hand to the other.

'At least she bought the best flavour. You can't beat tomato,' Susan said, catching sight of the label as Kerry shoved it to one side. 'You should have invited her in for a cuppa,' she added, watching her friend over the black and white pages.

'She's got a kind heart, but let's not push it.'

'Maybe too kind, I'm worried that she'll get hurt,' Susan said as she folded the paper, laying it down on the kitchen table. She felt her stomach tumble and turn, the pain still biting at her entrails.

'I'm still surprised Oliver's gone for someone so naive,' Kerry muttered as she grabbed at the newspaper, studying the black text that sat in mind-numbing columns.

'And some have a thing for arseholes, like Lewis for example,' Susan teased.

'I've got needs,' she said, her eyes piercing over the top of the paper.

Darkness fell over London revealing a cascade of stars.

'What a lovely evening to go to the pictures,' Oliver said, looking up at the sky.

'Isn't it just,' Colin said with a grin as he passed him, following the others into the cinema. Posters lined the walls in a colourful array.

'E-excuse me, you haven't paid yet,' a timid young man stuttered as he watched them enter the screening room with devilish expressions.

Harry turned back to him, laying his metal bicycle chain on the counter. 'Go on, fuck off,' he said as the young man obliged, bolting away from him as fast as he possibly could. As Harry turned his attention to the screening room, people flooded past him.

'Screaming won't get you anywhere,' Lewis exclaimed as he terrorised the remaining cinema-goes, a cosh cemented in his hand. Finn slashed the red leather seats with his beloved flick knife, divulging the padding withheld inside. The large screen turned blank amidst the carnage.

Colin punched a young man in the jaw, sending him to the ground with a thud. He recognised him to be the son of the boarding house owner who had called him and his father unwelcome scum on one-too-many occasions. With a satisfied smirk, he followed Oliver down a row of seats.

'Come on sweetheart, don't be scared, I'll be gentle,' Jack teased a teenage girl who sat in a petrified state. He wielded a bottle of whiskey in one hand and a large meat fork in the other, which he alternated in use.

'What the hell are you doing?' a boy, no older than sixteen said, running to her rescue.

'Your girlfriend in a minute,' Jack snarled, launching at him. A stab to the knee led his victim to stumble to the ground with an agonising cry. The girl burst into tears and Colin quickly pulled her to the door, saving her from having to witness the grizzly assault. As Jack proceeded with a repetition of punches, Colin looked at Oliver, concerned. He wasn't opposed to violence but murder he couldn't justify.

'Alright now, give it a rest,' Oliver ordered as Jack reluctantly abandoned his prey, revealing the severe damage he had inflicted. Blood trickled along the floor as the boy winced in pain, grasping his leg with shaking hands.

'You got a light?' Albie asked. He sat on a row with his feet up. 'I love this film, it's very minimalist,' he said to the girl beside him as she nervously fumbled for her lighter, the blank screen hanging before them. 'Cheers poppet, now off you go,' he said with a grin as he leant over, lighting the end of the cigarette. Letting it hang lazily from the corner of his mouth, he watched the last of the commotion. His eyes met the injured teenager who was wailing on the floor, the sound filling up the now empty screening room. 'Do the kid a favour and pull that sodding meat fork out of his knee, it's making my stomach turn,' Albie said.

Colin rolled up his sleeves, dropping to the floor before him. The boy scrambled to get away, but Harry grabbed onto his shoulders with his massive hands, holding him still.

Oliver offered up his belt which was forced in between his lips, salty tears streaming down his bruised face. As Colin grabbed a hold of the fork, the boy squirmed.

Jack leant up against the wall, smiling.

'Wipe that fuckin' grin off your face, before I smack it off you,' Oliver snapped.

'Why? Colin punched that bloke,' Jack countered as Albie grabbed the bottle from him, passing it to Colin who splashed it on the boy's leg as he sobbed.

'Punched, not stabbed, you lunatic. And he deserved it, he's been giving Colin shit for years. This poor sod did nothing to you,' Oliver said.

'From what I observed, he got in Jack's way.' Lewis glanced at the boy. 'I also don't believe you to be a moral authority on who deserves to be hurt,' he challenged.

Oliver seethed but said nothing. The underwhelming

reaction caused Lewis to aim for a more sensitive nerve. 'I saw Fran earlier, she said she was frightened of me, poor thing. I imagine she'll be frightened of you after she hears about tonight.'

With the speed of a rabid dog, Oliver grabbed the bottle from Colin's grasp, lobbing it full pelt at Lewis which slammed into his chest, sending him tumbling down the centre stairs.

'Bloody hell you've been so sensitive lately, especially considering Fran was sport from the start,' Jack said.

'She was what?' Albie asked.

'The dance hall, do you really think Oli would have gone for her if I hadn't made a bet with him first?'

Oliver's fists clenched in his pockets, feeling the anger build inside him as he thought of the way he had pursued her that night. It made him feel sick. He remained quiet, his silence letting the others know that it was true.

'You cretins,' Albie muttered.

A smirk played on Finn's lips. 'Well ain't that a revelation.'

'You've continued seeing her though?' Harry said, his hands still gripping the boy.

Oliver's brow furrowed. 'Because I like her.'

'I can tell, but she can't find out that you showed interest in the first place because of a bet, Oli, it'll upset her,' Colin said.

'Can we focus on the task at hand,' Oliver said, staring at Jack who simply grinned back at him.

Colin clicked his fingers in front of the boy's eyes which were now glazed over. 'Look at me, lad. It'll be over as soon as you know it, and I bet your girlfriend will be all over you for defending her.'

'M-my l-leg,' he said faintly through the leather in his mouth.

'I know, I'm sorry this has happened to you.'

'Go on Mother Teresa, do God's work,' Finn huffed impatiently as he watched Lewis pull himself up, brushing off his drape jacket.

With a sturdy yank, the meat fork released the teenager's flesh. Blood squirted into the air and he squealed at the sight of it.

Albie ripped off his blazer and wrapped it around his shaking limb. 'Women love a war wound, kid. Keep your chin up,' he said softly, taking the belt from his mouth and fastening it around his thigh to slow the bleeding.

'My mum is going to be so annoyed that I ruined my new trousers,' he wept.

Empathy flashed through Oliver's eyes as he glanced down at him. The boy was in agony but was more concerned about his trousers than the gashes. He knew what it was like to worry about clothes, how every piece his mum had managed to find meant the world to him. Reaching into his pocket he pulled out a wodge of pounds. The boy's mouth went dry as Oliver placed them in his lap.

'I know it won't fix your leg, but it's enough to buy you ten pairs of trousers, or maybe you could take that girl of yours on a few nice dates in the West End.'

The boy's expression was nothing short of shocked. 'Thank you,' he said quietly, placing the notes in his jacket pocket. 'I won't tell on you.'

'Good lad,' Oliver said.

'And the boarding house owner's son?' Harry asked, looking at Colin.

'Not a problem, he'd never risk being called a rat.' Colin smirked.

'There were no others that I recognised,' Harry said to

Oliver who nodded as the sound of sirens pierced through the theatre doors.

'That's our cue,' he said.

CHAPTER 7

THE HOT AND heavy weather was a testament to the summer that was now fully underway. Francesca sat, typing away the minutes as she wiped the sweat from her brow. Taking off her burgundy velvet blazer, her light blouse was a welcome relief from the suffocating fabric, allowing her skin to breathe. Watching the clock was the longest way to waste time, and what she normally ended up doing. Counting down the seconds, Mr Montgomery gave the stern command, dismissing her for lunch. An hour lunch break allowed her just enough time to deliver the usual homemade sandwiches to Charley.

Escaping the gaping entrance of the bank, Francesca battled against the countless suits and briefcases that filled the financial district. Despite the sunshine, it was all very grey and miserable with the menacing buildings and abandoned ruins standing stubbornly from Aldgate to Lombard Street.

The waterside was swarming with sweat ridden men going about their business while large ships sat patiently alongside the wooden landing stage. Shouts and commands were passed from worker to worker as thuds, crashes and disconcerting bangs could be heard from each end of the dock. Sitting upon the pile of brown hessian sacks, Francesca tried desperately not to get the dirt and grime on her pencil skirt.

'Hello, Charley.' She smiled as she caught sight of him, her hand raised to block out the sun which shrouded him in a blinding light.

'Hello, kid, how are ya?' Charley asked as he plonked himself down beside her. He took off his gloves, revealing the rough skin that lined his palms.

'Tired, but at least I don't have to do manual labour like you.' She laughed, looking at his hands. She reached for the ammo pouch which contained the usual cheese and pickle sandwiches.

'It looks worse than it is, besides, I'd prefer to be outside than cooped up on a day like this.'

'Perfect holiday weather,' she uttered, thinking of the trips she used to go on as a child to Southend-on-Sea.

'Yet we're both stuck in clammy old London, bloody typical,' Charley said as he munched on the sandwiches. 'What have you been up to then? Not getting into too much trouble with Elaine, I hope.'

'No, nothing newsworthy, but I have met somebody.' She grinned contently to herself.

'Is this somebody Oliver Thomas?' he asked, licking the tips of his fingers.

'Grandma told you, didn't she?' Francesca muttered.

'Be careful with that one, him and his friends aren't known

for their kindness to others,' Charley said, his tone serious.

'They can be a bit intimidating, but nothing I can't deal with.' She tried to reassure him, but he remained unconvinced.

'They can be bloody violent too. I just don't want you to get hurt.'

'Grandma said Oliver has a reputation along with every other 'Teddy Boy' type in the East End, but all the proof of violence has been exaggerated stories used by the newspapers to make young people look bad,' she spoke defensively.

'It's probably better if I just show you,' Charley sighed.

'Show me what?'

Charley reached around in his pocket. Pulling out a tightly folded copy of the morning paper's front page, he passed it to her. The newspaper headline read: *Terror inflicted on innocent cinema-goers as Edwardian clad youths vandalise local cinema.*

'What's this about?' she asked.

'Just read it,' he said as he watched the water. The absent breeze caused the Thames to appear calm and still.

Her eyes scanned the page. 'What's this got to do with me, Charley?'

'Keep reading.'

The heinous stabbing of a sixteen-year-old has left him with a severed knee. Various damages were also inflicted on the property, which will put the establishment out of use until adequate repairs are made. This disgraceful assault was one of many over the past year.

Charley looked at her with an uneasy expression. 'You hang around with them, don't you?'

'It could be anyone, you've seen how many angry young men walk the streets,' she stated.

'I saw him, Fran, your Oliver leaving out the back with the

others as bold as brass. We came out the pub to see the commotion and I recognised him instantly. I know the newspapers are hard to believe but trust me.'

'Is the boy ok? The one that got stabbed?' she asked.

'I can't say for sure. Knees take a long time to heal, but I think he'll live.' Charley gulped, thinking of the injuries he witnessed during the war, the memory of his friend's mangled flesh making his body tense. Eyes panicked, he sat there as the nurses tried desperately to clean the gash on his friend's chest, blood trickling, his agonised cries lashing against his eardrums. He shook his head, bringing himself back. *It's 1955, it's 1955, it's 1955* he repeated to himself in a quiet whisper.

Francesca stared at him. Even though she didn't understand fully, awareness flushed through her. Awareness of what he'd gone through. She wouldn't dare touch him, to console him, she'd noticed in the past that it would agitate him, make him feel confined. She simply repeated what he was saying, 'It's 1955.'

He sucked in a hard breath as he looked at her. 'Sorry, Fran, sometimes I get set off by the oddest things. It's never my own injury,' he said, gripping his shoulder, 'Just the thought of people I love, my—'

'It's ok, you don't need to explain yourself to me,' she said gently, sparing him the pain of delving further into his thoughts.

He flexed his fingers in a way the made Francesca wonder whether he was checking he was real, present. 'Anyway, what were we talking about? Oh, yeah, Oliver.'

She nodded at him. 'What should I do about it?'

'I promised your brother that I'd look after you and the last thing I want to see is you getting caught up in something like that, keep your guard up is all I'm saying,' Charley advised as he watched the passing boats glide gently down the river.

The darkness of the factory's interior shrouded the women in shadows and the vast cold metal walls stood bland and bleak. The steel walkways hung like spiderwebs, trailing their way throughout the body of the factory. It was cold inside and Charlotte rubbed her hands together. Eyes sore from concentrating on the needle of the machine, she looked up to meet the ugly grey ceiling. Watching the walkway, she noticed a young man leaving Mr Talbot's office. He was tall, almost too tall, with his gangly arms trailing at his side. To her, he was all too familiar.

Talbot's nephew, Jimmy, proved a considerable contrast to his uncle's butch frame, yet he was equally vicious. Catching sight of her watching him, he sent a slimy grin in her direction. She quickly diverted her eyes as he sauntered down the steps. Placing a knobbly elbow on her table, he stared at her. She tried to ignore him until he ripped the fabric from her grasp.

'Give that back,' she snapped, reaching for the material.

'Not until you tell me what I want to know.'

'What do you want to know?' she asked grumpily.

'What happened to my uncle? I know very well it wasn't an accident,' he hissed.

'I don't know anything.'

'Oh, I don't know anything,' he mocked, imitating her voice.

'Why are you so horrible?' She scowled at him.

'Tell me what happened,' he spoke sharply, causing her to sit stiffly.

'I don't know, and even if I did, I wouldn't tell you.'

'My uncle's hands are bruised to fuck, clearly from valiantly fighting off his attackers. His jaw is wired up, he can't speak, he can just about drink water.'

'Well, maybe it'll help him lose some weight,' she said snarkily.

'I know Harry did this, and the rest of your scum friends. I just can't prove it,' he pressed.

'You're paranoid.'

'And you're done for if I find out you're behind this,' he said, pushing her sewing machine onto the floor where it shattered into fragments. 'My uncle will probably dock your pay for a month to get a new one. You really should be more careful.' He smiled to himself as he left her to pick up the pieces.

The streets were rampant with cars stuck in heavy mid-day traffic. Lining the road in a coating of glistening metal, the vehicles sat impatiently. Tempers flared and people groaned in response to the intensifying heat. Glad to leave the red double-decker, Francesca hurried along the pavement. Her heavy handbag was full of migraine-inducing documents that pulled at her arm, the skin going red where the leather strap had branded her.

Turning right down Cheshire Street she met a depressing building with dishevelled brickwork. It could have been mistaken for a ruin considering the state of the surrounding area, which appeared neglected and abandoned. It was, however, an extensive structure. Formally a Victorian bathhouse, Repton Boxing Club held onto glimmers of its past life with high ceilings and somewhat graceful arches encompassing wide panelled windows.

Francesca entered nervously. It was not her choice of company and upon acknowledging the sour faces of a few battered old boxing coaches, she realised she was far from welcome. Their violent disciples pounded the leather bags that lined the wall with poised ferocity. Young men stood bruised and bloodied with cauliflower ears, the thickened cartilage sitting as a reminder of the various scraps and brawls endured.

The walls were coated in deteriorating promotional posters of bare-knuckle boxers, while photographs depicting mid-punch dramas clung desperately onto the brickwork. Images of past champions grimaced down at Francesca as she walked below them. Meeting the side of the raised ring that sat in the middle of the room, she was confronted by a set of twins who were sparring at the centre of the canvas.

'Where's Oliver Thomas?' she asked with false confidence, gripping the front page tightly in her hand.

'What's it to you?' the larger twin retorted.

'I'm the girl he's been seeing, and I've got a bone to pick with him. Now, where is he?'

'Oh, you must be Frankie,' the slightly better-looking twin said. 'Excuse my brother's rudeness, he's over there warming up on the bags.' He pointed to a heavy punch bag that hung in the corner.

Navigating the shadow boxers and skipping ropes, she approached him. Oliver was striking the leather sack with such force that she almost felt sorry for the inanimate object. The twins watched, leaning over the ropes as she met his side.

'Don't you think you've beaten up enough?'

'Frankie! What are you doing here?' Oliver asked, startled but equally impressed that she had the nerve to enter such a place alone. Leaning in for a kiss, she turned her head, his lips meeting her cheek.

'What's that about then?' he asked, looking at the newspaper in her hand.

'I think you know what it's about,' she said angrily, passing him the article. His eyes processed every word as his mind scrambled for an excuse.

'Oh, look, we're famous.' Jack smirked as he joined his sparring partner. He had already seen the morning paper and beamed at the fact that Francesca had put the dots together. Oliver sent him a warning glance, a silent command to keep his mouth shut.

'Why did you do that? Those people did nothing to you,' she asked them.

'Look, I can explain, things got out of hand,' Oliver said, trying to calm her.

'You put a boy in hospital.'

'He got in my way,' Jack blurted.

She stared blankly at him. 'You don't think you've done anything wrong, do you?'

'Nah, it was quite fun really,' Jack said, adding insult to injury.

'Shut it, Jack, you're not helping,' Oliver snapped.

'Maybe if you had the bollocks to tell her the truth, I wouldn't have to open my mouth,' he said with a crooked grin.

'Don't you dare,' Oliver said sternly.

'She deserves to know, honestly is key to a healthy relationship,' he lectured, waving a finger at him.

From the way Oliver was now staring at him, Francesca realised something was drastically wrong. 'What are you on about?' she questioned.

'He doesn't care about you, Fran, you were a game, and he won,' Jack took satisfaction in saying.

A lump built in her throat. 'What do you mean, a game?'

'I do care about you,' Oliver said, his heart thumping in his chest.

'Let me spell it out for you, that night at the dance hall, you were a bet.'

'A bet?'

'To see if Oli could win over someone like you, now granted, he didn't kiss you that night or take it further, so at least he saved you from that embarrassment. But he wouldn't have looked twice at you otherwise,' Jack informed.

'Is that true?' she asked with a mortified glance. Her stomach felt as though she'd been dropped from a great height.

Oliver realised there was no lie that could save her from the hurt she was feeling. 'That is true, but every moment after that night was real—'

'I thought you actually liked me,' she whimpered, attempting to stop tears from drenching her face.

'Look, Frankie.'

'My name's not Frankie, you're a horrible person,' she yelled, wiping her eyes with her sleeve as she ran out of the gym.

'That was bang out of order.' The bigger twin scowled.

'Come on, Ron, it's none of our business,' his brother said as they turned their attention back to the ring.

Isla looked eye-catching with her auburn hair bouncing as she walked. She had only just had it done and was not opposed to spending a pretty penny to create an image of perfection. Her nails were painted a coral orange while her lips were coated in a rich layer of scarlet red. The blazer she was wearing complimented the three-quarter-length denim jeans that hugged her thighs.

Her jade-green eyes met the exterior of the gym. Waiting

patiently for Jack, she looked at her image in a compact mirror. A group of boys leaving the decrepit building sent a few glances in her direction, as usual, she ignored them. Part of her did enjoy the attention and was one of the reasons she liked to linger outside the front entrance. Spotting Oliver out the corner of her eye, she immediately placed her compact back into her handbag. Approaching him, she could tell he was not in the best of moods.

'Looks like you've been through it, it's not like you to be the one with a bruised face,' Isla said, studying his flushed cheeks that had a slight hint of underlying purple.

'Got a fight in a few months, so training is getting harder. I'm not focused at all today,' he admitted, looking at his raw knuckles that gripped his gym bag.

'Why's that?' she asked.

'Because Jack opened his mouth and now Fran wants nothing to do with me. I should have told her the truth about that night and that stupid bet. We were getting along so well,' he explained.

'Jack told me about that in drunken mumbles, I didn't tell anyone else, if Lewis and Finn found out they would have had a field day.'

'They found out the other night, at least she didn't find out through them. But what does it matter now, she knows and she's not happy about it.'

'You went about it the wrong way, but when you introduced her to us I could tell you wanted things to work, you had no bad intentions,' she spoke softly. 'I'm sorry that Jack let that slip, he had no right to tell her. I know he's too stubborn to apologise.'

Catching sight of Jack, Oliver was quick to avoid him. 'Don't worry about it, it wouldn't be the first time he's pissed me off and it sure as hell won't be the last. I'll see you around, Isla, look after yourself,' he said, continuing along the pavement.

'So, what's all that about then? The poor boy's distraught,' she said with folded arms.

Jack was sweaty and the wraps that coated his hands were dirty and blood ridden. 'I might have taken things a step too far,' he said.

Isla sighed up at the sky. 'As usual.'

A waterfall of tears fell down her cheeks. Francesca was almost visionless due to her snivelling state. Her hands shook as she reached for her front door keys. With trembling attempts, she failed to unlock what felt like a great blockade. Hearing the scrapings that had been accidently inflicted on the wooden door, Stephanie opened it, meeting eyes with her daughter who stood in a very sorry state. She sat between her grandmother and mother on the sofa.

'I thought he cared about me,' she cried as both relatives consoled her.

'I know, men are ever such stupid creatures,' Vera muttered as she held her granddaughter's hand.

'I'm the stupid one because I believed him,' she wept.

'That's not true, you followed your heart, which is a very brave thing to do,' Vera assured her.

'Well, bravery is clearly stupidity,' Francesca said, frowning.

'Listen, there is no stupidity in having feelings for somebody else. If nobody tried, we'd all be heartless bastards. I know you feel embarrassed for falling for him so quickly, but this is the first of many,' her mother said, wiping her daughter's tears away with a handkerchief.

Vera looked at Stephanie in agreement. 'Your mother's right, there are plenty more fish in the sea. And just remember, the bravest of people are those who pursue the hearts of others despite failure.'

A knock at the door sent the attention of all three in that direction. As Stephanie opened it, she was met by Elaine who was wielding a large Dairy Milk Bar.

'I heard what happened,' she said as she watched Francesca from over Stephanie's shoulder. 'I brought your favourite,' she said, holding up the chocolate.

Entering the church with a creek, Colin trailed his way up to the main altar. The stained-glass windows projected colourful silhouettes onto the walls. Manifesting and moving, they danced up the centre aisle.

'Come to confess?' his father asked, sitting on the back pew.

'What are you doing back there?' Colin asked with a startled glance.

'Waiting for you.'

'Well, here I am,' Colin said reluctantly, looking around the empty church.

'Come and sit down. Don't worry, I'm not going to preach,' his father assured him.

'Good, because it gets tiring after a while. I want to apologise for what I said,' Colin admitted as he sat on the pew in front of him.

'No apology necessary, I know you didn't mean it.'

'Susan is my family, I care for her,' Colin said, sticking up for her despite his father's criticism.

'I know you do. I just worry that you'll get yourself into

trouble. You know you can always come to me if you need help,' he spoke, melancholy as he recognised his son's bruised knuckles. Colin quickly hid his hands as his father reasserted his gaze, staring at the main altar where a large cross hung. 'Do you remember Belfast?' he asked, reminiscing days gone by.

'Only a bit, why'd you ask? Are you homesick?' Colin questioned, concerned.

'I'm always homesick, but we needed a new start,' he sighed. 'You know, they made me choose between my faith and my love for you? I used to visit your mother in secret so I could see you. When she died, they tried to deny me my right to be a father completely, but I couldn't let them take you away. You are the last part of her that I have, and I have all my faith placed in you.'

'I love you too,' Colin uttered. He understood how hard it was for his father to admit such a thing. 'What did you do when you were young, before you became a Priest?' he asked.

'You know I served in the Great War,' he said.

'Yes, but before that? You've never really told me about your childhood.'

'From a young age I was sent to work down the docks, I helped make ships, it all felt like one big game, until I realised what I helped create,' his father answered.

1911

THE MAIDEN VOYAGE

SHE WAS NEARLY ready, years of hard work and sacrifice had led up to this. As the ship neared completion, thousands of workers whizzed about the Harland and Wolff Shipyard. There was a level of excitement and camaraderie in the air as the sound of clamouring and shrieking steel slowly drew to a close.

Joseph watched as the large vessel stood firm and proud. Working with steel was hard and laborious, but he enjoyed the feeling of getting the job done. Looking up at the huge propellers, he couldn't help but appear so small in the presence of such a marvel.

'Joseph Murphy, do you intend to stand there all day?' a sharp voice asked from above as the boy gawped at the magnificent man-made structure.

'No, Sir,' he said as his gaze remained fixed on the ship. He twiddled a gold crucifix between his fingers.

'Almost biblical isn't it,' his friend said from beside him, readjusting his flat cap.

'It's definitely something,' Joseph replied, barely able to take his eyes off it.

'Well come on then, they're gonna let the water in soon, and I'm sure you wouldn't be too impressed if you drown before seeing the ship sail,' he said humorously. He pulled Joseph to the rusting ladder that clung to the side of the concrete.

As the boys clambered out of the foundations, they met the top of the Thompson Graving Dock. Leaning over the railings, crowds of workers stared in awe at the fine piece of engineering; it was an almost godly construction. And so, the RMS Titanic sat proudly, waiting for her maiden voyage.

CHAPTER 8

TENSION ENGULFED THE room as the Thomas siblings stared one another down. Colin sat awkwardly between them at the kitchen table, slowly sipping his tea. He watched intently as both opponents eyed each other up. Like a referee, he was present to make sure neither of them hit below the belt.

'So,' Susan initiated, her tone nothing short of fierce.

'So?' he questioned, looking at his sister whose blue eyes were well and truly seeing red. She sat in a blazer with her mother's glimmering brooch. Her coal-black hair was tied firmly in a tight ponytail while her face developed a sharp expression that made her look as though she had sucked a sour lemon.

'Oh, don't you dare act like you haven't done anything wrong,' she snapped.

'I haven't, Susan, it was Jack who let it slip,' he said.

'Yes, you have you stubborn cow.' She threw a wooden rolling pin at his head which missed by an inch, bouncing off one of the kitchen cabinets with a thud.

'Easy both of you, I don't want a bloody domestic,' Colin pleaded.

'Ok, so I should have been honest with her, but I don't know why you're getting so worked up about it, you hardly knew her,' Oliver thundered, matching his sister's intensity.

'Yes, I did, but you were too fuckin' oblivious to see it. I was sick and who helped me home? Fran. Who checked up on me to see if I was ok? That's right, Fran. But you wouldn't know this because you were too busy acting like billy big bollocks with your so-called mates.'

'I didn't know she did that,' he said guiltily.

'She was good for you, and you went along and fucked it up. If you're not careful, you're going to lose me too 'cause you're neglecting those who you owe your attention and respect to,' she screamed, her cheeks flushed with frustration.

'I respect you,' he said.

'Don't you dare say that. I'm the one who's tryin' to keep us afloat while you're acting as if you deserve a prison cell. Where were those pound notes you promised me, Oliver? Gas and water won't pay for itself. I have about an ounce of respect left for you,' she spat venomously, glancing at that month's bills that were piled high on the table.

'Come on now that's not fair,' Colin interjected.

'Shut up Colin before I rip you a new arsehole too,' she bit, sizing them both up.

'I'm sorry if you're hurt,' Oliver said. He wouldn't dare tell his sister that he gave the money to that boy in the cinema.

Susan's gaze remained fixed on her brother who was now trying to avoid the confrontation entirely, shifting from one foot to the other as if he were about to run out the door. 'Hurt? I'm not the one you should be apologising to. Kerry has seen that girl in a state for the past two weeks and you haven't even had the bottle to do the right thing.'

'She won't want to see me,' he dismissed, pacing.

'She may not want to, but she needs to, for her own sake considering you've made her look like a bloody idiot. Hell, you've embarrassed yourself. Do you even care about her?'

'I did, but the damage is done,' Oliver said regretfully.

'You did care for her? Or you do? 'Cause I know in your heart you care even though you have a funny way of showing it,' she said, coaxing him to a confession.

'I do care,' he admitted.

'Then what the hell are you waiting for, talk to Fran, and if you're lucky, she might give you another chance,' she said firmly.

As both fled the scene, Susan resumed her calm and poised nature. Sitting back and taking in that day's post, she couldn't help but contemplate the situation.

'I've never seen her so cross,' Colin said as they walked along the pavement.

'Yeah, I really put her over the edge this time,' Oliver sighed, looking at his pocket watch.

Typing at a rate of knots, Francesca sat, wading her way through the countless letters before her. She placed them into envelopes, sealed and stamped them. It felt like an arduous task; one of which she wanted to complete by five o'clock. She fiddled with the first-class postage stamps that were content on remaining stuck to their packet.

Looking out the large glass window, she watched the sky as

it developed into a mixture of pastel pinks and purples. Swirling together, the coloured clouds took on the appearance of candyfloss. Patches of orange burned through as the sun gripped onto the remaining daytime, slowly falling to the ground like a rotating Ferris Wheel. Jolts of sunlight pierced onto the walls of Mr Montgomery's office as the man himself sat contently in his bulky leather desk chair, puffing smoke into the surrounding air.

'Smile and the world smiles with you,' he muttered, acknowledging her miserable expression.

'I don't care for the world right now,' Francesca said, keeping her fingers moving from typewriter, to envelope, to stamps. Even though she said this, she couldn't help but appreciate London's sudden caramelised beauty and the golden streaks that were bouncing around the office.

'Is there a reason for your recent moodiness?' Mr Montgomery interrogated as he watched his employee frown her way through the remaining minutes of the day.

'I'm not moody, just upset, sorry, Sir. The paperwork's nearly done,' she said quickly, trying not to involve her boss in what she recognised to be an embarrassing series of events.

'Bugger the paperwork,' he declared.

'Sorry?' she asked, puzzled. Looking at the large stack of envelopes that she had slaved over all day, she couldn't help but feel slightly offended.

'I said bugger it. Now what's the matter?' he repeated.

'I just feel like an idiot, a naive idiot. I trusted someone a little quicker than I should have.'

'This is about a young man, I assume?' Mr Montgomery speculated as he lit another cigarette.

'Yes,' she said despondently, placing the final letter onto the pile.

'A little advice, Fran, don't bother with relationships at your age, you'll only be heartbroken,' he said, turning to face the glass. The large window framed the sky perfectly and sat like a pretty picture behind his desk.

'I don't understand.'

'Men are difficult, and women are difficult, it's surprising we can even co-exist. But when you're young like yourself, relationships get even more complicated because you haven't yet figured yourself out,' he stated, exhaling a lung full of smoke.

'Then how are we supposed to learn how to love?' she asked, frustrated as she gathered her belonging into her handbag.

'You have to learn to understand your own heart before you can even begin to think about being accepted into anyone else's,' he said as the clock struck five.

Charlotte trailed Harry's footsteps. She took pleasure in weaving in and out of his shadow, amused as it moved along the pavement. Slipping her hand into his, she walked at his side. His hand was much larger and had a layer of labour applied calluses on his palm. Yet he was gentle and grasped hers softly as they wandered peacefully upon the glinting grass of Victoria Park.

'Oh look, a swing!' she said excitably, dragging him to a nearby oak tree with its sturdy branches. One of the branches was curved and had a rope fastened tightly around it. Attached to the rope was a bruised and battered tyre that swung with the gentle breeze.

'I think that's for children,' he said cautiously, looking at the weathered rubber.

'And I think you just don't wanna have fun,' she teased, circling him with adventurous eyes.

'No, I just don't want to fall on my arse. But go on, I'll give you a push,' Harry said as he watched Charlotte perch herself within the tyre, holding onto the rope with childlike excitement.

'Did you hear what happened to Fran and Oliver?' she asked as he pushed her carefully.

'I know roughly what happened,' he replied as Charlotte swung to-and-fro. He felt the sunlight beat onto the back of his black drape jacket.

'It's so awful, I really liked her and now she probably won't want anything to do with us,' she said with dismay.

'You did nothing wrong,' he assured her, watching the lake. The water was calm and a few ducks with trailing ducklings paddled their way across the murky green water.

'I'd be distraught if you did that to me, she didn't deserve that at all,' she muttered.

'Oli made a mistake, hopefully he can correct it.'

'I hope so. You should bring your little brother next time to play on the tyre swing,' Charlotte suggested as she felt his hand press into the middle of her back, sending her to swing forward once more. Harry only needed to use one hand as the little golden-haired creature before him weighed no more than eight stone.

'I don't think he'd enjoy it as much as you do, he's all about football now. He got into trouble the other day for fighting,' he mumbled.

'Takin' after his brother, then.' Charlotte sniggered.

'Why'd you say that?'

'Well, Talbot is still eating through a straw, and I saw the newspaper talking about the cinema incident, I'm not blind Harry. I'm not nagging either, I just don't want to see you get hurt,' she said, concerned.

He twisted the tyre around, so she faced him. 'Don't worry about me.'

'I worry a lot about you and the others, getting into tiffs and stuff. You could get into proper trouble for that, I just don't want to lose you 'cause of one silly mistake. Jimmy Talbot had a pop at me, saying he would hurt you and me if he found out it was you that did that to his uncle. Don't try and act like it wasn't you that did that, Albie told me, and I recognised the marks made by that bicycle chain you carry about,' she said as he knelt before her.

Looking up at Charlotte's freckled face, he smiled. 'Nothing is going to happen, and I'm here to protect you, I'll always protect you, Lottie,' he said, lifting a hand to her delicate cheek, kissing her tenderly.

The warm breeze navigated the compact roads and poky alleyways, finding its way out onto the open high street. Here, the narrow buildings towered high above the cobbles.

Stephanie was busy picking vegetables at the greengrocers, the produce sitting in large wooden crates stacked high into the air. There were all sorts of colours and textures available. She was set on finding the items written on her list, and was determined not to sway from it despite the temptation of rich plums and blueberries. Their colours were so bright that they looked almost artificial, the purples and blues resembling hard boiled sweets from the nearby sweetshop. As Stephanie placed a few hefty potatoes in her little basket, she recognised Charley's reflection in the shop's glass window. He was so broad that his silhouette masked her in shadows.

'Hello, Steph,' he said, grinning. He was carrying a huge

crate full of bananas. His friend stood at his side holding a crate of mangoes. 'You go ahead, Curtis, I'll follow in a bit.'

'Will do.' He smiled, entering the small shop. There he met the owner who inspected the ripe fruits one by one.

'These just came in fresh off the boat. The boss makes us deliver them by foot sometimes as it's quicker than loading the truck, especially for a little establishment like this,' Charley explained.

'They look wonderful,' she said, ogling the bright yellow fruits.

'How's Fran? I heard what happened.'

'She's ok, it's never nice to be heartbroken but unfortunately it's part of life. She really liked him.'

'It's probably for the best. Oliver is a known troublemaker,' he muttered.

'But weren't James and yourself quite the troublemakers back in the day?' she asked.

'I suppose, but even we had limits. Speaking of James, I think it's time you went back to church, you can't put it off forever. I know going back there's painful, but it's time you got closure.'

'No, you're right, Fran said exactly the same thing. Will you come with me?' she questioned, her dark brown eyes peering up at him.

Charley watched her for a moment. 'I don't see why not,' he agreed.

Leaving the bank, Francesca waved goodbye to Penny who was fixed to the telephone. The mellow evening left a docile impression on London as all were occupied by the entrancing heat. Francesca watched the retreating sun as she walked along the concrete, looping her blazer through the handles of her handbag.

'Fran!' a female voice exclaimed from behind her.

'I take it this wasn't a coincidence that you found me here,' Francesca said as Isla met her side. They hadn't interacted much, but she was cautious due to her prior involvement with Oliver.

'No, I followed you earlier, not in a creepy way though, I'm not a stalker,' she assured.

'I'm glad about that. What can I do for you?' Francesca asked, confused why the girl beside her had travelled, intending to bother her after a long day of work.

'Do you want an ice cream?' Isla questioned.

'I'm ok thank you, got a busy day tomorrow that I should prepare for.'

'Even more of a reason for you to relax now. Come on, it won't be more than half an hour.' Isla smiled.

'Well, if you insist,' Francesca reluctantly agreed.

Only a short distance from Fenchurch Street, the banks of the River Thames provided a much-needed sanctuary from the grizzly ruins and bustling pavements. There were fancy trade buildings made of marble and white stone. Victorian in design, they were a stark contrast to the Tower of London that sat prominently on the river's edge. The formidable fortress had many walls surrounding it. Looking at the White Tower sitting proudly at the centre, Francesca thought of the Tudors, wondering whether they would approve of the modern world that surrounded their history.

They pulled themselves onto a concrete wall that overlooked the river, a few rebellious waves crashing into Traitors' Gate below. Francesca enjoyed a chocolate ice cream cone and sat contently, her feet dangling over the jilting water. Isla perched with a raspberry ripple ice cream and was careful not to get it on her pale orange shirt. Long dark lashes framed her green eyes, while her auburn hair flowed gently with the warm breeze.

'He likes you,' Isla said, licking the raspberry dessert.

'He liked you too, by the sounds of things,' Francesca mumbled.

'Look, I know I'm not the most trustworthy source, but that boy likes you a lot. He made a mistake by starting things the way he did, but that doesn't mean it has to finish.'

'What happened between you two?' Francesca interrogated as she gripped the cone.

'I was young, we were both eighteen. I couldn't keep my hands to myself. Oliver nearly beat the lad to death when he found out. He hasn't been the same since. I haven't been the same, I seem to fall for anyone who will have me,' she admitted, a frown covering her face.

'I guess that's why Colin told me to be careful,' Francesca said.

'It was a stupid mistake. Ever since people have called me loose, or thought of me as a whore, even my closest friends. I'm not like that, please believe me, I'm no threat to you. You don't need to worry, I'm with Jack,' Isla said, her tone verging on desperate.

'I don't think you're a whore, or a threat, you wouldn't have come here to convince me to take him back if you were. You shouldn't let what people say get you down.' Francesca smiled. Inside, she scolded herself for judging her, she was always told not to judge others by her grandmother. Isla just seemed so perfect, like a china doll, but the more she watched her, the more she realised how many people had played with her, how many boys had used her, how many girls envied the way they toyed with her. Francesca had fallen into that trap, growing suspicious as soon as she drew their first comparison. There was no comparison, only two young women trying to make their way through the world.

'Thanks, Fran, I sometimes think words hurt more than a punch in the face,' she admitted.

'I understand, people call me boring and it gets on my nerves,' she admitted, gazing at her.

'Well, you're definitely not that. So, are you going to give Oli another chance?'

'I can't say I will,' she sighed, biting into the cone.

'There's no rush. Thank you for taking the time to hear me out, not many people listen to me, even Jack seems to look more than listen and he's supposed to be my other half.' She laughed, but Francesca couldn't help but see the sadness beneath her.

'Even if it doesn't work out between Oliver and I, I'm always free to listen to you. I think of myself as quite a good listener, I've survived nineteen years of religious sermons.' She smirked.

Isla hugged her suddenly, and Francesca, although taken aback, didn't pull away. She held her gently in return, something that Isla hadn't experienced in a long while.

'What's your bird called?' Oliver questioned from the end of the sofa. A cup of tea sat in his hands, yet it couldn't bring warmth to the frostiness that filled the room. Vera sat in her armchair, studying the young man before her with narrowing eyes. The budgie sat patiently in its cage, observing Oliver who was desperately trying to ignite a conversation.

'Houdini,' Vera answered bluntly, taking a long sip from her teacup.

'Like the escape artist?' Oliver asked as he watched the bird. He almost felt sorry for the little creature as it sat behind the barred structure.

'Yes, exactly.' Like a prison guard, she kept her sharp eyes on him. He shuffled nervously. It was unusual for Oliver to feel this uncomfortable. His pocket watch gripped his waistcoat, ticking the seconds by. Waiting for Francesca felt like an eternity, but he knew it was the right thing to do.

'What are your intentions with my granddaughter? Apart from making her upset of course,' Vera spoke suddenly, putting him on the spot.

'It was a misunderstanding, I just need to explain,' he said, realising that he was on very thin ice.

'My boy, sometimes you need to swallow your pride and say what's necessary. An apology will do, nothing more, nothing less,' Vera advised him.

'I didn't mean to hurt her. She probably won't even want to see me,' Oliver said pessimistically as he looked around the room, recognising the vase that sat in the corner.

'She's had those dying daisies up for weeks now. There is only one alive and even that's clinging onto life. Refuses to take them down because she cares about what they represent, whatever that may be.'

'She has hope,' he said guiltily.

'Yes, well, a word of advice from an old lady. Flowers need attention and care if they are to be kept properly, neglecting them for two weeks will kill off any possibility of their survival. You're lucky one is left standing,' Vera warned as she lifted herself from her chair. Spying Francesca through the window, she slowly ascended the staircase, leaving the two in privacy.

'Oliver, what are you doing here?' Francesca asked as she entered. Worried about the possible presence of her relatives, she looked around to make sure they wouldn't cause a fuss.

'I, um, just felt it was right to come here and apologise,' he said, his fingers tapping on the side of the teacup.

'Is that it?' she asked, placing her heavy handbag on the floor.

'I made a mistake. Yes, it didn't start out the right way, but I do care about you, the rest of it was real for me too. As soon as I saw you outside that sweetshop in your little dress and clumpy shoes, I knew I liked you, I think you're lovely, inside and out,' he pleaded, making his case as Francesca judged him from afar.

'You played with my feelings over a bet,' she snapped.

'I know, and that was wrong, so I'm sorry. And I'm sorry it's taken me weeks to talk to you, I'll do better. Please give me another chance,' he begged.

'Why should I?'

'Because we have something in common.' Oliver rose to his feet. Putting the cup down, he proceeded towards the glass vase.

'Oh yeah? And what's that?'

'Hope that we can try again,' he said as he picked out the remaining live daisy.

Francesca stared at it, concerned by its fragile nature.

'I suppose we can give it a try,' she said cautiously as she took the flower from him.

'Yeah?' he asked with sudden excitement.

'But you're in the doghouse,' she said firmly, watching the colour return to his cheeks.

'I know, I'll make it up to you, Frankie, I promise,' he assured her with a kiss on the forehead. Leaving the house with a proud grin on his face, he met Colin who was waiting down the end of the road.

'Took your bloody time. How'd it go then?' Colin asked.

'I got her back, Colin, I got her back,' he exclaimed.

As morning broke, it was filled with the prospect of a new day and new beginnings. The room was humid, and the sunrays pierced under the curtains. Susan sat upright on the bed in her nightgown, holding her stomach. Quickly running to the bathroom, she vomited. Rushing to her aid, Colin held her hair back and comforted her as she knelt in front of the toilet.

'I think there's something wrong with me,' she said. Visibly distressed by her unknown illness, her hands began to shake.

'I know there's something wrong, you've spewed your guts about three times this week already and it's only Tuesday,' Colin said as he rubbed her back.

'What could it be? Oh no. It can't be,' she spoke, horrified as she gripped her stomach.

'What can't be? Spill it, Susan,' Colin said anxiously.

She began to cry. 'Oh God, no.'

'What is it?' he fretted.

'I might be pregnant,' she snivelled as tears rolled from her eyes. 'I'm late and I've got no other explanation for why I'm getting poorly,' she said with a mortified expression, her hands now violently shaking.

'Jesus Christ,' Colin uttered, pacing.

'Fuck, we've gone and done it now,' she sobbed with regret. 'We're going to lose everything, Oliver will kill you if he finds out.'

'It's ok we can get it sorted, you might not even be pregnant,' he said, trying to think logically despite the panic he felt bubbling up inside him.

'But what if I am? I can't get rid of it, I won't get rid of it, we can't stay here, what are we going to do? I'm not even married,' she said fearfully, looking to her equally shaken partner.

'Ok, ok, one thing at a time. I'd never ask you to get rid of it. We are going to get through this together, all of us if that's the case,' he said. Holding her tightly, he felt her weep into his shoulder. 'We've got to keep this a secret until I can figure something out. You can't tell anyone.'

'I promise I won't,' she cried.

As weeks passed, their worst fear was confirmed. Scrambling for a way out of the situation, Colin realised that the problem could not simply be solved, and that they were both stranded in their self-made mess.

CHAPTER 9

THE GENTLE RHYTHM of pitter-pattering rain could be heard falling upon the pavement. Streaks of water cascaded down the glass windows of Albie's small semi-detached home. It sat at the centre of Bethnal Green Road and a few chirpy looking gnomes guarded the front door with large pointy hats.

His home was small, warm and welcoming. It was also filled with eccentricity from the bulky lampshades to the prominent sofa that took up most of the space in the front room. A withering pot plant watched the bay window, envious of the spitting showers; and a ceramic bulldog sat in the porch with a pair of colourful sunglasses perched on its head.

'And I present to you! The crème de la crème of art,' Albie announced proudly as he revealed the painting to Francesca. Isla posed half-naked over the sofa.

'Um, is that supposed to be her, you know?' she questioned, squinting at the painting whilst awkwardly avoiding eye contact with the real-life image.

'You better not have botched me up,' Isla teased as she pulled on a robe.

'I could never botch up such a fine frame. Maybe you two could pose together,' he said, holding a pencil up to Francesca, measuring her features with a mischievous grin.

'As lovely as that sounds, I'm not too comfortable getting my kit off in front of others.'

'Isla has no problem with that, do ya poppet,' he said cheekily as he watched his model wander to the bathroom.

'Piss off, Albie,' she joked as she fixed her hair in the mirror.

'So, why have you graced us with your presence on such a beautiful morning?' Albie asked, turning his attention to Francesca once again.

'It's miserable outside,' she said, looking out the bay window, then down to the soggy tights that clung to her legs.

'Everyone's perception of beauty is different. One person's storm is another person's sunny day,' he responded philosophically as he tended to his painting.

'Right, I'll keep that in mind when the rain drenches me again and makes me look like a London sewer rat,' she said, unconvinced. 'And to answer your question, Isla invited me as moral support.'

'Oh Jesus, Albie! Talk about proportions.' Isla gasped as she returned to the room, meeting the image of her supposed self.

'Have some imagination, it's like Vincent van Gogh,' he said, overly pleased.

'I'll show you Van Gogh when I cut your ear off for the mutilation you've done to my curves,' she threatened, looking at her perpendicular form.

'It's not too bad,' Francesca said, trying to hold back her

amusement.

'Fran, my hips are triangular!' Isla exclaimed.

'I'm sure they can be adjusted,' she suggested, only to burst into laughter.

'Who said I'm changing it?' Albie said with folded arms.

'You've done her boobs so round they look like my mum's cake tins,' Francesca said.

'A lot of women would kill for tits as big as cake tins,' Albie added.

'Well, it's certainly something,' Isla sighed acceptingly.

He turned to them with a prideful conclusion. 'It's innovation. One day your minds may be open enough to understand the meaning of art.'

'I'm not sure I want to understand it,' Isla said, adjusting her gaze from the painting to Francesca. 'Anyway, the girls want to meet up with you in your lunch break later, are you up for it?'

'Of course, that would be wonderful,' Francesca agreed.

Isla's hair was drenched and flattened. She hated looking imperfect, and as she caught her reflection in a nearby window, she felt as though she could scream. Black streaks of mascara stained her cheeks, her eyelashes clumped together.

She met the front door of her flat. It was on the seventh floor of a recently built tower block. The thunder grumbled in the distance as she let herself in.

'That's a new look for you, Isla.' Jack smirked. He was standing by a little table that had a fresh pot of coffee and two cups laid upon it.

'I need a bath,' she grumbled.

'Not before eating some breakfast, I prepared it especially,' he said, grabbing her by the hand, leading her to the table. 'I went down the market and got syrup, apparently the Americans love it. And I know you love American things, like films and fashion so I thought it was fitting.' He entered the kitchen and returned with two plates stacked with pancakes.

'They look wonderful.' She smiled, taking a seat. She shivered as her wet hair sent droplets down the back of her neck.

'Here, I don't want you gettin' a cold,' he said as he pulled a towel around her.

She popped a forkful of pancake into her mouth. 'They're delicious.' She smiled widely.

'So, how was it being Albie's art project?' He grinned.

'It was liberating, I lounged half-naked for a good hour.'

'Well, if there's any other bloke I'd let you get your kit off around, it's Albie.' He laughed. 'Do you want coffee?'

'Please,' she said, watching as the rich dark liquid trickled into the cup. Jack poured his own, adding to it a drop of whiskey that he kept in a hip flask.

'Have you been drinking this morning?' she asked, licking the sticky syrup from her fork.

'Only a little. It goes well with coffee and I needed some Dutch courage because I want to tell you something very important. That's why I've made you a special breakfast,' he said.

'Oh yeah, and what's that?'

'That I love you.'

Isla stared at him, her mouth wide with shock.

'I mean it with all my heart, I've loved you since school, but I never had the bottle to tell you,' he admitted.

Jumping onto his lap, she kissed him passionately. 'Well, I love you too,' she said.

'How about we get you out of these wet clothes?' He lifted

her up, her legs wrapping around his waist.

As the gloomy atmosphere continued its way throughout the day, Francesca sat at her desk and watched as the water spurted down the large panel of glass, the landscape behind it becoming distorted. As rumbles projected their way around the city, the inevitable lightning manifested above the clouds.

Her boss sat rigidly in his chair. Francesca watched her employer flinch as each lightning bolt cracked like a whip onto the surrounding surface of the earth. She couldn't help but think of the grizzly grey sky as a dark night during the Blitz; the clouds hiding a sinister force that was intended to cause great destruction. But she knew that this act of nature would pass, judging by the look on her boss's face, he thought otherwise.

'Afraid of lightning? It sometimes reminds me of the bombings with the loud sounds and bright light,' she explained as she typed away the seconds.

'I'll live. And I wasn't here to witness the bombings, only the aftermath,' he said, gripping the leather armrests tightly.

She filtered another piece of paper into the machine. 'It's ok to be afraid you know, everyone's afraid of something.'

'It's not something that I'm afraid of, it's someone,' he admitted.

'Who? Are you in trouble?' Francesca asked with a concerned glance.

'Not in this life,' Mr Montgomery replied as the thunder bellowed.

'You think you're in trouble with God?'

'I've done some things that I'm not very proud of, and I can't help thinking that he's coming for retribution,' he confessed with haunted eyes.

'What did you do in the war?'

'Terrible things.'

'You killed people? If they were shooting at you, then you had the right to defend yourself.'

'It's not that simple, Francesca. War isn't that simple,' he said.

'Then what are these terrible things? If you don't mind me asking,' she questioned.

He remained frozen in his chair. 'We started out bombing German industrial sites east of the Rhine, and eventually, civilian areas, Frankfurt and Hamburg to name a few.'

'You were just following orders.'

'I can't help but think that's a very sorry excuse to state when I reach the pearly gates. I've had the same dream every night to this day. Doctors say it's common for men returning from war, who thought war could work its way into your sleep.'

'What happens in this dream?' she asked.

'I see them all. Their faces are blood-covered and disfigured; they are the faces of the people I helped to kill. Men, women and children,' he confessed as the thought terrorised his mind.

'That sounds awful. How do you sleep?'

'These do the trick.' Taking a bottle of pills from the desk drawer, he shook them in the air.

'You're a good person, so you'll go to heaven. That's how it works,' Francesca said.

'I was a good person before the war, now I'm just a corrupted soul along with all the others,' he expressed pessimistically, hearing the roar of a thunderclap in the distance, making him flinch.

'When I first started here, you encouraged me to speak

honestly, so that's what I'm going to do. God will forgive you, I know he will. My grandma says that our lives are built on mistakes and lessons which we learn from. You made a mistake, but think of how many others have done the same. You think your acts are unforgivable, but you don't know the compassion of those above, those that have moved on and are now at peace,' she said with a smile, looking at him hopefully.

'And why should I believe that? Why should I believe a nineteen-year-old girl who's trying to comfort a nutter in a storm?'

'Because I have faith, and you should too. I take it that's why you've got all the aircraft antiques scattered about your office because you were a pilot?'

'It was a childhood dream, one that was retired in a nightmare. Doesn't mean I can't reminisce,' he said with a grin, looking at the objects. There was a globe, flight glasses, binoculars, the large propeller that sat on the wall, and some maps that laid stagnantly rolled up on a shelf.

'You've got some fancy bits and bobs lying around. What's that?' Francesca asked as a little bronze object caught her eye. She attempted to distract him as the storm slowly died down.

'Have a look, it's an American compass made around 1910. It was given to me as a child,' he explained as she examined the object. Its bronze exterior and chain were in immaculate condition and contained four directional points with a little needle at the centre.

'It's really stunning. I love how every antique has a story,' she said, fascinated by the piece of history that sat in her hands.

'Yes, it keeps me sane by learning the tales of others, makes me feel like a child again.'

'What do you think?' Francesca lifted the object to her

blouse, holding it in position.

'It suits you, makes you look like Amelia Earhart.' He laughed as she gently laid the object back on the desk. The storm rumbled in the distance, yet the worst was over. Only a few jolts of spitting rain remained as the clouds swirled into the horizon.

Francesca left for her lunch break wrapped in a bright yellow raincoat. The polka dot scarf sat tightly fastened around her neck, fighting off the disobedient gusts of wind as she met the busy street. She joined the flood of people, mainly businessmen who were navigating the broad pavement quickly to find refuge from the remaining rain.

Reaching Tower Hill, she watched as the fortress stood in a grizzly state. Tossing water from the sides of the uneven grey stonework that formed its formidable walls, a deep pool of water formed within the grass moat, the Tower of London springing back to life. A soggy Union Jack fought through the dampness, swaying violently with the aggressive blasts of wind that were tormenting the clouds.

Francesca approached the distinguishable pack of girls wielding bright umbrellas, one of which had turned inside out and flapped frantically in the air. Greeted by Charlotte who grabbed her in an enthusiastic embrace, they continued down the road.

'How's work going?' Susan asked, her voice was quiet, and she spoke as though her mind was in a different place.

'The usual business,' Francesca said as Charlotte and Elaine looped their arms around hers.

'Come on then, let's find somewhere to eat, you must be peckish,' Kerry stated, growing impatient with the pleasantries.

They walked down the pavement in two rows, three in front, three behind. With umbrellas in hands, they followed the stream of water that had developed in between the cobbles.

'I made a dress the other day for my little sister, and it had all different colours and textures, oh you'd love it, Fran!' Charlotte exclaimed.

'Or hate it as the case may be,' Kerry inferred from behind them.

'I'm sure it looks wonderful.' Francesca smiled, imagining the creation with its possible detailed embroidery, ribbons and taffeta. She shuddered as the air bit at her legs. They were coated in thin black tights that had only just dried off from that morning's onslaught.

'I'm glad you and Oliver sorted things out,' Isla said, peering down, recognising her suede shoes that had watermarks developing upon them.

Francesca glanced back at her with a grin. 'Thanks, what have you been up to today, apart from being Albie's muse?' She winked.

'If I told you, I'd have to kill you,' she said mischievously.

'Oh, come on, Isla, spill the beans,' Charlotte pleaded, looking to her friend with soppy eyes, almost how a dog looks at its owner when begging for scraps.

'Jack told me he loved me,' she announced proudly.

'Is this before or after you let him between your legs?' Kerry asked, looking at Susan with a judgemental glance.

'I'll have you know it was before,' she informed.

'I take it he was pissed when he said this,' Susan muttered as she gripped her oversized trench coat, the wind bullying the back of her neck.

'He might have been a little bit drunk, but he still meant it,'

Isla admitted, her voice growing despondent.

'If you say so,' Kerry sighed.

'He wouldn't have said it if he didn't mean it,' Francesca said encouragingly, causing Isla to beam.

'I like your coat, Susan. I think it's a bit baggy for you though.' Elaine observed the mass of khaki green fabric swallow the girl behind her. Its tortoiseshell buttons sat fastened, yet it failed to reflect Susan's elegant figure.

'It's a trench coat so it's supposed to be, and I think some things look better when they're oversized,' she explained, yet she knew it was a blessing that the weather was damp and groggy. She wasn't even showing, but the paranoia made her pick the baggiest thing in her wardrobe. If she wore a large coat on a hot day it would cause suspicion, especially from Kerry who was quick to catch her out.

'I do love an oversized jumper,' Elaine agreed.

'What's with the change of style all of a sudden?' Kerry interrogated.

'Just fancied it.' Susan smiled nervously.

They continued in silence for a while until they met the side of the Ye Old Tiger Tavern. It appeared to have a merry atmosphere with the singing of various drunken tunes, despite it being the early hours of the afternoon. Behind it was a vast empty space consumed by depressed brickwork and broken glass. The ruins spanned all the way from Tower Hill to Water Lane, leaving the rotting corpse of half-collapsed buildings in between.

'What is your favourite song, Fran?' Charlotte asked. The girls continued down the road, leaving the pub behind them, its inhabitants' singing becoming a slowly retreating echo.

'You better say Rock Around the Clock by Bill Haley,' Kerry blurted out.

'I prefer Shake Rattle and Roll,' Isla said.

'That is a good one I'll give you that,' she agreed.

'I don't know, I prefer more classic stuff, like Vera Lynn, The White Cliffs of Dover,' Francesca admitted awkwardly. Her answer was met with silence.

'Hm, it's not my style but each to their own,' Kerry said.

'Is there a reason you like that song?' Susan asked.

'Yes, it reminds me of someone I loved.' She smiled, thinking of her brother.

'Well Shake Rattle and Roll has the same effect on me, except I wouldn't say I loved him,' Isla admitted humorously as the girls burst into laughter.

They proceeded to a café on the corner of Lower Thames Street. From the Custom House to the Coal Exchange, the area appeared noisy and chaotic with hundreds of people rushing in and out of the establishments.

'We need to educate you,' Kerry said as they entered. The small space offered traditional foods, fish and chips, and all the good stuff. Steaming cups of tea warmed the hands of those chilled from the surprisingly cold rain. Pies and pastries were served while the girls took in the smell of the freshly baked goods. They sat around a little table tucked in the corner, watching the spitting showers hit the glass window.

'Wait until you see Carl Perkins, he's dreamy,' Isla said. Her cheeks grew red, matching her auburn hair.

'And James Dean, he's my favourite actor,' Charlotte added enthusiastically.

'Don't forget Marlon Brando.' Kerry grinned.

'How could we forget Marlon Brando,' Susan said with a sigh.

'Who's that?' Francesca asked, causing them all to stare.

'Please tell me you are takin' the piss,' Kerry said in disbelief.

'No, who is he?' she questioned. Looking to Elaine for assistance, she was met with equal confusion.

'He's absolutely gorgeous, Fran,' Charlotte said as butterflies filled her stomach.

'He's an American actor,' Susan informed.

'He's famous, you must have seen one of his films, The Men? A Streetcar Named Desire?' Isla continued, shocked by Francesca's revelation.

'A Streetcar Named Desire is my favourite!' Charlotte exclaimed.

'It doesn't ring any bells.' Francesca laughed. She and Elaine would often frequent the cinema, especially on brisk days. However, they were more pre-occupied with British films depicting historical dramas with homegrown stars such as Laurence Olivier.

'Girls, it appears that we have a lot of work to do,' Kerry said urgently as she ordered a plate of egg and chips. It was brought over instantly and she drenched the plate in salt and vinegar.

'Well, this Friday is the perfect opportunity, we are all going to the dance hall, you two better be there,' Susan said, stealing a chip from Kerry's plate.

'You can all come round mine beforehand to get ready,' Charlotte suggested.

'Is there enough room for all of us?' Francesca asked, knowing how cramped her little flat was.

'My dad's going to visit my uncle in the evening, and my sister is always out-and-about, we'll have plenty of space.'

'Lottie's it is then,' Susan agreed.

Elaine waved goodbye to Francesca as she entered the bank for the remaining hours of the day. Parting ways with the girls, she trailed her way back home, navigating the dampened red brick streets. Swinging the soggy and now folded umbrella in one hand, she watched the droplets as they ran down the material creating patterns on the thin green fabric. Entranced by the water crafted patterns, she failed to recognise the two boys that had stalked her down the road.

'Did you have a nice lunch?' Lewis asked. A cigarette clung to the corner of his mouth and smoke followed him as he walked.

'It was good, why'd you ask?' Elaine questioned suspiciously as she continued walking, eager not to stop for them.

'I'm just being friendly,' he answered, grinning at Finn who followed unnervingly behind her.

'You don't strike me as a friendly person.'

'Oh, is that so? You'd think otherwise if you got to know me.' He smiled through his teeth as he combed his wet blonde hair back across his scalp.

'Yeah, he's a lovely bloke,' Finn added as he met her side. Sandwiched in between them, there was no escaping their company.

'It doesn't seem that way, judging by the way you treat people,' she uttered.

'Not everyone deserves my care and attention,' Lewis said arrogantly.

She turned to meet his sharp glance. 'You're very full of yourself.'

'I try my best,' he said, throwing the cigarette down to the floor, letting it fizzle out in a passing puddle.

'But seriously, Elaine, we don't bite, feel free for a chat any day,' Finn said, yet his tone was consumed with contempt.

'Why are you two attempting to be nice? I can tell you don't mean it.'

'Because we see how Fran is neglecting you,' Lewis mentioned.

'She's not.'

'She most certainly is, ain't that right, Finn?'

'The other girls are very fond of her,' he agreed.

'You on the other hand,' Lewis said, looking Elaine up and down with judgement.

'Thank you both for your words of wisdom, but I know her better than all of you put together. She wouldn't forget me.'

'Forget you? Sweetheart you're already in the past,' Lewis said cruelly.

'She has spent a lot of time with Isla and Lottie, hell, she even went and visited Susan, brought her tomato soup and all,' Finn informed, putting ideas in her head.

'How much time has good old Frankie spent with you in the past month or so?' Lewis asked manipulatively.

'Not much, but she's not like that, I am her best and oldest friend.'

'Keyword in that sentence, oldest.' Finn grinned.

'I hate to break it to you but you're old news, better start looking for a new best friend because Fran doesn't want you anymore,' Lewis said as Elaine's eyes grew glossy.

'You're both really mean,' she whimpered as she hurried away from them, wiping the tears with her sleeve.

They watched her disappear down the end of the road.

'Poor thing, I think we hurt her feelings,' Finn sighed.

'I didn't think we could make her cry so easily,' Lewis said, satisfied.

As Elaine met the porch of her house, she looked up to the grim-looking clouds that dominated the skyline. The darkness of the mid-afternoon felt eerie, almost unnatural, and brought a melancholy atmosphere to the city. Entering, she threw her sodden wet umbrella to the ground.

'Are you alright, Elaine?' her brother asked.

'I don't want to talk about it, Charley,' she replied as she scurried away to her bedroom, slamming the door.

He pulled on his thick coat. 'Ok, well if you do, I've got to pop out for a bit, but we can have a chat later,' he voiced loudly so she could hear. Opening the front door, he faced the miserable weather. The house was only opposite, but in the lingering storm, it seemed to be of great difficulty to get anywhere without being blown backwards.

'Hello, Miss Vera,' Charley said as he stood at the front door of the Parmenter household. Grasping the umbrella that his sister had tossed to the ground, he stood in opposition to the heightening rain.

'Miss? I haven't been called that in a very long time. It almost makes me feel young again,' Vera said with a smile, looking up at him. His hair was slicked back, and his youthful face—which was particularly unusual considering he survived a war that would age many a man—contrasted his strong stature. His hand gripped the wooden umbrella handle that was pulling with the blustery wind.

'You're only as old as your mind wants you to be.'

'Say that to my joints,' she muttered.

'How's the arthritis?'

'Easing up, but without a doubt, it will be back by winter,' she sighed, wringing her hands.

'Let's not think that far ahead. The docks are deadly that

time of year, slippery wood and heavy objects never mix well,' he mumbled.

'I imagine it's quite the hazard, are you sure you don't want a cup of tea before you go, dear?' Vera offered as her daughter met the doorway.

'Thank you, Vera, that's very kind, but we best be on our way,' he said politely.

'Good afternoon, Charley, almost like the evening with this weather, isn't it?' Stephanie chuckled as she pulled on a coat and fastened a scarf around her head. Her dark hair fought to break free from the confines of the material.

'Tell me about it, I don't think the clouds could get any greyer if they tried,' he muttered.

'A great British summer,' she said humorously, stepping outside, meeting the cover of his umbrella.

'Are you ready?' he asked, offering his arm.

'As ready as I'll ever be.'

'Come on then, now or never.' He guided her down the pavement, their arms locked tightly.

The rows of houses that lined Coborn Road created a wind tunnel that not even the utility poles could escape, sending the electric cables thrashing violently in the air. Reaching the white panelled church that stood like a bright beacon shining through the darkness, they entered.

'I haven't been in here in a very long time,' Stephanie said as they passed the heavy wooden doors. She removed her scarf, looking at him with an expression stained with guilt.

'You and me both,' Charley admitted, guiding her down a pew. The church was quiet and empty.

'It hasn't changed one bit.' She reminisced as they took a seat.

'See, this isn't so bad,' he said.

'I suppose not. There are a lot of memories in this place. My wedding. My son and daughter's christenings. My husband's funeral. It's a shame my son didn't get to rest here, Mile End was his home,' she whispered, hugging his arm. 'I miss him.'

'I miss him too, Steph, I miss him too. Not a day goes by where he doesn't pop into my head,' he admitted.

'He haunts mine,' she said, frowning.

'You've got to let him go, for your own sake,' Charley warned, understanding that failing to release the past could damage her future.

'I know, it's just painful.'

'All goodbyes are painful, but you'll see him again one day. Memories are the imprints of people that we keep throughout our lives, and they re-introduce us in death like we haven't missed a day in each other's company.'

'I hope you're right.' She looked up at the large cross hung above the main altar, then back to Charley. 'I remember when we all went to Southend-on-Sea. You both were only little, and James fell down the sea defence, sent splinters all up his back.'

'And you and Vera had to pull them out one by one. What a trauma that was. There was that other time when Tom Turner picked a fight with me, and James showed him what for.' Charley recalled.

'I remember that nasty lad, James did him up good and proper. He never bothered you again.'

'I wonder why, he knocked two of his teeth out,' he said, smirking.

'You always protected each other, I never worried when you were together, it's the same way I feel about Francesca and Elaine,' Stephanie said.

'They'll never be separated, they're practically sisters, just like James and I were brothers. I'm sorry I couldn't protect him in the end.'

'I know, Charley, I lost my son, but you also lost a brother, and I can't imagine how hard it must have been for you. You had no responsibility to protect or save him, not in the end anyway. You couldn't help where you were sent. And James was so stubborn, wanting to join the Air Force.' Squeezing his arm, she felt compelled to ask, 'How's your shoulder holding up?'

'Apart from the scarring it's fine, got away lightly compared to most of the lads, I try my best not to think about Dunkirk, or the events after,' he answered, brushing off his injury.

'God bless them all,' Stephanie said with a heavy heart.

'So, do you think you are up for coming to a Sunday service soon? I know Fran and Vera have been trying to get you to come back for ages,' he spoke with bated breath.

'When this whole place is packed? I'm not sure if I can face that,' she said, gulping hard.

'It's been ten years since the war ended, Steph, it's time,' Charley encouraged.

'Will you come?' she questioned timidly, knowing full well that he had no interest in pursuing his faith.

'If you want me here, I'll come. I don't care for churches myself, so don't expect it to become routine.'

'Thank you, you're the closest thing to a son that I have left.' She looked at him gratefully.

'Anytime, family comes first.' He smiled down at her. 'Speaking of which, Elaine was upset when she came in, I was wondering if she had a falling out with Fran?'

'I don't know, I'll have a word with her when she gets in from work.'

As the two sat on the wooden pew, they were oblivious to the Priest who had caught wind of their conversation from behind the curtain. With a smile, he turned away, tending to his duties once more.

Kerry scraped an agitated hand through her soggy hair. She waited for a moment, clenching the handle of her folded umbrella. The cold wood pressed against her palm as she faced the front door, dreading the thought of stepping inside. And so, her hair got wetter, the drops running down her forehead and nose. Wiping her face with the sleeve of her drape jacket, she thumped on the door. Her mother answered, a sour expression covering her face. She was much shorter than Kerry and had a grubby appearance with a dirty pinnie clinging to her waist. Her sunken eyes looked to her daughter's piercing amber glance. She appeared as though she was about to utter something, but before she had the chance a harsh voice bellowed from behind her.

'Where the fuck have you been?' her uncle hissed. He lounged across the sofa, a lit cigarette clinging to his lips.

'Out,' Kerry said firmly, pushing past her mother.

'Go on, tell her,' he said.

'Tell me what?'

'Your uncle and I have been talking, and we've decided that if you continue to act the way you do, you'll have to move out,' her mother explained, looking at the ground.

'You mean he's decided,' Kerry said, watching her uncle.

'If you don't start doing what I've asked I will kick you out, I asked you to do the laundry before you left, and you haven't, I asked you to sweep—'

'I'm not your fuckin' servant,' she snapped.

'As long as you're under my roof, you are,' he said, smoke seeping out of his nostrils.

'This is mum's house, you only moved in when dad died because you saw an opportunity to live rent-free,' she bit. Growing angrier, her hand clenched the umbrella handle, oh how she'd love to drive the metal pointed end through his eye.

'Kerry, that's enough,' her mother said sharply.

'One day you're going to have to make a choice, me or him,' Kerry said before storming upstairs.

Oliver's hand grasped his pocket watch, raindrops falling onto the silver. He had been waiting outside the bank for about thirty minutes and his hair was drenched. He had no intention of leaving until he saw Francesca. He'd happily wait in a blizzard to lay eyes on her. Placing his pocket watch back into his waistcoat, he straightened out his drape jacket. Catching sight of her in her yellow raincoat, he quickly approached with a grin, amused by her outfit.

'I didn't expect to see you here,' she said, smiling.

'I was just passing through,' he said, leaning down, kissing her softly on the cheek.

She raised an unconvinced eyebrow. 'Fenchurch is a bit out of your usual territory.'

'Well, I make exceptions. I thought you might like the company on your way home,' he said.

'That's sweet of you.'

'Your raincoat is very fetching.'

'Well, it's better than being wet, now isn't it?' she said cheekily from under the safety of her hood.

'Put your hands out and close your eyes.'

'Why?' she questioned suspiciously.

'Because I told you to. Now put them out, don't be difficult,' he teased.

'Ok,' she said excitably, extending her palms.

Oliver felt the striped pink and white paper bag in the pocket of his jacket. It was so tightly packed with sweets that it was on the verge of bursting open. He placed it in her hands. 'You can open your eyes now.'

'That's the fullest bag of sweets I've ever gotten,' she exclaimed, holding it tightly.

'And I'm sure you'll make light work of them,' Oliver added. 'I got you an assortment. I remember you liked Dolly Mixtures and those different boiled sweets. I think we best be heading off before we get swept away,' he said, peering at the cobbles where a stream of water shot down between the stones.

Francesca leapt into his arms, her lips meeting his. He wrapped his arms around her, lifting her in the air. 'On second thought, a few more minutes wouldn't hurt,' he said, smiling as he kissed her.

CHAPTER 10

FRANCESCA WANDERED INTO the living room. Taking off her sodden wet raincoat, she placed it on the banister. The house was quiet, almost too quiet. Even Houdini sat silently, watching her as she passed him. She quickly snuck into the kitchen, careful as she reached for Winston. Nibbling on a piece of shortbread, she heard her mother's light footsteps wander down the stairs.

'Fran, I hope you're not scoffing biscuits, I'm about to make dinner. What have I told you about snacking?' Stephanie muttered.

'I'm not.' Francesca panicked, placing the jar back on the shelf. Using her blazer sleeve, she rubbed the crumbs from her mouth.

'Then why are their crumbs on the floor?' her mother interrogated as she stood behind her.

'I just had one, to see me through,' she explained.

'Hm, I see, pass me one then,' Stephanie said, putting out her hand.

Francesca grabbed Winston and pulled out a biscuit. As her mother munched, she noticed her soggy strands of hair.

'Have you been out?'

'Yes, I popped out for a bit with Charley,' Stephanie said as she licked the sugar from her fingers.

'You went to church, didn't you?' she questioned, a smile covering her face.

'Yes, I did,' her mother admitted.

'How was it?'

'Strange, but it felt like it was needed. I'm going to come back to church soon.'

'I'm proud of you for going, I know it's difficult,' Francesca said.

Stephanie smiled slightly. 'It's been tough, but of course you know that already. I thought it would be too painful to go back, but now it feels like I've closed the door on a dark chapter of my life. It seems silly because he died such a long time ago.'

'It's not silly, I always think about him, even though I was only little when he died. We shouldn't have lost him that way. It felt unjust, that's why it hurt so much.'

Stephanie fastened her pinnie around her waist. 'You're right, and it still hurts, but we need to try and make the most of our time here on earth, we can't spend it fixating on the past and the things we can't control,' she said, grabbing some hefty potatoes from the cupboard. 'Speaking of things we can control, Charley said Elaine was upset when she got home, do you know why?'

'I have no idea. She was fine when I left her earlier.'

'It might be a good idea to go over and have a natter,'

Stephanie advised, slicing the potatoes.

'I'll whizz over in a bit,' she agreed.

As the afternoon shifted to evening, the rain dispersed, resulting in a tranquil display of muted dark blue. The occasional star poked through the clouds that sauntered across the night sky.

Francesca, dressed in bright pink pyjamas, hurried across the road to reach the Anderson house. Grabbing a handful of pebbles from the flowerpot, she pelted one after another, aiming for the top window. As a messy mass of dark blonde curls appeared at the glass, Francesca looked around cautiously, careful not to be noticed. Dumping the pebbles back into the flowerpot, she looked up at her friend whose head was now stuck out of the frame.

'What's the matter, Elaine? Charley told mum that you were upset.'

'You should know why,' she replied bitterly, looking down at Francesca who was standing in her fetching slippers and matching dressing gown.

'Why?' she asked.

'Because you're abandoning me and leaving me behind to hang out with the girls,' Elaine said, avoiding eye contact.

'No, I'm not, you're my best friend, you're more important to me than anyone,' she declared, worried as to why she would think such a thing.

'Even Oliver?'

'Yes, even Oliver.'

'You don't mean that,' Elaine said mopily.

'I don't say what I don't mean. Everything was fine earlier. Did the girls say something to you after I left?'

'No, the boys.'

'Which ones?' Francesca asked.

'Lewis and Finn.'

'Those meddling bastards. They just want to cause trouble, don't you see? They want us to turn on each other,' she said passionately.

'Why would they want to do that?'

'I think it's because we are now part of their group, and they don't like it.'

'They were so mean. They approached me when I was all on my own,' she said.

'It's bang out of order, I'll have a word with Oliver. They should apologise,' she uttered.

'Don't worry, I don't need an apology from them, they won't mean it. All I need is you, you're all I really have apart from my parents and Charley.'

'And I need you,' she replied with a smile. The evening wind bit at her exposed ankles, causing her to march on the spot.

'I would give you a hug, but I'm a bit high up. Nice jimmy jams by the way, very stylish,' Elaine teased from above.

'What can I say, I'm a stylish person,' she replied, doing a twirl so Elaine could appreciate her late-night fashion statement. 'I better be off then, I don't want to catch a cold,' she said, rubbing her hands together.

'Yeah you best, if you do, I'll be sure to bring round some soup, tomato of course.' Elaine winked.

'Tomato is the best! You still up for Friday?' Francesca exclaimed as she crossed back over the road.

'Of course, if you're going, I'm going!' she shouted, nearly waking up the neighbours.

Charlotte's golden hair sat in two tight victory rolls. Francesca's in contrast was loose and fell gently past her shoulders. They walked the length of Spitalfields Market, the large, covered space playing host to stalls displaying fresh produce, a few selling fabrics and trinkets that caught the wandering eye. Nearby, the chugging trains could be heard leaving Liverpool Street Station, the steam rising high into the air, swirling above the city. It was a vibrant place with an equally vibrant history, made clear in the surrounding narrow streets filled with old buildings. From a Victorian tobacco factory to a one-hundred-year-old Jewish soup kitchen, the area appeared as though it hadn't been touched since the nineteenth century. There were old stone repositories and terracotta-coloured brick pubs, all tightly crammed together. But, there were a few skeletons of bombed buildings that lurked between, standing as an ugly reminder of the war.

Francesca followed Charlotte as they weaved in and out of the crowds.

'I need embroidery thread, I want to fix up one of my blazers,' she said, determined as her eyes scanned the stalls.

'What colour?'

'Anything but grey, I'm bored of seeing grey. Every time I go to the factory, I face twelve hours of dingy greyness. I want something that stands out, maybe gold?'

'Gold sounds like a good idea, like my locket. How is the factory?' she asked, hurrying to keep up with her.

'Exactly! That's the gold I want, we can use that as a reference. It got better for a bit but recently it's been awful, Talbot cut my pay because my machine broke,' she mumbled, searching through a wicker basket full of embroidery thread. The lady behind the stall was busy counting her coins, placing them in a little leather purse.

'But that's not your fault if the equipment was faulty,' Francesca speculated.

Charlotte stared into the basked, unsure whether to tell her about Jimmy. 'It will always be my fault, no matter what I do.' She shook her head, snapping herself out of it. 'But anyway, how are things with Oli? I hope he's on his best behaviour.' She grasped the gold thread, holding it up to her friend's locket.

'Things are wonderful, I was thinking I should get him something, he's bought me dinner a few times, flowers and sweets, I feel like I should get him a gift to show him I care,' Francesca said as Charlotte handed a halfpenny to the lady.

'Oh, I love presents! Do you have anything in mind?' she asked as they continued through the busy market, the shouts of stall owners piercing the air.

'I have no clue, but I just got paid so I can get him something proper.'

'What about something to match his pocket watch? A necklace maybe?' she suggested.

'What kind?' Francesca asked as they met the side of a little stall hosting a variety of trinkets. Jewellery glistened as it hung from tall display boxes.

'Well, what about something lucky, like this?' Charlotte questioned, pointing to a silver necklace with a horseshoe pendant hanging at the centre.

'I like that.' Francesca smiled.

'I think he'd love it, it's thoughtful.' Charlotte grinned, the dark brown freckles on her cheeks contrasting her pale skin.

'Ok, I'll get it,' she decided, rummaging through her purse.

'I'll knock a few bob off for ya darlin' 'cause you've got a beautiful smile,' the stall owner said. He was a man in his fifties wearing a friendly expression.

'That's very kind of you,' she said as he wrapped the necklace in a little paper bag.

'Talk about the gift of the gab, they always know what to say to make a sale.' Charlotte chuckled as they walked along the cobbles.

Francesca looked down at her. 'You know I was thinking we should do something as a group, something fun.'

'I agree, especially with the sudden nice weather. We need to make the most of it before it rains again,' Charlotte said as the sunlight met her face, her golden hair illuminating.

'We could have a picnic. I can make some cakes with my mum?' Francesca suggested.

'I love that idea! Oh, that would be so much fun. I could make little finger sandwiches like they do in the posh restaurants,' she said happily.

'Yes, a posh picnic in Victoria Park.' Francesca laughed.

The hair salon sat on the corner of Mile End Road. It had a distinctive atmosphere. Traditional with its appeal to middle-aged and older ladies, it was a sharp contrast to some of the new male salons in the area. They introduced high-quiffs and pompadour hairstyles in opposition to the short back and sides made popular during the war.

The salon was packed with women who sat under large hairdryers. A few flicked through magazines while others nattered loudly over the sound of hot air, spreading the latest gossip. There was a potent scent of setting spray, hair oil, and cream that created a smell so obnoxious that Francesca felt as though she could faint. She sat facing the window as her mother and grandmother had their hair tended to. Vera perched under a hairdryer while Stephanie had her hair set under thick netting. Francesca listened to the distant nattering of a few loose-lipped women. Mostly, their conversations were about their family, church gossip and other boring topics. Growing tired, she played with the buttons on her cardigan.

'Fran, dear, pass me one of those magazines if you would be so kind.' Vera put out her hand as she was passed a hefty Women's Weekly Magazine.

'You look awfully bored,' her mother said, watching her sulk.

'It's not exactly the most exciting experience,' she mumbled.

'I did offer you a cut, but all you wanted were your ends done,' her mother sighed, wishing her daughter would take more interest in her appearance beyond cardigans and contentedness.

'If I got anything else done, they'd make me look like a Brussels sprout,' she replied. A hairdresser scowled at her, causing her cheeks to flush with embarrassment. Her mother looked at her angrily, yet Vera was amused by the comment, hiding her smile behind the magazine. A knock on the glass window caused Francesca's eyes to light up. Albie grinned at her as he entered the salon.

'No need to look horrified I'm not stayin' long,' he said as a few women stared him up and down with distaste. His ginger hair had a distinctive wave to it that appeared to defy gravity. His suit was black, but his vibrant blue brocade waistcoat was bright and beautiful.

'So, what are you doing here in a place like this?' he asked, looking at a few sample hairstyles that were stuck around one of the mirrors.

'Just had my ends done,' she said.

'How adventurous,' he sighed, taking a seat beside her.

'I did offer her a new haircut,' Stephanie muttered.

'Ah, you must be Fran's lovely mother,' he flattered as he shook her hand. 'I completely agree, a new style would suit you,' he spoke, turning his attention back to her. Grabbing at her strands of brown hair, he pulled them into a tight ponytail, much to the horror of the women present in the salon. 'There you go, a simple solution,' he said.

'I think it suits you,' Vera agreed.

'See, it's not going to be long before you dress like us. A pair of trousers would go a long way on the set of legs you've got.' He grinned.

'I'm really not sure about the whole trouser situation,' Francesca said awkwardly, fearful of looking like Kerry and drawing attention to herself.

'You won't know until you've tried,' he encouraged.

The morning sunlight reflected onto the kitchen wall in an array of yellow and orange and Francesca couldn't help but think of the unbearable mid-day temperatures to come. Dressed for work, she grabbed her handbag; it was stuffed full of heavy files and tugged on her arm. A knock sent her hurrying to the door. She opened it to greet Oliver. He was surrounded by sunshine and she squinted as she laid eyes on him.

'Hello treacle, I thought I could pick you up some breakfast on your way to work, if you haven't had it already. Oh, and this is for you,' he said, passing her a single daisy with a mesmerised smile. 'You look gorgeous, I like what you've done with your hair.'

Francesca's glimmering eyes were warm and welcoming as

she accepted the flower. Her hair sat in a structured ponytail and melted with the immovable light, sending the smooth fibres past her shoulders and down her back.

'Thank you. That sounds lovely, I couldn't think of a better way to start the day,' she said, giving the flower a sniff as she quickly popped it in a fresh vase of water. Her absence from the doorway allowed Oliver to catch sight of Vera who sat firmly in her armchair deciphering the latest crossword puzzle. Houdini tweeted contently as he bathed in the influx of sunlight.

'Good morning, Vera,' he said politely.

'Good morning, Oliver, make sure she isn't late for work,' Vera said sternly. Taking off her reading glasses, she recognised the single daisy standing in the vase.

'You have my word, shall we?' Oliver asked as Francesca looped her arm around his, allowing herself to be led down the path.

'You've been quite the gentleman recently.' She grinned, looking at him with an optimistic glance. His black hair was slicked back and his face cleanly shaven. He wore his usual dark grey three-piece suit while a polished set of brogues poked out from beneath his trousers.

'It's how I should act everyday around you.' He smiled as they followed the cobbled street.

'You know the girls met me during my lunch break, on the day you came to see me after work?'

'Yes, you told me about it on the bus with your mouth full of sweets,' he said, amused.

Francesca blushed. 'Well, I had no clue until I got home, but Lewis and Finn cornered Elaine after she left the others.'

Oliver's eyes sharpened. A cold expression developed on his face and it made Francesca gulp.

She continued cautiously, 'They put it into her head that I don't care about her anymore, that I'm moving on without her. She was obviously quite upset, they made some less than savoury comments by the sound of things,' she explained.

'Those two are out to make problems. I'll have a word with them, but I can't promise an apology. As for Elaine, is she alright now?' he asked.

'She's fine, and she doesn't care for an apology. But why are they meddling, Oliver?'

'They're out to get you for some reason. Lewis has had his eye on you in particular since he first met you. And Finn, well Finn's just a nasty git,' Oliver huffed, growing angry as he thought of their scheming ways.

'Then why do you hang around with them?'

'Why? Because they've been by my side since we were kids and I can't exactly kick them out of the group. But I will have a go at them for what they said to Elaine.'

They followed the rows of terraced houses that were crammed together. Walking past a set of shops, Oliver scanned the surrounding area. It was a peaceful morning, as peaceful as it could be for the bustling East End. The faint whistles of passers-by were rivalled by the birds that sang a chirpy tune. They sat on the electric cables that zig-zagged above the street in glinting silver formations.

School children ran around and played. Make-shift hopscotch was drawn on the pavement with white chalk while skipping ropes twisted and spun in the air. Pinafore and pigtail clad girls played hide and seek around the nearby alleyways. Boys in shorts with youthful expressions played football on the road. One of the leather balls was sent crashing towards Francesca who flinched. Oliver quickly whacked it away from her with one calculated swipe.

'Easy there lads, always watch where ya kicking,' he said playfully as the ball was sent toppling back to them.

'Sorry, Oli, and sorry, Miss, didn't mean to startle ya,' a young boy said as the group moved along the street. Nursery rhymes serenaded the area as little girls played ring around the roses and other games.

'That's Harry's younger brother, good kid,' Oliver informed her, watching them disappear behind the school gates.

'I can tell, he's a lot taller than the other boys.' She laughed, seeing the resemblance.

They wandered to the greengrocers. Fresh fruit was displayed at the front of the shop on rows of wooden tables. There were peaches and pears, grapes and tangerines. Vegetables sat at the back with large carrots and cabbages taking up most of the space.

'So, what do you fancy,' he asked.

'I like apples,' Francesca said, overwhelmed by the variety of ripe and rich treats.

'Come on, be more adventurous than that,' he teased.

'Oranges and lemons?' she asked, listening to the children singing.

'Might be a bit sour.' He laughed. 'Look at the size of that,' he said, catching sight of a massive melon.

'If I ate all of that, I think I'd pop,' she exclaimed.

'What about cherries?'

'Strawberries are best at this time of year,' she suggested.

'Strawberries it is then,' he agreed, grabbing a punnet. Giving the shop owner thruppence, they continued down the road.

'How's Susan?' Francesca asked as she popped a large

strawberry in her mouth.

'A little off with me. But I think that was because of what happened with you. She was bloody furious, if I didn't go after you, she wouldn't let me live it down,' he answered, looking at her with amusement as she struggled to contain the strawberry. Clearly, she'd bitten off more than she could chew.

'Well, the past is in the past for a reason. The present is great, and the future is looking promising for us,' she said cheerfully.

'I'm glad about that.' Oliver grinned as he munched on one of the juicy fruits.

'I got you something, it's only little, but I thought you might like it. I picked it up at the market, and, well here,' she said with sudden nervousness, pulling out the little silver chain with its horseshoe pendant hanging at the centre.

'Oh, Frankie, that's sweet of you,' he said gratefully, accepting the gift.

'If you don't like it, don't worry, it's just a silly present,' she said, trying to brush off the gesture.

'No, I love it, really,' he said, planting a kiss on her lips which made her go redder than the punnet of strawberries they were eating.

'It's silver so it matches your pocket watch, and it has the horseshoe to give you luck. I know you're Catholic and all, but I never see you go to church or wear a crucifix. And I thought you could do with a charm to help you along the way.' She smiled as he fastened the chain around his neck. Safely placing it under his collar, they continued to the bus stop.

'You're the only good luck charm I need. Thank you, it's the nicest present anyone has ever got me.'

'It's no problem,' she said, looking up to meet his glistening blue eyes.

'How did you afford this?' Oliver asked.

'I got my pay this week and I thought it would suit you, so I got it,' she said happily as she caught sight of the red bus.

'You have no idea how much it means to me,' Oliver said, watching her intently as the double-decker pulled alongside the pavement.

'I better be heading off then, thank you for the strawberries,' she said, planting a kiss on his cheek.

Kerry sat at the kitchen table. She had her hands clenched in her trouser pockets, eyes narrowed in Susan's direction as she sliced a fresh loaf of bread. Obliviously, her friend tended to the bread, unaware of the golden-brown glare aimed in her direction. The house was getting warm, and Susan wiped her brow with the sleeve of her oversized shirt.

'Do you want to tell me what's wrong?' Kerry questioned.

'Nothing's wrong,' she dismissed, guiding the knife over a slice, coating it in a layer of butter.

'Why are you lying to me?' she persisted.

'I promise, Kerry, I'm not, everything's fine,' Susan said calmly, yet her heart thumped so fast it felt as though it could leap out of her chest. Turning, she met Kerry's unconvinced glance. 'Look, I just feel a bit rough—' She tried to explain as Oliver burst through the front door.

'You look pleased with yourself.' Kerry observed as he entered the kitchen.

'I've just had a good morning.' He smiled.

'How's Fran?' Susan asked as she passed Kerry a plate of buttered bread. Reaching into the cupboard, she grabbed a jar of marmalade and placed it on the table.

'She was wonderful as usual. I got her some breakfast, and she got me this,' he said, revealing the silver pendant that hung from his neck.

'That's lovely.' Susan grinned, taking a closer look.

'Have you asked her to be your girlfriend yet?' Kerry questioned as she coated her bread in marmalade.

Grabbing it out of her hand, Oliver took a huge bite. 'I'm going to ask her at the dance hall,' he said, placing the half-eaten slice back into Kerry's grasp, causing her to scowl at him.

'I'm glad you're making it official,' Susan said happily.

'Yes, official, and I'm not going to fuck it up this time,' he said, looking down at the necklace.

Music blurted out of the old gramophone that sat on the dusty chest of drawers. Cigarette smoke danced in the air as Isla offered them around.

'Are you ready?' Charlotte asked as she held a tub of hair grease in her hands.

'I'm not sure,' Francesca replied, looking nervously at Elaine.

'They're ready,' Kerry said with a grin as she fiddled with a variety of devices that were waiting to push and pull their scalps into submission. Makeup was strewn about the bed, enough to paint their faces ten times over. It was an intimidating sight with all four of the Judies ready for action.

'Get to it then, if we carry on at this pace it'll be morning by the time we're done with them and we'll miss the dance entirely,' Susan ordered as Isla and Charlotte tended to Elaine whilst she and Kerry took charge of Francesca's appearance.

'I don't think I'm going to look very good,' Elaine said, worried as they both went to work on her dark blonde curls.

'Patience is a virtue, just relax,' Isla said.

'So, is everything going smoothly with you and my brother?' Susan asked.

'Yes, as good as gold.' Francesca grimaced as Kerry combatted an uncooperative knot that had developed in her mass of hair.

'That's what I like to hear. I saw you got him a necklace too, it was very nice of you.' Susan smiled as she watched Francesca's amusing array of facial expressions.

'Why did you defend me?' she asked.

'Because you're good for him, Fran, maybe even too good, and he was too blind to see it. I couldn't sit back and let him bugger it up,' she muttered.

'Well, thank you,' she said appreciatively, feeling the strands being yanked into position on top of her head.

'You're one of us now, whether you like it or not. I mean that in a non-threatening way, of course,' Kerry said as she concentrated on her masterpiece.

'What Kerry is trying to say is that we have your back, like family,' Susan clarified, smiling at both girls.

The group sat around the kitchen table, illuminated by a fading light bulb that hung at the centre of the room.

'So, what's that then?' Colin asked.

'What?' Oliver questioned obliviously as he leant over the drinks trolley, the piece of jewellery falling from the inside of his shirt. A selection of intoxicating substances were being enjoyed; it can be added some more than others. Colin refrained as he always did, while at the other end of the spectrum Jack drank anything he could find.

'That thing that's hanging from your neck,' Harry said bluntly.

'It's a present,' he explained as he placed the silver chain firmly back under his white poplin shirt. Holding a glass of brandy, he watched them, ready for their judgement.

'It's a fuckin' collar,' Jack said, taking a swig from his whiskey.

'Yeah, Fran's made you her bitch.' Finn laughed as he hopped onto the worktop.

'Both of you piss off,' Oliver snapped, defending Francesca's declaration of affection.

'Somebody's getting attached.' Harry smiled. His knuckles were coated in large gold rings that tapped against the glass in his hands.

'Just don't do anything drastic,' Albie teased as he sipped his drink.

'Like what?'

'Get her pregnant and then marry her,' Jack suggested as he downed his whiskey in a few gulps. Colin looked at the ground with dread, recognising the statement to be a little too close to home.

'That's a long way off,' Oliver assured, a grin creeping across his face.

'But you've considered it.' Harry deciphered.

'Maybe,' Oliver said as the thought of Francesca occupied his mind.

'That girl has got you wrapped around her little finger, hasn't she?' Lewis asked, sending a disdainful glance in Finn's direction.

'Yeah, she bloody has,' he admitted.

'I hate it when you're like this,' Jack grumbled as he refilled his drink.

'Like what?'

'All soppy and loved up.'

'I heard you told Isla that you loved her, so you can hardly talk,' Albie informed. The others looked at him, surprised.

'That's none of your fuckin' business,' he snarled suddenly.

'Well, I agree, it's embarrassing, proper feminine behaviour if you ask me,' Lewis said.

'There's nothing wrong with being sensitive,' Albie defended.

'Not everyone's so proud to admit that,' Finn opposed. He flicked his knife back-and-forth, the blade reflecting the dim light in its cold metal.

'I can't help who I am,' he said.

'What, a queer?' Jack spat.

'Shut it, Jack,' Oliver bit back in Albie's defence.

'No, you shut up, I'm tired of you telling us what to do all the time.'

'Well, somebody has to have the bollocks to take charge, I don't see any of you stepping up,' Oliver said.

Jack stared at him with contempt. 'You're not our leader.'

'Yes he is,' Colin said calmly.

'You're such a submissive little slag,' Jack berated, shooting him a glance.

'And you've been drinking too much,' Colin said, watching his friend destroy himself with every word.

'What I'm drinking is none of your concern. Why don't you just do yourself a favour and go back to wherever you came from, you probably don't even know, do you? Do you even know who your mum is?'

'Hey enough of that, it's unnecessary,' Oliver said, concerned by his hostility. Only he and Susan knew that Colin's mother died when he was young. It was kept that way for a reason as Jack would only use it against him when he was inebriated. But he'd still find a way to poke and push those sensitive spots. He'd regret it the next day, the cruel taunts, as he always did when he sobered up. And yet he'd never apologise, even though Oliver knew it ate him up inside. Colin and Albie were his usual targets, but they'd never raise their voices, they wouldn't give his tantrums the time of day.

'You're hurting yourself by acting this way,' Colin continued.

'I'll hurt you in a minute,' Jack said nastily.

'You don't mean that.'

'Now how the hell do you know what I mean? You have no idea what's going on in my head,' he shouted, pointing at them all.

'We don't want to know,' Albie sighed.

'Come on now, you're embarrassing yourself,' Oliver said, trying to defuse him.

'All of you can piss off, especially you,' Jack hissed as his eyes latched onto Colin. As he left the house in a rage, the room fell silent. Lewis and Finn watched each other with devious smirks, taking pleasure in the confrontation.

The two girls stood in front of them in their new attire.

'Oh, you both look spectacular!' Charlotte declared.

'Our work here is most definitely done,' Susan said, satisfied.

Francesca had her hair pinned back in a messy bun with cultivated strands falling to the sides of her face. Her rolled up three-quarter-length trousers were paired with a tailored blazer that concealed a velvet collared shirt. Adorned with a pair of thick-soled creepers, she looked much different from her usual appearance. She stood awkwardly as she contemplated a world without plaits, day dresses, and most of all cardigans.

'I'm not used to wearing trousers,' she said, pulling at the fabric.

'You'll get used to them. It took me a while,' Isla reassured her.

Elaine stood beside Francesca in a similar fashion with her hair forced back in tight victory rolls. She too was in trousers but wore a frilly white blouse and a long black drape jacket lent to her by Kerry.

'My hair feels so stiff,' Elaine complained as she tugged at her scalp.

'It looks amazing. Stop touching it,' Susan ordered as she grabbed Elaine by the hand, leading her out the door. As the others followed, Kerry walked alongside Francesca.

'It suits you,' she said encouragingly, trying to ease her friend's discomfort.

'Thanks, I'm still not sure about the trousers.' She forced a smile as they walked along the pavement.

'I feel the same way in a dress,' Kerry admitted, looking down at Francesca who was a little shorter.

'When is the last time you wore one?'

'Quite a while ago.'

1953

A REGAL AFFAIR

As THE SUN shone brightly over Morpeth Street, people filled the outside space with smiling faces and welcoming embraces. The entire community had come out to celebrate and had decorated the road from top to toe. The walls displayed red, white and blue bunting while Union Jacks soared proudly. There was a long wooden table at the centre of the road that fitted everyone onto accompanying benches. As the street party continued, a seventeen-year-old girl couldn't resist dipping a finger into her mother's homemade trifle. Taking a lick of the fluffy cream, an enormous smile covered her face.

'Bring the trifle, Kerry, quickly now, and make sure everyone gets a helping,' her mother said in a hurry as she balanced the other homemade treats in her hands.

'I'm coming,' she replied, pulling at her red dress, making sure it was spotless. Her long platinum blonde hair fell softly down past her shoulders. Grasping the glass dish, she followed her mother outside.

As Kerry gave everyone a portion, she looked at her uncle who sat slouching, drinking the minutes away with a bottle attached to his hand. Taking a seat for the first time all day, she was quickly accosted.

'Get me another drink,' he snapped from his chair.

'But I've just sat down,' she protested.

'I'm not gonna ask again girl,' he spoke firmly, holding up the empty glass bottle for her to retrieve.

'Do what your uncle tells you,' her mother said as she rushed about the benches.

'It's not fair, the men have been sitting on their arses all day,' Kerry opposed.

'Watch your mouth,' her uncle sneered.

'You treat us both like rubbish,' she continued, trying to make her point.

'That's enough, Kerry,' her mother muttered, tending to some empty bowls.

'I wish you'd treat us with some respect,' she said stubbornly, not willing to let the subject lie.

'Well, when you grow a pair, wear trousers, and cut your hair short, I may consider it. But for now, get me another bloody drink,' he mocked, looking at the now red-faced girl before him.

'No,' she stated defiantly.

'What?'

'I said no.'

Kerry was yanked by her ear to the kitchen. She was pushed to the floor, her tailbone cracking as she met the ground. With a wince, she braced herself as her uncle clutched his belt firmly. Bringing it up to strike her, he was interrupted by two young men.

They met eyes with Kerry. She wasn't crying or whimpering, but sat with a furious expression. She looked at them both as they stood in their unusual Edwardian suits.

'I don't think you should be doing that,' one of them uttered. 'It's the Queen's coronation, remember, a woman's day. Now it would be quite the insult to hurt a woman on a day when we are celebrating one,' he continued, combing back his strands of blonde hair.

'She's not a woman, she's a disrespectful little girl that deserves a good hiding,' he hissed.

Growing impatient, the other one pulled out a flick knife and began to play with it. Recognising the strong stench of alcohol, they looked at each other.

'Ok, let's make this a little simpler for your tiny little brain. You leave that girl alone or I'll make sure you never make it down the pub again, which I'm sure will be a hardship considering that's how you appear to spend most of your time,' he threatened, his tone sharp and unwavering as he placed the comb back in his pocket.

'And what are you gonna do then, you gonna use that?' he asked, lowering the belt to his side as he recognised the blade in the young man's hand.

'Oh no, I'm sure we can think of something much more creative.' He grinned, feeling the blade between his fingers.

'You little rats,' he spat as he retreated outside.

'I've never been called a rat before. Never thought of myself as a rat.' The blonde one pondered, pulling a packet of cigarettes from his pocket.

'Thank you, nobody has the bottle to speak to him like that,' Kerry said, looking up at them.

'Well, clearly you do, and I think it's quite admirable.' He smiled, lighting a cigarette, sending smoke whirling up to the ceiling.

'Come on then, up you get. My name's Finn by the way, and that's Lewis,' he introduced as Kerry was helped to her feet.

CHAPTER 11

THE CONCRETE FOLLOWED their every step as they made their way under the clear night sky. The clarity allowed starlight to shine down upon them in a persistent gleam. As they moved among the shadow illuminated city, their broad silhouettes crept under the light of distant lampposts. The rows of houses watched them as they walked. It was quiet, deceptively quiet. The group moved quickly, their thick creepers and beetle-crusher shoes meeting the pavement with a repetitive thud.

'I don't want you talking to Elaine like that again,' Oliver disciplined.

'That's a shame, I was enjoying myself,' Lewis said, smirking.

'Both of you need to pack it in. Jack has already scared Fran off once.'

'I think you'll find that was a result of you and you alone, you should have just been honest with her,' Lewis said.

Harry, Albie and Colin walked in front of them, listening to every word, yet were reluctant to partake in the conversation.

'Yeah, you played the poor girl like a fool,' Finn added insult to injury as he puffed smoke into the crisp night-time air.

'Enough, what's done is done,' Oliver snapped.

'The damage is done,' Lewis said under his breath.

'Just leave them both alone.'

'We'll try our hardest, can't promise anything,' Finn said.

'If you have the decency, apologise to Elaine,' Oliver said as he walked ahead of them.

'Why should we apologise? 'Cause she got upset that we told her the truth?' Finn questioned as he threw the cigarette to the ground, letting it fizzle out on the cobbles.

'There is no truth to what you said, you just have it out for them, why?' Oliver asked, frustrated as he turned back to them.

'They're different,' Lewis snarled with surprising hostility.

'Oh yeah, and what makes them different from Kerry? You remember the way she was when you found her.'

'Kerry's another matter entirely,' Lewis said.

'She needed somewhere to belong. Those two have belonging already,' Finn said.

'Francesca belongs with me so you're gonna have to get used to it,' Oliver said sternly as they reached the dance hall.

As they entered, they were met with quite the atmosphere. No longer dark and gentle with watching stars, the room took on multi-coloured appearance, and the sound enveloped any remaining silent spaces. The air was diluted by cigarette smoke that swirled between the swaying bodies. Some moved gracefully while others turned and tumbled in each other's arms. Francesca and Charlotte had peeled off from the group, dancing amongst the many. Oliver approached them, tapping Charlotte on the shoulder.

'You mind if I take it from here?'

'Go for it, Oli, she's all yours.' She smiled happily as she eyed up her next reluctant target. 'Come on, Harry!' she exclaimed, pulling him to his feet.

'You look a bit different.' He laughed.

'The girls insisted,' Francesca explained with reddening cheeks, still embarrassed by what she was wearing.

'It's certainly something. You look a bit like my sister wearing that shirt,' he teased, making her even more self-conscious.

'This collar is really itchy,' she fussed whilst pulling at the constricting velvet.

Taking her hands, he guided her into his arms. 'You look really lovely,' he complimented.

'Well, you look very handsome, as always,' she said, looking up at him.

'I wanted to ask you something.' He paused, nervousness overtaking him. 'Will you be my girlfriend?'

'This is quite a difference from the last time we were in a dance hall,' she said with a mischievous grin.

'It didn't start off the right way, but I need you my beautiful Frankie. I want to look after you, to be your partner,' he admitted, running his hands through the strands of hair that dangled at the side of her face.

'I need you too,' she confessed, kissing him.

'Fancy a kick and prance?' Lewis questioned, putting out his hand.

Giving him a pacified smile, Kerry answered, 'I thought

you'd never ask.' Taking his hand, she was led to the commotion, leaving Susan on her own.

'So, what are we going to do, I'm starting to show to the point where it's noticeable, Colin. They're not thick, sooner or later they're going to clock it. You need to tell Oliver,' Susan said, looking at him fearfully.

'I'll tell him when the time is right,' Colin insisted, looking down at her with equal distress.

'The time is right now! By your 'right time' the baby will already be in my arms,' she muttered. She didn't want to cause a scene, but recognising that the inevitable was imminent made her feel a certain level of dread. *Sooner better than later*, she thought to herself, navigating the possibilities in her mind.

'I'm not going to tell him now, he's so happy with Fran and all,' Colin tried to justify, yet he was met with no more than an angered glance.

'That's exactly why you should tell him. Fran will calm the storm, he won't act up in front of her 'cause he's still on thin bloody ice. Now go and tell him before you end up walking on thin ice too,' she threatened.

'Fine, I'll pull him aside,' he said, reluctantly giving in. With a slow pace, he approached Oliver. Standing behind him, he laid a hand on his shoulder.

'I need to talk to you about something.'

'Right now?'

'Yeah, it's important,' Colin said, his tone unusually serious.

Acknowledging his friend's worried eyes, Oliver agreed to listen. Susan watched with bated breath as the two proceeded to the entrance. Somebody pushed past them with such force that they jolted backwards and one of the doors was left hanging on its hinge. A guttural shriek pierced the air, and they both knew who was responsible. Jack was ramming his fist into the face of a young man, the first body he could find. People screamed and ran in different directions, and the music abruptly stopped. The two of them pulled Jack from his victim, hoisting him up by his jacket and shoving him outside.

'Go, go now,' Oliver said furiously.

As the rest of the boys followed swiftly, they caught sight of their disgruntled friend who was being forced down the road by his collar. Throwing him to the ground, Oliver paced.

'What the hell is wrong with you?' he snapped.

'Shit, he's gonna to get done for that one, that's the Detective's son,' Colin panicked.

'I'll warn him against telling.' Harry decided, turning back to the building.

'No the fuck you won't, he'll rat out the lot of us,' Albie said as he sent a scowl in Jack's direction.

As the girls caught on to the commotion, they saw the flushed face of the young man on the floor, his nose dripping a constant stream of red. Isla watched him as they continued out of the building, catching his bruised eye.

'Quiet, let me think,' Oliver said, studying the people flooding out of the dance hall in response to the one-sided scuffle.

'Fuck you all, wankers the lot of ya,' Jack slurred from the floor, looking up to the group surrounding him who appeared to be in sets of two.

'Harry, put him out of his misery,' Oliver ordered as his friend obeyed. Sending a fist into the side of his head, Jack's body slumped.

'Sorry about that,' Harry said nonchalantly, the truth was he rather enjoyed it. So did Albie who tried to contain his developing grin with the sleeve of his drape jacket.

'Was that really necessary?' Isla tutted. Dropping to Jack's side, she cradled his head.

'If we're lucky it might have killed him. One well-placed punch from Harry would do the job,' Lewis sighed.

'Yeah, let's face it, if Jack was a racehorse, they'd have shot him by now,' Finn added.

'Oh don't be so horrible!' she exclaimed, staring angrily at them both.

'All of you, that's enough, Jack's got a thick skull, he'll be fine,' Oliver dismissed.

'Thick in the head more like,' Lewis said quietly, making Finn smirk.

'What happened in there?' Francesca asked.

'Jack happened,' Oliver replied.

Susan had a face full of detest as she looked at the floor. As he moaned his way back to consciousness, Jack was met with the judgement of all those trying to clean up his mess.

'I need you to work your magic girls, otherwise he's in big trouble,' Oliver said, glancing at Isla and Kerry. He knew they were more than up for the challenge. 'Frankie, you and Elaine need to go home before somebody clocks you with us,' he added firmly. Understanding the seriousness of the situation, they both quickly disappeared down the road.

'I take it it's the Detective's kid who's squirming on the ground?' Isla asked, letting go of Jack as he drunkenly mumbled.

'That's the one.'

'Say no more,' Kerry uttered as they trailed their way back.

Meeting eyes with the swelling face of the battered young man, they knelt beside him as the room cleared.

'I've never seen anyone take a beating like that before,

you're so brave,' Isla initiated.

'Yeah, that black eye makes you look like a bare-knuckle boxer, all tough and roughed up,' Kerry said as she stroked his face.

'And not to mention handsome,' Isla said as she looped a hand around his bicep.

'My dad's going to—'

'Now, now, you've taken a heavy blow let's not think irrationally,' Kerry said. Peering through the broken door, she watched the group disappear down the road.

'Look what he did to my face,' he spat.

'All the girls are going to be after you now, looking like one of those bad types.' Isla smiled as she ran her hand through his hair.

'Yeah, you're going to be the talk of the town,' Kerry said.

'You think so?' he asked, looking into her golden-brown eyes. Like hypnotists, they manipulated the boy to their benefit.

'I know so. But you better keep your mouth shut for the sake of your reputation. Nobody likes a rat, not around here anyway,' Kerry warned, dabbing his nose with a handkerchief, causing him to wince.

'Ok, I won't tell,' he agreed as he fell for their empty compliments.

'Good, now let me get some ice for that eye.' Isla grinned.

The two sat on the front doorstep. They looked up to the clear dark skies that sat above Bethnal Green. It was three o'clock in the morning and the distant chirps of birds could be heard as they fluttered in and out of the tall red brick chimneys. A pint glass filled with water laid in Jack's hands as he rubbed his recovering head. Recognising his friend's weary state, Oliver took the opportunity to make his case.

'You need to stop doing this.' He passed him a wet cloth to clean his bloodied knuckles.

'I know,' Jack said bluntly, the crisp air biting at his skin. His brain pounded as he took a sip from the icy water.

'You say that, but you keep doing it. Are you sobering up?' Oliver asked.

'Yeah, but I've got a banger of a headache,' he admitted, grasping his head in his hands.

'Serves you right.' Oliver smirked.

Jack looked at him whilst rubbing his bloodshot eyes. 'Thanks for earlier.'

'You can thank Isla and Kerry. We can't save you every time. You know you're lucky to have her, many girls would go running.'

'I know,' he grumbled.

'I can't have you acting like that, you need to stop drinking.'

'I can't,' Jack confessed. He closed his throbbing eyes only to feel nauseous due to the rocking sensation inside his head.

'You can't or you won't?'

'There is no point in trying, I can't stop,' he admitted. It was like he was a young child getting told off by a parent, sitting to attention whilst being lectured on how to behave.

'Well, you need to try harder, 'cause even though you're hurting other people you're more importantly hurting yourself,' Oliver said.

'I will try.'

'For your sake, I hope so. I can't see you like that. I worry that you'll end up like my old man.'

'I know it's hard for you.'

'What?' Oliver asked.

'Escaping him.'

'It's not hard,' he dismissed.

'If it wasn't hard, then why do you still wear his pocket watch?' Jack asked, looking to the piece of silver that sat tightly in Oliver's pocket.

'I wear it out of principle,' he spoke bluntly, trying to end the conversation.

'Oliver and his principles, how far will you go for those things?' Jack teased as he chugged the remaining water.

'As far as what's necessary,' he said. 'Right, I've got business to attend to, feel free to sleep in my bed while I'm gone. And for fuck's sake don't wake Susan up, otherwise you'll have more to worry about than a bloody headache.'

'I'll be as silent as a mouse,' he promised as he stumbled indoors. Turning back, his curiosity got the better of him. 'Must be quite important business if you're going to tend to it at this hour.'

'More important than you could ever know,' Oliver replied, grinning.

Lewis stood in front of her, watching her with his inquisitive blue eyes. Kerry pushed him onto the end of the bed and straddled his lap. She undressed, popping the buttons on her loose shirt. He sat silently as she threw the material to the floor. Placing his hands on her hips, his palms met her delicate skin. It was surprising considering her rough demeanour, but under the layers of carefully crafted fabric, he found a soft, gentle being. Normally hidden from public view, he knew her exposed skin made her feel vulnerable, yet she let him in. The moonlight pierced through the curtains as her amber eyes glimmered through the darkness. He trailed her stomach with his hands, feeling the lace of her bra between his fingers. She shoved him back, laying on top of him.

'I'm going to get rid of him, I've been thinking about it for a while,' she breathed.

'Your uncle? It's about bloody time,' he said, running a hand through her hair, feeling the soft strands between his fingers.

'Whatever happens, I want you to know that I care about you a lot. You're one of the few people that's ever made me feel safe,' she admitted.

'I care about you too, more than you could ever understand,' he said as she kissed him firmly, pulling at his belt.

As his thick-soled shoes navigated the concrete, Harry kicked at anything that got in his way. A few bits of rubbish met the end of his leather while weightless leaves tumbled across the ground. The disembowelled greenery took on a living form as it twisted and trailed around him in a swirling formation. The streetlamps illuminated the path. His shadow followed him eagerly as he walked, its every movement projected onto the red brick wall beside him. It appeared and disappeared as the moonlight flicked and filtered in between the tightly compacted houses.

His broad frame was coated by his large drape jacket that fought off the jolts of cool night-time air. The streets were quiet, and Harry kept his glance directly ahead of him to the darkness of distant alleyways. Unfortunately, he had not seen what was coming up behind him.

With a blow to the back of the head, Harry recoiled. He

felt his nerves shudder as a heavy object was planted into him once more, sending him toppling to his knees. A looming set of figures appeared in his vision as the backdrop of the early morning lamplights filled the void around them.

'Tut-tut, Harry, you knew that was a bad idea,' a male voice said. The figure held a now bloodied claw hammer in his hand.

'Jimmy Talbot, you insufferable twat, took your bloody time,' Harry gasped as he felt the blood rise from the back of his throat. Spitting the violent red liquid onto the pavement, he recognised the two boys at his side. One was wielding a crowbar and the other a set of knuckle dusters. 'They look a bit big for you they do, did you borrow them from your mum?' he antagonised, recognising the brass jewellery that loosely fit the boy's fists.

'Shut your cunting mouth,' he hissed.

Harry grasped the back of his head. Blood trickled from the wound, developing into a crimson puddle on the ground.

'That little girl of yours is gonna get it too, thinking you can have one over on my uncle like that. You know his jaw has just healed so he was quick to explain why he looked so worse for wear. But it's fuckin' nothing compared to what we're gonna do.'

'If you dare touch Charlotte—' He tried to find the strength to stand but his head spun, sending him falling to his knees once more.

'Trust me, I have no interest in her, my uncle is going to deal with her personally.'

'If that fat git touches her, I'll cut his hands off,' Harry snarled.

'You're nothing but empty threats,' the boy with the crowbar uttered from behind.

'You and I both know it's not a threat.'

'Save your breath, you'll be seeing the gates of hell before you see sunrise,' Jimmy said sadistically as he grasped the hammer, lifting it high into the air, it glistened under the moonlight. Ready to strike a deadly blow, Jimmy was interrupted by a voice that bellowed through the shadows.

'I wouldn't do that if I were you, lad.'

'Oh yeah, and why's that?' the boy with the surprisingly small hands spat as he looked to the darkness.

'Because I said so,' the man spoke sternly.

'This is none of your business,' Jimmy hissed. He squinted, trying to make out the man's face.

'It became my business when you spilled blood on my streets,' he informed, looking at Harry.

'That's Charley Anderson,' one of the boys panicked.

'I thought you were blown to kingdom come during the war?' Jimmy asked.

'I was. Now on you go before I knock you all senseless,' he threatened, cracking his knuckles as he walked. 'Go on, piss off,' he said sharply as the boys obeyed, running back to the shadows.

Charley stared down at the bloody pavement, it was so clear and clean, not polluted with mud and sand and vomit as he had known it. That stench, he'd never forget it.

They know nothing of war but want to act like soldiers. Not soldiers, animals. In 1955.

He shook his head, despairing. How London must have shuddered seeing these youngsters tear each other apart. The odd scuffle wasn't new to it, of course, but these young men had their lives ahead of them and didn't have to fight in a war like he did, or the generation before, and yet they still chose violence.

'Come on then, up you get.' Charley smiled, extending a

hand as quickly as his change of demeanour. 'You're one of those Teddy Boy types that hangs around with my Elaine, aren't you?'

'Yeah, that's me, cheers Charley,' Harry said thankfully, brushing himself off.

'A word of advice, always check behind you before stepping forward,' Charley said as he wandered down the road.

'Is that somethin' you learned in the war?'

'No, it's a lesson I learned here. Now get that stitched up before those bastards come back for round two,' he answered, disappearing.

As Harry pulled himself together, he felt the gash between his fingers. It was cascading blood down the back of his neck. He clambered along the wall, careful not to lose consciousness. Thinking quickly, he understood that going to a hospital would cause more harm than good, so he set his sights on the only person he knew that could put him back together again.

'Lottie, open the door, it's me,' he said with a few frantic bangs.

Shuffles could be heard from inside the front room as Charlotte, clad in her teal nightgown and tight hair curlers, unlocked the door.

'Harry, what are you doing at my doorstep at this hour?' she asked, rubbing her drowsy eyes.

'Had a little incident, was wondering if you could patch me up,' he said as calmly as he could, turning around to reveal his bloodied head.

Charlotte's eyes widened. 'Oh God, what happened? I'm not a nurse, Harry, what am I supposed to do?'

'You've got the best needlework in the whole of the East End,' he flattered only to be met with her concerned glance.

'I-I'm not qualified!'

'I can't go to a hospital, it'll only make it worse for both our sakes, trust me,' he admitted as he leant against the wall, trying to remain upright.

'We can't have you bleeding out on my doorstep, come in quickly and try not to wake up my family. Here, put your weight on me,' she insisted as she pulled his arm over her shoulder.

'I'll crush you to death,' he hesitated as the little blonde creature burrowed herself under his armpit.

'Don't be silly, it'll take more than that to kill me,' she said, determined.

'We can't tell the others about this otherwise it could get messy.'

'Messier than it already is?' Charlotte asked, carefully sitting him down at the kitchen table. She studied the wound, prodding it slightly.

'A lot messier. Just dab some alcohol on it.' He flinched as his flesh bit back at her touch. Taking off his heavy drape jacket and shirt revealed the trail of blood that was navigating its way down the crevices of his sculpted back.

'I knew something like this would happen. It was Talbot's nephew that did this, didn't he?'

'Yeah, he had two mates with him.'

'I didn't think he had the nerve to do this by himself, the weasel,' she said angrily.

'What's done is done. I'm over all this, Lottie, I just want to be with you,' Harry sighed.

'And I want to be with you,' she whispered. 'I warn you I have no clue what I'm doing. Brandy or whiskey?' She fumbled through the shelves, grabbing a tea towel.

'Both. Brandy to clean the wound, and whiskey for me,' he answered as she passed him the bottle. Taking a gulp, he prepared himself for the stinging sensation to follow.

'Ok, deep breath,' Charlotte said as she took a deep breath of her own. Harry winced in response to the volatile brown substance that splashed against his flesh. 'Try not to struggle,' she said as his face scrunched.

'I'm not.'

'Well, stop moving then, I can't focus if you keep fidgeting,' she muttered as she removed the towel, tossing it into the sink. As Charlotte disappeared into the other room, she searched the dark floor for her special tin that contained her needles and threads. Placing the old McVitie's biscuit tin on the table, she rummaged around its interior. Pulling out the perfect needle, she looped the thread through.

'I warn you, I've never done this before,' she said, hesitating.

'There's a first time for everything.'

'Pass me the brandy.'

'But you've already cleaned the wound?'

'It's not for the wound,' Charlotte said as he handed her the bottle, taking a swig before burying the needle into his skin.

A pebble ricocheted off the glass with a tremendous thud, sending Francesca to the window. Her eyes were heavy and unfocused, her hair a messy mass of tangles and hair product.

'Do you realise the time? It's four in the bloody morning,' she whispered as she poked her head out.

'You didn't answer my question properly.' Oliver smiled, fully aware of the time.

'And what question was that?'

'Come down and I'll remind you.'

Francesca hesitated as she looked down the street, making sure they weren't being watched by a nosy neighbour. 'I'll let you in through the back gate, I can only let you as far as the garden, can't risk waking everyone up,' she said quietly.

'The garden is good enough for me.' Oliver grinned, proceeding to the wooden gate that clung to the side of the house. The brown paint was peeling and it looked like it would be of better use at the bottom of a bonfire than as a barrier. On the opposite side of the gate, a few shuffles could be heard, followed by the unlocking of a rusty bolt.

Francesca greeted him in an embrace, his hands meeting the fabric of her fluffy pink dressing gown. As she led him to the dark little garden, they found themselves isolated.

Oliver could make out the rope of a washing line with a few pegs left clinging onto it. There was a familiar structure at the back of the garden that was overgrown with weeds, soil and shrubbery of all descriptions. Oliver approached the Anderson Shelter with ghostly remembrance. Looking at the air raid shelter, he could make out the exposed iron sheets that formed its semi-circular shape.

'I remember these things all too well,' he said.

'My brother and Elaine's brother made it for us when the war broke out, said it would keep us safe when the bombs came,' she explained as she met his side. 'Mum wasn't convinced, so she'd drag us to the Underground instead. I think she just couldn't handle another second stuck in that tin can with my grandma.'

'I don't think anyone could bear these things, but I'd rather spend a night in this than meet a German bomb,' he said as his fingers pushed open the rusting door.

'I'd prefer not to go in there. My dressing gown has only

just been washed,' she protested as Oliver ducked inside the dirty structure, taking a seat on one of the remaining wooden benches.

'At least in here we'll have some privacy,' he said cheekily, patting the place beside him.

'I don't want to get my dressing gown dirty, my mum will have a fit if she has to wash it again,' Francesca objected.

He grinned. 'You'll just have to sit on my lap.'

Giving in, she heaved up the material and perched on his knees.

'So, will you, my beautiful Frankie, be my girlfriend?' Oliver asked.

'Of course I will,' she answered, leaning in for a kiss. Meeting her lips, Oliver pulled her close, her body pressing against his. His fingers teased the rope of her dressing gown and slowly released the fastened bow. Francesca undid his shirt buttons one at a time as he kissed her neck. With a gentle kick, the door slowly closed, leaving the two in darkness.

Facing the church, Stephanie grimaced as she caught sight of the Priest greeting people through the large wooden doors. She looked to the steeple, following it back to the ground with a nervous glance. It was a bright Sunday and the birds tweeted as they flew around the church garden.

'I don't think I want to do this,' she said reluctantly as Charley tried to move her forward, her hand tightly gripped around his arm. With Francesca and Vera ahead of them, they paused for a moment of contemplation.

'Of course you do.' Charley smiled as he caught the Priest's attention.

As he walked towards them, Stephanie recoiled at the

thought of an interaction. 'Do you think he'll judge me?' she asked, worried as she watched the approaching figure.

'No, only God can do that.' Charley winked.

Victoria Park was lush and green. Butterflies fluttered across the grass as bumblebees flew from one flower to another, the scent of pollen filling the air. The girls sat on a large tartan blanket under an old oak tree. The leaves moved with the gentle breeze, and the protective branches shielded them from the sun. A few wicker baskets laid open on the blanket containing fresh fruit, a Victoria sponge cake made by Francesca's mother, and many sandwiches supplied by Charlotte.

'Fran, your mum is ridiculously good at baking,' Kerry said, licking the jam from her fingers.

Francesca tilted her head back, feeling the warm breeze meet her face. 'Does your mum bake a lot?'

'Not really anymore, she used to make lovely carrot cake, now she only ever cooks for my uncle, and it's normally some sort of disgusting stew,' Kerry muttered.

'I didn't know you lived with your uncle,' she said, watching her intently.

'More like he lives with us,' she tutted.

'Do you not like having a man around? I sometimes miss my dad, but I was always closest to my mum.'

'No, I don't, not that type of man anyway, he's a brute. My dad died during the Normandy landings. Mum was never the same after, she became weak and timid, and my war shy uncle took advantage of her,' Kerry explained.

'I'm sorry to hear that,' she said, frowning.

'It's fine.'

Charlotte helped herself to a cheese and ham sandwich. 'My dad has never been the same since he got back. He has nightmares, bad ones, some so bad that he'll scream and it scares my sister half to death. It's almost like his mind turns to scrambled egg anytime he thinks about the war.'

'Mr Montgomery said he has the same thing. He takes pills to help him sleep.' Francesca remembered.

'My dad has tried lots of pills, none of them work. If anything, they make him seem like he's not all there. That's why I have to work long hours at the factory, because he ain't stable enough to keep a job,' she sighed.

'He makes bloody good sandwiches though, Lottie,' Susan said, taking a bite from one that was filled with cheese and pickle.

'We were up all morning preparing them, he's a really wonderful baker, he makes the bread from scratch, and if there are leftovers he makes a delicious bread and butter pudding. If I have money spare from my wages after flat payments, I try and get him the best ingredients. He always cooked and baked, even before the war because mum was always poorly. I think doing it now takes his mind to a better place.'

'He's done a wonderful job,' Isla agreed.

'My brother and I used to bake together with my mum, it was so much fun, but half the ingredients would be on the floor rather than in the bowl, our faces would be covered in flour,' Francesca said, smiling brightly.

'Used to?' Kerry questioned.

'My brother was a pilot, he was shot down,' she explained, feeling the locket that sat around her neck. She opened it to reveal his portrait. The girls huddled in close to get a better look.

'I'm sorry you lost him,' Kerry said, staring at the black-and-white image.

'He was handsome.' Charlotte grinned.

'He was kind too, and was really close to Elaine's brother,' Francesca said, looking at her best friend.

'Charley was never the same after he found out James died,' Elaine admitted, taking a swig from a large flask containing Robinsons Lemon Squash.

'It looks like we've all got loss in common,' Kerry said, brushing the crumbs off her three-quarter-length jeans.

Isla's eyes shone like polished jade, yet they appeared saddened. 'I never knew my dad, so I guess you can't lose what you've never had.'

'Do you want to find him?' Francesca asked.

'No, I've fended for myself for a long time now, just like Susan and Oliver,' she said, looking at Susan who sat quietly.

'Life has dealt us all a rough hand, hasn't it?' She observed, running her fingers through her long black hair that sat loosely.

'Doesn't matter how rough the hand if you know how to play it right.' Kerry smiled.

The boys were busy kicking about a football on the open grass. It was hot and the sun caused their faces to appear glossy and red. As the ball passed from one to the other, they looked back to the group of girls who sat nattering under the old oak tree.

'Where's Harry today?' Colin asked, the leather ball meeting the side of his foot.

'Lottie said he's working,' Oliver explained, smiling at Francesca who waved at him.

'Bit odd on a Sunday afternoon for him to miss something like this, it's even odder for Lottie not to drag him to it.' Jack ran a hand through his messy, greased hair.

'I'm sure he's ok, she'd tell us if something was wrong,' Oliver said as the ball was sent toppling towards him. The lake sat behind them, the gentle jilting water catching the sun's reflection. The large fountain could be seen in the distance, its spire reaching high into the summer sky.

'So, the word about town is that you've made it official with Fran.' Albie grinned.

'I have,' Oliver admitted, a large smile covering his face as he sent the ball to Finn.

'I'm pleased for you, she's a lovely girl,' Colin said.

'But have you made it 'official' official,' Jack pried.

'We've done things, but I'm not going to pressure her. We're going to take our time.'

'What things?' he questioned, smirking.

'I'm not telling you nosy sods,' he said, the warm breeze meeting the open collar of his white poplin shirt.

'Jesus, she's turning you into a gentleman,' Finn uttered, sending an unimpressed glance to Lewis as he kicked the ball in his direction.

'It shows you care about her. I think it's admirable not kissing and telling, even though it's always entertaining,' Albie said. His face was so red from the heat that it matched his ginger hair.

'I'm going to try and be a better person, only fighting unless it's competitive or for a good reason,' he said, looking over to Francesca again.

'Good for you,' Albie commended.

'I'm surprised she's managed to change you so quickly,' Lewis said, kicking the ball a little harder than expected.

'It's my choice to better myself, not hers. She's just shown me that there is more to life than this.' Oliver stopped the speeding ball with the arch of his foot.

'It makes you look weak, it makes us look weak,' Lewis said irritably as Oliver sent the ball tumbling back to him. The others stood stiffly, sensing the tension that built between them.

'There's nothing weak about change, what's the difference between me and Frankie, and you and Kerry.'

'I never changed for Kerry,' Lewis sneered, booting the ball into Oliver's arms.

'But Kerry changed for you,' he said, gripping it firmly.

Susan walked alongside her brother, the sun setting, shielding them in a golden-orange glow. The gothic style fountain stood before them, looking out of place on such a bright summer's eve. It would be much better suited to a grizzly day, surrounded by heavy showers. The pink marble and granite columns lifted high above; the eight sides linked by intricate engravings. A pool of cool, clear water filled the large basin as the various statues watched over it.

'Fran and Lottie did a wonderful job,' she said, taking a seat on the side of the fountain.

'They did. Do you remember playing in this when we were little?' Oliver asked, dipping a hand in.

'Yeah, I remember you drenching me with water, but I'd always get you back,' Susan said smugly.

'You did, and mum would shout at us for ruining our clothes.' He laughed, running a wet hand over the back of his neck, cooling himself down.

'I never knew what all the fuss was about, it's only water at the end of the day,' she tutted with folded arms.

'She struggled to afford them, and I suppose she did have to wash them and ring them out by hand.'

Susan raised an irritated eyebrow. 'More like I had to sit there and do it as punishment. You just got a whack on the wrists.'

'Or a black eye.' Oliver recalled.

'He always took it out on you, I'm sorry,' she said, frowning.

'What's done is done, it gives me motivation when I box. Speaking of which, I've got a big fight coming up, will you come?'

'Of course, I'll always come and support my big brother, even though it's a pain when I have to patch you up after. Have you invited Fran?'

'I'm going to, I want her to experience it. I need to talk to you about something, Susan, it's bothering me.'

'Well, spill the beans,' she said, the water falling gently behind her.

'Lewis and Finn seem on edge, especially when I talk about Fran.'

She looked at her brother, his eyes glinting. 'They've always been a bit sly, they like causing trouble. I think Lewis is probably annoyed because you got the pretty girl before him, and she's taking your attention away from the boys.'

'We can't cause chaos together forever, I'm twenty-one now, I need to get my life in check,' he said.

'I'm glad to hear it, I'm pleased to see you so happy.'

He smiled widely. 'As long as I've got you and Fran, that's all I need, and Colin, he's the only friend I truly trust. Speaking of which, do you know what Colin wanted to talk to me about the other night? You were both sitting together before he came over, did he tell you?'

Susan's heart sank. For most of the day she had managed to forget about her circumstances. 'No, he didn't,' she lied.

As Francesca ascended the staircase, she fiddled with the Dairy Milk Bar nestled in the pocket of her velvet blazer. Pushing the door open, she met eyes with a weary Elaine who laid on her bed in the foetal position, a hot water bottle clutched to her stomach like a second skin. Her hair was messy, and her face was flushed from the never-ending cramps.

'I heard you weren't doing so well. I brought some chocolate to cheer you up.' She smiled, revealing the purple packaging.

'That's made my day,' Elaine said as her friend sat next to her with crossed legs. Trying to sit upright another bolt of pain accosted her. She retreated into a ball once more, her face firmly pressed against her lilac bed sheets. 'I hate this time of the month,' she winced.

Watching empathetically, Francesca broke the chocolate into chunks, allowing them to become manageable small bites. 'Don't worry, I'll feed you. How long have you been in your jimmy jams?' she asked as she popped a slither in between her friend's lips.

'All day, and I don't care for wearing anything else until the crimson tide retreats,' she said humorously.

'You almost sound as poetic as Albie.' Francesca laughed as she helped herself to some chocolate. She quickly licked her fingers clean to avoid staining her work clothes. Elaine on the other hand couldn't care less, and her dressing gown hosted a variety of stains.

'I don't even think Shakespeare could be as poetic as Albie.

I like your ponytail, it's a nice change from your usual plait,' Elaine complimented as she welcomed another piece of chocolate into her mouth.

'Thank you, it's Albie's doing,' she explained, feeling the fastened strands of brown hair between her fingers.

'Why am I not surprised.' She grinned. 'Can I ask you a question?'

'Of course, you can ask me anything.'

'Have you, you know, done it with Oliver?'

'Nearly.'

'Nearly?' Elaine asked, confused.

'Um…' She paused, attempting to form an adequate explanation. 'It hurt too much, so we did other stuff,' she replied, growing embarrassed.

'Other stuff?'

'Yeah, other stuff,' Francesca repeated with reddening cheeks.

'Lottie, what was all that commotion the other night? Not to mention my diminishing stash of alcohol?' her father asked. His face was weathered, yet his expression was kind.

She threw down her heavy bag, noticing her red raw hands stained with visible cuts. Quickly, she hid them behind her back. She didn't want him to worry about her wellbeing, especially considering the fragile state of his own.

'I had to borrow some of it to sterilise something,' she said cagily, watching her father with his oven glove clad hands. He was wrestling with a homemade cottage pie that he appeared to be very proud of. Placing it on the kitchen worktop, the steam rose high into the air.

'Is that something to do with that Harry boy?' he persisted as the smell of beef and gravy filled the room.

'Yes, he got himself in to a bit of bother at work, cut the back of his head,' she said cautiously, repeating the excuse Harry had prepared for her.

'Who works in the early hours of the morning? And couldn't he get to a hospital?'

'It wasn't bad enough. And he decided to work late,' she said quickly.

'I think it was considering the bloody tea towel that was left in the sink,' he said, catching Charlotte red-handed.

'Sorry dad, I forgot that was there, he just wanted me to sort him out.'

'Of course he wanted you to sort him out,' her potty-mouthed sister interrupted as she sat on the tatty sofa. Her face was dirty with crumbs and her fingers were smothered in the remains of a few unfortunate bourbon biscuits.

'Bugger off,' Charlotte snapped, her eyes piercing into her fifteen-year-old sister who looked at her smugly.

'Be civil girls, and what did I tell you about eating before dinner? It ruins your appetite. Now come on, it's ready,' he said, their eyes lighting up at the prospect of a hot meal.

Morpeth Street loomed with its tightly compacted run-down houses lining both sides of the road. The end of the street was cut off by the overground rail service. It created vibrations that rippled their way under the foundations of the buildings, causing them to shake on occasion. A nearby chemical works stood large and ugly and created a nauseating stench that infected the area.

Clothing and bed sheets swayed gently along the hanging

lines. It created a playground for local children who darted in and out of the material. Women sat on their front doorsteps, tired expressions overtaking their faces. Their hands rinsed clothes in water-filled buckets, the dirt and grime of East End life being squeezed out only to return days later.

As Kerry wandered along the cobbles, a couple of the women sent hardened glances in her direction. Knowing she wasn't welcome, Kerry scowled back at them, content on showing her equal disdain.

With a deep breath, she entered the house.

'Speak of the Devil,' her uncle snivelled.

'And she shall appear.'

'Kerry, you were supposed to do the housework,' her mother snapped. Her dirty pinnie sat loosely wrapped around her waist.

'Why?'

'Because your uncle told you to,' her mother said, turning to reveal a swollen, bruised eye. Her hands were shaking violently.

'Nobody is going to marry a girl who has no domestic skills,' her uncle spat from the sofa.

Kerry felt the rage build with every beat of her heart, yet she remained calm. 'Who says I want to get married,' she said stubbornly.

'Well, nobody is going to want to be with you full stop if you have that attitude.' He tended to his beer bottle, taking an obnoxious gulp.

'I beg to differ.'

'Go upstairs. I've had enough of you for one day. And change out of those ridiculous trousers, you look like a man.' Her mother stared at the ground out of shame, not for her daughter, but for the words that were coming out of her own mouth.

'I think they make me look like a respectable woman.'

'You look like a queer,' he mocked.

'And then a queer I'll be.'

He stood from the sofa. 'You stubborn little—'

'Little what? I'm not a small child that you can hit anymore.' Her fists tightened in her trouser pockets.

'We'll see about that,' her uncle sneered, wrapping his leather belt around his knuckles.

'Stop it, she doesn't know what she's saying,' her mother pleaded.

'I do know actually, mum, and I'm going to say it. You are going to leave us alone. Leave me and my mum alone, you're not welcome in this house,' she yelled. Her claws were slowly pointing in his direction like a lioness preparing to defend her pride.

'Stop it, Kerry, it'll do more harm than good,' her mother cried.

'I'm tired of you giving in to him. You don't do it out of love, you do it out of fear, you always have.'

'You're getting too big for your boots,' he said, grinning as he approached her.

Throwing herself in the way, her mother was sent tumbling to the floor.

'Did you not hear what I said?' Kerry continued. She tried to maintain a firm stance with her feet cemented to the floor.

'You will have nothing without me. You'll lose everything, I'll make sure of it,' he said as he threw a punch, missing Kerry as she ducked.

She sent a blow to his forehead and he fell to the ground

with a thud. Her mother ran to her aid, yanking the belt from his knuckles. He tried to stand, but Kerry was too quick, sending her fist into his throat. The punch was thrown with such force that he fell flat on his back gasping for breath, his Adam's apple dislodging, invading his windpipe. His eyes bulged, dripping with tears.

'I can't breathe,' he wheezed, his eyes darting between Kerry and her mother who watched him with disgust. A large bruise was developing between his eyes, the skin split, and he gripped his neck in agony as it swelled.

'It's not nice feeling helpless, is it?' Kerry asked with folded arms. 'Now get out of our house.'

'You're gonna get put away for this,' he hissed at her, semi-conscious as he staggered to the door.

'Oh, so you're gonna tell the police that a girl did that to your face, what are your mates gonna say when you tell them that too? You'll never hear the end of it,' her mother said, smiling as she held her daughter in a protective embrace, the belt now sitting firmly in her hand.

He looked, realising he had lost his power over them.

'I'll send your belongings to the second-hand shop, there's no need for you to come back here,' she continued.

'You bitch.'

Kerry pulled the belt from her mother's hand, her uncle fleeing at the sight. 'You know what? I don't think I'm done yet.'

He stumbled along the cobbles holding his throat. The women sitting on their doorstops called to their children to get out of the way as they watched, horror-stricken.

'Apologise,' Kerry shouted at him, sending the belt across his back, the leather cracking against his spine.

'I'm sorry,' he screeched, falling to the ground.

'Somebody needs to put a stop to this,' one woman said to another.

'Would you like to try? My daughter and I will slap you stupid,' Kerry's mother snapped at them.

'Sorry to who?' Kerry asked sternly as he dragged himself along the cobbles.

'To you and your mum, I'm sorry for what I've done—'

'And what have you done?'

'Hurt you.' He stared up at her.

'How? Go on, tell all these women and children what you've put us through.'

'I abused you both,' he shouted.

To this confession, the children threw stones at him. He cowered more than he already was.

'But of course you knew that already, didn't you ladies,' Kerry called out to them as they sat, stunned. 'You heard the screaming, yet you did nothing, shame on all of you. Even when you saw it in person at street parties, you did fuckin' nothing.'

A few women hung their heads, others dragged their children inside. A couple of boys in their early teenage years shouted at the bruised man to keep off their street, while the younger children stuck out their tongues and blew raspberries.

'So, what are you going to do now?' Kerry's shadow loomed over him.

'Leave and never return.'

'Get on with it then.' She kicked his leg and he bolted down the end of the road.

Francesca examined the final piece of paper, making sure she hadn't made any mistakes. With a satisfied smile, she placed it on a gigantic pile of bank statements that she had managed to complete in record time. She turned to Mr Montgomery who was focused on a mind-numbing file, his fingers tapping methodically on the desk.

'Done, Sir,' she said, watching him.

He looked at his wristwatch, unconvinced. 'Already? There better not be any mistakes,' he warned.

'There isn't, I've read through every statement to make sure,' she said cheerfully, gathering the documents into her arms.

'I'm impressed you've typed them so quickly,' he commended.

'Well, as you said, Sir, people from our neck of the woods get shit done.'

He tried to stop himself from grinning. 'Take those through to Penny and have your lunch break early, you deserve it.'

'Thank you,' she said, feeling awfully proud of herself as she left the office.

Tower Hill Garden was beautiful with its flourishing shrubbery and assorted roses. The surrounding Trinity Square was lined with deep cobbles that were reminiscent of old England. They were busy with the footsteps of commuters and marked by the heavy tyres of black taxis.

Francesca sat on a marble bench that overlooked the centre of the green; it was paradise amongst a concrete jungle. It was peaceful, but she had heard stories of it being the site of executions. She considered how such a beautiful space lined with marble and exquisite flowers could hold such dark secrets. A war memorial had been placed within the green, adding to its morbid history. She looked at it as she munched on a warmed jam sandwich that had been stuffed into her handbag.

'You sittin' all alone?' Lewis asked.

'Yes, is Finn not with you?' she questioned, unnerved as he sat beside her.

'Funnily enough we're not joined at the hip, he's busy doing God knows what.'

'What do you do?'

'Bits and bobs here and there, nothing you'd be interested in,' he said cagily. His shoes were a polished pair of intricate brogues that reflected the sunlight into Francesca's eyes.

Squinting as she looked at him, she felt the need to ask, 'Do you enjoy hurting people?'

'I do, actually,' he spoke, almost proudly.

'Why were you so mean to Elaine? Do you have something against us?' she asked, quickly brushing the crumbs off her velvet pencil skirt.

'No, only against you,' Lewis answered.

'Why?'

'Oh, keep up, I've explained this to you before. You don't fit in, and you never will despite what the others have led you to believe, or more specifically, what Oli has led you to believe,' he said bluntly.

'I don't want to fit in.' She looked at him defiantly.

'That's exactly the problem, sweetheart, and it's starting to get irritating. You're changing him, making him soft, and you're spoiling our fun.'

'I haven't changed him, he's a grown man and makes his own decisions, you just want to blame me for the fact that your mate wants rid of you.' She paused, feeling her temper flare. 'What fun?' she asked.

He flashed a sinister grin. 'I thought you would have caught on by now. You know, whenever we go out it always ends in violence, a cracked jaw, a busted nose, a meat fork to the knee, and that's only in the past few months—'

'It doesn't help that he's encouraged by people like you,' she snapped, cutting him off.

'People like me? I'm not even going to acknowledge that type of insult. Unfortunately for you, he will always listen to us over you, he's known us since we were kids, and he's known you for less than a year. And don't forget, Fran, you may now be his 'girlfriend' but he pursued you because of a fuckin' bet. I'm actually surprised you'd be thick enough to take him back after he led you on and made you look like a dumb little bitch.'

'Don't you dare talk to me like that, he apologised, and I forgave him,' she said quickly. Gathering her things into her handbag, she hurried to escape his presence.

'And that's the biggest mistake you could have made,' Lewis sighed, watching her disappear.

Isla knocked on the door. It was opened instantly by Stephanie who was holding a basket full of washing. She placed it on the ground so Isla had her full attention.

'What can I do for you?' she asked politely.

'I'm Fran's friend, I was wondering if she was in?'

'As luck would have it, she is. Head up the stairs, first door down.' She ushered her in.

'Thank you, you have a lovely home,' she complimented as she ascended the stairs, peering at the family pictures that lined the walls.

'It's not much, but it does the job,' Stephanie said, heaving the basket back into her arms.

Isla poked her head through the door that sat ajar. 'Fran?'

'Isla? Did mum let you in?' She smiled as she caught her reflection in the mirror.

'Yeah.'

'Come and sit down, I was just rearranging my vanity, my makeup drawer is a mess. I can go and make you a cuppa if you'd like?' she asked as Isla closed the door.

'Oh, I'm ok thank you, I came over here because I heard you might need some help. Elaine told me you had trouble with Oliver.'

'Goodness gracious that girl can't keep her mouth shut.' Francesca bristled.

'It's normal for it not to be perfect the first time.'

She held her face in her hands. 'Isla, it wouldn't even go in. It's like I clamped up. I don't think my parts work.'

'You just got nervous, that's all. Did you do anything else?'

Francesca went pink, matching her champagne-coloured bed sheets. 'He touched me, it felt good, and I did the same to him, but that was it. I've never really been told what to do, and when he was pressed against me, it stung.'

'Well, that's a start. The main thing with it is that you need to feel comfortable, to know your own body,' she said without judgement.

'Um, well it needs to go up there, I know that much,' she muttered.

'No, I mean you need to know what *you* like.'

'I don't understand.'

'Well, what do you think about when you, you know, touch yourself?'

'I haven't.' Francesca shuffled uncomfortably.

'What do you mean, you haven't?'

'I mean, my own body frightens me,' she whispered, making Isla chuckle.

'That's the silliest thing I've ever heard.'

'No, it does, honestly. I've been taught to be scared of my body since I was little. My mum and grandma have always been encouraging, saying it's only natural, but I've been told over and over that it's sinful.'

'You've been taught to feel shame for feeling good, that's all. What he did to you, you need to do to yourself. It's how you'll get confident with your body, and once you've done that, it'll get easier. I promise it will.'

'Are you sure?'

'Yes. Take control, teach yourself.'

'Ok, I'll try,' she gulped, still unconvinced.

'One more thing, has your mum or grandma spoken to you about contraception?' Isla asked.

'My grandma once told me that the man should pull out near the end, but apart from that, not really.'

'That's rubbish, it doesn't work. Women can still get pregnant if you do that,' Isla informed her.

Francesca looked shocked. 'I suppose it's a good thing we didn't go all the way then,' she said, relieved.

'I know I have a bit of a reputation for sleeping around, but not once have I ever been caught out, I always make sure it's safe. You need to be safe too, Fran. I brought one of these for you, I know a woman down Holloway who gets them in,' she said happily, passing her a little rubber object.

Francesca accepted it into her grasp, but stared at it, confused.

'It's a cervical cap, think of it like a barrier. So, before you have sex, you need to put it up there, and it'll stop you getting pregnant. It's rubber so it won't hurt too badly. It might be a little uncomfortable but it's better than needing some dodgy backstreet abortion later down the line. The main thing to remember is that you take it out afterwards and clean it. I find that knowing you're as protected as you can be makes you relax more,' she explained.

'Nobody has ever looked out for me like this. Thank you.' Francesca smiled widely, putting the cervical cap in her vanity drawer.

'I tried to tell the other girls about it, but they dismissed me. I think they see me as the last person to come to for sexual advice.' She frowned.

'I think they're stupid not to listen to you. I really appreciate you coming round to talk to me about it. I had no idea cervical caps were even a thing,' Francesca said.

'Well, I heard they're doing experiments with a pill to stop women getting pregnant, but we'll be the last ones to get it I imagine. I can picture the morality campaigners already, screaming about how it'll corrupt the youth,' she muttered.

'There are a lot of people out there who still think like Victorians.'

Isla grinned. 'And what a boring way to live. How's work going?'

'It's been surprisingly good, I'm getting on quite well with my boss. But Lewis found me during my lunch break the other day and was absolutely horrid,' she huffed.

'It's because of the picnic,' Isla said, smirking.

'What happened at the picnic? I hardly spoke to him.'

'Not you. Jack told me Lewis and Oli had a bit of a back-and-forth, and Oli said something that really got under his skin.

It's nothing for you to worry about, he was just lashing out because he got embarrassed.'

'He called me a bitch. I've never really been spoken to like that.'

'Join the club, you should hear the list of things he's said to me in the past.' She rolled her eyes. 'He's even called Lottie some nasty things, he wouldn't dare say anything about Susan though for obvious reasons. He's not that cretinous, at least, I think he's not.'

'What's his problem then?'

'He has a Madonna-whore complex,' she said.

'What does that mean?'

'Susan told me about it, she read it in a book. To put it bluntly, Kerry is his Madonna, like a saint that can do no wrong, and every other woman is seen as a whore, below him—'

'I didn't even realise they were together.'

'It's a bit complicated, he was Kerry's first, and she has been loyal to him. But they've never been in a boyfriend-girlfriend relationship. He desires other women, has slept with loads, but he could never love them like he does Kerry, even though he'll never admit it, but Kerry is almost too much for him, she's too strong, too powerful.'

'She challenges him?'

'Not many men like to be challenged by a woman. He takes it out on other women who aren't as strong as Kerry, or at least he thinks,' she said.

'You should be a psychologist.'

'That sounds like a brainy job.'

'You need to give yourself more credit. I think you explain things well,' she complimented, making Isla blush.

CHAPTER 12

THE MILK BAR sat on the corner of Eric Street and was a stark contrast to the tarnished buildings within the area. The interior was art deco in style and had black and white square tiles lining the floor. Bar stools stood occupied. It was loud with the nattering of young people and the distant rhythm of a large jukebox that sat in the corner of the room, glimmering with its polished chrome. The long counter displayed an assortment of ice cream from cherry to caramel and chocolate. A couple of young Greek men in matching uniforms were busy scooping the different flavours into multi-coloured concoctions. They were tall and twin-like in appearance. Francesca recognised them from when she was at school and sent a smile in their direction as she sat down with the others. She remembered them flogging sweets on the playground for mere farthings, now they owned their very own sugar-filled shop.

Francesca ordered a chocolate milkshake while Oliver

settled for vanilla with extra cream. Charlotte ordered a knickerbocker glory sundae but knew her eyes were bigger than her stomach. Harry sat stiffly with a coffee as Albie ordered a scoop of pineapple and peach ice cream.

'How's everything going then?' Charlotte asked, clinging onto Harry's arm.

'It couldn't be better.' Francesca smiled. Oliver clasped her hand under the table as one of the men arrived with a tray full of desserts.

'Everyone seems to be at peace for a change.' Albie observed.

'It probably won't last long,' Harry muttered, sipping his bitter looking coffee. Charlotte in opposition had her extravagant knickerbocker glory in a tall glass. It contained the sticky mixture of ice cream, cream and fruit. Diving in with a long spoon, her lips were soon coated in sugar.

'It definitely won't be peaceful when Jack and I fight those lads from that South London gym,' Oliver said.

As Francesca took a large gulp from her chocolate milkshake, she looked at him, concerned. 'Could you get hurt?'

'It's always a possibility, but I've been doing it for a long time now, I know what I'm doing, Frankie, don't worry I'll be fine,' he assured her.

'When is it?'

'Soon, I want you to come and cheer me on,' Oliver invited as he sipped his vanilla milkshake slowly.

'I've never been to a boxing match before, of course I'll come,' she agreed.

'We'll all be there so you can sit with us, Fran.' Albie smiled as he finished his ice cream. 'And we can watch Jack beat someone half to death,' he added, Francesca's face souring at the thought.

'I had to perform surgery on Harry the other week,' Charlotte blurted out, her lips covered in cream. It was only when she wiped her mouth with a napkin that she realised what she'd said.

'I can see that. It looks like a nasty gash. What happened?' Oliver asked as Harry calmly sipped his coffee.

'Is that why you didn't come to the picnic?' Albie questioned suspiciously.

'It happened at work, just an accident,' he dismissed.

'Sounds like a load of bollocks to me.' Oliver scowled.

'It's nothing, Oli, honestly.' Harry's eyes grew worried as he watched his friend.

'I suppose it could be worse, you could have lost an eye or something. Cockney types love taking an eye or two,' Albie stated, recognising his injury to be more than just a happy accident.

'Why do you say that?' Francesca asked.

'Haven't you heard the stories?'

'What stories?'

'Don't listen to him it's exaggerated nonsense,' Oliver said as he sent an unamused glance in Harry's direction.

'No, I want to know, tell me,' she pleaded, leaning over the table.

'I want to know too,' Charlotte said as she licked her spoon.

'You know the pub down the road, the one with the big red doors?'

'Yeah, that's the Blind Beggar,' Charlotte said.

'Well, there was once a notorious gang that used to, shall we say, inhabit it back in the day.' He rose, setting the scene. 'And one day a bloke went in there and looked at them the wrong way. Before he knew it, they pinned him to the ground and bang!' He thumped his fist on the table. Charlotte and Francesca jolted backwards with fright. 'He had the end of an umbrella stabbed four inches into his eye socket. Apparently, if you look hard enough, you can still see the bloodstains on the floor,' he concluded, looking at them all individually.

'That's bloody disgusting.' Charlotte cringed as the image occupied her mind.

'Yeah mate that is a bit of a rank story to tell while we're trying to eat.' Oliver looked at the remaining foam that sat at the bottom of his glass with sudden distaste.

'So, did he survive?' Francesca asked, fascinated by the tale.

'It went into his brain, there is no coming back from that,' Albie said.

'Did they catch the man that did it?'

'He got away with it,' Oliver interjected. He had heard the story when he was a child, *don't go near that pub or Bulldog Wallis will get ya*. However, he was never sure how much of it was true. The group regularly went drinking in the Blind Beggar but never heard a peep out of anyone, so it was reduced to Cockney legend spoken only in whispers.

'Nobody was dumb enough to stand witness,' Albie said.

'I fear for your children and the stories you'll tell them at bedtime.' Francesca laughed.

'At least there will be a moral at the end of every story,' he justified.

'And what would that be?' she asked, amused.

'Don't get caught looking at people the wrong way.' He grinned.

The moonlight sent silver streaks onto the shadow-laced walls. The curtains fluttered with the gentle breeze, shapes wandering softly across the room, gently distorting. The breeze met Francesca's exposed back, working its way up to her neck, cooling her down. She sat on top of him, sweat dripping from her body as her thighs twitched, tightening around his waist. Oliver stared up at her, a satisfied smile covering his face.

'That was unexpected,' he said, reaching for a packet of cigarettes.

'I've been practicing,' she panted, causing him to raise an eyebrow. 'Not with other people, just—'

'With yourself?'

'Exactly.' She collapsed beside him, her head resting on his muscular shoulder.

'Good, because that was bloody spectacular. You're spectacular,' he said, lighting a cigarette. Smoke slowly rose into the air and Francesca watched it, transfixed as it danced with the shadows.

'I think you are too. I've never felt that way before,' she said, yawning as her eyelids tugged across her drowsy pupils.

'I haven't either,' he admitted.

'Of course you have, I'm not your first,' she dismissed, snuggling into him.

'I don't mean the sex, it made me feel complete. It felt like what love should feel like.'

'Love?' Francesca gulped with anticipation as she peered up at him.

'I love you,' he said.

Those three special words she had waited her entire life to hear. For some reason, she thought she may never hear them, or that if she did, they wouldn't feel any different from someone telling her that her outfit was nice, or that she had done a good job at something. She was always curious to hear someone say them to her, wondering what the words would feel like. They felt spectacular.

'I love you too,' she said.

The East End enjoyed the last of the summer days. Children played under the dying sunset as the streets were gripped in a warm embrace. As Francesca wandered down the road at a merry pace, she pulled at her blazer and skirt, making sure she still looked respectable after a hard day's work. Trailing the red brick walls, she knocked on the door, a grin encapsulating her face. She was met by a flustered Susan who was attempting to move a cardboard box filled with paperwork.

'He's not in, Fran, should be back in a jiffy,' Susan said, lifting her hands to her hips, attempting to catch her breath.

'Do you need a hand?' Francesca offered.

'Please, I'm having a bit of bother.'

'It's unlike you to accept help,' Francesca said as she grasped the box in both hands. Taking it up the stairs, she returned to Susan who was tending to the kettle. 'Are you ok, Susan? I mean, have you been feeling ok?'

'Yeah, I'm fine,' she said.

'Fine is what people say when they aren't fine.' Francesca sat at the kitchen table.

'You don't want to know,' she sighed, pouring the boiling water into two mugs.

'I do. Whatever is troubling you, there is always a solution.'

'I'm pregnant.'

'Oh my God.' She sat frozen. The words weaved their way

into her brain creating a lattice of panicked thought.

'Do you want sugar in your tea?' Susan asked calmly.

'How?' Francesca questioned.

'Please don't tell Oliver, he'll go mental,' Susan said as she slowly poured in the milk.

'Are you keeping it?'

'Yes.'

'Who's the father?' Francesca asked as Colin wandered obliviously into the room. 'Oh fuck,' she exclaimed.

He turned to Susan furiously. 'You told her?'

'I wish you didn't,' Francesca said.

'I needed to talk to someone about it, you're hardly talkative about the fact that I'm carrying your child,' she muttered.

'And you know why? 'Cause I'm trying to figure things out. All you needed to have is a little patience,' he snapped.

'I don't possess patience! I'm bloody with child and it's showing. The more patience I have, the more likely I am to lose you,' she wept suddenly, tears flooding her cheeks.

'You're not going to lose me. I will talk to Oliver,' Colin assured, embracing her tightly. 'Sorry you've got caught up in this, Fran,' he said as Susan buried her head in his chest.

Seeing how distressed her friend was, Francesca felt her heart grow heavy. 'I won't tell anyone,' she promised.

Blackfriars Road was quiet, the only noise a gentle murmur from the movement of distant traffic. The wind slowly curled around lampposts and a few docile trees, the leaves gently swaying in the air as the sun beat down upon them.

The buildings around the area appeared deformed. Christ

Church sat crumbling amongst the grass and gardens that surrounded it. A few colourful roses climbed the grey walls, leading them to meet a shattered stained-glass window. It was damaged but beautiful in its destruction, the glass projecting colours onto the ground in arrangements of red, yellow, and navy-blue. Children played amongst the ruins, imagining them to be a world away from the hustle and bustle of city life. The colours were almost magical, the decaying stones resembling an Arthurian castle from centuries past.

A peculiar looking circular building sat in decrepitude not far from the gardens. It was hidden away by tight formations of tall houses that stood firmly along the road. The exterior of the building was enormous with its deteriorating columns and outer wall. Rubble laid about the ground intermixed with broken glass. The air was still, but it wouldn't be for long. As people gathered amongst the ruins, the building was brought back to life. A raised square canvas was placed in the centre, four sets of ropes linked to each corner.

As Francesca approached, she looked at the ruins, slightly unsettled.

'It's alright, Fran, you won't get hurt or anything,' Albie assured as they walked up a steep rubble bank.

'This is a very odd-looking building.'

'Do you not know what this place is?' he asked as he brushed off his dust-covered hands.

'I don't know,' she replied, looking at Elaine who was equally clueless.

'It was originally a chapel, made circular so there were no corners that the Devil could hide in,' he explained.

'But why are they boxing here? Seems unholy to be fighting in a church,' she protested.

'The church fell to tatters a long time ago. It's owned by a woman named Bella Burge, or Bella of Blackfriars as she came to be known. She was a boxing promoter in the 20s. After her husband died, the building was passed over to her. Some of the biggest fights took place here back in the day,' Kerry said as she scaled the bank, meeting their side.

'She ran it herself?' Francesca asked with a certain level of disbelief. She remembered the time she entered the boxing gym and felt utterly out of her depth. The idea of a woman running fights was a completely new concept to her and one she began to admire.

'She's quite the woman, my dad knew her.' Kerry smiled.

'She sounds fantastic.'

'Bella should be here today, first time she's been back since the Blitz blew this place to hell,' she continued.

'She's got more balls than most of the men in the East End,' Albie added with a grin.

'I don't doubt it.' Francesca laughed as they looked down at the makeshift arena.

Vast crowds gathered around the ring. It was almost as though nothing had changed. Weathered men placed their bets as excitable children clambered onto the walls to get the best view. Francesca was helped onto a large piece of charred concrete that was now occupied by the rest of the group. Charlotte munched on some boiled sweets as she sat on Harry's large drape jacket. Kerry watched as Colin and Susan approached, her eyes narrowing as she recognised the paleness of her friend's face.

'You look rough.' She observed.

'She's had an upset stomach,' Colin said.

'She can speak for herself.' Kerry helped Susan onto the

concrete slab. Francesca stared at the ground, remembering the desperate situation she had found herself in.

Isla approached the group with a satisfied smile.

'You look happy.' Francesca recognised.

'There's something about blokes beating each other to a pulp that is extremely appealing.'

'Oh, I completely agree,' Albie said.

'It's all fun and games until Jack ends up flat on his face,' Kerry mumbled.

'That's not going to happen.'

'Oh yeah, and why's that?' Colin asked as he leant against the concrete, looking up at Susan who stared blankly to the distance.

'Because Oliver gave me this,' she said, presenting his knuckle duster which made Kerry roll her eyes.

'Isn't that cheating?' Francesca questioned.

'It's not cheating, just enhancing.' She winked as she disappeared to the side of the ring.

'Don't worry, Oliver ain't the cheating type,' Kerry assured her. 'It's just 'cause Jack's technique is shit, and he'll tire himself out by the end of the first round so he needs a helping hand.'

There was a slight uneasiness to the atmosphere as the first few fights played out before them. Francesca recognised the twins from the boxing gym that made light work of their opponents. It was like watching Shakespeare, but with an unrulier crowd and more blood and guts. The audience grew louder with every punch and every drop of blood.

Jack emerged from the side of the building and leapt into the ring. Leaning into the corner, he looked at Isla who stared up at him. As she ascended the side of the squared circle, she kissed him, the crowd watching her intensely. In their distraction, she passed him the knuckle duster, the metal now coating his right fist as he put on his leather gloves.

The young man opposite looked at him with a grimace, grinding his teeth that were protected by a thick layer of rubber. His coach stood at the side of the ring, watching the two stare each other down. It was a rivalry that had gone on for decades, each side of the river fighting to prove their superiority. As Jack's gloves were fastened, he sent a devilish smile in the direction of his opponent.

A referee stood between them.

As the bell rang, the two met each other at the centre. Shouts and screams filled the air as the crowd erupted into chaos. Jack was quick to attack, forcing the young man into the ropes. Body shot after body shot caused the cracking of his opponent's ribs. There was a horrible discolouration to the abdomen, the skin turning a deep and unsightly purple.

The young man winced, trying to fight back before dropping to the ground. The referee began the count. Blood dripped from his mouth as he slumped to his side. The fight was over.

Jack sent a satisfied smirk in Isla's direction as she clapped enthusiastically. He stood upon the ropes in celebration.

The Devil hides in corners.

'Anyone would think he's got knuckles made of brass,' Lewis muttered as he met Kerry's side. He looked at the canvas that was now stained with blood. Francesca played with the hem of her dress, trying to distract herself from the surrounding commotion.

'You're late,' Kerry said irritably.

'We had some business to attend to,' he said as he met Francesca's uneasy glance. 'Won't be staying long,' he added, combing his blonde hair. Finn stood beside him, playing with his flick knife, cutting into the concrete block.

'And why's that?' Kerry asked.

'Because I already know how this is going to end.' He grinned.

Oliver entered the boxing ring, his eyes focused on his opponent. He felt the gentle breeze meet his face. The day was reaching its peak and the sunlight fell upon him, illuminating the canvas at his feet. The crowd fell silent as they prepared to face each other.

'I feel sick,' Francesca said as she watched Oliver approach the centre of the ring.

'Don't worry, if there's anyone I'd put my money on, it would be him,' Albie said confidently.

Oliver looked into his opponent's eyes. They were very similar in build and he knew he was in for a tough fight.

'You're going to be leaving here on a stretcher,' his rival hissed.

Oliver didn't reply, he just stared back at him, unflinching.

The crowd erupted as they swung at one another. Round after round went by and they both appeared bruised and bloodied, their muscles tired, their bodies exhausted. Oliver's white shorts were coated in a sticky red, although it was a mystery as to whether it was his blood or his opponent's.

'Why's this going on for so long?' Francesca asked anxiously.

'You really don't understand fighting, do you? He's tiring him out, waiting for him to make a mistake,' Kerry informed her.

'They are certainly putting on a good show,' Albie commended as he sat entranced.

'Do you know how to defend yourself?' Kerry asked as she looked down at her own bruised knuckles.

'As you said, I don't understand fighting so how can I fight,' she dismissed.

'Give me your hand.'

Francesca reluctantly extended her arm.

'Never hold your thumb when you punch otherwise it'll break,' she said, placing Francesca's delicate fingers into position. 'Now punch my palm.'

'I'm not doing that,' Francesca muttered.

'You better or I'll hit you,' she threatened. Knowing Kerry wouldn't say something she didn't mean, Francesca quickly sent a jab into her hand. 'Try it again, but twist your arm out as you punch,' she instructed. Francesca struck her again, this time with greater force. 'There you go, much better,' she said, satisfied.

The girls failed to notice a venerable woman watching them from afar, a slight smile covering her face. She turned her attention back to the fight, her fierce glance locked on the ring below.

'These lads aren't half bad, Bella,' a man at her side said.

'Young, angry and frustrated, just like they were after the first war, makes for good fighters, but bloody terrible men,' she sighed.

'I'm sure I wouldn't stand a chance in a proper fight,' Francesca said pessimistically.

'That's why you've got to be clever, your mind is just as much of a weapon as your body. Pick up anything you can, throw it, punch, scratch. Aim for the delicate bits like the nose or throat, testicles if it's a bloke,' Kerry informed.

'Why are you telling me this?'

'Because I'm sure at one point or another you might need

to defend yourself, it's part of life, especially here,' Kerry explained.

Francesca nodded as she focused her attention on the fight once more. There was blood and saliva dripping from the corners of their mouths. Oliver had a hideous black eye, however, his opponent looked considerably worse. His nose was cracked, split open like a ripe peach allowing a cascade of blood to trickle down his lips and chin. His cheeks were flushed and swollen; his eyes now fearful. Oliver ducked as he swung at him in desperation. A well place uppercut sent the young man's head back with such force it looked like it induced whiplash. His limbs stiffened as he fell to the canvas with a lifeless thud.

The arena fell silent as Oliver retreated to his corner calmly.

The referee quickly ended the contest, dropping to the floor to tend to the injured man.

'Are you ok? You seem distracted,' Oliver asked as he watched Francesca with his unusually peaceful blue eyes. His face was clean but bruised with one eye appearing horribly swollen. His knuckles were red raw and contrasted the black swallow tattoo that sat on the back of his hand.

They sat facing each other on the stairs, their legs intertwined. Both held onto a mug of hot tea that sent steam swirling around them. Even though it had been a warm summer's day, the evening presented a chill that caused Francesca to grasp her mug tightly.

'I'm ok, just contemplating life,' she answered, pondering the unfortunate scenario she had wandered into. She didn't know what to do about Susan, or what to think, but a promise was a promise and she intended on keeping it.

'Oh yeah, and what does this contemplation involve?' He grinned, looking at the girl before him who was tucked snugly under his drape jacket.

'The future.'

'Of you and me?' he asked.

'Maybe.'

'Where do you see yourself in ten years' time?'

'Happy,' Francesca said simply, taking a sip.

'Good answer.'

'What about you?'

'I can't really top happiness now can I?' Oliver said, recognising that his happiness was sitting right in front of him.

'I don't think so, but besides happiness?' Francesca asked as her fingers tapped lightly on the side of the ceramic mug.

'I want children and a family.'

'I want that, just not here,' she said.

'But this is your home, ain't it?' he questioned, confused.

'Yeah, but I want to travel and see things I haven't seen before, to make the most of any opportunities that come my way,' she said, remembering what Mr Montgomery had told her. 'I've realised now how little I know about my own city, let alone the whole world, it's exciting,' she added.

'Your head is in the clouds,' Oliver teased.

'And your head is in the ground, look at all the chances and possibilities around us,' she said enthusiastically.

'Possibilities for what?'

'I don't know, Oliver, life, there's just more to my world than the East End, I can see it,' she spoke with a twinkle in her eye.

'You're right, your world can be whatever you want it to be,' he encouraged, pulling her onto his lap.

'It's my grandma's birthday at the end of September, I'd love it if you could come,' she invited.

'Am I welcome? I'm not sure Vera would be too amused about me turning up to a family event,' Oliver asked cautiously as Francesca played with the buttons on his shirt.

'I consider you family, and I want you there,' she insisted.

'It's a date then,' he agreed. With a pause, he looked at her, running a hand across her pale cheek. 'I love you, Frankie,' he said.

Francesca nestled into his shoulder, her hands stroking the back of his neck. 'I love you too.'

As Oliver left the house, he sent a final cheeky grin in Francesca's direction before darting off into the darkness. As she closed the door, she threw herself on the sofa. With tired eyes, she looked at Houdini who sat with a beady-eyed expression. His bright feathers ruffled as he perched within his cage. He let out a few chirps as Vera made her way down the stairs. With her reading glasses on, she plonked herself down in her armchair, picking up a nearby newspaper.

'Everything alright, Fran?' she asked, acknowledging her granddaughter's drained expression.

'It's just been a long day,' she said. She sat with her legs crossed, fiddling with the hem of her dress.

'And is there anything that has made this day particularly gruelling?'

'A friend of mine is in trouble,' Francesca said.

'What kind of trouble?'

'I suppose it's best not to say.' She pondered.

'Can this trouble be solved easily?'

'I'm normally good at solving things, but this has me puzzled,' she admitted.

'Well, it sounds like you're in a pickle, tell me what's wrong, it won't be repeated,' Vera assured her as she took off her reading glasses.

'My Friend, specifically Oliver's sister, is pregnant by his best friend. It's Colin, from church,' she revealed timidly.

'Oh dear, that's not good at all.'

'They're young and out of wedlock, different faiths, and Oliver will be furious with Colin if he finds out,' she said, panicking.

'But I take it they've got one thing that'll keep them together, love. I'm speaking from experience,' Vera spoke calmly.

'But love isn't going to get them out of the situation, grandma. What can I do? I'm only one person,' she said with frustration.

'You need to support Oliver's sister, this is going to be the hardest thing she will ever face, I take it she's keeping it?' Vera asked, aware of the consequences of keeping the child.

'Yes.'

Thinking quickly, she conjured a plan. 'Then they need to get married, for them and the child's sake. They need to get far away from here and have a fresh start, a new beginning. Colin needs employment to support the family. Nobody can know where they go, not even Oliver, he'll need time to cool down. They need to figure things out for themselves without the judgement of others.'

'Where can they go?'

Vera paused. 'Scotland, Gretna Green. It's just over the border and they can get married, a new start up north until things can settle here in the south. I have a friend from my Air Force days that can find Colin work on his farm, it's not much but it'll see them through the winter.'

'Oliver's going to hate me if I don't tell him.'

'Sometimes we have to put others above ourselves in order to help ourselves. It's the right thing to do, it's the Christian thing to do,' her grandmother said.

'How do you know that it's the right thing to do?' she questioned.

'Because somebody paid me that kindness a long time ago, they helped me when I had no other options. Us women have to help each other, no matter how difficult it may be or how many it will turn against us.'

Francesca pulled herself from the sofa. 'I'll do the right thing.' With newfound confidence, she bounded up the stairs.

'I know you will,' Vera whispered as she watched her granddaughter disappear. She remained seated in her armchair, reflecting on her past, and how a simple act of kindness changed her life forever.

1913

SAVING GRACE

A YOUNG VERA whimpered her way down the alleyways of London's underbelly grasping a small child in her arms. She struggled to follow the red brick walls that were distorted due to the tears that welled in her eyes.

People within the district looked tired and broken, their eyes sunken and their expressions unwelcoming. They wore rags and had matted hair; some had no shoes upon their feet. Children played in the street with nothing but their imaginations to occupy themselves. That imagination would be ripped from them by the various factories in the area, reducing them to yet another cog in the manufacturing machine.

Stepping quickly over the dirt ridden cobbles of Bow, she gripped her daughter tightly in a protective embrace. Residing in a corner, her mind became muddled by the financial predicament she had found herself in. Vera and Albert tried to maintain the best standard of living for their daughter, giving her everything they had even though it was little.

'Can I help you?' a lady asked as she poked her head out of the window.

'I don't think anyone can,' Vera answered, her hands shaking from the cold.

'Getting in a state won't do you any favours, come on, in you come.' The lady beckoned them to the front door. She had an accent, one that Vera was yet to decipher.

'I won't intrude on you, Miss, I don't even know you,' she said, wiping her tears on her tatty sleeve.

'I insist, you'll catch a cold in this autumnal frost.' The lady welcomed them into her home. The house was large by Vera's standards. She watched the old grandfather clock that stood proudly at the end of the hall and marvelled at its gold detailing. Meeting the lounge, she looked at a variety of delicate Royal Doulton figurines that sat upon the open fireplace. These wonderful curiosities were contrasted by peeling wallpaper, proving the woman to be a new resident of the area with her beautiful objects placed in such a miserable interior. Why she chose this area of London Vera couldn't quite understand. Bringing in a hot pot of tea and a few fresh scones, the kind lady sat poised as she watched the teenage girl before her.

'My husband, Albert, had an accident in the factory he works in, and they won't give him compensation. His arm is mangled, we can't survive the winter without his wages. I work my fingers to the bone every day for that blooming factory, but my wage alone isn't enough to put food on the table.'

'I see,' she said, passing Vera a steaming cup filled with fresh tea.

The little girl sat contently on her mother's lap, growing more curious upon realising her new surroundings. With big brown eyes, she watched the fire as her mouth gaped open.

Vera found herself captivated by the woman before her. She had her hair sculpted and respectably tied back and wore pear-drop pearl earrings the caught the flickering light of the open fire. Her dress had an elegant and dignified high lace collar, indicating the expense of her clothes. Vera gulped, looking at her own bedraggled sleeves. 'There's nothing I can do, they'll take her away from us and put her in an orphanage, or worse, a workhouse if we can't feed or clothe her. I'm failing as a mother,' she cried.

The lady passed her a handkerchief that was decorated in floral embroidery. Vera rubbed her eyes quickly so her daughter didn't see her tears.

'You most certainly are not, and you are stronger than you think.'

'How can you say that so confidently, how do you know how hard it is to live in these parts?' Vera asked, conflicted by the woman's optimism, it was hard for her not to be insulted by it.

'I'm from Manchester originally, then I moved to Chelsea, then to the East End. I fancied a new start in order to gain support for my campaign. I rent this property as a gathering place for my supporters.' The lady smiled, passing the little girl a scone, her eyes lighting up upon the first bite. She watched as the child scoffed it down, leading her to devour the crumbs that laid on her grubby dress.

'What kind of campaign? Are you some sort of politician?' Vera questioned.

'In some sense, yes, but my priority is helping women who are less fortunate than me.'

'I'm not sure how you can help.'

'I may not understand your struggle, but I stand beside you, arm in arm. You will see better days, I promise you that, and your little one.' She smiled brightly. Wandering to an oak desk tucked to the side of the room, the woman fiddled with an envelope. Passing it to Vera, she sat back down.

Vera gasped as she looked at the contents of the envelope. The pound notes withheld inside were enough to see her through to the following autumn. 'I can't take this, Miss, I hardly know you and I'll never be able to pay you back,' she objected, her hands shaking even though they were being warmed by the large open fire.

'It's yours, I insist,' she said graciously, refusing to take the envelope back. 'And come to one of our rallies if you wish, we need as many women as possible,' the lady invited as she led them to the door.

'Of course, what's your name?' Vera asked, turning back to her with a grateful glance.

'Sylvia, Sylvia Pankhurst,' she introduced.

CHAPTER 13

SEPTEMBER HAD COME quickly, almost too quickly for some. The darkness flooded the East End, streetlamps guiding those late-night wanderers that were caught in the blackness. Stepping out of the shadows, Colin and Susan approached the house hand in hand. They took a deep breath, facing each other in the peaceful nothingness that was contained in the night-time air. Walking had cleared their heads, and they had decided that the inevitable was now upon them. Susan kissed Colin's hand as they entered. Feeling her palm shake within his, he understood the consequences they may face.

'Everything will be ok, I promise,' Colin said, smiling. Yet even he felt the knots develop within his stomach, and the muddle of words inside his voice box, there was no easy way to say it. 'Oli, can I have a word?' he spoke with false confidence as they entered the kitchen.

Oliver was sitting at the wooden table with a glass of

whiskey in his hand and a large bottle beside him. Colin was panicked by this as he knew the volatile nature of the liquid, yet, he found comfort in the fact that Oliver might not remember the conversation the next day.

'Yeah, what's the matter?' he asked, looking at them both. 'You look like a deer caught in headlights,' he said to his sister who lingered nervously in the doorway.

'I have something to tell you, we both do, and you're not gonna like it so hear me out,' Colin said cautiously.

'What's going on? Susan?' Oliver asked, confused by the tension that was developing between them.

'I'm, well, with Susan,' he admitted.

'With?'

'And I'm with child, Oliver,' she confessed timidly, holding Colin's arm in a nervous grip as she met his side.

'Sorry, you're going to have to repeat that,' Oliver stated as his confusion turned into a slow-burning rage.

'Susan is pregnant.'

'Are you taking the piss, Colin? My fuckin' sister,' he said fiercely.

'I know, I should have told you earlier,' Colin admitted, trying to remain calm.

'But we knew you wouldn't act reasonably,' Susan added, looking at her brother with his flushed cheeks and piercing eyes.

'And how am I supposed to act knowing that my best mate has had his way with my nineteen-year-old sister?' he thundered.

'It's not like that, I love her.'

'You only love her because she's pregnant, you hear that, Susan? He only loves you because he feels guilty for knocking you up,' Oliver shouted.

'Don't say that,' Susan said, tears drenching her face.

'I do love her, no matter what you say or do,' Colin said, gripping Susan's hand tightly.

'How dare you.' Oliver smashed the whiskey bottle into a serrated weapon. Launching at Colin, he held him to the wall with the glass pressing into his windpipe.

'Oliver, don't!' Susan screamed, trying to yank her brother back.

'Or what?'

'If you hurt him, I swear to God you will never see me again. Do you hear me?' she hissed, managing to break the two apart.

'You should be ashamed of yourself, don't think I'm gonna let you get away with this,' Oliver spat, pointing the bottle in Colin's direction. 'And you, what a disgrace you are,' he said venomously, looking at his tearful sister.

'Fuck you,' she snarled.

'Get out, you're not welcome here anymore,' Oliver said coldly, flinging the half-empty glass at the wall behind them as they left, a trail of whiskey trickling down.

The clamour of machinery echoed within the factory's interior. The women looked as though the life had been sucked from them as they too had become machinery, working in aimless loops, filtering the material in between their fingers. Their feet pressed the pedals in a rhythmic sequence while the whites of their eyes became sore and bloodshot.

Charlotte tried to the best of her ability to move unrecognised across the darkened factory floor. Some of the women watched her, but she ignored them. Reaching her sewing machine, she scanned her workspace in an almost frantic manner. Catching sight of her missing scarf under the table, she grabbed it only to cringe at the sound of Mr Talbot's voice.

'My office, Lovett, now,' he ordered.

Her hands shook as they met the metal railing, her heart beating faster with every step. Mr Talbot sat at his desk; he rubbed his fierce moustache as she stood stiffly before him.

'Did you think you'd get away with it?' he asked smugly.

'I don't know what you're talking about.'

'You know exactly what I'm talking about. Give me one reason why I shouldn't sack you,' Talbot said sternly.

She remained silent, avoiding eye contact.

'Because I'm a generous person, I'll let you make it up to me.' He smiled, leaning back in his chair, it groaned under the weight.

Recognising his intentions, her face heated and she wanted to scream, but she knew she didn't have a choice. She grinned back at him, slowly moving towards the desk. Leaning over the surface, which was cluttered with paperwork, she looked at him with her large blue eyes. The freckles on her face were illuminated as she met the dim light of an old lamp. His hands were now placed on the wood, excited as he leant forward.

Enough is enough, Lottie. A voice she'd repressed for so long broke free, and her anger erupted.

She picked up a fountain pen and struck it down into the back of his hand. With a shriek, he jolted backwards, the pen firmly gripping his flesh. Blood trickled from the incision, navigating its way down his arm.

'I'd rather quit this blasted job than go anywhere near you. I don't need your employment, I'll find my way on my own,' Charlotte said as she stood up from the desk, a triumphant grin covering her face.

'You stupid bitch, my nephew will teach you some respect, clearly the beating he gave your boyfriend wasn't enough,' he threatened.

'Let him come,' was all she said.

Francesca knocked on the door. She held her heavy handbag that had her work blazer looped between the handles, the heat beating uncomfortably down upon her. Oliver opened it and she was shocked to meet his troubled eyes. She was used to seeing him calm and in control. She grew more concerned as she followed him inside, spotting the alcohol that stained the hallway wall.

'Mum said you called, you said it was urgent?'

'I needed to see you,' Oliver said, cupping her face in his hands. 'I don't know what to do, I don't—'

'Ok, try to calm down, tell me what's happened,' she said, her brown eyes staring up at him.

'He got my sister pregnant,' he said furiously.

Francesca felt physically sick, the breath catching in her lungs causing her to wheeze a response, 'Who?'

'Colin. I'm going to kill him I swear to God, Frankie.' He let go of her face, his fists clenching at his side.

'Have you told anyone else, any of the boys?' she pried, worried her plan was set in motion too late. She and her grandmother had the perfect scheme, but it was useless if Colin was already beaten to a pulp.

'No, not yet, but when I do,' he said grimly.

Francesca laid a hand on his chest, feeling his heart race. 'One thing at a time, do you know where they are?'

'I kicked Susan out, I haven't seen her,' he said desperately.

'But what if they're in love? You can't deny them that, surely,' she said softly.

'It's disrespectful, they should have told me,' he snapped.

'Maybe they were worried about how you'd react?'

He turned to the doorway. 'I'm going to find them—'

Francesca quickly stepped in the way. 'They wouldn't have gone far. It's been a long day, deal with it tomorrow when you've got a clear head,' she suggested.

'No, I need to sort it out now.'

Francesca's mind rushed to think of a distraction. As he grabbed the doorknob, she latched onto his hand. Pulling it to her face she wrapped her mouth around two of his fingers, sucking gently. Oliver's eyes softened as he watched her, desire swirling behind his pupils.

Removing them, she kissed his hand. 'I think you're pent-up and need to relax.'

'I suppose it can wait till tomorrow.' He nodded as she guided him upstairs.

The curtains were drawn in the bedroom, making it cooler than the rest of the house. Francesca undressed herself and laid on the bed, the cold sheets meeting her shoulders.

'Take your hair down,' Oliver ordered, pulling off his belt.

She did as he said, the silky strands falling down her chest.

'Lay on your front.'

Lazily she turned onto her stomach, a grin spreading across her face. Oliver, who was now dressed in nothing but his trousers pulled her by her feet towards him, yanking her hips up so she was pressed against him. He licked her back, meeting her neck.

'You shouldn't tease me,' he said in her ear, nipping at it. 'Tell me what you want.'

'I want you,' she said.

He reached a hand in between her legs, making her arch her back. She let out a soft moan as his fingers moved against her. 'I'm not convinced,' he said.

'I want you,' she repeated, her voice desperate.

'That's more like it,' he said, undoing his trousers.

The marketplace stalls attracted nosy passers-by who were enjoying the last of the pleasant weather. The sun was starting to set, and the sky looked as though it was on fire, burning orange and yellow colours onto the streets below. Funnelling her way through the vast crowds of people, a gloomy-looking Susan tried to mask herself from sight, hurrying through the commotion. She was exhausted. Her melancholy expression contrasted her wide eyes that were frantically darting left and right, looking for an escape. She was trapped within the red brick confines of the district.

She walked the roads she grew up in, but now, she felt like a mere stranger. Trailing her movements, Francesca clutched a paper bag firmly in her hands. Meeting her friend's pace, she pulled her aside. Susan looked at her with a panicked glance as she was shielded by the shade of the nearby alleyway.

'I'm not here to hassle you, Susan, I'm just here to help,' Francesca assured her startled friend who appeared to be on the brink of tears. She swiftly handed her the bag, knowing that there wasn't time to spare.

'What's this?' she asked, puzzled as she grasped it in her shaking hands.

'Open it,' Francesca insisted.

'That's a lot of money,' Susan said in awe, a stack of pound notes filling the bag.

'And it's yours, for a new start, for all of you,' she explained.

'I can't take this from you, this must be all your wages,' Susan said, distressed by the gesture.

'It doesn't matter how much it is, there is no room for debate.'

'And what's this?' she asked, reaching into the bag, grasping a little white slip of paper.

'All the details for your new life. The note has the contact information of a man just over the Scottish border. He's a friend of my grandma, a veteran who now owns a farm in the countryside near Dumfries. He can give Colin work and put you up over winter until you can afford a place of your own. Nobody will find you there, you'll be safe.'

'You've thought this through.' She studied the slip, the golden ticket for a way out.

'It was my grandma's idea. She found herself in a similar situation when she was young. There is a place called Gretna Green where you can get married in secret.'

'I'll never be able to repay you for this,' she said gratefully.

'There's no need for repayment, just go today, both of you before the last train leaves, promise me you will,' she fretted.

'We will, what will you tell Oliver?' Susan asked as she gripped the bag tightly to her chest.

'I won't,' she gulped.

'I'm scared, Fran, this place is all I've ever known,' Susan said.

'But think of all the things you are going to know, what you will know when you get away from here,' she said as she hugged her snivelling friend tightly.

'I'm abandoning my brother,' she cried into Francesca's shoulder.

'Don't worry about Oliver. Your priority is that baby. Now go, you need to find Colin,' she said as she wiped the tears from her friend's eyes.

'Thank you,' Susan said as she returned to the bustling street.

They hoped for their conversation to remain a secret, but they failed to recognise the two rats that were scheming in the alleyway. The boys retreated out the other side of the cobblestone maze, grinning like Cheshire cats.

'Tut-tut, somebody's in a lot of trouble,' Lewis said.

'Should we tell Oliver before they leave?' Finn asked as he looked at his conniving friend.

'No, let them go, it'll only make the situation worse for Fran,' he said sadistically.

As the sun fell to the demands of the night sky, Francesca sat on Albie's back porch watching the stars. Her stomach twisted and turned as her head fought a back-and-forth battle over her actions. Albie passed her a hot chocolate that had an obnoxious amount of whipped cream and multi-coloured sprinkles. She sent him an amused glance as she sipped his creation.

'Can you hear it?' Albie questioned.

'What?'

'Silence, ain't it beautiful?' He smiled, staring at the sky.

'You know you find beauty in the strangest things.' She laughed.

'It's because they are the things that are most overlooked. So, when you find the beauty in them, they can be the most spectacular thing,' he explained. His eyes glistened as he watched the full moon.

'You're a wise man, you know that?'

'Most people beg to differ. They call me strange or different,' Albie dismissed. 'I don't tell many people this, but sometimes I wish I could fit in, you know, to be normal. The way I look, the people I love, even my artwork, I'm constantly scrutinised,' he admitted.

'But what even is normal? If you think about it, no one person is the same, so I don't know why people make a fuss about others who don't resemble their own difference. You are who you are, and you should be proud of that,' she said confidently, taking another sip from her mug.

'You really think so, poppet?'

'Yes, I think so, Albie.'

He looked at her with amusement as a layer of cream coated her top lip. 'You should be proud of yourself.'

'Me? I'm not sure why,' she said.

'You've put up with Oliver, which is no mean feat, and you've won over his friends, which can be considered even more of a challenge.' Albie recognised.

'I haven't won over everyone,' she sighed.

Albie fiddled with his ginger hair. 'If you're referring to Tweedledum and Tweedledee, I wouldn't worry. Lewis has the emotional intelligence of that comb he carries about, and Finn's just a berk. They are the only people who have ever successfully introduced anyone to the group, and let's face it, Kerry wouldn't take no for an answer.'

Francesca, tickled by Albie's comparisons, sat giggling. 'I'm hardly like Kerry.'

'But you've made your mark in your own way, Oliver has somewhat mellowed out, Lottie has someone else to pester other than Harry, Isla feels a little less misunderstood, and Susan—'

'What about Susan?' she asked quickly, too quickly as Albie sensed the panic in her voice, causing him to raise an eyebrow.

'Is somethin' bothering you?'

'Oh, no, I'm just tired, I've had a long day,' she said, staring into the mug.

'I can tell, you've had cream covering your top lip for the past five minutes.'

'Why didn't you tell me!' she exclaimed, turning bright red as he passed her a handkerchief.

'I thought it suited you.' He grinned.

Colin carried their bags, looking behind to make sure Susan was keeping pace. As they bundled onto the carriage, he pushed their minimal items into the compartments above their seats. They had little baggage due to Susan's inability to return home and collect her belongings, alongside Colin's fear of facing his father, which had resulted in a carefully crafted letter left in the doorway. They were now entirely on their own. Susan gripped her mother's rose-shaped brooch tightly. She watched with a glossy gaze as the train left the dark station, her eyes scanning what she could to memorise the East End. As a tear fell from her eye, Colin held her hand. Not a word was uttered between them, yet they knew exactly what each other was thinking; how leaving could be considered running away, but they saw it as running towards a brighter future.

As the Priest returned home, he called for his son but there was no response. Reading the letter that sat strategically in the doorway, he took in every word. With a silent sorrow, he gripped the paper close to his chest. Dragging himself up the stairs, he passed a picture of his late love holding their infant son in her arms. He looked at her image with distress, and she looked back at him with a smile.

CHAPTER 14

ELAINE WATCHED HER friend as she shuffled nervously along the wooden pew. Francesca always felt a little uncomfortable at church, but today she appeared extremely anxious. Her hands fidgeted in her lap and she was biting her bottom lip. The Priest was behaving strangely too. He appeared stern and cold, more than usual with his icy glance passing over his congregation. He began the sermon with a forceful tone, his voice unrelenting. Elaine followed the Bible as he read a lengthy passage from Corinthians. It spoke of fornication and sexual sins against the body. A few people nodded in agreement, as usual, she thought it was a load of rubbish. Vera seemed to think so too, her eyes despairing as she peered at the Priest.

Elaine looked at Francesca again, her gaze remaining firmly on the stone floor. As the service finished, she pulled her behind a pillar. 'What's bothering you, Fran? You look dead behind the eyes.'

'I've done something, Elaine, and I feel really guilty,' Francesca replied, glancing at the Priest as he disappeared behind the curtain.

'Well, what is it?'

'I was round Susan's a while ago and she told me that she was pregnant.'

'No, how?' Elaine exclaimed.

'Nobody can know,' Francesca uttered, panicking. 'But worst of all it's with Colin, that's why the Priest looks so miserable.'

'I'm very confused. Why do you feel guilty?' Elaine questioned, scanning the inside of the church.

'Because I helped them get away to Scotland, it was grandma's idea. You know how violent Oliver and the others can be. They would have mauled Colin to pieces,' she fretted.

'How exactly did you help them get to bloody Scotland?'

'I gave them my combined wages,' Francesca explained.

Elaine grabbed her hands. 'You did the right thing.'

'You think it was the right thing to do?'

'I think so. You helped them out of a real sticky situation. But now you've put yourself smack bang in the middle of it.' She recognised.

'I know.'

'Does Oliver know what you've done?'

'No, he'll go mental,' she said, dreading the thought of him finding out.

'There's no way he'll know you've helped them, so try not to worry,' Elaine assured her with a smile.

As the church cleared, Vera trailed her way up to the main altar.

The Priest appeared from behind the curtain, standing with crossed arms. He was holding his arms so tightly that his fingers were going white, and the fabric crinkled under his grip.

Vera positioned herself at his side. 'That was quite the performance.'

'Performance?' His sharp glance latched onto her, but she simply smiled.

'Well, you surely can't believe what you were saying.'

'I've always made it clear, that sort of behaviour is unacceptable.' It took every ounce of energy to maintain his composure as the old lady deciphered him.

'But today seemed particularly forceful, you might frighten the young ones spouting such nonsense,' Vera said.

'They need to hear it, so they don't make mistakes.'

She stifled a laugh. 'Mistakes are important, and if I remember correctly, you committed the exact act that you are condemning. You're a man of God, Joseph, how can you claim to be when you don't even forgive yourself.' She laid a hand on his shoulder before leaving him to his thoughts.

Monday morning was chilly and Jack pulled at his leather jacket. Whitechapel Road was overflowing with traffic, and the rumble of the Underground could be felt pulsing under his feet.

'Good morning, Jack,' Lewis said with a grin. He was walking along the pavement with Finn who had a trail of smoke following him, a cigarette cemented firmly between two fingers.

'Mornin' boys,' he said.

'You on your way to work?'

'Yes, another day of cutting up animals and taking orders from my dad who I can never bloody please. So, where are both of you off to at such an early hour?' he asked.

'We're actually on our way to Oliver's,' he explained.

'Oh yeah, and why's that?'

'Haven't you heard?' Finn questioned, rolling the cigarette between his fingertips.

'No, I haven't, go on, tell me then,' he said impatiently.

'Susan's pregnant.'

'Piss right off, by who? I bet Oliver has already killed the bastard.'

'Colin,' Lewis revealed.

'Where is he now?' he asked with balled fists, his eyes narrowed.

'Gone,' Finn said, looking at Lewis.

'It's like they've vanished into thin air,' Lewis sighed.

'Well, he better not fuckin' appear in these parts again, Oliver will have his head, or I certainly will,' he said grimly.

'I don't doubt it, anyway, we best be on our way. We're going to make sure he's ok,' Lewis said, continuing along the pavement.

Francesca gathered her belongings together in a fluster. Vera glanced over her daily newspaper, studying her granddaughter through strong lenses as she bolted out of the door. Houdini sat in his cage, chirping the minutes by as Stephanie cleaned the kitchen worktop.

'That girl is impossible to get up in the morning,' Vera tutted as she sipped her tea, her gaze fixed back on the black and white text.

'Sounds like somebody I know.' Stephanie smiled.

'I hope you're not referring to me, dear, in the Air Force

they never allowed us to sleep in.' She reminisced, flicking through the pages.

'Is that why you're making up for it now? You may not be in bed, but you sure do like a good nap in that chair.' Stephanie smirked only to be met with Vera's unimpressed glance.

Oliver's eyes were aflame. Lewis and Finn sat before him with meddling expressions. The kitchen was still, and the light crept in through the half-open curtains.

'So, what is it?' Oliver asked numbly, his sleep-deprived brain finding trouble functioning.

'We have some information that you might find... interesting,' Lewis spoke slowly, savouring every word.

'Your sister and Colin have left London,' Finn said calmly, waiting for Oliver's blood to boil like a scientist watching over a chemical experiment.

'And how do you know this?' Oliver asked, his head in his hands.

'Because we saw someone help them get the last train out of the city,' Lewis said.

'Oh yeah, and who would be bloody stupid enough to help them?' he questioned, growing angry at the thought.

'Your Frankie, that's who. We didn't hear all of the conversation, so it's probably best that you ask her yourself where she's sent them,' Lewis informed him.

'You're lying.'

'We saw it as clear as day,' Finn confirmed.

'We just thought you should know that your girlfriend went behind your back. What are friends for if we can't tell each other when we're being lied to,' Lewis spoke with false sympathy.

Oliver gripped his knuckles tightly; he sat silently, his face depicting a thousand phrases.

As the clock ticked its way towards mid-day, Francesca typed quickly. A mountain of paperwork sat before her in a messy pile. Mr Montgomery rushed into the office, red-faced, staring in her direction.

'Is something wrong, Sir?' she gulped.

'Fran, you have made a monumental fuck up,' he yelled.

'I-I'm not sure what you're referring to,' she stuttered, taken aback by his tone.

'You sent out the wrong paperwork to some very important people. And you've cost this bank a lot of money,' he said furiously, slamming the wodge of paper down in front of her.

'It was an accident,' she panicked.

'If it were deliberate, the outcome would still be the same. So why should I care if it was an accident?'

'It won't happen again,' she said timidly, trying to hold back tears.

'You're damn right it won't. You've been very distracted lately and it's starting to get on my nerves. I suggest you get your act together if you want to remain in my employment,' Mr Montgomery warned as he left Francesca sat in a startled state behind her desk. 'Go for lunch and sort yourself out,' he dismissed.

Truthfully, Francesca was distracted, more so conflicted by her actions and the possible harm they could cause. The only thing that was keeping her from guilt was the fact that Oliver didn't know it was her that sent his sister away.

As she wandered onto the street, she took a deep breath. Catching sight of Oliver, her mood lifted ever so slightly. With a smile, she walked towards him, yet her heart sunk as she recognised his unfriendly expression.

'Oliver, what are you doing here?' she asked, trying to maintain a cheerful demeanour even though she could tell that something was drastically wrong.

'How about we take a walk,' Oliver suggested.

As they met the side of the River Thames, Francesca looked at him, concerned. His face was flushed, and his eyes were unkind. Nobody was around and she wrung her hands nervously.

Did he know?

The Tower of London stood behind them; the waves could be heard, colliding with the metal of Traitors' Gate below.

'Where's my sister?' he asked, trying to contain his temper.

Her stomach dropped. 'I don't know.'

'Don't lie to me.' Oliver could barely look at her, so he stared at the river.

'I'm not lying,' she pleaded. He had never spoken to her in such a cold manner. It put her on edge, and she flinched at the slightest sound.

'They saw you.'

'Who?'

'Lewis and Finn. They saw you with my sister. I know you have something to do with her and Colin's sudden relocation.'

'It's for their own good,' she admitted, sitting herself down on an old wooden bench.

'What is? Taking her away from me?' Oliver exploded.

'I didn't take her anywhere, I only gave her a choice,' Francesca replied. She sat frozen, the words lodging in her throat.

'I'm going to ask you one more time, where is she?'

'I can't tell you,' she said, her heart pounding.

Oliver sent the palm of his hand into her face with such force that her head snapped sideways into the wooden bench at her back. Wincing with pain, she held her cheek as tears cascaded from her eyes.

'Tell me,' he demanded.

'I would be breaking a promise if I told,' she whimpered as the tender skin bit back at the touch.

'A promise to who? My sister? Who are you to think you can get involved in this? You're not family, Francesca, you never will be,' he snarled as he left her sobbing on the bench.

Hurrying back into the bank, she pushed her way through the large entryway with its high marble ceiling. Businessmen watched her as she quickened her pace, their judging glances making her feel even more embarrassed. She stood in the ladies' toilet looking into the mirror, the developing bruise tarnishing her pale skin. As her watery gaze fixed on her blurry reflection, a copper silhouette wandered up behind her.

'Fran, what happened?' Penny asked, meeting her side.

'I've just had a really bad day,' she answered as she met Penny's warm embrace.

Francesca sat back at her desk, her head hung with shame.

'Sorted yourself out?' Mr Montgomery asked as he walked past, oblivious to her discomfort. He sat behind his large oak desk. Upon hearing no response, he looked at her, acknowledging the bruise on her cheek and the tears that she used her blazer sleeve to conceal.

'Who did that to you? Was it your boyfriend?' he asked, a

sudden gentleness consuming his voice. Nodding in response, Francesca's shaking hands attempted to set up the typewriter. 'No man hits the woman he loves,' Mr Montgomery added softly.

'It was my fault, I did something I shouldn't have,' she attempted to explain.

'No situation gives a man the right to do that, Fran. Take the afternoon off, Penny can sort out the rest of the paperwork.'

Morpeth Street was busy with women rushing each and every way. They were sorting out the various washing lines that trailed the road, their hands rough from the labour of washing fabrics by hand. They watched Isla with displeasure as she walked along the pavement, she was an entirely new type of women. Her hands looked as though they had never seen a day's work, and her fingernails were coated in pristine pink nail varnish. Her blouse and tight denim jeans hugged her body while her auburn hair gently flowed with the cool breeze. Knocking on the door she played with her hair, sending a few unfazed glances at the women who judged her from afar. Kerry answered the door and welcomed her into the front room.

'Have you heard?' Isla asked as she perched herself on the sofa.

'What?'

'Colin got Susan pregnant,' she revealed.

'I bloody knew it,' Kerry said as she paced.

'You did?'

'She's been acting odd for quite a while, and him for that matter.'

'Why didn't you say anything?'

'I asked her what was wrong, and she just wouldn't tell me. I was hoping she wouldn't be that stupid. Colin is going to be in a world of trouble now,' she muttered.

'Well, they've left.'

'What do you mean they've left?' she questioned sharply.

'I don't know. Jack said they've done a runner to God knows where,' Isla explained.

'I think I'd do the same if I were in their position. You know what Oliver's like when he's angry,' Kerry sighed.

'Charley! Nice of you to pop by for a change,' Elaine said sarcastically as her brother entered the house.

'You cheeky little git, you know I'm working extra shifts. You could always visit,' he said, kicking off his thick boots.

'Down those grimy docks, I don't think so,' she said as she filled the kettle with water.

He eagerly leant across the kitchen worktop. 'Come on then, tell me the gossip.'

'Well, Colin Murphy done a runner with Susan Thomas. The word is that she's pregnant,' she informed him, reaching for two mugs.

'Bloody hell,' he said under his breath.

'The Priest hasn't been himself, he's like a ghost that sits there at the main altar, and not even the holy spirit could bring him back to life.'

'So, how did they get away, this is that Oliver's sister?' he asked, watching his little sibling, her curls bouncing as she darted around the kitchen.

Passing him a steaming mug, she told him what she knew. 'Yes, and I'll let you in on a secret, Fran helped them get away on the train to Scotland, gave up all her wages. Vera told her it was the right thing to do. You can't tell anyone, Charley, especially the Priest. Fran said it would do more harm than good.'

'I can see her point. But if she is hiding this from Oliver, he's not going to be happy when he finds out,' he said uneasily.

'He wouldn't hurt her, he loves her,' Elaine said.

'I wouldn't put it past him. I better go and check on her, just to make sure she's ok,' he said, unnerved.

'You can't tell her that you know, it's supposed to be a secret! And mum's gonna be home in a minute, I think we've got corned beef again for dinner.' Elaine scrunched her nose in protest as she stirred her tea.

'I'll be discreet about it. And tell mum I'll be back in a jiffy,' Charley said, pulling on his heavy boots once more.

In a trance, Francesca continued to rotate the wooden spoon. She watched the butter, flour, eggs and sugar combine into a thick batter. Attempting to hold back tears, she pulled her sleeve to her eyes, absorbing the salty droplets. Her hair was tied up, and the bruise was fully visible on her delicate skin. She lied to her mother and grandmother, telling them she had a fall at work, hence the reason she was sent home early. It would be stupid to imagine that Vera believed this lie. She sat and watched her granddaughter miserably stir her birthday cake. Francesca forced a smile every time she made eye contact, but this was not enough to deceive her. She felt guilty for lying, but most of all she felt angry for Oliver raising a hand to her. As Stephanie rushed about the kitchen in her floral pinnie, she grabbed a metal baking tray.

'You can lick the spoon after we're done? You always liked

doing that when you were little,' she encouraged whilst pouring the mixture into the tray.

'Maybe another time,' Francesca said, clearly in a state of melancholy as to deny the yellow goodness in front of her.

As the doorbell rang, Vera pulled herself from her armchair. Answering it, she met a concerned-looking Charley who peered over her short frame. Recognising the bruise on Francesca's cheek, his eyes sharpened. He looked down at Vera who met his glance with equal fury. They both knew that the black and blue colours upon her were no happy accident.

'May I have a chat?' he asked.

Guiding him upstairs, Francesca sat stiffly, gripping her champagne pink pillow. Charley sat opposite her on her silver vanity stool.

'Do you want to tell me what happened there?'

'I fell.'

'What really happened?' he asked again.

'He was cross.'

'About his sister?'

'I knew Elaine would tell you, I needed to tell somebody.'

'He made a big mistake doing that to you,' he said sharply, lifting her chin so he could examine her face.

'He didn't mean it,' she said in denial.

'If he didn't mean it, he wouldn't have done it in the first place,' he thundered.

'Please don't get involved, Charley. I know you made a promise to my brother to protect me, but please don't,' she said, beginning to cry.

'I can't let him get away with this. More importantly, you can't let him get away with this. We can go down to the police station,' he continued, determined not to let justice slip from her hands.

'I don't want to,' she said, burying her head in her pillow.

'Let me talk to him,' he persisted.

'We both know that won't end well.'

'I'll be civil,' he said, looking into her bloodshot eyes.

'Please leave it, nobody needs to get involved.'

Charley paused, realising he was getting nowhere. 'If that's what you want, I'll leave it. But if you change your mind, you know where to find me,' he said as she hugged him tightly. He ran his hands through her hair as she wept into his shoulder. It broke his heart to feel her shake in his arms. 'It's ok, Fran, you have every right to feel upset. You've done nothing wrong and I'm so proud of you for standing up for what you believe in and helping someone in need.' The words wouldn't take the pain away, but her crying calmed. She fell asleep in his arms and he gently placed her in her bed. Charley stroked her head until her face relaxed completely, and her mind tumbled into a dream. He sat by her side for two hours, making sure she felt safe. Making sure she felt loved.

The darkness flooded into the gym through the broad Victorian windows. It was quiet with only a few men left. Some were sweeping the floor, while others sat unwrapping their hands. The canvas at the centre of the room was still, the moonlight shining upon it.

'Call it a day, Oli, you're gonna hurt yourself,' a coach called out as he locked up the changing room.

Oliver took no notice as he continued to beat the bag relentlessly. Jack watched him, troubled by his unhinged nature. Normally poised and calculated he favoured technique over brute strength, but at that moment, he appeared wild and erratic.

'I know it's normally the other way around, but do you want to talk about it?' he asked as he sat on a stool in the corner, his exposed shoulders meeting the cold brickwork.

'No, I don't want to bloody talk about it,' he snarled, continuing his onslaught.

'Is this about Susan and Colin? Lewis and Finn told me about it,' Jack pressed.

'I bet they didn't tell you about Fran. She helped Susan and Colin get away to God knows where,' he said. Stopping his assault, he turned to him.

'Why would she do that?'

'I don't know. I don't understand how she could lie to me, how Colin and Susan could lie to me,' he hissed. His cheeks were crimson, a mixture of infuriation and exhaustion.

'He's a little sod for keeping that from you, he's lucky he made it out of London,' he said, cracking his knuckles. 'As for Fran, I don't know what to suggest.'

Albie sauntered into the gym, his ginger hair proving a bright contrast to the bland, decrepit walls. 'I thought you two would be here,' he said.

'Well, you found us,' Jack muttered.

'What's all this gossip then, are they really gone? Isla told me roughly what happened,' he asked nosily.

'Yes, and it was Fran who helped them get away,' Oliver stated.

'How do you know that?'

'Because I fuckin' asked her, that's how.'

Albie paused, recognising Oliver's hostility. 'You didn't do anything to her, did you?' he questioned.

'What if I did?' he sneered, throwing his bloody hand wraps

to the ground.

'You hit her, didn't you?' he said, his eyes wide with disgust.

Jack watched uncomfortably from the corner. For once he didn't have a snarky remark or joke to crack.

'I needed to know what happened,' he justified.

'That gives you no right to hit her, fuck, Oli, what possessed you to do such a thing?'

'I'm not in the mood for a lecture right now, Albie,' he spat, grabbing his gym bag from the ground.

'I want no part of this or anything to do with you, you should be ashamed of yourself,' he said angrily, leaving the two of them.

The weekend was a welcome break. It was filled with the festivities of Vera's Birthday. The house had been decorated with makeshift banners and a perfectly iced sponge cake sat at the centre of the buffet table. Stephanie fussed over the tablecloth, making sure it was strategically aligned. Houdini had been placed upstairs, yet his defiant tweets could be heard from above.

Pulling on a peach-coloured satin dress that was purchased especially for the occasion, Francesca couldn't help but feel overly formal in the glamorous garment. It was not as if she was going anywhere, and the cinched-in waist and billowing mid-calf skirt made her feel more akin to a Christian Dior model than a working-class girl from Mile End. However, her mother had insisted and was kind enough to buy it for her, so she knew she had to wear it despite feeling uncomfortable. Combing her long hair, she fiddled nervously with the ends. Vera helped her cover up the bruise on her cheek with some makeup, yet it was still slightly visible.

Isla was busy preparing the little table for dinner, placing cutlery down as Jack stirred the gravy. The small flat was consumed by the smell of sausages and boiled cabbage. As Isla served a helping of mashed potato onto each plate, she grinned as Jack hummed to himself.

'Does that help get the lumps out?' she teased.

'It does, I serenade the gravy into submission.' He smirked.

Isla popped the cabbage and sausages onto the plates. 'You make it sound like you're fighting it.' She laughed. 'Speaking of fighting, how was training the other day?'

'It was fine. I didn't work myself too hard, I don't want to cause an injury. Oliver on the other hand—'

'What about Oliver?' she asked quickly.

'He just went a bit mental I suppose, things have turned sour between him and Fran,' he said, pouring the gravy on.

'What happened? They've been going pretty strong and make such a lovely pair,' she asked, shocked.

'Well, I think they're done for good this time,' Jack said vaguely, taking the plates to the table.

'What gave you that impression?'

He shoved a forkful of mash into his mouth. 'I just get the feeling that they weren't right for each other. I think Oliver hit breaking point with the Susan and Colin situation. From what I heard, Fran helped them both leave London. It didn't help that Albie came and pissed him off more than he already was.'

'How did he piss him off?'

'Albie was just Albie, he took Fran's side, 'cause of course he would.' He rolled his eyes, making Isla stare.

'What's that supposed to mean?'

'He's very, never mind, he just has no loyalty to me or Oliver, or any of the boys.'

'Well, you haven't exactly been kind to him over the years,' she said defensively.

'He's just odd.'

Isla glared at him. 'Don't be an arse. Albie has a good heart, he was there for me—'

'What, when you cheated on Oliver?' he said snidely.

'There's no need to bring that up.'

'Why? It's the truth, ain't it? When you buggered it up, Albie was the only forgiving one, 'people make mistakes', it was one hell of a mistake, Isla.'

'You know it's moments like this that make me question my love for you.' She left the room in tears.

Oliver sat at the kitchen table, tapping his fingers against a glass that contained a hefty amount of brandy. As Lewis helped himself to the last of it, he noticed the whiskey stains that marked the wall.

'That was a waste,' he muttered.

Finn played with his flick knife. The night was dark, and the kitchen sat dimly lit by the dying lightbulb hanging from the ceiling.

'I've made a mistake,' Oliver said suddenly.

'How?' Lewis asked as he took a sip from his glass.

'I hurt her.'

'And she hurt you. We warned you about her,' he spoke carefully.

'I shouldn't have reacted the way I did, Albie came to the

gym and made me see sense, I need to speak to her.' Oliver pushed the drink away.

'You're not thinking straight,' Lewis said, watching him.

'I don't know what to think.'

'You know what would help take your mind off things?' he said, looking at Finn with a devious smile.

'What?' Oliver asked, his head hung low.

'Finn, why don't you give Isla a ring.'

The party reached the height of its celebrations. Francesca and Elaine sat at the top of the stairs, avoiding the antics below. The large buffet hosted a selection of home-made food, including her mother's attempt at canapés comprising of spam, olives and anchovies. Feasting on some scotch eggs, Elaine watched her sombre friend whose eyes remained fixed on the door.

'He's not coming, Fran,' she said, her face stuffed with food.

'I know, but he agreed to come to grandma's birthday.' She frowned.

'Has he apologised for that?' Elaine asked, recognising the bruise that tarnished her friend's delicate skin.

'No.'

'You can do better than that, look at what he did to you. You deserve an apology,' she said.

'You're right, I do deserve an apology,' Francesca agreed.

'Well then, we'll go over there now, he's only a short distance away,' she said, shovelling more food into her mouth.

'Right now?' she questioned reluctantly.

'Yes, right now. You've already been hospitable to everyone. You even survived a conversation with Judy and her Italian fella,' Elaine said.

'Ok, I'll be as quick as possible,' she agreed.

'I'm coming with you.'

'No, I need to speak to him on my own, and I need you to cover for me until I get back.'

Elaine gulped but nodded. 'Be careful.'

Leaving the house, Francesca shuddered as she was met by the pending autumnal chill. With folded arms, she navigated her way down Coborn Road, the rows of houses watching her as she hurried past them.

'You wanted to see me?' Isla lingered in the doorway. Oliver sat at the end of the bed silently as she approached. Straddling his lap, she unfastened her hair. Popping the buttons of her blouse, she pulled his hands to her hips. She attempted to kiss him but was met with his cheek. His eyes were no longer passionate like she remembered, but glazed over in frozen concentration.

'You love her, don't you?'

'She'll never love me after what I've done, but I do love her,' he admitted.

Isla looked at him guiltily. 'I never should have come here.' She pulled herself from his grasp, fastening the buttons on her blouse.

Walking down Vallance Road, her mind raced. Her thoughts were scrambled, and she felt defeated. Meeting the doorstep, Francesca took a deep breath. She still didn't know what she was going to say. Strangely, the door was unlocked, allowing her to walk into the hallway.

'Well, look what we've got here, this is a nice surprise,'

Lewis said as she entered the kitchen. He had a lit cigarette between his lips.

Francesca went rigid, taken back by their presence at such a late hour. 'Where's Oliver?' she asked.

Finn was perched on the kitchen worktop. 'He's a little preoccupied with Isla, givin' him a go I imagine,' he answered.

'That's not true.'

Lewis circled her, exhaling the digested smoke in her face. 'You wanna bet sweetheart, we may be many things, but we're not liars. Pretty dress by the way, what is it? Satin?' he said off-topic, getting a little too close for comfort. Tossing the cigarette into the sink, he took pleasure in tormenting her.

'I don't believe you,' she said firmly.

'Looks like satin to me.' Finn grinned, hopping down from the worktop. Francesca took a step back. He stood in the doorway, lending a sinister glance to Lewis.

'Let me leave,' she demanded.

Finn stared down at her. 'Now why would we do that?'

'You have caused quite the disruption to our nice little group,' Lewis said. He positioned himself behind her, so she was sandwiched between them.

'Yeah, it has instilled a fair bit of animosity,' his friend added. 'But forgive and forget, I guess,' he said insincerely as he moved to let her pass.

Francesca walked through with unease.

Lewis's hand gripped her wrist tightly, pulling her backwards so fast that she didn't have time to react. Pushing her up against the kitchen cabinet she felt her back slam against the granite worktop, bone meeting stone. One of his hands sat firmly over her mouth, while the other clenched her now bruising wrist. Her other arm was free and frantically searched the surface behind her.

Bringing his lips to her ear, a sharp smile developed on his face. 'Come on, Fran, you know Oliver didn't really want you, I did try to warn you, I told you you'd get hurt but you just didn't listen. You know, I could have shown you a real fuckin' good time if you weren't so uptight.'

Francesca's fearful eyes cascaded tears down her face, mascara staining her cheeks. She tried to scream, but his fingers were pressed hard against her lips.

The wood of a hefty rolling pin met her palm. Swinging it quickly, it clipped Lewis's nose, breaking instantly into a distorted position. He released her as blood seeped from his face, his body dropping to the floor in shock. Francesca threw down the rolling pin and bolted for the door. Finn grabbed a handful of her hair, yanking her to the ground. She shrieked with pain. The sound of her screams vibrated the walls, and Isla and Oliver looked at one another with dread.

Reaching for the flick knife in his pocket, Finn held her tight, his balled fist ripping her scalp. The pain was like nothing she had ever experienced, and all she could do was beg for him to stop.

'Please, you're hurting me,' she said, looking up at him.

'Teach that bitch some manners,' Lewis hissed, his face busted.

Finn held the blade to her cheek, the cold metal pressing into her flushed, tear-stained skin.

'What the hell are you doing!' Isla interrupted as they burst into the room.

Meeting eyes with Francesca who was crying uncontrollably, Oliver scowled. Realising he wanted no part in a fight with him, Finn released his grip, allowing Francesca to run into the hallway and out the front door.

'This shirt is worth a lot of money,' Lewis spat as he gripped his gushing nose. Red stains were developing on the white fabric in bloody streaks.

Finn quickly hid the knife from view. 'Come on, Oli, we were just having a bit of fun, remember she lied to you—'

A metal-clad fist met his stomach and he leant over the kitchen table in agony. Isla glared at them as she hurried after Francesca.

Oliver pointed as he clutched his knuckle duster. 'If you ever touch her again—'

'You're gonna what?' Lewis snarled.

'I will kill you both,' he threatened.

Running out of the house, Oliver's manner turned soft and gentle. Ordering Isla to stay back, he went after Francesca alone.

'Leave me, Oliver,' she cried, cradling her injured wrist as she hurried along the pavement. A few neighbours turned on their lights to the commotion. With nosy intentions, they stared through the netting that lined their windows.

'I'm sorry, Frankie, please wait, whatever they did I'll make them pay for it,' he pleaded.

'I don't give a toss about them, it's you I'm upset about. You're only sorry because you got caught, I can't believe you slept with her,' Francesca shouted at him, her face marked with watery black streaks.

'I didn't sleep with her,' Oliver denied.

'Don't lie, what was she doing upstairs with you? You hit me and made me feel terrible, and I was the one who felt guilty for it. How dare you humiliate me like that, getting with her and letting those two hurt me,' she spoke, her voice breaking with every word.

'Please, just let me explain,' he insisted.

'No, I'm done with you,' she said, running away from him.

The sunrays pierced through the heavy clouds. Kerry looked out the window, observing the children who were running across the cobbles. Lewis sat behind her, a smug smile covering his face.

'You shouldn't have tried your luck with her. You knew very well that she was taken,' Kerry said. Grabbing an apple from the fruit bowl, she tossed it from one hand to the other.

'It's a shame really, would have been fun.' Lewis smirked, quickly wincing at the pain of his broken nose.

'Well, I'm glad she took my advice and made you pay for it. I didn't know she was your type,' Kerry pressed as she guided a blade around the apple's flesh.

'Feminine?' he taunted.

'I was going to say innocent,' she said bluntly as the blade cut into the apple, a little deeper than expected.

'I thought it would make a change,' Lewis teased.

'If you wanted innocent, you should have said so. We both know you can't handle me when I'm sinning,' Kerry muttered as she took a bite.

'You don't think I can handle you?' he questioned.

'I'm the only woman in this world that you can't handle,' she said firmly, gripping the apple. 'Don't try anything like that again.'

'Don't tell me you're actually fond of her,' he uttered in surprise.

'Yes, I am, and if you go near her again, I'll make your bollocks into a pair of earrings,' she warned as she tossed the mutilated apple into his lap.

Oliver slumped against the wall. In misery, his hands fumbled through a pile of photographs. He missed his sister. He missed Francesca. He felt the horseshoe necklace that was gifted to him, manipulating the silver pendant between his fingers. He sat in the hallway, avoiding the sunlight that hurt his inflamed blue eyes. Bloodshot and sore, he looked down at the photographs of his sister, tears dropping onto the black and white pictures. In one image she hugged him tightly, almost as though she would never let him go.

1951

A DISTANT MEMORY

SOUTH BANK WAS completely transformed. The area was no longer consumed by charred concrete and mangled metal. Now, a giant dome sat at the centre of the area welcoming people back to the previously abandoned site. It was a symbol of prosperity, with exhibitions surrounding discovery and innovation filling the dome's interior. It allowed the exploration of magical worlds, from distant space to the bottom of the ocean. Pickled creatures sat in jars for people to gawp at in astonishment while large model planets hung from the ceiling. One display contained a taxidermy polar bear that bared its teeth at passing children. They hid behind the legs of their parents as the creature looked down at them. A twelve-ton steam engine sat prominently within the exhibition. It had realistic smoke that puffed into the air. People stared at it in wonder, its tracks embedded in a layer of fake snow.

'Five-shilling entry, what a bloody liberty,' Oliver

grumbled.

'Oh, come on, when will we be able to experience something like this again?' Susan said, a wide smile covering her face.

'What a load of stuffed and pickled animals? I could think of better things,' he said, unimpressed as he looked at the hands of his pocket watch.

'It does look a bit strange,' Susan somewhat agreed, looking at the little creatures who had been bent and broken behind the glass.

'They could have used the money they spent on all this to rebuild half the homes in the East End. They only care about making South Bank look good for the tourists,' he huffed.

'What does it matter what the government does with its money, the East End will always be forgotten. The main thing is that we've got each other,' Susan declared.

'Yeah, and that will never change.' He grinned, looking down at her.

A woman approached them, a thick black box cemented in her grasp. 'Do you want ya picture taken?' she asked as she lifted the Hawkeye camera to her line of sight.

'Sure,' Susan agreed, grabbing a hold of her brother.

CHAPTER 15

AS WEEKS PASSED, autumn helped itself to the surrounding shrubbery. Tainting the formerly green leaves with golden brown and yellow, they fell to the ground, creating a runway of speckled amber. Walking in her wellington boots, Francesca smiled as she watched the leaves tumble to the puddle ridden pavement.

She wandered through Victoria Park and observed the different animals that prepared for hibernation. A little hedgehog caught her eye. It was going about its business, pushing its way through the soggy strands of grass, eager to find a cosy bush to hide in. She smelt the air, it was rich with the scent of freshly fallen rain. It was a sweet relief from the stuffy summer days. She looked around her, taking in the peace of the post-rain atmosphere. A Chocolate Labrador with muddy paws and wet fur bounded around the greenery, leaving a distinguishable set of prints in the grass. It turned its attention to the lake with its high reeds and soggy ducks. The dog's owner let out a horrified gasp as it jumped headfirst into the lake, causing a tsunami of water and the quacking of unimpressed ducks who were sent into retreat. Francesca attempted to hide her amusement behind the hood of her raincoat as the animal sat proudly upon the marshy bank.

Acknowledging the oak bench that she and Oliver shared pleasant memories on, she couldn't help but feel a change of mood. It was like she was mourning someone, missing the sudden disappearance of closeness and familiarity. She no longer recognised him, he wasn't so clean kept, and isolated himself from the world. He was now a ghost to her.

Francesca continued her drizzled journey to the docks. Meeting the banks of the River Thames, she watched it for a moment. Its current was violent and sent vessels jolting up and down. She could feel the salt invade her nostrils. She breathed deeply as the air stung the back of her throat, forcing its way into her lungs. It was surprising considering the Thames was a calculated concoction of salt and fresh water, yet the aroma was so potent that she imagined herself at the foot of a Dover cliff, facing the ocean head on, watching a dramatic display of crashing waves.

She fiddled with her wrist. The bandage concealed any evident bruising, yet the pain prevailed with every movement. Elaine did the best she could with gauze from her mother's first aid kit, but it did little to ease the discomfort. A scarf was being tossed and beaten to the ground by the bullying wind. Taking pity on it, she grabbed it quickly which resulted in a shot of pain being expelled from her wrist in protest, her face contorting in a wince.

'Thank you, the wind seems to want to make my life

difficult,' a female voice said with relief. She had an accent that Francesca was not familiar with.

Standing from the ground with the scarf firmly in her hand, she met eyes with the young women who stood before her. She wore her black hair fastened tightly, the thick curls sculpting her delicate dark skin. Her lips were coated in poppy red, while her eyes were the colour of rich mahogany. She wore a full willow-green skirt and matching polar neck paired with little white pumps and a white coat. Her beauty was captivating, her image a picture of perfection.

'It's no problem, if it makes you feel better, you're not the only one, I feel like I've ingested enough salt to supply every fish and chip shop in London,' she said politely as she passed the accessory back to its owner.

'I'm sure I've spotted you around here before. My name's Jackie,' the young woman introduced as she placed the scarf back around her neck.

'I'm Fran, and my friend works down the docks, normally around the Western Basin, I visit regularly,' she spoke, a bit embarrassed as she stood in her yellow raincoat and muddy green wellies.

'So does mine. Maybe they know each other,' Jackie said curiously.

'It's highly possible. My friend seems to know everyone. I better be off before we're both blown over Tower Bridge. It was nice meeting you, Jackie,' she said, giving her a final glance.

'And you, Fran, I'm sure we'll meet again soon.' She smiled, walking in the opposite direction.

The wind was so strong that it whipped the clouds into a rotating cream, caramelised by sudden jolts of golden sunlight. Sitting on the usual pile of brown hessian sacks, Francesca looked around as she swung her legs to-and-fro. The distant warehouses sat stiffly, their grey metal a grim sight atop the water. She fiddled with the bandage that poked out from under the cuff of her coat.

'Hello, kid,' Charley said as he tossed a large sack onto the pile, missing her by an inch. As he plonked himself down beside her, he removed his gloves revealing his calluses-clad palms. They were red raw, and his skin appeared cracked from the cold weather.

'How are you today?' she asked.

'The usual, more importantly, how are you?'

'I'm ok, I met someone today, somebody you might know,' she said, handing him a cheese and pickle sandwich that had been kept safely in the pocket of her raincoat.

'That's good, you could do with meeting some new people,' Charley mumbled as he devoured the sandwich in a matter of seconds.

'I'm surprised you don't get indigestion scoffing it like that.' She laughed.

'Nah, my insides are made of tough stuff, remember I did survive a war.' He smiled, rolling the silver foil into a ball in the palm of his large hand.

'How could I forget, how is the shoulder?'

'A bit stiff, but expected at this time of year. So, who was this acquaintance?' he asked.

'Her name's Jackie, she's very well dressed, looks a bit older than me, nearer your age I'd say, said she knows somebody who works here,' Francesca informed, acknowledging the choppy water splash against the side of the landing stage.

'I know the Jackie you speak of. Her friend works with me.'

'I had a feeling you'd know, you don't seem to forget faces.'

'I don't forget many things. I know pretty much everybody

on this side of the river. He fought in the war, her friend I mean,' Charley explained.

'Was he hurt?' she asked, watching a large boat that was being forced to the stage by men heaving thick ropes.

'He's got a scar on his chest, but don't let that frighten you. He's a lovely man and a respectable one at that.'

'Are you trying to set me up?' She asked, recognising Charley's sales pitch.

'I'd never, merely a suggestion, kid.' He grinned to himself. 'Speak of the Devil, Curtis!' he called out.

'Hello, Charley, and who's this lovely lady?' he questioned, approaching with a friendly smile. His accent wasn't as thick as Jackie's. He was well built, similar to Charley's stature. He wore a loose and dirty white linen shirt with braces that held onto his broad shoulder blades. Kind eyes illuminated his face as he came closer. Taking off his gloves, he shook Francesca's hand with surprising gentleness.

'This is Fran, Fran meet Curtis,' Charley introduced as the two stared at one other.

'It's a pleasure to meet you,' Francesca said, her cheeks growing red.

'The pleasure is all mine, now I best be heading off, got to offload that thing of God knows what. Are you still up for the pub later?' Curtis asked.

'Of course, when am I not up for a pint,' Charley agreed as his friend pulled himself onto the boat.

The cold air slipped in through the window that sat ajar. It invaded the kitchen, the dark room feeling even more uninviting. Oliver sat stiffly at the wooden table, a cigarette burning beneath his grip. As Isla watched him, he exhaled a deep, smoke-filled breath.

'I'm sorry, I didn't know what I was thinking, on the phone Finn said that you and Fran were done and dusted for good, Jack suggested the same thing,' Isla explained. Bags pulled at her eyes and her face looked paler than usual.

'I thought you were her friend?' he asked.

'I am.'

'And Jack?'

'I love him,' she said, hanging her head.

'Then why?'

'The truth is, I never got over losing you. Jack and I got into an argument, it tore open old wounds,' she confessed.

Oliver looked at her, frowning. 'Isla, it's been years.'

'I know that, but I couldn't help but think we could have tried again, it would've been like the good old days,' she admitted.

'What you did back then, it really hurt me, you understand that? Every time I look at you, it hurts me.'

'I hurt myself doing what I did to you,' she said, her eyes welling with tears.

Oliver lifted her chin, so she faced him, her dulled green eyes meeting his. 'That night was my fault, I shouldn't have let you come. I wasn't in the right frame of mind, and before I knew it, Lewis and Finn had called you round. I'm to blame for this, Isla, not you.'

'I shouldn't have been so stupid as to believe them, I should have known better. The way you looked at me that night, it wasn't how I remembered. You didn't want me, you wanted her. I knew that from the moment I first saw you two together, and yet I still came to your house like a blind fool believing you'd want me back in an instance,' she spoke honestly.

'Don't say that about yourself, don't put yourself down. I want her back. But she won't want me after what I've done. She thinks I slept with you. I broke her heart,' he lamented.

'I can't look at Jack the same after that night, I betrayed him. I betrayed Fran,' she sobbed.

'We won't tell him, it will send him over the edge if he found out,' he said, passing her a handkerchief.

'I lied to him, I said I came round to collect one of your shirts to give to Lottie to repair. I said I walked in just as they were hurting her. Will Fran tell him the truth?' she asked, dabbing her wet cheeks.

'She's not that type, she wouldn't be spiteful, it's not in her nature,' he said.

'I'll help you get her back,' she uttered.

He ran a hand through his messy black hair. 'It'll do no good.'

'I'll just tell her you want to meet, to discuss things. Say next Friday in Victoria Park, you have some good memories there so maybe she'll reconsider? I don't want to be responsible for ruining your relationship,' she said, fiddling with the handkerchief.

'And I don't want to be responsible for ruining yours, but don't worry, I had already caused enough damage on my own before you even entered the picture,' he muttered, angry with himself. 'I hit her, Isla, because she helped Susan and Colin I slapped her in the face. I didn't realise how hard until I saw the bruise.'

Isla winced at his words. 'Why on earth would you do such a thing? Good God Oli and you wonder why Susan and Colin left?' She massaged her temple with her fingers. 'I made Fran trust me, and now she probably thinks I had bad intentions all along, I need to talk to her, to make sure she understands.'

'She probably won't understand, Isla, be prepared for that.'

'I will. I'm going to go now, I think it's best that we try and avoid each other,' she said, saddened.

'I think that's a good idea,' he agreed, watching her leave.

As Isla walked the length of Vallance Road, she kept her eyes locked on the cobblestones. She walked delicately along them; her blue suede shoes contrasting the light grey stones. She looked up to meet Lewis and Finn standing in front of her. Stopping dead in her tracks, a lump built in her throat.

'Are you alright, Isla? You look as though you've been crying.' Lewis observed.

'You've been round Oliver's, haven't you?' Finn said.

'You manipulated us both to hurt Fran,' she spoke angrily, her cheeks turning a bright red that matched her nail varnish.

'You should be thanking us,' Lewis said, grinning. His face was still damaged with purple and green patches marking the side of his nose.

'Why?'

'Because we've given you what you've always wanted, we gave you Oli back,' Finn said.

'I'm with Jack, I care about him,' she said, clenching her jaw with frustration.

Lewis's glance turned cold and sinister. 'You just make the same mistakes over and over don't you, you can't help acting like a little slag, it's just who you are.'

'I'm not,' she said tearfully.

Finn stood smugly with folded arms. 'We didn't force you

to do anything, you came on your own free will, and now you have to live with that.'

Francesca fought her way through the blustery gale. She navigated the different alleyways leading her to spill out onto the cobbled high street. The road was busy with people hurrying to get themselves out of the cold. As Francesca continued, she pulled at her raincoat, shuddering as she walked. She glanced at the array of colourful treats presented in the sweetshop window; she looked to the earthy assortment of vegetables in the greengrocers' display. Walking past the butchers, she was called to by a voice she recognised all too well.

'Oi, Fran, come here.'

'What do you want, Jack?' she asked, walking into the small shop to see him behind the counter cutting meat with a large cleaver. Sausages and steaks lined the counter while pork joints hung from hefty hooks.

'Just a word,' he said, carrying on with his business. The slicing of raw meat stained the air with a characteristic stench of blood.

'Well, make it quick,' Francesca said impatiently. She had no want for a conversation with him.

'You've ruined that boy you know, he's not been himself ever since you left him,' Jack stated.

'And why do you think I left him in the first place? You don't think I'm bloody hurt after what happened,' she said defensively.

'It wasn't right for Oliver to hit you, and they shouldn't have done that to you, Isla told me what happened,' Jack said, noticing that bandage that Francesca quickly attempted to conceal.

She paused, feeling her cheeks grow flushed with irritation at the mention of their names. *He didn't know.* Oh, the trouble she could cause by telling Jack the truth. She pondered it, the words sitting on the tip of her tongue. But at that moment, she realised causing more damage wouldn't repair the damage done to her. She wasn't like them and wouldn't cause trouble for the sake of it. 'It'll heal,' she said quietly.

'Fran, what are you doing in here?' Albie said, poking his head around the door frame.

'Leaving,' she said, yet her eyes remained fixed on Jack.

Albie grabbed her hand. 'Let me walk you home.'

'Always the gentleman, aren't you Albie,' Jack remarked, gliding the cleaver through a rack of ribs.

'I could give you lessons if you'd like?' Albie said sarcastically, amusing Francesca as they walked out the door.

The Prospect of Whitby Pub was filled with all sorts of characters. It was frequented by merchants and those who worked by the water due to its riverside location. The pub stood as it had done for hundreds of years, and the different personas of past and present had left their mark through carvings engraved on the old bar. It was the site of bare-knuckle brawls and animal fights. Pictures of boxers were hung proudly upon the walls alongside images of Victorian trade ships. The smell of tarnished wood and cigarette smoke filled the interior, adding to its nostalgic presence.

They sat opposite one another at a secluded table. Charley watched, taking in the different people and their drinking preferences. The alcohol soothed the soul and drove passion into the spirit, some a little too much.

'She's a sweet girl. James's sister, right?' Curtis asked.

'Yeah, she's lovely, going to be twenty next March.' Charley smiled as he took a sip from his pint.

'Bloody hell, time flies. I remember James talking about her. I wish he could have been here when I arrived back from Trinidad.'

'You'd be a good match for her,' Charley suggested.

'There's a mighty fine age gap between us,' he dismissed.

'She's had a rough time lately with a lad who has put her through the wringer. She could do with the influence of a more mature man, a sweet man.'

'I may be a mature man, but I still have nightmares of that war. No woman should have to deal with that,' Curtis said honestly as he watched his friend.

'I do too,' Charley admitted.

'Even when I get dressed, I'm faced with that war.'

'You're not alone in that. My shoulder still looks mangled, I can barely stare at it for five minutes before my stomach turns,' Charley said as he finished his drink, gulping down the last of the foam.

'Well, I look like I've fallen into a mincer. I don't think she'd look twice in my direction if she saw my scar,' he uttered, feeling the large wound that marked his chest.

'You'd be surprised.'

'I haven't been surprised yet,' Curtis sighed.

Charley took a deep breath as he remembered the sight of his friend's chest. How as soon as he heard Curtis was injured, he had fought tooth and nail to get to him despite the threat of punishment from his superior officers. The dishonourable discharge that quietly stained his name, that turned its back on his sacrifices as he made his way to that field hospital. When he had found Curtis, the doctors had done what they could, but it was a messy affair. The large, strained stitches attempted to contain skin and crushed bone. A miracle they said, it was a miracle he was alive. It was a miracle Charley had found him again, and he remained by his side as he healed, as he cried through the endless nights.

Curtis sent his friend a solemn smile, as though he knew exactly what he was thinking. They could joke about it as much as they liked, but the wounds on the outside held no comparison to the damage on the inside.

'You ain't welcome in here,' a drunken voice blurted out, pointing a finger in their direction. A straggly old man stood in dirty attire, his face weathered and sunken.

'Why don't you take a seat and sober up,' Charley muttered.

The old man couldn't make out his face, so he staggered over. 'No, fuck you, I don't want none of them in here,' he spat, staring at Curtis.

Them, the word rung in Charley's ears like a detonated grenade. It was said with such spite, such unprovoked hatred. His brother in arms, and this scrawny excuse of a human had the gall to use that tone.

'I think you're the one that should leave,' Curtis addressed him calmly.

'Who the hell is you to tell me what to do?' he said, getting a little too close for comfort.

'I think you need to show some respect,' Charley bellowed.

'Oh Charley, I'm sorry, didn't realise he was with you,' the man said.

'It doesn't matter if he's with me or not, he has the right to drink in here if he pleases.'

'They have no right,' the old man continued.

Charley's eyes were set ablaze. It was rare that he lost his temper, but when he did, it was enough to frighten the Devil.

'Charley, don't worry about it,' Curtis said.

'I'm not worried, I'm pissed off.' Charley rose from his chair. The old man swung at his head with a bony fist, only to be met with a massive fist in return which shattered his chin. Dragging him to the bar, Charley smashed his head repeatedly on the wooden surface, every hit giving way to a crack and a snap. Pulling the bloody mess of a man to the door, he tossed his lifeless body outside. Everyone sat silently as he returned.

'Does anyone else have anything to say?' Charley asked angrily, looking around at the remaining people. 'I didn't fuckin' think so.' Taking his seat, Curtis looked at him with a satisfied smirk.

'Next pints are on me then.'

CHAPTER 16

MONDAY MORNING WAS heaving, sending Francesca swerving in and out of her fellow commuters. Taxis stood in standstill traffic. They looked like shining black beetles ready to scurry into London's various cracks and crevices. The red double-deckers resembled ladybirds, darting quickly in and out of the bus stops, flying at a speedy pace back onto the bus lanes. Crossing the road swiftly, she looked at her watch; she was early despite the jam-packed roads.

'If you're coming in his defence, I don't want to hear it,' she hissed with dismissal, catching sight of Isla who had clearly been lying in wait for her amongst the mass of office workers and flustered bankers.

'Please, just give me a moment to explain.'

'I don't need an explanation, and I certainly don't need Oliver. You can have him.' She turned back to her.

'He doesn't want me, you're the only one he wants. The

truth is I tried to—'

'I know exactly what you tried to do,' Francesca spoke bluntly.

'But he wasn't interested, I promise you that nothing happened between us. We were both manipulated by Lewis and Finn, I know that's no excuse. Oli wants to meet you in Victoria Park on Friday after you finish work,' Isla persisted, trying to keep pace with her.

'I can't trust your promise. You know, after telling me how much you hate being called a whore, you sure as hell acted like one that night,' Francesca snapped. Isla's eyes grew glossy with tears. 'Oh, and Jack spoke to me the other day—'

'Please tell me you didn't say anything to him, it was a mistake,' she fretted.

'I have no interest in getting involved in your business so don't worry, it's your responsibility to tell him the truth, not mine,' she said coldly.

Isla looked at her with relief. 'I am truly sorry for everything that's happened, I know from the outside it looks bad. The boys told me you were finished for good, and I was stupid enough to believe them. I got in a fight with Jack, my head got all messed up. Surely my apology means something,' she pleaded.

'Your words mean nothing to me, all I want is silence so please, leave me alone,' Francesca said, her tone emotionless.

Isla obeyed her wishes. Slowing down, she was engulfed by the swarms of people that buzzed around London's busy financial district.

Charlotte staggered upstairs in her nighty, a tray gripped tightly in her hands. She pushed her way through the door to the bedroom. Plonking herself down proudly, she planted the tray on the lap of the man who was snuggled under the bedcovers.

'I made you breakfast, scrambled eggs on toast, and I made the egg into a smiley face on the toast. I thought you'd find it funny,' she said with self-amusement. Her blonde hair was messy and tickled her cheeks.

'You never fail to put a smile on my face,' Harry said as he propped himself up, rubbing his groggy eyes. As he acknowledged Charlotte's efforts, he couldn't help but grin.

'Go on, try it,' she said, watching him intently. She fiddled with the ring that her finger had recently acquired.

'It's lovely, but I have a taste for something else,' he said, pushing the tray to one side.

'Oh, you are silly, eat up, you've got a busy day at the garage.'

'The garage can wait,' Harry replied, pulling her towards him. Swiftly, he rolled her onto her back, kissing her neck as she giggled.

Jackie wore a fuchsia pink coat and a matching pair of baby doll heels. Careful not to get them dirty, she chose her steps wisely as she navigated the dock. Meeting the side of a large rusting ship, she peered over the railing. It was filled to the brim with wooden crates piled with fruit and sacks containing sugar and tea.

'How are you, Charley?' she asked, watching him with a smile as he swung a large sack over his shoulder.

'Not too bad, Jackie, your beautiful self?' he asked.

'I'm wonderful. Thank you for what you did the other night, Curtis told me what happened.'

'It's no problem, I don't like my friends being disrespected,' he said, leaning over the railing.

'You know I don't believe in violence,' she said, glancing at his bruised knuckles.

'You know I don't either, but I will use it when it's necessary,' Charley spoke firmly.

'Hopefully it'll get to the point where it's no longer necessary, but again I thank you.' She paused for a moment, looking at Charley guiltily. 'Was the man badly hurt?'

'He'll live.'

'I'm glad to hear that.'

Charley watched her intently. 'Your compassion for people never fails to amaze me. I remember you rushing about on the wards during the war, when other nurses ignored the cries of injured German soldiers, you were the only one who would help them.'

'We're all human, Charley, if we all acted so cruelly, we'd be no better than wild animals,' she said as he stepped off the ship.

'Unfortunately, some people within this city aspire to such standards,' he sighed.

She rubbed her glove covered hands together, fighting off the autumnal chill. 'I met a friend of yours, Fran?'

'Yes, she told me. I introduced her to Curtis the other day,' he answered, the breeze meeting his pale cheeks.

'She seems like a kind girl, beautiful big brown eyes just like her brother's were.'

'I thought you'd put the dots together,' he said, grinning.

'Where does she live? I'd like to invite her round for tea, her brother was always kind to me.'

'15 Coborn Road, just opposite my house,' he informed her.

Albie ogled the different treats as Francesca made her decision.

'You didn't have to come and buy me sweets during my lunch break, Albie,' she said, amused.

'Sugar make everything better, poppet, choose whatever you like.' He smiled.

The large containers reached the ceiling, the different boiled sweets standing colourfully against the old walls, taking on the appearance of wallpaper.

Francesca met his side, peering at the display. 'I normally go for Sherbet Lemons, Dolly Mixtures or Pear Drops.' She frowned, remembering the times she shared sweets with Oliver.

'Fran, in a shop full of every treat you could desire you choose possibly the most unadventurous ones. Let me surprise you,' he said, rolling his eyes.

'Ok, I'm expecting big things.' She laughed as she followed him.

Albie approached the shop owner who stood in a white apron, a friendly smile covering his face.

'What can I get for you?' he asked, the many jars lining the counter.

'We will have eight Matlow's Milk Bottles, six Fruit Salads, and a Barratt's Sherbet Fountain with a stick of liquorice,' he ordered.

'No problem at all,' the man said as he collected the sweets into a little white and pink striped paper bag. Handing the bag to Francesca, Albie paid the man, giving him sixpence.

As they wandered onto the street, Francesca popped a Fruit Salad in her mouth, her eyes wide as the raspberry and pineapple flavour met her taste buds.

'Good, aren't they?' Albie asked smugly.

'They are, thank you for getting them for me,' she said

happily.

'You're welcome, I thought you could do with cheering up.'

'Do you know everything that happened?' she asked.

'I know Oliver put his hands on you and it disgusts me. I didn't want to bring it up the other day when Jack accosted you, I thought it might be a bit raw,' he spoke, his tone contemptuous.

'I appreciated you doing that. I'm meeting him, to talk,' she said.

'Go for the closure, but don't you dare take him back, he doesn't deserve you,' he said firmly.

'I won't.' She ran a hand over her loose brown plait.

Albie spied the bruising that marked her delicate wrist. 'I heard rumours about what happened that night, they hurt you too, I see.'

'Well, I whacked Lewis in the face with a rolling pin.'

'I'm sorry, you what?' he questioned, trying not to laugh.

'I cracked his nose with a rolling pin, he pushed me up against the worktop, and I used whatever I could find,' she explained, smiling slightly.

'I have to say I'm pretty impressed you took Kerry's advice on board.' He smirked.

At the garage, Harry fiddled with the underside of a car that had seen better days. Its rusting exterior sent flakes of angered orange metal onto the floor. Pulling at its pipework, the vehicle groaned in response. He was covered in dirt and oil and had sweat running from his brow. Hearing the shuffle of footsteps, he rolled himself from under the car.

'Oliver, you scared the life out of me,' he said, pulling himself up, feeling the world swirl around him as he gripped the scarring wound on the back of his head.

'I need her back,' Oliver admitted, a melancholy expression staining his face.

'I heard you put hands on her, you can't be treating women like that. You know Lottie wants nothin' to do with you, she was fuming. She's been sending Fran embroidered hankies, the poor girl probably has about ten at this point.' Harry spoke defensively. He wiped his hands with a cloth, marking it with streaks of oil.

'I know, I shouldn't have done it.'

'Oliver Thomas admitting he's wrong, what a day it is to be alive. It's nice to see you put somebody else before your pride for a change,' Harry muttered.

'Damn my pride, I need her Harry,' he declared.

'I know you do. The question is does she need you?'

'She couldn't have moved on that quickly,' Oliver said.

'I doubt she has, but you hurt her, she may forgive you but she might not want you.'

'I love her,' he admitted.

'Tell that to her not me,' Harry said bluntly, pulling himself back under the car.

The swirling grey clouds gave way to spurts of rainfall throughout the day. As Francesca looked out the window to confront the grumbling sky, she heard a knock at the door. Opening it, she was greeted by Jackie who was wielding a large umbrella.

'Charley told me where to find you. I was wondering if you

wanted to come round for a cup of tea?'

'I don't see why not, that would be lovely. Just give me a minute to grab my things,' she said with a surprised smile, dashing upstairs to retrieve her raincoat.

They walked down the cobbled street slowly, following the rows of regimented houses that lined Coborn Road. Jackie had a firm grasp of the umbrella. She held it perfectly above her guest, making sure she didn't get a single drop on Francesca even though she wore her thick yellow raincoat.

'So, what do you do?' Francesca asked.

'I'm a nurse, what about you?'

'I work in a bank as a secretary, to tell you the truth, it's quite boring.'

'I can imagine, can't you look for another job?'

'I'm comfortable in my position.'

'But there's no fun in being comfortable, maybe you should look around for something different,' Jackie suggested.

'I could do with a change of scenery I suppose. All I do is type and stare at the clock, or out the window.'

'Back in Trinidad, I had a job as a secretary for a while. It was worse than boring. But at least when I looked out the window, I could see views across the Island.' She remembered, smiling.

'I bet you're fed up with the weather here,' Francesca said as the rain fell upon the puddle-ridden pavement.

'It has grown on me, I do miss the heat and the beaches, and the music.' Jackie reminisced, the sky above growing to be a sinister sight of gunmetal grey.

'The beaches here probably don't compare, they're all stony.'

'They have their charm, but the pebbles really hurt your

feet when you paddle. And I certainly don't fancy a swim in the Thames any time soon,' Jackie said humorously.

'Yeah, I wouldn't advise it. You're right about the pebbles, sometimes they even manage to get into your shoes, I can never figure out how that happens. I'd love to go abroad, I've never been. The furthest I've gone is Southend-on-Sea,' Francesca explained, her cheeks growing red from the cold.

'Then that's a good place to start to find a new job. You could work on a cruise liner or an aeroplane?'

'Only one problem, I get motion sick. I went out on a boat once when I was little, I remember being sick everywhere.'

'Oh, that puts a slight spanner in the works, but I'm sure there are other options,' Jackie said.

'I do like the thought of working in a different country, or maybe even just outside of London itself. How long have you been a nurse?'

'As long as I can remember, I was stationed here during the war, I looked after injured soldiers. Curtis was stationed here too, that's how we met Charley, and your late brother,' she informed.

'You knew James?' Francesca asked with brightening eyes.

'I did indeed, he was one of the finest men I ever met.' She recalled.

As they walked, Francesca looked to the Underground station with its gaping mouth. People hurried inside, content on getting home amidst the rush hour. The Police Station sat firmly on the corner of Addington Road. A few weathered police officers stood outside enjoying a cigarette while others grappled with an unruly man in handcuffs. As they passed them, one officer sent a menacing glance in their direction before flicking his cigarette down, the embers suffocating in a deep puddle. Francesca stared back at him, confused by his ugly expression.

'Why was he looking at us like that?' she asked.

'Because you're walking with me,' Jackie said simply.

Bow as a district was no different from any other in the East End. It had red brick houses that lined each street. The odd warehouse or factory stood as an ugly reminder of the previous century, and Francesca could hear the distant screeches of the overground. Turning down a lengthy road by the name of Tomlin's Grove, they soon came to a standstill outside a run-down terrace house. It was quite contradictory when looking at Jackie in her clean and pristine state.

'Here we are,' she said as she leant her soggy umbrella up against the wall. 'I'll introduce you to the others.'

Francesca smiled nervously, trying her hardest not to judge the building by its exterior.

'Curtis, we've got company,' Jackie called as they entered the hallway. A few shuffles later and he was standing before them, his large frame filling the doorway.

'Hello again,' Francesca spoke politely as she met eyes with him. This time he was in fresh clothes and had his hair neatly combed back. His kind eyes were the same, and Francesca found comfort in them.

'I'll go and find the others.' Jackie grinned, turning her attention to locating the remaining members of her household.

'It's nice to see you, Fran. If you need anything just give me a shout,' he said as he guided her through to the small living room. Politely, he took her coat, hanging it on the stair banister in the hallway.

She scanned the space, recognising the peeling wallpaper and a dishevelled set of sofas. They were covered hastily by blankets and fraying cushions. A dying plant sat sombrely in the corner of the room, while an oval wooden coffee table filled the centre, balancing on its uneven legs. The carpet was a muted grey with a concoction of brown shapes that, if you stared at too long, became an optical illusion of moving fragments. The house looked as though it hadn't changed since the 1930s.

'Fran, meet Ricky and Wilma,' Jackie introduced as the others followed her into the room.

'Pleased to meet you both, your house is—' Francesca scrambled for a compliment as she met eyes with Curtis once again.

'It's ok, we know very well it's shit,' Ricky said abruptly. He sat slouching with a pompadour haircut that framed his moody face.

'Watch your language. It's not much, but it's home.' Jackie's eyes narrowed in his direction.

'Home sure as hell ain't here,' he said stubbornly.

'This is our home now, Ricky, whether you like it or not,' Jackie said, retreating to the kitchen where she filled up the kettle and let off some steam.

'So, what do you both do?' Francesca asked, anxiously fiddling with the hem of her skirt as she took a seat.

'Ricky's a porter at Liverpool Street Station, carries people's luggage about, and I work in one of those fancy houses over the other side of London, I clean and do ironing,' Wilma said. She had a friendly expression that welcomed Francesca into conversation. Her thick black hair was held under a large headband, and she had two plastic pearl studs in each earlobe.

'Why did you choose London? I know the prices are dearer here in the city,' Francesca questioned.

'We didn't have a choice, we've had no choice since we got off that damn boat at Tilbury. Got told where to go and what to do since day one,' Ricky muttered.

'We were invited here because of the labour shortage Ricky, and the fact that Curtis served, be grateful for that. There are better opportunities here, don't try and deny it,' Jackie said, reappearing with a large tray filled with steaming mugs of tea.

'What opportunities?' He scowled at her.

'I'm not going to stand here and argue with you. Stop sulking and pull yourself together it's embarrassing, especially in front of a guest,' she disciplined, passing a mug to Francesca. She graciously accepted it, pulling it to her lips to avoid the mounting tension. 'Speaking of guests, feel free to pop round any time, and bring friends as well, they're more than welcome,' Jackie added softly as she returned to the kitchen.

Curtis, who was leaning against the peeling wallpaper, looked down at Francesca with a grin. 'When I arrived, I was housed in an air raid shelter under Clapham South Tube Station with a load of other people. Then everyone was dispersed across the country. I was supposed to be sent to the midlands, but I got in contact with Charley and he saw to it that I got to stay in London. The others followed not long after. At first, nobody would house us, but Charley managed to pull some strings,' he explained.

'Charley's a good man.' She smiled.

'Yes, there are many good people here, you've just got to open your eyes and see the bigger picture. Look beyond the signs and the comments, they don't account for the opinions of everybody,' he lectured, staring at Ricky who rolled his eyes. 'Come on, I want to show you something.'

As Curtis led her up the narrow staircase, Francesca carefully gripped the mug between her cold hands. 'I sense some tension there,' she said as she entered his bedroom.

It was quaint with a single bed covered in a plain white

duvet and pillow. He had a few photos that lined the tiny window space, and a stack of old books on a small chest of drawers which he began to rummage through. As he latched onto a newspaper, he turned back to Francesca who was sitting patiently on the bed.

'Ricky takes things personally and only acknowledges the bad in this world. He has a foul temper, and it worries me. As you can see, Jackie is far more optimistic,' he said, taking a seat beside her.

'Jackie said you were both stationed here during the war?'

'Yes, I was stationed in many places, I met Charley and James as soon as I arrived, it was an utter coincidence considering we were in completely different branches of the military. I was in the Navy, Charley the Army, and of course your late brother in the Air Force, but they had all merged at Dover, and so that's where we stayed for a while, and we became close. Jackie worked in the underground tunnels at Dover too, caring for the wounded.' A smile covered his face for a moment in reminiscence. 'On the day I arrived back here it was a far different Britain than I remembered, the city seemed broken, the people seemed broken. We were greeted well at first, I picked this up on the day we arrived,' he said, passing her the newspaper.

'I remember my grandma reading a paper like this.' Francesca held it in her hands. As she scanned the paper, the headline read: *Welcome Home! Evening standard plane greets the 400 sons of the empire.*

'See, it's not all bad,' he uttered, smiling.

'But is it? I've seen the signs placed in the windows of boarding houses, and the looks people give Jackie just for walking down the street.'

'I don't care for signs, Fran. I don't get worked up by the opinions of others. I did my bit for this country and I've been rewarded for it,' he spoke gratefully.

'By having to live here, by having to work down that dock?' she asked, unconvinced.

'It's no different a life than Charley's. By moving here, we have been given a new start, new opportunities if not for us then for our children that'll come after,' he justified.

'I suppose, what was it like?' she asked, looking at the black and white image of the large vessel spread across the page.

'What was what like?' he questioned.

'Being on the Windrush,' Francesca said, pointing.

1948

NEW BEGINNINGS

WHAT A SIGHT it was, not the vessel but the distant island it would find harbour in. It was a peculiar little nation all to itself, surrounded by the vast ocean. The saltwater seeped inland and accumulated streams, rivers and lakes. It brought in fishermen and traders. It produced battleships and concealed shipwrecks on its coastline. But most of all, it brought people, new people to this little island which influenced lands much bigger than itself.

As the Empire Windrush neared the completion of its voyage, it met the shores of Essex. As the passengers looked over the railings, they met eyes with the distant houses and settlements. Trees and greenery were manipulated by blustery winds as the murky water collided with the side of the ship. It wasn't like home at all, but they were all hopeful that it would welcome them as though it was.

Appearing on the top deck, Curtis watched with relief as

the vessel crept closer to shore. He clutched the metal railings that were painted a bright white, much to the contrast of the grey destroyers he had become accustomed to during the war. The sea was rough, yet he remained calm. He was lonely, yet he knew it wouldn't be long before the others joined him. He'd made conversation with the other passengers, including a group of Polish refugees who were promised a new life after being ferried to Mexico by the allies. One woman and her daughter were a grateful reminder that he was no longer on a warship. There was laughter and the Windrush was busy, full of languages and accents he didn't know. But he didn't get too close to anyone, apart from the small Polish girl who had asked to look at one of his books as he'd sat reading. With a nod from her mother, he had lifted her onto his lap and read to her until she fell asleep, distracting her from the relentless rocking of the ship. Thinking about it, Curtis realised that the young mother, Zofia, had sent her daughter over as a distraction after noticing his fear, the fear that seeped into his eyes when the water got choppy and his memories drowned him. He knew that her husband had fought and died, maybe she recognised the fear after seeing it in her husband's eyes, or even in her own reflection, he had heard stories of the goings-on in Poland, and as he cradled her child the fire to fight again blazed through him. But he was tired, so very tired of it all. Zofia was too by the looks of things, her beautiful face weathered. He knew as soon as they docked he'd never see her again, so he had made no attempt to get to know her beyond the pleasantries. It was better that way.

His eyes reflected the minimal light from the dark clouds, making them dull. He hadn't slept much, but it didn't bother him. After the war he hardly ever slept, afraid of what he might see when he closed his eyes.

CHAPTER 17

FRANCESCA WALKED HOME in the damp and drizzle. The pavement looked as though it was a mirror, the steps of her green wellie boots warping her reflection. She caught sight of a familiar face within the rippling water. The approaching figure was a bitter looking Kerry who swiftly caught up to her, distorting the image completely with one large stomp.

'It's nice to see you have loyalty to your own,' she said.

'What's that supposed to mean?' Francesca asked, her focus remaining on the path ahead.

'Why are you hanging out with those people? I know who lives in that house,' she said judgingly.

Francesca's fists tightened in her raincoat pockets. 'If you must know, I went round for tea, Jackie and Curtis knew my brother. They were nothing but nice to me.'

'Were you left alone with him?' she pried.

'Who?'

'This Curtis you speak of. I've heard stories about their kind, especially the men.'

'I don't follow.'

'Put it this way, I'm sure he'd jump at the chance to take advantage of you,' Kerry said snarkily.

Francesca had had enough, with all her might she shoved Kerry, her back smacking into a lamppost. 'He's a good person. They are good people, unlike you and Lewis. I can't believe you still stand by him after what he did,' she snapped.

Kerry stared back at her, enraged. 'You've got some bloody nerve—'

'Please piss off and mind your own business,' Francesca yelled as she left her under the blackening sky.

Throwing off her wellie boots, Francesca huffed her way into the kitchen. Vera watched her through strong lenses. She was occupied with a bowl of jellied eels that sat in her lap, the stench of fish invading the air.

'What's the matter, Fran? You seem glum.' She watched her granddaughter return with Winston. Sitting on the brightly printed sofa, Francesca held the biscuit jar at her side, helping herself to a piece of shortbread.

'I just don't understand some people,' she said angrily, taking a bite, a cascade of crumbs falling on her dress.

'What's happened, dear?' she asked as she munched on the last eel, the bone hitting her teeth.

Feeling sick at the sight of her grandmother slurping up the animal like a sea monster, Francesca placed the lid back on the jar. 'My friend, at least I thought she was my friend, Kerry, took a swipe at me for hanging around with Curtis.'

'Charley's friend?' Vera asked.

'Yes. You know him?'

'He's a lovely chap, I've bumped into him a few times when he's bringing in fresh produce for the greengrocers,' she said, licking the jelly from her fingers.

'He is lovely, so I don't understand why it got her back up,' she said with folded arms.

'Excuse my bluntness, but I imagine it's to do with his skin,' Vera said, placing her bowl to the side.

'Why does it even matter?' she grumbled.

'I don't know, but people, especially around these parts are hostile to people who differ from them, even though they have every right to be here. Your friend is probably just ignorant, and what did I tell you?'

'Ignorance can be dangerous.' Francesca recalled.

'You know, a long time ago I fell in love with a G.I. that came over during the Great War, his family were from Angola and settled in Cleveland, I always wanted to visit America.'

'What about grandad?'

'Love is complicated. Your grandfather suffered greatly when they brought him back from the trenches. I'm afraid he had no love left for me or your mother,' she admitted.

'I never knew about this,' Francesca said, leaning forward with fascination.

'He was the sweetest man, but he knew the dangers we'd face if I left with him. It's hard enough now, let alone back then, and America is so cruel, even to this day 'mixed' marriages are illegal, it's a disgrace. Britain has no laws of that kind, only social attitudes but it didn't make it any less dangerous. So, we were stuck between a rock and a hard place. He left for America after the war was done and I never saw him again. He did, however, give me Grace, I had a fascination with the figurines from when I was young, so he bought her for me as a parting gift,' she explained, pointing to the Royal Doulton figure that sat proudly on the dining table.

'So that's why Grace is so precious?'

'Yes, a reminder of the one who got away.' She smiled slightly. 'People have no right to tell you who you can or can't hang around with, Fran, if you want to spend time with Curtis then that is your choice,' she encouraged.

'I can't believe she had the bottle to talk to me like that, or to push me,' Kerry vented as she paced.

The living room was surprisingly large now that all her uncle's belongings were gone. She and her mother could now enjoy their house and fill it with everything they ever wanted. This was evident as a new television set sat in the corner of the room.

'Maybe you should let it go, she doesn't want anything to do with us,' Isla said, watching her agitated friend from the comfort of the sofa.

'I never wanted anything to do with her in the first place,' Kerry grumbled.

'That's not true, I know you liked her.'

'And she had the nerve to talk about Lewis,' she continued, disregarding Isla's comment in favour of the sound of her own voice.

'I'm not sure why you're in Lewis's defence,' Isla interrupted, fed up with her friend's incessant pacing.

'Why shouldn't I be?' she asked, stopping.

'What did Lewis tell you about that night?' Isla questioned, curious to what information Kerry had been led to believe.

'That he tried to put it on Fran, and he got a mighty whack to the face for it, which I don't doubt he deserved. I gave him an earful for that by the way, the cretin shouldn't have joked around with her like that, I told him long ago not to mess about with her,' she muttered.

'But he didn't tell you about how he grabbed her wrist so hard it almost snapped. Or how Finn nearly carved her face with that bloody flick knife he carries about. She was in tears. What they did was no joke, they attacked her. If Oliver hadn't intervened, I wouldn't put it past them to have taken it even further,' Isla gulped as she watched her friend's face turn from a shade of red, to as white as a sheet.

'That can't be true, they wouldn't hurt her like that.'

'I was there, I know what I saw, haven't you seen her walking around with her wrist all wrapped up? There's a reason she wants rid of us. Just be grateful that she didn't tell the police otherwise Lewis and Finn would be in a lot of trouble. I know they've done a lot for you in the past, but being associated with them is not good for you.'

'I want them here now,' she said, a sudden sharpness consuming her tone.

'But it's late,' Isla objected, looking to the clock hanging on the living room wall, its hands just reaching eleven.

'I don't give a rat's arse what time it is, get them here now,' Kerry ordered, her hands trembling.

The two sat in front of her. Watching her narrowed glance, they knew she was far from amused.

'Do you want to tell me the truth about what happened that night?' she interrogated.

'Nothing of significance happened,' Finn said, brushing off the incident.

'Tell me the truth about Fran,' she pressed.

'What truth about Fran?' Lewis asked with folded arms.

'What you did to her,' she snapped suddenly, causing them to sit stiffly.

'You're gettin' worked up over nothing,' Finn dismissed, looking around the room for an escape.

'You're both a disgrace,' she hissed.

'Kerry, look—'

'Don't Kerry me Lewis, how dare you do that to her. What if that was me?'

'It was just a laugh.'

'From what I heard she wasn't laughing, in fact, I heard she was crying,' Kerry said furiously.

'It sounds like you've taken this personally,' Finn said.

'Yes, I have. I thought you knew better than to hurt a woman like that. You have no idea what it's like,' she said, her voice breaking ever so slightly.

'I'm sorry,' Lewis said softly. She was the only woman that he had ever loved, even though he was too stubborn and prideful to admit it. He would never hurt her, but he could see that what they did to Francesca had hurt her, and that broke his heart.

'I don't care for your apology, what matters is that you attacked her, and I can't forgive you for that. I want you both to leave,' she demanded.

'If that's what you want.' Lewis frowned.

'Leave London, and don't fuckin' return.'

'Kerry, you can't be serious.' Finn panicked.

'I am deadly serious,' she spoke sternly, pointing a finger.

Finn's brow furrowed. 'You can't make us leave.'

'God knows I can. You should think yourselves lucky that you've not been put away, that's where you should be right now. If you're not gone by tomorrow, you'll wish you got put behind bars. Trust me, my version of justice will have you beggin' for hell,' Kerry warned, her face flushed.

'We helped you, before us you were nothing,' Finn snarled, but Lewis placed a hand on his shoulder with just enough firmness to make his lips tighten.

A smile spread across Kerry's face, sinister in a way that made Lewis wince. 'How could I forget my knights in shining armour who saved me from my twat of an uncle. I took what he gave before you came, and I took it after also, you were just an interlude, 'cause trust me, the night after that street party I was taught what it was like to really suffer at the hands of a man. The only thanks I owe you is for the suit inspiration. I must admit, I do wear them better than you.'

Lewis felt his heart shatter in his chest. 'I didn't know he did that to you, I thought—'

'That he used to beat me and that was it? Not even my own mother knows what he did, so why on earth would I tell you? He wouldn't touch me once I put on trousers, ain't that funny?'

Finn gulped as Kerry stared into him.

'That night will mark me for the rest of my life, just as I'm sure that night will now mark Fran.' Her face was stained with disappointment, so much so that Lewis couldn't look at her.

'We will leave tomorrow evening,' Lewis reluctantly agreed, head grasped in his hands.

'Morning. And don't think I won't notice if you're still here,' she spat, turning her back on them.

Curtis wiped the sweat from his brow. He was hot and bothered despite the night that sent a cool wind twisting along the landing stage. The sky was clear, so clear he could make out the constellations, the stars bright enough to illuminate the dock. His large eyes looked for Charley who had also signed up to work the extra shifts, or twilight hours as the workers called them. Most of the men found the idea of spending the evening working to be an annoyance, but Curtis enjoyed it, he enjoyed the quiet, it was the closest he could get to sleep without having to sleep, which is when his thoughts would get the better of him. *Better to work in the dark than be consumed by it*, he thought to himself as he wandered across the weathered wooden panels. His shoes were scuffed, there was no way to avoid scuffing them, and his linen shirt was dirty. He tutted himself a reminder to be more careful. He hated how Wilma had to scurry off to find a launderette when most of their washing was his, but she gladly did it.

Approaching a rusting hulk of a ship, he pulled himself over the railings with ease, his thick-soled shoes meeting the metal floor. Entering a room caked in orange flakes of iron, he paused. There was someone here with him. He could hear it, sobbing. He knew exactly who it was. His heart dropped so far it could have scraped the riverbed.

Charley.

They'd got used to each other's cries over the years, during and after the war. Curtis walked down a small set of stairs, the old ship screeching in protest. The room was brightened by the starlight that forced its way through the portholes. Against the wall were crates of tobacco, the labels weren't visible but he recognised the smell, pungent against his nostrils. Between the crates sat Charley who was crying into his palms, muttering between exasperated breaths. He clutched his ammo pouch between his knees, no sandwiches to be found.

'Hey big man,' Curtis said, sitting before him with gentleness not often attributed to a man of his size. 'It's 1955. You're home.'

Charley lifted his head, eyes raw from the tears that shot down his cheeks. His hands shook. 'I can't stand it, I can't stand feeling this way,' he wept, his eyes returning to the darkness of his palms.

'There is nothing wrong with how you are feeling, Charley. What happened to you would haunt any man. There are nights when I can't stand it either.'

Charley met his glance again, wide-eyed like a frightened child.

'Can I take your ammo pouch for a moment?'

He nodded, and Curtis took it from him, placing it behind his back. He shuffled, taking something from his back pocket. Placing the item inside, he closed the pouch and handed it to Charley who winced as he his fingers met the fabric.

'Open it,' Curtis told him.

Charley's face was drained of colour. As he slowly slipped a hand inside, he grasped a wrapper. Curtis sat patiently, he'd sit there all night if it was necessary. Pulling it out, Charley's lower lip quivered.

'What is it?' Curtis asked him.

'A Mars Bar,' he replied, wiping his tears on his sleeve.

'What do you like about Mars Bars, Charley?' he questioned softly.

'The way the chocolate sticks to the roof of my mouth. How I would buy one with James, Elaine and Fran when we were young and we'd share a bar between us, fighting over who got the biggest bit even though we cut it into four equal parts. How we did the same in Dover, and we'd share a bar between Jackie, you, me and James.' He reminisced, his painful thoughts receding as he peered down at the wrapper.

'Open it,' Curtis said to him.

Charley's shaking hands opened the wrapper, and he broke the bar in half, handing a section to Curtis who munched on it. A smile covered Charley's face as he ate his half, leading him to lick his fingers. 'It tastes like happier times,' he said, staring at him.

Curtis wouldn't dispute that, he wouldn't try and act as though all was well, it would be the greatest insult. 'It wasn't our fault. What we did during the war was what we had to do, we had to survive.'

'I sometimes wonder if it was worth it,' Charley said, his thundering heart like a bomb inside his chest. He grasped his shoulder, the scarred tissue was rough against his shirt.

Curtis gently lifted his hands and cupped Charley's face. 'Of course it was worth it, don't you ever question that.'

Charley nodded, and Curtis let go.

'I wouldn't be here without you,' Charley said, grinning at his friend.

'And I wouldn't either, you've pulled me back when I've felt so trapped in my thoughts I could go mad,' Curtis admitted. 'Now I think you should come and stay the night, you need a hearty meal and a good natter with Jackie.'

As they left the ship, Charley found himself again. He took a deep breath as he stared at the stars, the cool wind sweeping past his burning cheeks. 'How many Mars Bars do you have stashed away anyway? You pull them out like a rabbit out of a hat.'

Curtis smirked. 'It's probably best I don't answer that otherwise you'll think I have gone mad after all. I just know that they are the things that pull you back, that remind you what you fought for.'

Jackie was quick to greet them. She was dressed in her nursing uniform and looked immaculate despite having worked a twelve-hour shift.

'You didn't fancy getting into your pyjamas, Jackie?' Curtis asked, aware of the time and the fact that she'd been in her uniform at least four hours more than she needed to be.

'You know I always wait up, dressed and ready to go in case you need me,' she said, smiling brightly. 'Charley, come in, you look like you've had a long day.' She welcomed him into her arms, and she knew by the look in his eyes that he had got himself into a state. 'I'll prepare a bed for you, but not before you get some supper. There is stewed rice and chicken in the kitchen, then you can listen to the horror of a day I've had at the hospital. Somebody managed to vomit and it sprayed the ceiling. It was quite spectacular, and a sight I'll never be able to unsee.'

'I'll happily sleep on the sofa.' Charley laughed.

'No, you will take Curtis's room. I have a double bed, small but enough for two. I think I can tolerate my massive lump of a friend sleeping beside me, it wouldn't be the first time, as long as he doesn't snore or I'll smother him with a pillow.' She pinched his nose making him yelp.

Days passed, and the old oak trees appeared bare. Francesca walked underneath them, her boots meeting the pathway that was covered in decaying wet leaves. She wore a new dark blue suede coat that her grandma had bought her out of disgust for her yellow raincoat, but she missed its baggy embrace. A large red letterbox stood at the edge of the park where the grass met the concrete. She quickly funnelled a few letters into it before walking onto the marshy green.

Catching sight of Oliver who was sitting on a bench, she approached slowly. He had a portion of fish and chips wrapped in newspaper on his lap and a daisy firmly gripped in his hand. He wore a large drape jacket as he always did, yet his image was shattered and broken. As she sat beside him, she felt her eyes well up with tears. Her mind became heavy and conflicted.

'I brought you some food, thought you might be hungry.'

'Thank you, but I can't stay long,' she said, facing the murky lake.

'Well, at least take this. How have you been?' he asked. Passing her the daisy, she accepted it into her grasp.

'Healing, what about you?'

'Hurting, I'm so sorry for what happened, Frankie, please forgive me, I never should have lost my temper,' he confessed. 'I should never have let Lewis and Finn get into my head, I wasn't thinking straight, and they called Isla round—'

'I don't want to hear anymore.' She cut him off quickly. 'I forgive you, but I'm not taking you back,' she said firmly, gripping the daisy to the point where the stalk bent under the pressure.

'I love you, you know that?' he spoke desperately.

'I loved you too.'

'Loved. So you don't anymore.' He recognised.

'After what happened, no I don't. I'll always care about you, but this won't work between us, I think we can both see that.'

She stood from the wooden bench.

'Come on, have a little bit of hope,' he said as she walked away.

'Hope for what, Oliver? There is no hope for us, not anymore. I think it's best that we both move on,' she said with a final glance, tears visible as they ran down her rosy cheeks.

As the five individuals met, a series of pleasantries were exchanged. Harry wore drainpipe trousers with a plain white T-shirt. In contrast, Charlotte wore a flowing navy blue skirt with a matching blazer, her hair in her usual tight victory rolls. Elaine was amused by Albie's pair of obnoxious pink socks. They blinded Francesca as the material met the rays of sudden sunlight, a sweet relief from weeks of continuous chilliness.

As they walked along the cobbles, Charlotte presented her good news. 'So, I suppose you're the only one who doesn't know, Fran,' she said with a huge grin on her face.

'Know what?'

'That we're engaged,' she exclaimed, thrusting her hand into Francesca's face, revealing the gold band with a little crystal at the centre.

'Seriously!' she squealed with excitement, examining it.

'As serious as that bloody ring,' Harry muttered from behind them.

'I'm so happy for you both! When's the wedding?' she asked, turning back to him.

'At Christmas time, the sooner the better, and I want you to be there,' Charlotte insisted.

'Of course I will,' Francesca agreed in an instance.

'So that's going to be a pricey event.' Albie laughed.

'That's why I'm working extra shifts at the garage,' Harry said.

'Oh, I love weddings, the last one I went to was for my cousin. All the bridesmaids wore mustard yellow.' Elaine reminisced.

'Whatever possessed them to choose mustard yellow, a hideous colour for a wedding,' Albie concluded.

'I know, it was very unflattering,' she agreed.

'There will definitely be no mustard dresses at our wedding,' Harry said.

'The colour theme will be purple, like the royals.' Charlotte smiled.

'A royal wedding it is then.' Francesca laughed as they met the doorstep.

Even in the sunshine, the outside of the building proved to be menacing with its cracking walls and poky windows. As Jackie welcomed them in, they sat on the tatty sofa waiting to be introduced to the others. Wilma bundled down the stairs and sat adjacent to them. Her hair was neatly braided, and she fiddled with the plastic pearls that decorated her earlobes. Curtis shortly followed and placed himself next to her, his warm brown eyes meeting Francesca's. Ricky slouched in the corner out of protest. Jackie returned with a tray of steaming mugs. Growing irritated upon recognising Ricky's grumpiness, she looked at Curtis with displeasure.

'Sit up,' he said sharply, causing the boy to reluctantly obey.

Francesca introduced them all one by one. Albie sat studying the room while Elaine slowly sipped her tea. Charlotte watched the gentle sun rays hit the glass of a nearby window.

'You lot dress funny.' Wilma observed. From Harry's chunky creepers to Albie's flamboyant brocade waistcoat, she sat fascinated.

'Oh, wait until you meet Kerry.' Charlotte grinned.

'Who's Kerry?' she asked.

'The female version of them, trousers and all,' Charlotte informed her.

'I'd like to meet her. She sounds interesting,' Wilma said, her expression curious.

'Maybe one day,' Francesca said, growing angry at the thought of her.

'I like your blazer, not half bad with a needle are you,' Jackie commended.

Showing off her embroidery, Charlotte smiled. 'I did it a while ago, I'm thinking of adding to it.' Harry, with his broad shoulders sat snugly on the sofa as she placed her small hand in his.

'I can always help you with that if you want, I'm partial to a bit of needlework,' Jackie suggested.

'Oh, I'd love that!' she said, looking at Harry excitably.

'So, what's up with you?' Ricky asked, sending a captious glance in Albie's direction.

'I'm not sure what you mean.' He ran a hand through his perfectly placed hair.

'You don't look normal,' Ricky muttered.

'Watch yourself,' Curtis warned.

'There's no fun in being normal,' Albie said proudly as he looked at Francesca.

'You're very—'

'Queer? I am queer if that is what you're getting at,' he informed. 'May I smoke?' he asked quickly, turning to Jackie.

'Of course you can, you're brave to admit that,' she said kindly, watching him pull out a packet of cigarettes. She glanced at Wilma who grinned contently.

'You're not the only one, Albie,' she admitted.

The group looked at her, surprised.

A smile spread across Albie's face. 'Well, to being who we are,' he said, lifting his mug in a toast. The others lifted their steaming mugs, repeating him, bursting into laughter as they drank.

'Can I go now?' Ricky grumbled, their presence appearing to be an adequate inconvenience.

'We'll chat later,' Curtis said as he disappeared upstairs.

Dear Fran,

I'm not great at this writing stuff, so I'll make it quick. I apologise for the way we treated you, we had no right. By the time you read this Finn and I will already be in Newcastle, and I've been warned of what will happen if we return. Out of respect for Kerry, I won't return. I hope you can forgive me, but only you can make that decision.

Lewis.

Francesca scanned the letter. She sat on the end of her bed, fiddling with the frills at the bottom of her pillow. Her wrist was still faintly bruised and a little swollen. She figured that pushing Kerry had hardly helped matters. Luckily, she managed to hide her discomfort from her relatives, keeping the angered skin covered by long sleeves.

She was not quite ready to forgive him.

Placing the letter on the window seal, she imagined the harshness of Kerry's words to cause him to write such an apology.

Conflicted, she sought the advice of those much wiser than herself.

'How do I forgive someone I despise?' Francesca asked as she bundled down the stairs, confused by a supposedly simple concept. Her mother was wiping dishes with a bright green tea towel as Vera tended to Houdini with some bird feed.

'It's a hard thing to do, but it'll bring you peace once you've done it,' her mother answered as she stacked the porcelain plates neatly in the cupboard.

'But how can I forgive somebody who hurt me?' she asked again.

'I take it this person apologised, but you can't find it in yourself to forgive them yet?' Vera pressed as she formed a suitable answer.

Francesca nodded as she sat opposite her.

'A little advice, Fran, not all people deserve forgiveness, but as your mother said rightly, you deserve peace, so forgive while you can because you will lead a better life for doing it,' her grandmother explained.

'I suppose,' she said, unconvinced.

'But it's entirely up to you. Sometimes it takes a while for wounds to heal, and forgiveness to be found,' her mother added with a smile as she fiddled with the bow on her pinnie.

'So, it doesn't have to be instant?'

'Of course not, it might take an eternity, but life's too short to hold grudges,' Vera advised as she fed the little bird some more seeds.

Charlotte walked down the road. Her golden strands of hair were muted by the fading sky that passed over her head. She looked into a compact mirror, checking her cherry blossom lipstick. The gold ring that sat around her finger caught her eye. Admiring it, she bumped into someone. She jolted backwards as she saw who it was.

'What on earth do you think you're playing at? I leave this city for two seconds, and I come back to find my uncle with a punctured hand,' Jimmy snapped, refusing to let her pass.

'He had it coming, and you hurt Harry,' she said, looking up at him, her eyes sharp and angry.

'He deserved it, and you'll get what's coming to you, I'll make sure of it. I can't believe you had the nerve to stab him yourself rather than relying on your guard dogs, I'm almost impressed,' he said, grinning thinly.

'Well, what are you waiting for?' she asked.

He circled her like a hyena stalking a fresh carcass. 'The perfect moment.'

'You're just saying that 'cause you haven't got your mates to back you up, you're a fuckin' weasel just like your uncle,' she yelled.

'Oh, look at you gettin' all angry, little Lottie tryin' to act tough,' he said.

'Only my friends can call me that. They won't let you hurt us,' she said as she pushed past him.

'We'll see about that. Oh, and congratulation on the engagement, but I doubt you'll both make it down the aisle,' he said.

Curtis stood opposite Ricky in the kitchen, tensity mounting as they stared at one another in silence. Jackie sat in the living room, her fingers occupied by the wool that twisted and turned around the knitting needles in her hands. She listened for the pending confrontation.

'What was that about then?' Curtis asked calmly.

'What do you mean?' Ricky hissed.

'You were extremely rude.'

'I can't be bothered with this,' he said, attempting to escape. Curtis stepped into the doorway, blocking his path with his large frame.

'You should be, why are you so angry?' he questioned.

'Why are you letting them into our house?'

'Oh, so this is about their skin,' Curtis sighed.

'They were judging us,' Ricky spat as he paced the length of the small kitchen.

'From my observation, you were the one being judgemental.'

'I really don't care,' Ricky muttered.

Jackie had heard enough. She placed her knitting needles down and proceeded to the kitchen. 'Give them a chance, they've given us one,' she said, trying desperately to convince him.

'I don't want to,' he said bitterly.

'Then how do you expect anything to change?' Jackie asked, frustrated.

Ricky found himself stuck, unable to answer her as his mind struggled for a response. Barging past them, he retreated to his room, slamming the door behind him.

There was a crispness to the air that was intensified by the night sky. Vallance Road was quiet with the distant whirling of taxi cabs and drunken individuals bundling out of the Blind Beggar or one of the many other pubs within the area. Oliver looked dishevelled, his hair was out of place and his eyes looked gaunt.

'I've properly ruined it with Fran,' Oliver said. Jack leant against the wall as he watched his friend lament.

'Yeah, you have, what you did was unacceptable,' he said, taking a swig of whiskey.

'You're the last person that should be talking to me about behaviour,' Oliver snapped suddenly.

'Oh, and why's that? Go on, Oli, tell me,' Jack questioned.

'Because half the time you can't even stand straight, you know you're messed up, and you just kept pushing and pushing. You always lost control and we had to clean up your mess like you're a sodding toddler.'

'At least I don't carry around a pocket watch that belonged to my abusive father, and after you hit Fran, it seems that you're turning into him, maybe you even enjoyed it,' he said venomously.

'Shut your mouth,' Oliver said, incensed.

'Or what?'

'I'll say something I regret.'

'And what's that? Nothing you say can hurt me, I've heard it all before.'

Oliver paused, staring at him. 'That night before Fran came round, Isla paid me a visit.'

'Yeah, to pick up a shirt for Lottie to repair, don't try and twist it,' he said with crossed arms.

'That's a lie. She wanted to sleep with me, she said she missed me, you can ask her yourself if you don't believe me.'

Jack stared at him, his eyes wide with shock. 'You're lying.'

'You know very well I'm not,' he said firmly.

'Fuck you,' Jack said quietly, turning to the door. Oliver

sat, surprised by his under-reaction, he was expecting a punch to the face, but instead, he got the back of his friend's long drape jacket. 'While we're being so honest with each other, I suppose I should tell you, Fran's been seen getting real close to a lad that works down the docks, has even been round his house a few times,' he uttered coldly.

'Get out,' Oliver said.

'With pleasure.'

'Tell me it's not true, Isla,' Jack said, furiously pacing. Her small flat was lit by a few dull lamps, the light following his angered shadow across the walls.

She sat with her head in her hands, the tears falling into the darkness of her palms. 'I'm sorry, I don't know what I was thinking,' she wailed.

'For fuck's sake Isla, I thought you loved me.'

'I do, I didn't sleep with him,' she said, looking at him desperately.

'But you went round there with the intention of sleeping with him,' he said sharply.

'Yes, but it was a misunderstanding,' she tried to justify.

He looked down at her, his eyes burning with tears. 'Don't try to make excuses, I'm leaving.'

'Where are you going?' she asked.

'To do something I should have done a long time ago,' he said, slamming the door.

As Francesca pondered the dying daisy that was placed on her desk, she caught Mr Montgomery watching her out of the corner of her eye. Despite this, her gaze remained fixed on the dying flower. The room was filled with cigarette smoke that passed over the many artefacts on his desk. The smoke navigated its way around the large propeller, resembling clouds slowly moving in the sky.

'Are you going to sit there and stare at it all day?' he asked.

'No, Sir, just lost my train of thought,' she replied, turning her attention to the typewriter once again.

'That wouldn't happen to be from your estranged lover, would it?' he said, acknowledging the hypnotism that the wilting flower possessed.

'He's not my lover,' she dismissed.

'But he was something. Don't be stupid enough to take him back.'

'Do you like flowers, Mr Montgomery?' she asked.

'I guess so, why'd you ask?'

'Do any flowers have special meaning to you?'

'I suppose, what are you getting at?' he said impatiently.

'Daisies now have quite an odd meaning to me, both good and bad,' she said as she studied its delicate petals.

'Roses have always reminded me of my mother. Hell, that's why I've got one tattooed on my arm,' he explained.

'Can I see?'

'Yeah, here you see, it's got the petals and the thorns.' He pulled up his sleeve.

'When did you get it?'

'When I got back from the war, she died of a heart attack while I was out in a bomber over God knows where. My biggest regret is not being here to say goodbye. Whatever happens in life, Fran, don't miss the opportunity to say goodbye.'

'I'm sorry you lost her,' she said, examining the artwork.

'It's not your fault. But if I can tell you one thing is that no matter how hard goodbyes are, they are a necessary part of life, so we can close one door and open another without fear of us going back on ourselves. Now, if I were you, I'd put that flower in the bin before you make a mistake.'

'But it's just a flower, it's doing no harm,' she said.

'Every moment you look at that rotting thing you're considering going back and clinging on to the past, let it go, say goodbye,' he said, continuing his paperwork.

As Francesca left the office, she turned back to the decaying daisy sitting sorrowfully in the bin. As she walked upon the pavement, she heard footsteps coming up behind her.

'Answer me one question,' Oliver insisted as he met her side.

'What do you want to know?' she asked as the chilly breeze bit at the back of her neck.

'How could you move on so quickly?'

'The truth is, I haven't, I haven't moved on even though I want to,' she admitted.

'You're seeing somebody else, aren't you?' His eyes were cold as he cast his icy glance upon her.

'We're not together anymore, Oliver, who I see is up to me.'

'Just answer the question,' he spoke with stern persistence.

'I've just made some new friends, not that it is any of your concern.' Francesca watched the road, hoping desperately for a bus to appear.

'I can't believe you'd—'

'Oh, don't take this personally.' She cut him off quickly.

'You're the one that's made it personal,' he hissed, charging down the pavement.

'By meeting new people?' Francesca asked.

'By moving on,' he shouted.

'Maybe you should try it because it's making you into a wreck of a man,' she snapped as he disappeared down the bottom of the road.

Oliver looked down at his scuffed brogues as he sombrely followed the cobbles of Vallance Road. *She's right*, he thought to himself, realising the state he was in. He had lost everyone he had ever cared about because of his poor judgement.

'We agreed not to tell him,' Isla said furiously, storming towards him.

'I lost my temper,' he admitted.

'Because you lost your temper, I've lost the person I love.'

'I'm sorry,' he said.

She looked up at him, recognising the despair in his tired eyes. 'I should have just told him the truth. He left last night, said he's going to do something he should have done a long time ago, whatever that means, just watch your back,' she warned, walking in the opposite direction.

As the train reached the platform, hundreds of feet met the concrete of Liverpool Street Station. The area was thick with smoke. The sound of train horns and screeching tracks pierced the air. As Susan stepped onto the platform, she held her stomach that had now developed into a fully formed bump. The baby was growing as it should, sending a few little kicks into the skin here and there. Waddling along the concrete, she held Colin's hand; two thin gold bands glistening on their fingers.

'Do you need a hand with that, Sir?' a porter called out before being politely declined.

They had no intention of staying long, but the guilt of leaving home was too much to bear. They both had bright faces and looked at one another contently. The Scottish air had done them both good and they longed for the countryside once more.

'Come on then, the quicker we make peace, the quicker we can go home,' Susan said as they left the station.

Colin pushed his way through the heavy church doors. He met eyes with the centre aisle and the rows of benches that followed its direction. Looking at the large wooden cross, he couldn't help but feel guilty for abandoning the church. He felt even more guilt for abandoning his father. His mind filled with dread at the thought of their possible reunification.

'Welcome home,' a voice bellowed from the front pew. His father sat, concentrating on the candles that flickered upon the main altar.

'I have a new home now,' Colin said as he walked slowly up the aisle, mustering up the courage to confront him.

'I know. You did the one thing I was afraid of.'

'Everything's going to be ok, Susan is healthy, the baby is developing as it should,' he said optimistically.

'You know I don't approve of her, and you went behind my back. And then you ran away,' his father said, his tone unwavering.

'I did what was necessary,' Colin justified as he sat beside him.

'Running from your problems, running from me?' he said irritably.

'Running with Susan. She is my priority, will always be my priority.'

'Why have you come back?' his father questioned.

'To make things right.'

'With whom exactly?'

'God.'

'Well, I'm glad you still hold your faith in high regard, despite your choice of wife,' he said coldly, acknowledging the ring on his son's finger.

'I love her.'

'I should hope so.'

'I wish you would accept her. I know why you won't, but at least try to consider the fact that she makes me happier than anyone else in this world,' he confessed proudly as he passed his father a small slip of paper. 'Here is our new address in case you have a change of heart, we'll be leaving in a few days.'

'Goodbye, Colin.' His father dismissed him, scrunching the piece of paper in his hand.

'Christ, I must be seeing things. Is that really you?' Kerry said as she opened the front door to meet her elusive friend.

'Yes, in the flesh.' Susan smiled as she entered.

'I hope you haven't brought Colin, it's not safe you know,' she said cautiously, her eyes scanning the road before shutting the door.

'Yeah, I know, that's why we left in the first place.'

'Then why have you come back? If it's not purely on bad judgement,' Kerry said bluntly as she watched her friend waddle to the sofa.

'I need to make things right with Oliver, Fran has been

sending me letters, telling me he hasn't been doing well. She also told me how you gave Lewis and Finn a good bollocking.' She plonked herself down.

'What's done is done. As nice as it is to see you, I really don't think you should have come back,' she said, concerned as she sat opposite.

'Oliver won't hurt Colin.'

'I've never seen him so unstable, Susan,' Kerry warned.

'Well, hopefully he's had time to calm down.'

'Where do you live anyway? I'm supposed to be one of your closest friends and I don't know where you've moved to. Hell, you didn't even tell me you were pregnant,' Kerry said irritably as she looked at the growing bump.

'We live in Scotland now, just over the border in Dumfries. I should have told you, I was just scared. Come here, you can feel the baby kicking.' Susan reached out her hand.

'I'd rather not. The whole baby inside you thing makes me uncomfortable.'

'Don't be silly, come here,' Susan persuaded as Kerry reluctantly offered her hand. Placing it gently on her belly, Kerry felt the little movements made by the mini human inside.

'Feisty little bugger just like its mum.' She smiled as she retracted her arm.

'Fran spoke well of you in her letter, even though you had a go at her.'

'I did what I did to Lewis and Finn for myself. It had nothing to do with Fran,' Kerry said firmly.

'You always were a stubborn git. But you're a stubborn git with a heart of gold,' Susan said.

'There are many people who would disagree with you there,' she muttered, her short platinum blonde hair contrasting her deep amber eyes.

'You'd be surprised at what people think.'

'So, where is Colin? Have you let him off the leash?' Kerry teased.

'He's at the church. He'll be back later.'

'Oh, that can't be fun, his dad is a scary piece of work.'

'Yes, he is. But Colin's not there to see his dad, he wants to make peace with God.'

'Well, I'd prefer to make peace with an invisible being than a pissed off father. Speaking of churches, I see you got married.' She observed the little band that sat around her friend's finger.

'Yes, in a blacksmith's workshop, got the papers so that's all that matters,' Susan said with amusement.

'Oh, how romantic.' Kerry laughed.

'It was no fairy tale, but it was good enough for me.'

'Let's see that ring then,' she said, sitting forward to examine the new piece of jewellery.

Susan extended her hand. 'It's only simple, but it's all Colin could afford so it's special.'

'It's lovely, I'm glad you didn't get Albie to design it, otherwise it would be an atrocity.'

'Oh God, if it's anything to go by his paintings, I probably wouldn't have a finger left for the ring to go on. How are Albie and the others?' she asked.

'I don't see them very much anymore, Susan, I burnt those bridges.'

'There are no bridges burnt that can't be rebuilt.'

As Francesca sat on the end of his bed, she sifted through the small stack of books left on the chest of drawers. They were heavy and her wrist ached slightly with every page turned. They were old and run down, yet they had a certain beauty to them. As Curtis walked into the room, he watched her keenly as she held onto the vintage leather. Trailing her hand over the novels, she touched the weathered pages that felt as though they had encountered an adventure all to their own.

'Can you read me a story?' she asked, looking at him with adventurous eyes. She held a copy of Jules Verne's *Twenty Thousand Leagues Under the Sea*.

'And why would a young woman like yourself want to be read a story?'

'To escape. Isn't that the beauty of it?'

'To run away?' he questioned.

'I've imagined a life outside of London, but I think films and books are the closest I'm ever going to get to escaping this city,' she answered.

'Well, it's a good thing I have plenty of books.' He smiled as he sat beside her, taking the old novel from her grasp.

As he began to read, Francesca laid her head on his shoulder, his gentle voice meeting her ear. Two chapters in and her eyes grew heavy. He stiffened as she nuzzled into him, hardly realising she had fallen asleep. Sliding one arm under her knees and the other behind her shoulders, he laid her down, her head meeting the soft pillow. Leaving the room, he returned with a blanket, covering her.

Despite the blanket, she shivered, and Curtis scolded himself for not thinking of giving it to her sooner. There was no heating in the house which left it in a Baltic condition and even he, as a muscular man standing over six-foot, had to rub his hands together to keep them from getting stiff.

He ran a finger down her cheek. 'Fran, I think I better walk you home, I don't want you to freeze,' he said gently.

'But I'm so tired.' She gripped his finger in protest. One drowsy eyelid lifted to see him sitting on the edge of the bed. 'I'd like to stay a little longer, I enjoy being around you.'

Curtis couldn't help but smile as he saw her fingers placed on his. 'I'll go and get some more blankets,' he said, rising from the bed.

Francesca rubbed her groggy eyes. 'I don't mind if you'd like to lay next to me,' she said shyly. 'You'd be warmer than a blanket,' she quickly added, feeling her cheeks redden.

'I can if you'd like.'

'I would like that.'

He nodded as she shuffled backwards, the single bed leaving little room for manoeuvre. He laid beside her. She could sense how tense he was, almost as if he was frightened of her. She was so close to him, and could see his chest rise and fall, reminding her of his past, what Charley had told her. She pulled the blanket over him as they faced each other, their eyes meeting.

'Why are you being nice to me?' she had to ask. He'd invited her round on her own on multiple occasions. He had cooked for her and they had played cards together, a competitive game of rummy which lasted hours. He taught her chess and dominoes and she had laughed in a way that made her stomach hurt. She had gone out of her way to walk with him to the docks on some mornings, and she had made him sandwiches alongside Charley's. The three would sit and chat for every minute of their lunch break before Francesca had to scurry back to the bank.

'Because I like you.'

'Not just because you knew my brother?'

'At first I was curious, I wanted to see if you had his spirit, which you do. But that has nothing to do with me liking you.'

She sighed, 'I'm nothing compared to my brother, I don't have his confidence. I have ambitions, but part of me is too scared to pursue them.'

'Give yourself more credit, Fran. Confidence comes with age and experience. You have his kindness, you've looked after Charley for all these years.'

'He's looked after me,' she countered.

'You've been kind to Jackie and I, a lot of people from these parts aren't.'

'That should just be second nature,' she said. 'Why did Charley never tell me about you?'

'I imagine Charley wanted to wait till you were older, till you healed a bit. I think he knew you'd bump into us at some point of your own accord.'

Francesca grinned. 'Can you tell me more about James?'

Curtis's lips twitched upwards in reminiscence. 'We all bonded over the fact that we lied about our ages to get in, all being sixteen. The three of us were well built and looked older than we were. James told me that your mother was livid when she found out, but gave in after a while.' He shook his head, recalling how his friend had refused to take no for an answer many times.

Francesca considered whether that was why her mother had felt so much guilt after his passing. 'He was so incredibly young, you all were.'

'Even Jackie lied about her age. But she had been working since the age of thirteen and was wise beyond her years, so she fooled them. But nothing could have prepared her for what she saw. Charley was just seventeen when he was injured at Dunkirk but went back to fight after he healed. I was twenty when I was on the brink of death a few years later. War doesn't care about who we are. We all suffered at its hands.'

Francesca gulped, realising that she would be twenty in March, the same age that Curtis was when he had been injured. She started counting on her fingers. 'So, you're thirty-two? Like Charley?'

He nodded. 'I'm a fair bit older than you.'

'It doesn't mean we can't be friends.' A mischievous smile spread across her face.

CHAPTER 18

VICTORIA PARK WAS illuminated by an enormous bonfire at its centre. With months of preparation, it had been constructed out of collected branches, old wooden planks, and the occasional door. This combined with a healthy dose of gasoline sent the blaze high into the night sky, the smoke masking the stars.

The bonfire party was a tradition, proving to be an excuse for many to feast on seasonal confections such as treacle tart and toffee apples. Jacket potatoes were roasted in the ashes and were filled to the brim with cheese, while others helped themselves to homemade vegetable soup. Children waved sparklers in the air, imagining them to be magical wands that manipulated the light. The entire neighbourhood had come out to watch the flames as the festivities continued into the early hours.

Francesca sat with her mitten-clad hands. She was feasting

on a hot potato that sent steam into her face, warming her cold skin. Elaine sat with a toffee apple, licking the sticky layer, her lips caked in sugar.

'Oliver and I got in an argument.'

'There's no surprise there, what was it about?' Elaine asked, taking a bite.

'He was annoyed that I've been trying to move on.'

'He still cares about you, otherwise he wouldn't get so cross,' Elaine analysed.

'He has a funny way of showing it,' Francesca muttered, stabbing the potato with her fork.

'Do you care about him?'

'I don't know.'

'What he did was unforgivable, don't take him back,' her friend said with a concerned glance.

'You'd be surprised by how many people have told me that. I can forgive him, but I won't take him back, I would be disrespecting myself if I did,' she said, stuffing a forkful of cheesy potato into her mouth.

'You're a better person than me. If someone did that to me, I'd get Charley to kill them.'

'Charley was ready to kill him, but I didn't want him to get involved. I just want to put it behind me.'

Laying her head on her friend's shoulder, Elaine looked up at her. 'I never want to see you hurting like that again.'

'I know you don't.' Francesca smiled, glancing down at her.

'I shouldn't have told you to go round there that night, it was my fault.'

'Don't be silly, you weren't to know they were there.'

'How is the wrist doing?'

'Good as new,' she replied, wiggling her arm in the air.

A straw-stuffed body, supposedly resembling Guy Fawkes was wheeled through the crowd amidst cheers from excitable children. A dodgy brown wig was placed on its head in hopes of making the figure seem more realistic. It was hoisted onto the top of the bonfire and burnt within a matter of minutes. Francesca almost felt sorry for the body as it was reduced to ashes.

'So, Curtis seems nice, I saw the way you were eyeing him,' Elaine said, munching.

Francesca grinned but said nothing, choosing to watch the bonfire instead.

'He looks older, him compared to Oliver is like a man being compared to a boy. It's not very fair.'

'I know, it's made me think,' Francesca sighed.

'And he's handsome, I couldn't help but notice,' Elaine added with a wink.

'Very handsome.'

'Is it going to go anywhere?'

'I don't know. He's just lovely to be around,' she said.

As Susan twisted the key, she panicked at the thought of confronting her brother, a thought that had stopped her from coming for the past couple of days. Colin followed slowly behind her. For now, the space was empty, and they were left alone with the stench of alcohol. The house was a mess. Rubbish littered the floor, including mountains of bills and paperwork that Susan knew were important. Gathering them into her arms, she placed them on the table. The kitchen worktops were coated in a layer of grime. Dirty plates and pans were piled high in the air. She sighed as she took a seat. Looking around, she couldn't help but imagine the clutter as a parallel to her brother's mind, troubled and twisted, but most of all difficult to untangle. Reaching for a few old photos scattered on the ground, she placed them on the worktop. She sat back with a glazed glance. She no longer recognised this place. She hoped she'd still recognise her brother. With a thud, the door swung open. Colin stood at Susan's side.

'What are you two doing here?' Oliver hissed as his eyes latched onto them.

'I have a key, I used to live here, remember?' Susan snarled.

'You know you're not welcome.'

'We both know that's not true, Oli,' Colin said.

'You have no idea what I think.'

'I do know actually, and I'm not afraid to tell you what I think,' Susan said, mustering up the courage to tell him what for.

'And what is it that you think, Susan?'

'That you need to pull yourself together, look at this place it's disgusting,' she muttered, kicking a month-old newspaper that laid on the floor.

'You've got some nerve,' he said angrily.

'And you've got a broom in the corner that I suggest you use before you can no longer see the carpet,' she said with unintentional wit.

Oliver's lips quirked. 'Colin, pass me that broom will ya.' He reached out his hand. 'So why are you back?' he questioned as he gathered the rubbish, the bristles dragging reluctantly across the floor.

'To see if you're alright, I see now that you're not,' Susan said, saddened.

'I thought I'd lost you forever.' Oliver stared at her.

'You haven't, I was doing what was best for us,' she said, holding her protruding bump.

'And Fran was our saving grace,' Colin added calmly.

'I don't want to talk about Fran,' he dismissed with a quick swipe of the broom.

'We don't have to. But it's Fran that has been writing me letters, telling me how you are doing even though I know it hurts her to do so,' Susan explained.

'She wants nothing to do with me.'

'That may be the case, but bumming around like this isn't going to leave a good impression now is it? You look like you haven't showered in a week.'

'Where are you staying?' he asked.

'A bed-and-breakfast,' she said.

'Well, this is your home, and you have the right to stay in it,' he said, gathering the dirt into a pile.

'Hand me that dustpan and brush, we'll get this place cleaned up in a jiffy.' Colin grinned as the two siblings smiled at one another.

'Have you seen your dad?' Oliver questioned.

'Yes.'

'How did that go?'

'As expected, but I said what I needed to say,' he said, kneeling to gather some of the grime into the pan.

'He's never liked us. Just because we're Catholic,' Oliver tutted as he wiped the kitchen surfaces.

'Catholic, Protestant, same cake different flavour icing. Religion shouldn't be able to tell us who we can and can't love.' He smiled at Susan who looked at him with brightening eyes.

'I'm pleased for you both,' Oliver spoke sincerely as he noticed their wedding bands.

'You really mean that?' his sister asked.

'Of course, it was just a bit of a shock to the system.'

'I should have told you,' Colin said.

Oliver placed a hand on his shoulder. 'I overreacted. I see now that you had no bad intentions.'

Jackie swayed with the music. Her body was loose and her hair was down, falling past her shoulders. She wore a red dress that fitted her like a glove, the ruffled hem sitting just above her knees. The Eldorado Club was a place where Jackie could truly relax. Here she didn't have to be so perfect and pristine, an appearance she knew she needed to uphold when she was amongst the Cockneys. She had only ever brought one Cockney, Charley, to her little slice of heaven in East Dulwich. He had danced with her all night, and had danced with her friends also, all of whom she had met at the hospital.

Curtis and Charley were her best friends who she trusted would love her for who she was. Not Jackie the nurse, not sisterly Jackie who Ricky and Wilma relied on, just this. A young woman who by circumstance had grown up too soon. She tilted her head back, feeling the cigarette smoke move around her as the jazz band continued to play. The music was like honey, rich and potent. Curtis handed her a glass of rum, and she sniffed it before gulping it down, savouring every smell, every touch and taste.

'You've got every man in this room looking your way, Jackie.' Curtis was standing beside her, a wide smile on his face.

'That's a shame, I'm in the mood for a woman this evening,' she replied, grinning.

'Keep moving the way you do and you'll have your pick of the whole place.'

She met his gaze and looped and arm over his broad shoulder. Her perfume wafted up his nostrils, warm lavender.

'And what about you?'

'I need time, I've had one too many disastrous attempts at finding someone,' he said. There had been three attempts. The first woman he had danced with here and had taken home, but she fled as soon as she saw his scar. The second was a local councillor's wife who had flirted with him to piss her husband off, which he wasn't aware of at the time. As soon as they were one-on-one, she also ran away after seeing his war wound. And possibly the worst and final attempt was with a woman he met on the Tube who slept with him 'for the experience' as she had said afterwards. It made him feel sick. *Used.*

Anger flared in Jackie's eyes as she thought of those women. 'I know it has been difficult for you. And what about Fran? Don't act like you're not interested in her in that way, I've clocked the way your eyes light up when you see her, and I know she's been round our house a fair few times,' she whispered into his ear.

'She's a sweetheart. Charley told me she's had a rough time lately with a previous partner, the least I could do is show her how she deserves to be treated. Even if it's not with me in the long run. You remember how difficult it was at that age trying to figure out what you want, who you want.'

Jackie nodded but let out a sigh. The truth was that she never got to figure such things out at that age. Her young life was controlled entirely by the war, even after it was over. She was still haunted by what she saw, the amputated limbs, the look on their faces as soldiers and civilians alike died. Even though she never took up arms, Curtis and Charley always treated her with respect, understanding that the things she witnessed left mental scars no different from the ones branding them.

Curtis guided her into his arms and hugged her. He knew exactly what was happening when her eyes glazed over in that way, what she was reliving. He didn't know how she did it, how she continued to be a nurse to this day, the Lord knows he'd rather die than join the Navy again.

'It was nice of you to invite Fran and her friends round.'

Jackie shook her head free of the thoughts that plagued her. 'We hardly ever have English guests apart from Charley. It's important that Ricky and Wilma make friendships with others around their age who are from here.'

'To protect them?'

'You say that like I'm scheming,' she tutted.

'No, but I understand we don't live in an ideal world, if they make some connections, it'll only serve to benefit them.'

'Just like how we benefited from making friends with Charley and James, and vice versa.' That beautiful smile spread across her face again. 'I have a feeling they're going to need each other, you've seen things are getting more hostile. Even after that wonderful evening at the Lambeth Town Hall earlier this year, there have been a number of attacks on people and establishments who encourage co-existence,' she sighed.

Curtis remembered that cold February night. The Anglo-West Indian Committee had hosted an evening which encouraged black and white people to dance together. Sure, it was a little awkward at first, but after the initial rounds of mambas, jives, and fox trots they were laughing and drinking together. It was almost utopian. But Curtis knew it was an uphill battle. How the younger generation would face even more scrutiny despite the efforts of the Committee. Tensions were rising, and even The Eldorado had been attacked by the press for being a 'coloured club' as they put it.

'Enough worrying,' he said as he offered her a cigarette.

She took it and he lit it for her, the embers glowing against her dark skin. The smoke whirled around her as she backed away from him and started to dance again.

The night-time darkness was contrasted by the laughter and light of the Thomas household. Colin and Oliver sat together as though nothing had changed. Susan's face lit up, ecstatic as she witnessed the two arm in arm. The kitchen worktops were clean, the floor was clear; the house was spotless again. Oliver sat in a fresh set of clothes. He had his black hair slicked back and was freshly shaven. Once again, his pocket watch sat proudly in his hand, ticking the seconds by.

A few loud bangs sent Oliver's attention to the front door. Opening it, the darkness flooded in. *Jack*. Not a word was said, but his manner was all too familiar. He had that look in his eyes, a concoction of alcoholic anarchy that swirled within his pupils. Pulling out a revolver, he forced Oliver back to the kitchen with the weapon aimed at his chest.

Susan's face turned to a picture of horror as she watched the situation helplessly. Colin stood from his seat slowly, but Jack acknowledged his presence, rendering him useless. Oliver closed his eyes as the metal barrel was pressed to his forehead. With a drunken smile, Jack pulled the trigger.

Colin dropped to the floor with a lifeless thud.

Susan's screams made themselves heard like sirens in a state of tragedy. A ghastly mixture of suffering and confusion filled the room as the neighbourhood awoke to the nightmare before them.

Susan fell to the ground like a wounded animal next to Colin. Oliver turned into an animal himself. Tackling Jack to the ground, he forced the revolver out of his hand. Holding the metal to Jack's head, he heard his sister's pain-filled cries.

'Go on, aren't you going to pull it?' Jack mumbled, no longer resisting.

'No, because I'm not a monster like you,' he spat, throwing the weapon down.

Days passed and Susan sat loyally at his bedside, clinging onto his hand in hopes of feeling a reciprocating grip. She had faith for a while, but after that while all that was left was misery.

The Priest walked slowly into the room as he watched his dying son. He met Susan's glance with mirrored distress.

'How long has he got?' he asked, trying to process the situation before him.

'The doctors won't say. I just want him to come back to me,' Susan answered, breaking down into tears.

Walking towards her, he welcomed her into his arms. 'I know, I want him to come back too,' he spoke softly. 'You want to know something?'

'Anything,' she said with desperation, hugging him tightly.

'My wife was a good woman, a Catholic too, just like you. Back in Belfast as a young Protestant man, it was obscene to think of such a match. And especially a match with a child out of wedlock. I know what you are going through, I managed when I lost my Annie.'

'I'm not losing him,' she said defiantly, looking up at him.

'Of course you're not.' He embraced her again, trying to comfort her even though the inevitable would be upon them shortly.

CHAPTER 19

SHE STOOD OVER the grave.
The winter air was crisp and whirled the powdered snow across the vast grounds of Tower Hamlets Cemetery. It was peaceful. It was silent. It was beautiful with the gentle flurries of snow from the night before that had solidified into a thick white layer. This layer engulfed the landscape, not a statue could be seen, not a blade of grass to be recognised. It sat upon the many tombstones like a coating of royal icing.

As Francesca walked up behind her, she watched as Charlotte carefully placed a bouquet of roses on her mother's grave. Catching sight of her out of the corner of her eye, Charlotte tried to conceal the tears that fell down her cheeks.

'I was just passing by and noticed you standing here all alone. It's ok to be upset,' Francesca said.

'I'm not alone, I'm with mum,' Charlotte said with a snivel and a sniff as her friend passed her a handkerchief.

'You know you can always talk to me.'

'I quit my job a while ago, I couldn't bear it anymore, and now my savings are running out and I'm struggling to find work. My former boss has been spreadin' lies about me, saying I'm mentally unstable and unfit to work in the other factories in the area, so none of them will employ me. You know Harry had that cut on the back of his head, well it was Talbot's nephew that did that. They hurt him because of me, I'm worried they'll do it again,' she confessed.

'Oh, I'm so sorry, Lottie, is there anything I can do?'

'No, it's fine, honestly, just means we have to put off the wedding for a bit until we can get the funds and wait for things to settle down,' she said, forcing an optimistic smile.

'I'm sure we can think of something,' Francesca said as her mind began to scheme.

'How's Colin? Harry and I brought up some flowers the other day. Susan looks like she's in a right state.' Rubbing her hands together, she fought against the frosty air.

'It's not looking good, there's only so long they can keep him hooked up to those machines.'

'I'd be in a wreck if that was my Harry.'

'Yes, it's awful. And the fact that Jack was let go,' she said, disgusted.

'How?'

'The Priest somehow got him released, even though he put his son in hospital.'

'Harry wanted to kill him when he found out, I don't think I've ever seen him so cross. Luckily, the police got there first,' Charlotte said.

'That boy has got away with so much, and yet there is no justice for the people that get hurt.' Francesca's thick green wellie boots crunched against the snow-lined grass.

'When we die, do you think we have a trial before we go to heaven or hell?' Charlotte asked, looking at the many gravestones surrounding them.

'Maybe, I like to think God is an understanding person, a good judge of character.'

'So, he forgives people?'

'Maybe if the people ask for forgiveness,' she replied.

'I think that's what Jack needs to do, for his own sake.'

'Unfortunately, only he can make that decision,' Francesca said.

Shuddering in response to the icy breeze, Francesca held her suede coat in a firm embrace. Continuing down the road, she looked at her wellie boots that had accumulated a thin layer of ice upon their soles. Careful not to slip, she walked upon the powdered layer that had masked the cobblestones. It was disorientating how East London transformed. The rows of houses sat with icicles hanging from their roofs, their red bricks coated in frost. It was as if nature was back to reclaim its territory, engulfing the distant ruins in snow.

She met the end of Morpeth Street. A pack of men were attempting to reclaim the area before them, shovelling snow out of the road. Children played, throwing snowballs at one another. The word snowballs seemed entirely too pleasant, for they were more like ice clusters that left bruises and red marks on their faces. Nevertheless, the children let their imaginations flourish in the flurries and icicles, transforming the streets into Antarctica or a new world entirely.

As Francesca reached the door, she gave a few soft knocks

with her numb hand. She stood patiently as she waited for a response. As a bright-eyed woman appeared, Francesca politely introduced herself. 'Hello, I'm Fran, is Kerry in? I'd like to talk to her.'

'Of course.' Kerry's mother smiled as she rubbed her arms, the breeze invading the warm entryway. 'You've got a visitor!' she called.

'What can I do for you?' Kerry asked stiffly as she met the doorway.

'I wanted to say thank you for what you did, with Lewis and Finn,' she said, looking up at her.

'Don't mention it.'

'Can I take you somewhere?' Francesca questioned.

Kerry looked at her suspiciously. 'Not gonna push me in the Thames, are you?'

'No, don't be silly, you'd push me in before I even got the chance,' she said, grinning.

A smirk covered Kerry's face. 'Bugger it, I've got nothing else to do today.'

As they walked down the road, Kerry's thick creepers embedded in the snow, leaving a trail of deep footprints behind her.

'You know Lottie lost her job a while ago,' Francesca informed.

'Her boss was a twat, it's probably for the best,' Kerry said, pulling her drape jacket around herself.

'I think she's in trouble. She said something about his nephew hurting Harry.'

'Oh, that little wanker,' Kerry hissed.

'You know him?'

'He's a slimy git, and a nasty piece of work if he wants to

be.'

'How do we stop him?' Francesca asked, fiddling with her polka dot scarf.

'Look, I don't want to involve you,' Kerry said, turning to her with a concerned glance.

'I want to help,' she said quickly.

'Well, if you're up for getting your hands dirty, I'm sure we can come up with a plan. But don't get upset if you don't like what you see,' she warned.

'I can handle it.'

As they reached the rundown house with fading paint, Kerry felt a few snowflakes hit her cheeks. 'I don't know what you're playin' at bringing me here, but this better be good, I'm freezing my tits off,' she huffed.

The area was quiet, eerily quiet, putting Kerry on edge. The bright white snow hurt her vision if she stared at it for too long, so she retired her gaze back to the shabby looking front door.

'Don't worry, we can warm up inside.' Francesca said as she pulled her reluctant friend by the arm. Knocking on the door, they were greeted by Jackie who welcomed them in.

'Tea?' she asked as the two found refuge in the living room.

'That sounds lovely,' Francesca said.

Kerry looked at her with a piercing stare as she paced the small interior. She wasn't judging it, she was judging them.

'They're good people, Kerry, just give them a chance. I introduced the others to them, and they got on like a house on fire,' she encouraged, but was met with no more than a grumble.

Ricky wandered into the room and took a seat.

'So, who's your friend?' Jackie asked from the kitchen.

'This is Kerry, Kerry, meet Jackie and Ricky, where's Curtis?' she asked.

'Working, as usual, he should be back later, feel free to stay as long as you like.' Jackie grinned as she placed the tray down. It had a few mugs of steaming tea accompanied by a selection of pink wafers.

'So, tell us about yourself,' Ricky said, studying Kerry's scowling expression as she sat on the sofa opposite him.

'There is nothing to tell,' she said bluntly.

'Hello, and who's this?' Wilma asked as she peered into the room.

'This is Kerry,' Francesca introduced.

'Ah, this is Kerry, your friends told me about you. I love your eyes, they're very unique.' Wilma smiled, taking a seat beside her, a little closer than Kerry would have liked judging from the way she bristled.

'Thanks.'

'You don't talk much, do you?'

'I talk when I want to talk.'

'Well, my name's Wilma, and I'm very talkative so you might find it difficult to resist my conversation,' she said. Francesca grinned as she refused to take Kerry's silence for an answer. 'Where did you get your jacket?' she asked.

'The Ladies' Market.'

'I've only ever passed through there on the way home from work, but the little stalls look lovely, you'll have to take me some time,' she suggested.

'That's a great idea,' Francesca said enthusiastically as she sipped her tea.

'I better be off,' Kerry said in a bid to escape, despite only being there a mere five minutes.

'I'll walk you home,' Wilma said.

She sent her a sharp glance. 'I can manage.'

'I don't doubt it.' She beamed, jumping from her seat.

'Everything will work out you know,' Oliver assured as he cradled his sister. Her eyes were swollen from the tears that assaulted her face.

The snowy landscape could be seen out of the hospital window despite the frozen layer that had developed on the glass. Two robins jumped on and off a tree branch, their little feathers fluttering through the chilly wind.

'He's going to die, ain't he?' she snivelled, glancing at his motionless body. His gold crucifix glowed against his unnaturally pale skin.

'I don't know, Susan, I'm not going to lie to you and say he'll recover, but things will work out, I'll look after you no matter what happens.'

'The Priest has been coming up every day,' she said, looking out the window to distract herself.

'I hope he hasn't been giving you trouble,' Oliver said defensively.

'No, quite the opposite, he's been kind,' she informed him with a slight smile as she watched the two robins dance before her, fluttering from one branch to another.

'I'm glad to hear that.' Oliver avoided eye contact with Colin. He felt his stomach drop with every glance, so he too watched the robins.

'Fran popped by. She told me that Lottie quit her job and that they won't be able to afford a wedding, it's not fair this world.'

'Surely there is some way around it.' He pondered.

'That's exactly what Fran said. Maybe you should go and

talk to her, as a reconciliation.'

'Now why would I do that?' he questioned reluctantly as the birds flew out of sight.

'Because it's the right thing to do,' Susan said simply.

'I've never really been to Victoria Park,' Wilma spoke merrily as she wandered about, in awe of the winter wonderland.

'Well, now you can tick it off your list,' Kerry said, reluctant to make conversation.

The afternoon presented a corrupted blanket of snow with boot marks and paw prints embedded in the crunchy ice. A few blades of grass were forcing their way through while other areas remained encased in the powdery substance.

'You seem to me like you're a reserved person,' Wilma assessed.

'It seems that you're out to annoy me,' Kerry said gruffly, continuing her path through the ice and dirty snow.

'Hey, that's not very fair, don't judge a book by its cover,' Wilma said, picking up a clump of snow, forming it into a ball. As she lobbed the snowball, it hit the back of Kerry's drape jacket with a thud.

Kerry stopped, irritably spinning on her heels to face her. Before she could say a word, another snowball was sent hurtling towards her, combusting on her chest making her stagger backwards. 'You're in for it now,' she exclaimed as she grabbed at the ground.

As the two waged war, they ran about the park, hiding behind trees, benches, anything to defend themselves from one another. Snow exploded on the objects, sending shards of icy shrapnel into the air. As Kerry lobbed a final ball, she was met with a giggling voice lurking behind an old oak tree.

'Truce,' she pleaded as Kerry lowered her arm.

'Ok, truce.' Kerry grinned, watching Wilma with childlike admiration as she met her gaze.

'You know I won,' Wilma said.

'Piss off you won,' Kerry said, brushing off her hands.

'Yeah I did, I lowered your defences,' Wilma exclaimed as she shoved a concealed handful of snow down the back of her opponent's neck. Running away and unable to contain her laughter, she looked back to see Kerry hot on her trail.

Oliver hadn't ventured to Coborn Road in quite some time, but he knew exactly who he would be confronted by if he dared to knock on the door. With a pause, he stood outside, taking a moment to form the right words, the sentences ingrained in his mind like a script. With a deep breath and one quick motion, he tapped on the wood.

Vera scowled as she opened the door. 'May I ask why you're here?'

'I just wanted to talk to Fran.'

'I think you've done enough,' she objected, standing firmly in the doorway.

'Please, Vera, it'll be five minutes at the most, I need to make things right.'

She stared at him for what felt like an eternity. 'I don't know what went on between you two, and I have too much respect for my granddaughter to pry, but she seems happy, happier than she has been for quite some time, and things are only looking up for her, don't you go and spoil it. I understand that your young life hasn't been fair, but hers hasn't either, and my dear, she is far too good for you. Come in, and make it quick,' she muttered, letting him through. She felt her painful joints crack as she retreated to the comfort of her armchair.

As Oliver walked up the stairs, he felt his heart thump. Knocking on the bedroom door, he was greeted by Francesca's confused expression. She looked left and right, trying to figure out how he managed to get into the house.

'Who on earth let you in?' she asked coldly.

'I see you're still into the habit of wearing your dressing gown at four thirty in the afternoon.' He looked at his pocket watch. 'But answering your question, Vera let me in.'

'You must have been bloody persuasive, and you have no right to judge my fashion sense considering your recent appearance.' He was well-groomed which caught her off guard, and she looked him up and down several times as he entered the room.

'I can't say she was pleased to see me.'

'I wonder why that is,' she muttered, sitting with her legs crossed at the top of her bed. 'I take it your sister is behind this?'

He watched her intently as he sat on her vanity stool. 'Of course she is. I'm sorry for everything that's happened to you, and everything that I've put you through,' he said, acknowledging her wrist that still had the faintest shades of green and yellow surrounding it. Francesca quickly hid it under the fluffy material of her dressing gown. 'I also had no right to tell you who you could spend your time with, I got cross, and said some things I shouldn't have,' he added.

'It's ok.'

'Susan told me everything, how you wrote to her.'

'She was worried about you.'

'You didn't have to do that,' Oliver said thankfully.

'That's what friends are for. She wanted to know you were alright. How's she doing?' Francesca asked.

'Not good, she spends every waking moment at his bedside.'

'How are you doing?'

'I could be better.' A lump built in his throat. 'It's all my fault.'

'Why do you say that?' she questioned.

'Jack and I had an argument, I said he was an embarrassment, and I told him about Isla.' Oliver looked at the ground. 'Then he came back with a revolver, I imagine the bullet was meant for me, but he aimed it at Colin instead, he knew that would hurt me more.'

'This isn't your fault. He's unstable and you couldn't tell what he would do. The past is in the past, all we can do is worry about the present because that's enough stress in itself.'

'You always know the right things to say,' he said, smiling. 'Speaking of the present, I want to talk to you about Lottie and Harry, Susan was thinking we could figure something out for them,' he continued.

'I've been thinking about them too, they deserve a little positivity,' she agreed.

'So, we're on the same page?'

'Yes, I've got an idea in mind, but I need to put some clothes on, so if you could wait in the hallway that would be great,' Francesca said as she leapt to her wardrobe.

'Are you sure this is a good idea?' Oliver asked cautiously as they stood outside the white panelled church.

'Have you got a better idea?' Francesca tutted, mustering up the courage to enter the building.

'I think the Priest is a little pre-occupied for a wedding, don't you?'

'It'll take his mind off things,' she said optimistically.

'What things? His dying son?' Oliver said. He would rather be any place but there. The Priest had never liked Oliver and was not afraid of showing it in the past.

'Look, you don't have to come in, but it's worth a shot,' she said, pushing open the doors. Catching sight of the Priest lighting candles at the main altar, she walked up the centre aisle with Oliver in reluctant pursuit. 'Can I speak to you for a minute?' she requested shyly as he turned to greet them both. He looked intimidating with his tall stature coated in his usual black robes and white collar.

'Of course, Francesca, what can I help you with?' he questioned, continuing to light the candles.

'I was just wondering... I mean, I know it's a bad time, but I was hoping...' She scrambled for the right words, but they wouldn't come out.

'Spit it out, child,' he said, blowing out the match in his hand.

'That you could do a wedding,' Oliver interjected.

'Of course I can do a wedding, but for whom are you asking, I hope not yourselves?' His eyes narrowed.

'Oh no, of course not, it's for my... Our friends Lottie... I mean Charlotte Lovett and Harry Marchal. The problem is they can't afford it, but we're willing to pay,' Francesca blurted out. She looked at Oliver who stared back at her, unaware of the financial obligation.

'No payment necessary, when is this wedding?' the Priest asked, his stern Northern Irish accent softening slightly.

'We were hoping in two weeks' time,' she suggested.

'Two weeks? Have they got any paperwork, confirmation from the Church of England? Have they even been attending this church?'

'No, but—'

'Then it's going to be a bit tricky,' he stated with folded arms.

'Yeah, we see that now. Don't worry about it, thank you for your time,' Oliver dismissed.

'Now hang on a minute, I said it would be tricky, not impossible. I'll see what I can do, but don't get your hopes up. Now on you go, I need to prepare for this evening's service,' the Priest concluded as he turned his attention to the altar once more.

It was a slow day at Liverpool Street Station. Due to the recent snowfall that had caused havoc on the tracks, the trains were infrequent to say the least. Engineers had been rushing along the railway lines, trying to fix problems caused by the melting snow and broken branches that had fallen into the path of oncoming steam trains.

Ricky had to wait between two and three hours for the overground carriages. As a porter, he had to carry passenger's bags to nearby taxis, which he despised, yet today, he almost missed it. Waiting around in the cold for the few trains made his blood boil. He stared at the station clock, its large hands taunting him.

The nearby Underground was operating as usual, allowing hordes of people to leave the darkened tunnels. As Wilma walked up the stairs, the winter breeze bit her cheeks, making them go rosy. She wore a thick wool coat that met her knees. A mischievous smile covered her face as she noticed Ricky sitting grumpily on a station bench.

Sneaking up behind him, she nicked the cap off his head. 'You always look so mopey,' she said, tossing it from one hand to the other.

Startled, his head snapped back angrily. 'Well, you get to work in a house, I have to sit in the cold all day. And at least your boss likes you, she makes you hot chocolate. I don't even get water.'

Wilma's smile grew wider. 'She's a lonely old lady who lives in a massive house all on her own, I think she employs me more for the company than domestic service. I spent today making beds that haven't been slept in for fifteen years.'

Rising from his seat, he tried to grab the cap from her, but she was too quick, darting from his grasp. 'Give that back, they took ten pounds out of my wage as a deposit for this stupid uniform, and I won't be impressed if you ruin it.'

'You think you're the only one that has it tough. I have to wear a silly uniform too. I just get to change out of mine when I leave. But I suppose your one is particularly ridiculous,' she said, poking out her tongue as she popped the cap on her head.

His brow furrowed. 'You're getting on my nerves.'

'Well, it doesn't take much.'

'Why do you say that?'

'You're in a constant state of grumpiness, if you're not careful you'll get a permanent frown. You're a bit like Kerry,' she said.

'Don't compare me to her, she's nothing like me.' He stopped, wondering if she was right. 'Why are you interested in her anyway? She hardly likes your company.'

'I beg to differ, I think she's just set in her ways, just like you. And as you heard me say before, I love her eyes.' Her smirk reappeared.

'On you go, girl, he doesn't get paid to chat,' a conductor bellowed from the end of the platform.

'Sorry, Sir, I was just asking for directions,' she said, winking as she tossed the cap into Ricky's arms.

Francesca stood, staring up at the window. With a handful of pebbles, she aimed, hitting the glass. Elaine was quick to stick her head out. Her bouncy curls dangled out of the frame as Francesca lifted two Dairy Milk Bars.

'So, why did he come to the house?' Elaine munched on the chocolate as she sat on her bed.

'Well, he apologised, and we came up with a plan of how to make this wedding happen for Lottie and Harry,' Francesca said.

'Do you miss him?'

'Only when I'm alone. But then again, I suppose that's the time when you'd miss anybody when you're alone with your own head.'

'It can be scary when you're alone and think things you shouldn't. I doubt myself. I have a go at myself for no reason like there's a little voice inside my head telling me off,' she admitted whilst playing with the purple wrapper.

'Don't worry, Elaine, I get it too, I think we're our own worst enemy,' she assured.

'And mum's pressuring me to get a job. I don't even want to work, but she said it's about time I pull my weight, and Charley agrees. But I refuse to do manual labour or factory work,' she said with disgust at the idea of getting her hands dirty.

'I'm sure you'll find something.' Francesca laughed.

'I hope so, 'cause that voice in my brain is getting really irritating. Enough talking about my head, how's Colin's?' she asked, shifting focus from one mind to another.

'It's not looking good.'

'I suppose that was a stupid question to ask. What happened to Jack? I heard rumours that he got away with it.' Elaine frowned.

'He was released. The Priest did it out of mercy,' Francesca informed her.

'Jack should be begging on his knees with gratitude, he could be behind bars right now.'

'We both know he's too thick to realise how lucky he is, but I don't think even the Priest's words will save him if Colin dies. I don't know how the law works, but it'll be classed as murder, and there is no way around that,' Francesca muttered.

The lamp illuminated them as they worked. The blazer was placed between them, being decorated with a variety of buttons and threads.

'I just don't know what I'm gonna do,' Charlotte sighed as she fiddled with the needle, a metal thimble cemented to her finger. She sat on the sofa with its run-down material and tatty patches of visible stuffing.

'Why don't you become a nurse? That's what I do, and I get decent pay for it,' Jackie suggested as she sipped her tea, warming her hands with the steaming mug. They were wrapped in blankets and quilts.

'I'm not qualified.'

'The National Health Service will train you. I was transferred to civilian service after the war like a lot of the other women across the Empire,' she explained as she picked up a needle, threading it with ease.

'I have always liked the little outfits with the hats, and my grandmother was a nurse in the Great War,' Charlotte said happily, imagining herself in the smart uniform.

'There you go then. I'll have a word with the Matron if you'd like?' Jackie asked.

'That would be wonderful, I stitched Harry up once, but I wouldn't say I did a very good job of it.' Charlotte remembered.

'As long as you close the wound, you're on the right track. So, when are you going to get married?' she questioned, recognising the delicate ring that sat around Charlotte's finger.

'Well, we're so excited, we wanted to tie the knot as soon as possible, but that's not going to happen now. My mum died at this time of year and I hoped getting married in it would bring some joy, but a few things have come up which have halted our progress.'

'I understand. Don't worry, you'll be married soon enough,' Jackie assured her as she pierced the material, her hands manipulating the delicate gold thread into calculated patterns.

'I want to invite everyone, all my friends and family, and of course that includes you and the others.' Charlotte smiled, her eyes bright and hopeful.

'I'm sure it will be a wonderful day.' Jackie grinned.

'Jack, what are you doing here?' Isla asked, startled as she entered her flat. The foul stench of alcohol filled the room and intoxicated anyone unfortunate enough to step inside.

'I need you Isla, please forgive me for what I've done.' Jack was slumped against the floral wallpaper. He looked up at her with bloodshot eyes, a bottle of whiskey clenched between his knees.

She glanced at the revolver that laid glinting on the floor. Kneeling in front of him, she pulled off her coat and scarf. 'I need you too, even after what you've done. But you can't hide in my flat, you need to take responsibility for your actions.'

'I'm not hiding,' he said, placing a lit cigarette in his mouth.

'Who are you trying to fool?'

'I'll get eaten alive if I go outside.' The truth was that he'd been hiding in a back room at the butcher's shop, but his father had kicked him out. Not because of what he'd done, his father was well aware of that. But rather the vulnerable state of his son, which made him snarl and tell him to 'grow a pair.'

'I think people have got bigger things to deal with than coming after you.'

'I'm not sure about that, people hold grudges,' he said, paranoid.

'Put that bloody bottle down. You need to get yourself together.' She grabbed the bottle, placing it out of his reach.

'And do what exactly?' he questioned, exhaling a cloud of smoke.

'Go to the church and apologise to that man for what you've done. And thank him for getting you released, anyone else would want to see you rot. You need to make things right, Jack, you hear me? Because if Colin doesn't make it through, you will go to prison, no matter what the Priest says. Oliver and Susan will testify against you, you've taken it too far.'

'He's not dead yet.' He looked at her only to meet her flushed face.

'Yet. Do you even feel the slightest bit of remorse?' she asked.

'I didn't know what I was doing,' Jack said, looking at the half-empty bottle that he longed for.

'You didn't know what you were doing but you still done it. You need help.'

'It was an accident,' he proclaimed.

'An accident? Listen to yourself. What you did was your fault and yours alone, I don't care what Oliver said to you, or what you have against Colin, and most of all I don't care what you drank.'

'He called me a monster,' he admitted with self-loathing.

'And I agree. But even monsters deserve a second chance if they are willing to ask for it,' Isla said, pulling the cigarette from his mouth.

The evening coated London in a blanket of bleak mid-winter blackness, shrouding the snow ridden pavements in shadows. He walked along the dark concrete, the only light coming from a few distant streetlamps. His fists were bloody, and his eyes were tired, a rough night indeed.

The floor was coated in a deadly layer of thin black ice. He stumbled, sending him to retreat onto the grass of Tower Hamlets Cemetery. It was quiet and stagnant, and the blades of grass stood frozen amidst the shrubbery. An owl could be heard hooting from a distant tree while a fox scurried past, its stomach full from feasting on a pile of rubbish down a nearby alleyway.

As a figure walked toward him, he was taken aback. He rubbed his eyes, trying to focus on the encroaching silhouette. It had long brown hair and a thin figure, hardly a sight of intimidation.

'Jimmy Talbot?' she asked.

'Yeah, what's it to you?' he snapped, almost falling over a tuft of grass.

'I have a message.'

'From who?'

'From Charlotte,' she replied.

'Ah fuck.'

A second figure appeared. Recognising its short platinum blonde hair, he knew he had made a serious mistake.

'Remember me?' Kerry gritted her teeth as she pulled him by the collar to a nearby tree. She held him by the throat, her face only a few inches from his.

'Look, Kerry,' he pleaded as her grip tightened around his neck. Francesca watched with unease, a bag sitting loosely over her shoulder.

'You fuckin' cretin, did you not think this would happen?' she snarled, her expression furious.

'I can explain.'

'Fran, give me the hammer,' she ordered, putting out her hand.

Francesca looked down at the claw hammer that sat in the bag. She hesitated, realising that there was no going back. Handing the weapon over, she turned away, her face growing pale and sickly. She imagined the bloodiness to follow, anxiously wringing her hands.

'I know you're fond of using this on other people,' Kerry said, pressing the metal to his cheek. Throwing him to the ground, she stalked him, swinging the hammer to-and-fro. Trying to crawl from her grasp, he was slammed to the ground by her thick creeper that pressed firmly in between his shoulder blades. Gabbing a hold of one of his arms, she held out his hand, the metal now hovering a few inches above it.

'I'm sorry, I'll never go near them again,' he cried as she lifted the weapon, ready to strike.

'Your apology means nothing to me,' she spat venomously.

Francesca looked at him, her eyes distressed, yet she said nothing.

Kerry paused as her glance met Francesca's, her grip on the weapon unwavering. 'If you go near them again, I'll take your hand off,' she hissed, releasing him.

'I-I promise I won't,' Jimmy stuttered as he scrambled to his feet. He sprinted across the grass, disappearing into the darkness.

Tossing the weapon down, Kerry looked at Francesca. Normally she would have felt angry at herself for not going through with it, but for the first time in her life, she felt a sense of peace. 'Let's get you home,' she said, guiding her off the green.

As the door creaked open, Jack snuck into the church. His eyes scanned the empty interior, yet his sight was occupied by the mass of flickering tea lights that had been placed at the main altar. He walked over to them, feeling the light on his face. The Priest, armed with a stack of Bibles, wandered down the centre aisle. He quickly stopped, sensing the new presence within his church.

'Can I help?' he asked, scaring Jack half to death.

'I'm the one that—'

'Yes, I know who you are, how can I help,' the Priest repeated firmly.

'I want to apologise.'

'It's not me you should apologise to,' he said, looking up to the large cross that hung above their heads.

'You can't be referring to God? I'm not religious, so that ain't gonna happen.'

'That is exactly who I'm referring to,' he spoke calmly.

'Why did you get them to let me go? After what I did, didn't you want justice?' Jack asked as he watched the Priest go about his business.

'No man can ever truly decide a course of justice, only the divine can do that. But what I am giving you is time to find peace. If my son passes on, it won't just be his life lost, but yours too. Prison is no place for a young man like yourself,' he explained.

'I don't understand.'

'Why don't you believe?' the Priest questioned.

He pulled a disrespectful face as he looked around the church. 'What, in all of this?'

'Yes, this,' the Priest continued.

'It's just stupid.'

'And why's that?'

'I just can't believe.'

'You can't or you won't?'

'A little of both.'

'I think that you need to step back and acknowledge all the good in your life, all the gifts that surround you, then realise that they are there for a reason.'

'Yeah, yeah, because God put them there,' Jack muttered dismissively.

'No, because you put them there, now, start to have a little faith in yourself and you might begin to find it in others. And for goodness' sake stop drinking, you smell like a brewery,' he said as he tended to the back pew, placing a Bible upon each seat.

Jack stood still. The Priest's words filtered their way into his brain, and for the first time in his life he realised the importance of that word, *faith*. That faith that Colin had always had, what he didn't understand until that moment. It wasn't believing in some mighty being, or those responsible of spreading the word of God, but finding faith within himself, bettering himself to find the betterment in others. The holiest thing a person could do, and he'd done a shoddy job of it so far. 'I'll try,' he said quietly.

'Why don't you come to a Sunday service? It might do you some good,' he suggested.

Jack sent him an uneasy nod as he left the church.

Frith Street was bustling. Francesca walked alongside Curtis. She was unfamiliar with the area and was taken aback by its vibrancy. From the many theatres to the London Casino, she imagined it to be a place of cheap thrills and debauchery. There was a certain charm to the area with its eccentric buildings and equally eccentric people. Proceeding across the road, Francesca was amused by a few men who wore large fur coats, their faces adorned with makeup.

'You look surprised,' Curtis commented as they moved along the pavement.

'I just haven't really seen men wear makeup,' she admitted.

'And yet they wear it better than most women. Don't tell Jackie and Wilma I said that.' He smirked. Francesca grinned as they met the outside of a small building called the Moka Bar. Entering the space, she gawped at its interior.

'Don't tell me you haven't been to an espresso bar before?'

'I haven't, not like this one anyway.'

'Well, there's a first time for everything. Let me introduce you to the owner,' he said, guiding her to the bar.

Francesca took in the smell of fresh coffee and the sound of the high-pressure machines. The burbling chrome monsters were large and sent steam up to the ceiling. It wasn't like the usual coffee houses Francesca was accustomed to. This espresso bar was modern, almost innovative in its design. From the chrome stools to the bubbling contraptions, everything appeared to be new and exciting. The walls were coated in framed pictures. They depicted people and places from all over the globe. She looked at them with fascination.

'And who's this little lady?' the man asked from behind the bar. He wore a pure white apron that contrasted his tanned skin. His hair was black, and his eyes were the colour of oak leaves.

'I'm Francesca,' she said politely.

'Fran, this is Pino,' Curtis introduced.

'Francesca is a strong Italian name, are you Italian?' Pino asked, tending to his machines.

'No, only English. My mum just liked the way the word sounds,' she admitted, a bit embarrassed.

'You have dark eyes and hair like an Italian.'

'But I'm way too pasty,' she said, looking at her pale arms.

'Nothing a little sun won't fix.' Pino smiled, pouring the rich liquid into two cups. 'Here you go, tell me what you think.' He placed the cups before them. Leaning against the bar, he waited patiently for their response.

'It's quite bitter,' Francesca said, her face scrunching as the flavour assaulted her taste buds.

'That's because it's real ground coffee, other bars only use essence. But here we use the real thing, so it tastes authentic,' he explained.

'It's fantastic as usual. Trust me, you get used to it after a while,' Curtis said, gulping down the coffee as though it was water.

'I think I prefer tea,' she said.

'The English and their tea,' Pino muttered as he retreated to a back room that contained his precious coffee beans.

'Not long ago this was a launderette, damaged by the bombings. Pino saved this place and made something of it,' Curtis explained.

'It's wonderful, who is that?' Francesca asked, looking at a picture that was hung on the wall. It depicted a man singing in a back-end Chicago club.

'That's Joe Williams, the best of the best. American Jazz musicians will make you feel things you've never felt,' Curtis said.

'Do you play?'

'No, music does run in the family though. My mother played the piano, even performed on stage a few times,' he spoke proudly.

'Is she in England?'

'She passed just after I left the Navy. She didn't have the chance to come here with me,' he said, saddened.

'I'm sorry to hear that. My father died of sickness when I was little,' Francesca said as she attempted to take another sip from the cup.

'It can't be easy, losing a parent is never easy.' He looked at her empathetically.

'I have my mother and grandmother, Charley and Elaine, and I had James,' she said with a pause, feeling the chain around her neck.

'I take it he's in that locket?' Curtis asked.

'Yes, so he can stay close to my heart.'

'It's beautiful. I'm lucky I have Jackie and the others. We all grew up together. Jackie is my best friend. Ricky and Wilma are like little siblings. Even though they have the habit of testing my patience, I love them like family.'

'I can see that. Thank you for bringing me here,' she said.

'Anytime, Soho is a nice change from the East End don't you think?' He winked.

'It is. I hope one day I can see other places.' Again, she looked at the pictures that decorated the walls.

'I'm sure you will. I've seen the world from the inside of a destroyer, a view I wouldn't recommend.'

'So, you're done with travelling then?'

'Yes, I just want to live a normal life with a normal job, and most of all I want to be happy.'

The launderette hosted nine huge baby blue washing machines, all but one sitting unoccupied. A thin pine wood bench spanned the centre of the room. Albie sat, staring at the clothes that swirled around, the soapsuds splashing up the glass. He was perched on his drape jacket with folded legs, a sketchbook sitting in his lap. The machine buzzed as he continued drawing.

'This ain't a bloody studio,' the owner huffed from the corner. She was a stocky lady in her fifties, a dirty pinnie wrapped around her waist, and her thick grey locks of hair sat messily in a wonky bun.

'I've paid to use a machine, and I'm quietly waiting for it, would you rather I sing and dance?' he asked sharply.

She grumbled, slouching back into her seat. 'I don't serve your kind, love, it's bad for business,' she said quickly as Wilma entered.

She was wielding two large bags of washing that pulled at her arms. 'I'll be quick, and I've got the money, I've been turned away from three today already. I'll have to go as far as Limehouse to find another launderette,' she said desperately, revealing the coins that sat in her closed fist.

'That's not my problem, leave now before somebody spots you,' she said, now scowling.

'Wilma, isn't it?' Albie asked, placing down his sketchbook.

'Hello, Albie, it's nice to see you again.'

'This ain't a caff,' the woman said, standing from her seat.

'But it is a launderette, and there are eight empty machines, and by the looks of it you could do with the custom, so let her wash her stuff,' he said.

'I said no.'

'It would be a fuckin' shame if this building burnt down, wouldn't it? Maybe because of an electrical fault, I've heard that happens a lot.'

The woman stared at him nervously, realising who she was talking to. 'Use it, but you're paying double,' she said to Wilma, her hands firmly placed on her hips.

'Because of your rudeness she's not paying anything, now sit down before I make you,' he snapped.

The woman dropped quickly into her chair.

Wilma looked at him gratefully as she stuffed the machine full of clothes. 'It can be a nightmare sometimes,' she said, closing the door. As she sat on the pine bench, she watched as the clothes began to tumble and turn inside the machine.

'Don't worry about her, she's just horrible because her husband won't touch her at night,' he said, grinning. To this Wilma laughed, a little louder than expected.

'What are you drawing?' she asked.

'Just somethin' I've been working on. It's a teapot, but instead of it pouring tea it's spurting out the Thames River, and the Queen is in a swimsuit falling through, it's like Alice falling down the rabbit hole.'

'Alice falling down the rabbit hole?' she questioned, amused.

'Have you never read Alice's Adventures in Wonderland? It's got a talking rabbit, a Queen of Hearts that loves tarts, a mad hatter,' he explained.

'No, it sounds like something completely unusual, and utterly fantastic,' she declared. 'You know, I've never admitted that about myself before to anyone other than Curtis, Ricky and Jackie. Even though it's who I am, Jackie says I have to be careful who I say it to. Jackie has been in relationships with women, but says we have to be careful because people would only use it against us, especially those who have already shown their dislike of us being here.'

Albie smiled empathetically. 'My preferences have been used against me my entire life, my mum kicked me out the house when I was fifteen because of it. Of course, I'd never understand how it feels to experience struggles as a young woman like yourself who has ended up, well, in a not very forgiving place. I don't think we should have to admit anything we don't want to. We should just be able to be who we want to be, love who we want to love, and not have to explain ourselves to anyone,' he said, tending to his drawing.

'I agree. I'm sorry your mum did that to you, it's her loss. And I'm sorry Ricky was a bit rude to you, he can be very confrontational sometimes. He struggles to understand Jackie and I, let alone a man liking men.'

Albie shrugged his shoulders. 'Don't worry about it, I've heard it all before from my... Well, people I used to call friends.'

'I like Kerry, Fran introduced me to her. She's very sure of herself.'

'Yes, well, if anyone questions Kerry, they get a broken nose or a black eye.' He smirked.

'We're going to go to King's Road together,' she informed, watching him sketch.

'I warn you she's a tough nut to crack, she doesn't let people in easily.'

'Well, she's never met a person like me before,' she said confidently.

Albie watched her, inspired by her determination. 'Ricky seems like a tough nut too.'

'Yes, he most definitely is. It didn't help coming here either,' she explained.

'Maybe he's lonely, he seems very closed off. He needs to be able to express himself. I can tell because I was the same way before I started making art.'

'I think you might be able to help him with that.'

'I might indeed,' he agreed.

CHAPTER 20

'Busy day?' Jackie asked.

The crisp air followed him as he walked through the door, making her shudder. Curtis was worn out from a day of lugging heavy shipments along the slippery landing stage. His face was dirty, and his hands were red raw.

Jackie was perched on the sofa. Wilma sat on the floor in between her legs, just as she had done when she was a child. Jackie battled with an unruly knot that had developed in her thick locks of hair, a comb cemented in her hand.

'Very busy day, but I'd rather be down the docks than endure that,' Curtis said, looking at Wilma with her wincing expression.

'You and Fran seem to be progressing,' Jackie said, smiling.

'Yes, she's lovely, but I won't let it go too far. She has adventure in her eyes, just like James did. Who am I to hold her back?'

'I understand. It's only natural for a young woman like herself to fly the nest, I mean look at us, we did the same,' she said, peering down at Wilma who grinned back at her.

One thud came after another, inducing Francesca's annoyance. Pulling herself from her frilly bed sheets, she made her way to the window. Sticking her head out of the frame, her hair trailed down the brickwork. She recognised the familiar face as she rubbed her groggy eyes.

'What do you want, Jack? If your intentions aren't to break my window at seven in the morning,' she said grumpily. A fresh layer of snow had covered the ground, the brightness hurting her eyes.

'I'm sorry,' he stated. Nothing more, nothing less, just an apology which took her by surprise.

Francesca raised an unconvinced eyebrow. 'Sorry for what?' she asked, content on dragging out his confession.

'For everything, and I mean everything.'

'Well, everything is an understatement. Susan will never be the same after this.'

'Look, I went to the Priest.' Jack rubbed his hands together, the icy breeze nipping at his skin.

'You came here to tell me you finally did the right thing? Don't expect any sympathy from me.'

'I don't expect anything from you. What I do want is for us to be good with each other,' Jack requested.

As she contemplated his suggestion, she avoided his line of sight, leaving him to shiver in the cold a little longer. 'We're good.'

'I was wondering if I could come to church with you and

Elaine this Sunday coming?'

'I suppose, but as long as you take it seriously, it isn't a joke,' she said defensively as she watched the frosty world around them. The roof tiles glinted like distant crystals as the clouds slowly moved above them.

'I promise,' Jack said.

As Kerry approached King's Road, she kept to a steady pace. She felt Wilma beside her, bouncing with energy. The houses that lined the street were large and opulent, displaying their wealth with huge crystal chandeliers that glistened through broad windows. Groomed, snow-covered shrubbery lined the pathways. There was a certain arrogance about Chelsea that Kerry disliked very much. Despite this, the streets were filled with normal people going about their business, just as Wilma did daily after cleaning one of those presumably arrogant houses.

'I can't believe you've never been to King's Road,' Wilma said.

'I can't afford half the stuff here, so what's the point.'

There were carefully crafted buildings on each side of the road, the most prominent being the Town Hall. Its granite columned entrance led to vast, smooth marble floors. Kerry imagined them to be reminiscent of the Romans, yet the columns were far more Victorian in construction. Recognising the different classical rhythms coming from inside the building, Wilma moved along the pavement in a little dance.

'Not partial to a bit of classical music?' she asked as she shuffled along to the beat in a ridiculous manner.

'Can't say it's my cup of tea,' Kerry spoke quickly, trying not to laugh.

They met a row of boutiques with huge window displays. One appeared to specialise in fine furs and fabrics which were presented on pristine white mannequins. Others showcased rubies, emeralds, and precious metals manipulated into rings and necklaces.

'Aren't they pretty? I'd love to own jewels like that one day. It would be a nice change from these plastic pearl studs,' she said, feeling her ears.

'They'd suit you.' Kerry stared through the glass, eyes sharpening as she caught the rejective glance of a shop assistant.

'You don't have pierced ears I noticed.'

'No, I most definitely do not.'

'Would you let me pierce them?' she asked sweetly as they continued down the road.

'Not a chance.'

'Why, are you scared of the pain?' she challenged, making Kerry swallow hard.

'Of course I'm not scared,' she huffed.

'Let me do it then. If you're not frightened, you have nothing to worry about.' She smiled so widely that Kerry felt like giving her a slap, but she restrained herself. The reality was that she was enjoying her company, though she'd never admit it.

'So, what do you think?' Wilma asked.

'I think that this is the most pretentious place I have ever been to in my life. I bet it costs an arm and a leg to buy a portion of chips around here,' she mumbled as she watched the luxury cars that lined the road. A Bentley and Rolls Royce the colour of burgundy and bottle green sat alongside the pavement, resembling the jewels on display. 'But I guess there is no harm getting ideas until we can buy knock offs somewhere cheaper,' Kerry continued.

'I heard that some new shops have opened here that have more of an open mind, selling designs aimed at young people. They're even owned by young people, who would have thought.'

'I bet they're still pricey, I think I'll stick to what I know,' she grumbled, peering down at her shiny shoes.

'You have an interesting fashion sense, I've never really seen a woman wear a suit before,' Wilma said, looking at Kerry's black blazer and drainpipe trousers. A bolo tie sat tightly around her collar and her short hair was carefully brushed back. People watched her as she continued down the road, some in awe and others slightly horrified.

'It's just the blazer that does it, no need for fancy buying,' she said as they entered a boutique.

'If you don't mind me saying, I think your style is magnificent, in fact, you're one of the most beautiful women I have ever seen.'

Beautiful. Nobody had ever called Kerry beautiful. She blushed out of shyness, possibly for the first time in her life. 'This place should give us some inspiration,' she said, focusing on the task at hand.

The shop contained many objects from hats and bow ties to colourful skirts, shoes and even a few dangling necklaces.

'That's very pretty,' Wilma said. She was drawn to a silver chain with a little heart pendant at the centre.

'How much is it?' Kerry asked as she met Wilma's side.

'It's more than I can afford.' She frowned as she walked away from the glistening necklace. As they wandered back onto the pavement, Kerry gently gripped her arm.

'Maybe you could save up for it, that's what I do when I like something I can't afford. Come on, let's look in some other shops,' she encouraged.

Wilma nodded in agreement. 'You should be a tailor, you know that? You seem good at picking fabrics.'

'I'm not delicate, I would probably bugger up the material or make some stupid mistake,' Kerry dismissed.

'Well, tailoring isn't supposed to be delicate, it's supposed to make a statement. Blazers, trousers, you could do the lot.' Wilma smiled as they came to a halt.

'That, that's it!' Kerry exclaimed as she spotted the white dress in the window, it was simple, but it looked to be a perfect size. It was sitting at the front of a posh second-hand shop but appeared as though it was brand new.

'That's perfect,' Wilma said, grinning as she pulled Kerry by the hand inside.

Francesca had persuaded every friend and acquaintance of the couple to do all they could to make their special day a reality. Clubbing their money together, they had saved up enough to buy Charlotte a proper wedding dress.

Francesca walked beside Charley. The snow was melting and had left layers of sludge on the pavement. The heaps were no longer a pure white, but a mucky grey that camouflaged the landscape in clusters of dirty ice.

'So, where are you taking me?' she asked as her mitten-clad hand gripped his sturdy arm. She wore a baby blue hat and scarf that had been knitted for her by Vera the previous year.

'Now if I told you that, it wouldn't be a surprise,' Charley said with a grin, clearly pleased with himself.

'It better be good for us to be out in the cold,' she joked as they met the patchy grass of Victoria Park. Francesca scanned the bleak area, catching sight of a few reindeers that stood contently in an enclosure at the centre.

'I thought you might like to come and pet the reindeers, just like your brother took you to do when you were little.' Charley smiled as they approached the animals.

Francesca's eyes lit up as they met the beautiful creatures. The sound of the bells around their necks rang out, creating a pleasant melody. Their faces were buried in buckets containing a combination of oats and barley. As Charley paid the man, she knelt next to a reindeer that she recognised from a familiar white spot on its coat.

'Do you remember me?' she whispered. Taking off her mittens, she gently stroked the reindeer's fur. A couple of grunts persuaded her that it remembered the little girl that used to find so much joy in the company of animals.

'Big old things, aren't they?' Charley said.

'Marvellous creatures,' Francesca spoke with a huge grin. She fought against the crisp air nibbling at her exposed fingers as she petted the animals, feeling their soft coats. 'Thank you, Charley,' she said gratefully.

'No problem, kid.'

Albie knocked on the door. He watched the road as he waited. Halfway down the street, a decrepit set of ruins sat between the compact houses. The crumbling bricks invaded the path, deforming the pavement.

Curtis opened the door swiftly. 'Albie, how can I help you?' he asked.

'I was just on my way to the record shop, and I thought I'd ask Ricky if he wanted to come with me?'

'You're lucky, it's his day off. I think that's a wonderful idea. Do you mind waiting here for a second?' he questioned, smiling.

'Of course not.'

'Ricky!' Curtis called out as he shut the door.

'What do you want?' he asked grumpily, meeting the bottom of the stairs.

'I want you to go with Albie, he's invited you to go with him to the record shop.'

'I'm not doing that,' Ricky snapped, attempting to bolt back upstairs.

'Yes, you are,' Curtis said sternly, pulling him to the doorway by his arm. 'You're going to give him a chance, remember what Jackie said,' he uttered.

'Fine, but this is the only time and I'm doing it for Jackie,' he said stubbornly, forcing a scarf around his neck.

The robins danced with one another in the crisp air. The branches were a playground for all sorts of animals, from owls to squirrels. Susan had watched them all as she sat holding his motionless hand.

'You'd love the robins, Colin,' she said as a tear fell down her cheek. 'They swoop and glide, and keep me company while I wait for you, while we both wait for you.' She placed his hand on her bump. She smiled as she felt a little kick. And then another movement, but it wasn't from the baby. Colin's thumb moved. Then his hand motioned back-and-forth. Then his fingers gripped hers. She watched in disbelief as his eyes opened, proving there to be life in him once again.

The shop was a sharp contrast to the bleak winter palette of the outside world. It was bright and colourful with obnoxious wallpaper favouring a chaotic mixture of geometric shapes. It was filled to the brim with records that sat in cabinets at the centre of the room. From Bill Haley to The Platters, the shop had it all.

Albie's nose was red from the brisk wind, mirroring his ginger hair. Wiping it with a handkerchief, he turned to his reluctant acquaintance. 'Bloody cold today,' he said as he placed the handkerchief back into the pocket of his thick drape jacket. Albie looked more garish than usual. His navy-blue three-piece suit was paired with a set of aqua green socks.

'I'm only here because Curtis told me to come, you know that, right?' Ricky mumbled.

'Well, I admire your honesty. Do you listen to much music?' Albie asked as he flicked through the records.

'Not really,' Ricky said impatiently.

'You're missing out, come here and look at this,' he said, beckoning him over.

'What about it? It's just a vinyl,' Ricky dismissed.

'But not just any vinyl, it's art, I promise it'll change your life,' Albie said optimistically as he held a record by Johnnie Ray, one of his personal favourites.

'I'm not convinced.'

'You'll be surprised.' Albie smiled.

Ricky reluctantly sat on a stool in the listening room as Albie fastened the headphones over his ears. He set up the record, its peculiar sound meeting Ricky's eardrums.

'It sounds odd,' he protested.

'It's expression, expression is all about thinking outside the box,' Albie insisted.

'I don't like it.'

'Well, what about this one. You hear the guitar in it?' he asked.

Ricky paused. 'It's catchy,' he admitted, listening to the Rock 'n' Roll beat. 'This music is different from what I've heard before.'

'That's because it's not just music, it's a gateway into the artist's soul, it's love, it's sadness, it's a rebellion. As men we've been told not to express ourselves, to have a stiff upper lip, it's nonsense. Art is emotion, the good and bad. It takes a real man to be able to understand his own soul.'

Kerry laid stiffly on floor with a towel placed under her head. Her bedroom was filled with records and magazines and Wilma was busy taking it all in.

'I haven't got all day,' she spoke irritably, however Wilma ignored her, choosing instead to try on her black drape jacket.

'I'm the one holding the needle so I wouldn't get mouthy if I were you.' Her lips curled into a grin. 'Do you think this suits me?'

'Not one bit,' Kerry grumbled, crossing her arms.

'How does the floor feel?'

'Hard and uncomfortable, so can we please get this over with.'

'You're scared, admit it.' Wilma towered above her as she held the needle.

'If you don't hurry up—'

Wilma plonked herself down, legs either side of Kerry's waist, her full weight on her stomach and hips making her yelp.

'You little brat,' Kerry groaned.

'You told me to hurry up,' she said playfully, shuffling to

make herself comfortable. The drape jacket fell from her shoulders.

'Is it really necessary for you to sit on me?'

'Do you want me to get off?'

Kerry stared up at her. Wilma's face hovered over hers, and Kerry felt one of her braids drag across her chest, her breathing turning a little heavier than usual.

'That's what I thought.' Wilma bopped her on the nose, her face resuming its usual scowl.

'Please tell me you've done this before,' Kerry said as she held the needle tight above her left ear.

'No, but Jackie did mine, so I know roughly what to do. You don't know the trouble I went to stealing this needle out of her sewing kit. That woman is a hawk, notices absolutely everything,' she muttered. 'Now try and stay still for me. If it hurts, grab my thighs or hips, please God do not punch me in the face.'

'I wouldn't do—'

Kerry gritted her teeth as the needle pierced her earlobe. Wilma quickly wiped it and slotted a silver earring through. Cleaning the needle, Wilma motioned her to turn her head. Kerry obeyed, this time grabbing a hold of her thighs tight, not out of pain, but anger. Noticing this, Wilma quickly pierced the other lobe. Getting off her, she watched intently as Kerry peered into the mirror, examining the two studs.

'Pain makes you angry.' Wilma observed.

Kerry turned to her, smiling slightly. 'Pain makes me feel vulnerable, I don't like feeling that way, so I get angry. Did I hurt you?'

'Not one bit,' she said, sitting herself on the bed.

'I'm sorry for being so cold, for judging you when we first

met. I think you're... You're wonderful in every way.' Kerry shocked herself by being so open, especially with someone she had known for such a small amount of time. Nervously, her gaze lifted to meet Wilma's. There was something about her rich russet eyes that set a fire in Kerry's heart, desire burning through her. A feeling she had never felt, not even with Lewis. She continued, 'A lot of people are frightened of me, but you're not, why?'

'Because I can tell you mean well, even if you call me a brat.' She smirked.

'You just caught me off guard.' She laughed as her mother wandered in holding a tray containing mugs of tea and two slices of homemade carrot cake.

'Thought you both might be peckish after the procedure,' she said cheerfully, placing it on the bed.

'You make it sound like I had a limb chopped off.' Kerry rolled her eyes.

'Thank you, I'm starving,' Wilma said, grabbing a plate.

'You've done a wonderful job, for years I've tried to get Kerry to have her ears pierced.'

'I think they suit you, they complement your face,' she said, smiling as she took a bite from the cake.

Kerry blushed and her mother noticed.

'Why don't you stay for some supper, Wilma?' she asked.

'As long as I'm not intruding—'

'Don't be silly my sweet, you're more than welcome, isn't that right, Kerry?'

'Yes, I'd like you to stay,' she agreed.

The bullying gale caused the metal gate to swing violently into the old stone wall, forcing its way through the wooden panels of the church. The Priest stood in his dark robes, watching the congregation leave as he rubbed his hands together.

'What did you think of that?' Francesca asked as they bundled out of the building.

'I didn't really know what was going on,' Jack answered.

'To be honest, I didn't really know what was going on, and I've been part of this church since birth,' Elaine said as they walked through the garden.

'Well, that's alright then.' Jack laughed. 'I might bring Isla next time, she's the one that persuaded me to come in the first place.'

'I didn't think she was the religious type,' Francesca said bluntly.

'Neither was I, but here I am.'

'The more the merrier, I guess,' she sighed.

The Priest watched the three of them with a smile. Looking up at the sky, he followed the clouds that twisted and twirled above his head. Concentrating on the robins that fluttered amongst the dying branches of a nearby tree, he heard a peculiar sound. It was that of a wheelchair, but nobody from that morning's service was in a wheelchair. Looking down, his eyes welled. Colin was being pushed by Susan along the pavement. He appeared before him in the small church garden, the stiff wheeled contraption grinding to a hasty halt. Susan's face flooded with tears as the Priest embraced his son. Colin's head was heavily bandaged, and his skin looked as grey as the sky above. Despite this, a wide grin covered his face. Francesca ran to Susan, hugging her tightly.

'I'll see you around,' Jack said, his glance fixed on the floor. He should have felt relieved, but he was crippled by shame.

'You don't have to go,' Elaine said, but he had already vanished in the opposite direction.

Vera sat down with a painful sigh, her bones cracking as she descended into her armchair. Looking at Houdini, she marvelled at his bright feathers that sat in pretty alignments upon his wings.

'Here we are,' Stephanie said as she placed a tray down; it had two cups and saucers upon it. A teapot sent steam curling into the air as she poured the liquid into each cup, followed by a drop of milk. 'Are you alright, mum? You seemed distracted yesterday?' she asked.

Vera was normally on the ball, but not recently. At church, she was off-key when singing and lagged behind everyone else when saying the Lord's prayer.

'I have something to tell you.'

'So tell me before I worry,' Stephanie said.

'I'm sick,' Vera admitted as she attempted to grip the teacup.

'What kind of sick? Is it to do with the arthritis? If so, we can go to the doctor and get you some more—'

'I've already been to the doctor,' Vera informed her.

'And what did he say?'

'That I've got cancer in my bones,' she said calmly, taking a sip.

Stephanie dropped her teacup, it shattered into pieces as it met the ground. Her mind rushed, trying to process the information without completely shutting down. 'Surely there is something we can do?' she said, distressed.

'It's too late, I've got three months left at the most,' Vera revealed.

'I don't understand.'

'Neither do I, but it's my time and I accept that. The doctor said I've had it for quite a while. It explains why my arthritis has been getting worse, I thought it was just the cold weather, but I was wrong,' she said. Her voice was slow and hopeless.

'How are we going to tell Fran?' Stephanie panicked as tears poured down her cheeks.

'We are not going to,' Vera said.

'We can't not tell her,' she objected.

'At the moment, it'll do more harm than good. You've got to let her spread her wings, you promise me that? That girl is made for bigger and better things.'

'I will let her,' Stephanie agreed as she wiped her eyes with the back of her hand.

'And she can't do that if she knows I'm dying, now can she?' Watching Stephanie, who was snivelling uncontrollably, Vera welcomed her into her aching arms. 'Everything will be ok,' she spoke softly as she held her daughter as tightly as she could.

Sitting at the top of his bed, she watched as the darkness poured in through the small window. An old novel sat in her hands. Curtis, clad in his dirt ridden clothes, turned away from her as he removed his linen top, exposing his muscular shoulders. As he rummaged quickly through the drawers for a fresh one, Francesca pulled herself from the bed. He felt her presence behind him but refused to turn and reveal his disfigured skin.

'It's ok you know, I'm not bothered by a little scarring.'

'I can assure you it's not little,' he said.

'Ok, that was a poor choice of words, but I don't care how bad it is,' she breathed as she placed a hand on his back, his warm skin meeting hers. Curtis gulped and closed his eyes. He hadn't been touched gently by a woman in a long time. Turning around, he revealed the scar, its silver strained tones pulling and contorting the dark skin on his chest. 'Can I?' Francesca asked as she cautiously lifted a hand.

He nodded.

Delicately running her fingers along the scar, her heart ached for him. 'How did this happen?'

He stared at her, expecting her to be disgusted, but she wasn't. She kept her hand on his chest, her touch tender and considerate. 'I'm not sure you want to know,' he gulped.

'I do.' Her large eyes peered up at him.

1943

DEAD IN THE WATER

SITTING IN HIS bunk with his hands behind his head, Curtis twiddled his thumbs in anticipation of the coming day.

'Do you ever fall asleep?' a young man asked. He watched his wide-eyed friend whose gaze remained fixed on the surface not far from his head. It was cramped, and hardly a picture of home with lines of tight metal bunk beds.

'I can't fall asleep here,' Curtis said as he finally retired his gaze. 'It's not natural for people to be in water, if that was the case then God would have given us webbed feet,' he spoke humorously as he wiggled his toes.

'Well then, why did you sign up to the Navy?'

'Because I was asked too,' he answered simply with a smile, turning over to meet the metal of the destroyer.

Curtis was awakened by a great jolt that sent every able man to his feet. As water trickled in from below, they looked at one another with dread.

'Torpedo!' a man screamed from the narrow corridor as the disorientated sailors pulled themselves from their bunks. Men flooded through the metal maze with its cramped stairways and dead ends.

'This way!' Curtis exclaimed as he pulled his friend up the stairs. The water behind them invaded the air quickly, helpless cries using up the remaining oxygen.

Trudging through the water, the lights began to fail, the ship was going down. With a few buzzes and cracks, the remaining light left the dying ship, leaving the men in darkness.

'Well, that's just great,' his friend said.

'Come on, this way, one more deck to go,' Curtis said determinedly. Losing his grip on him and blinded by the dark, he had no choice but to go on alone.

Another torpedo sank into the already wounded ship. Curtis was met with a mighty light followed by the roaring heat of a fire. Shock was starting to take effect as he felt the water gaining on him. The salt stung his eyes, and his hands shook, yet he managed to pull himself up the final set of railings.

'U-boats, we're done for, we've gotta jump!' a young sailor exclaimed as they clung onto the capsizing destroyer. As Curtis looked down, preparing to enter the icy black water, he saw his friend's body float calmly, motionless to the chaos around it.

'Quickly, quickly,' the sailor shouted as he threw himself over the side, meeting the frozen depths below.

Another harsh beam of light was expelled from the ship, sending mangled and charred metal into the warm skin of those still unfortunate enough to be on board. Curtis toppled into the water with a violent splash. Trails of blood moved around him as the salt bit at his open wounds. His head rose with a gasp, but he no longer felt like life was worth living.

CHAPTER 21

CHARLEY WAS STRUGGLING desperately to peel a mango with his large fingers, the knife inflicting awkward slashes. Growing increasingly frustrated, his brow scrunched.

'Having trouble big man?' Curtis teased as he prepared his ingredients. There were long rolled-up dasheen leaves (or overgrown spinach as Charley called them) alongside peppers, split peas, ground roasted geera and saffron powder.

'It'll be worth it in the end, it always is, I find myself dreaming of saheena. Bless my mother, but if I eat another plate of potatoes and corned beef, I think I'll rot on the inside.'

'That reminds me of the food during the war.' Curtis smirked as he tended to a hot pan bubbling with oil.

'My mother cooks like it still is.'

'Considering Britain has access to spices across the world, I am surprised by how little they are used. You're lucky I found dasheen today, I had to ask around for it. Jackie is the one who knows where to get them.'

'And you didn't ask her because?' Charley questioned, slicing into the mango, nearly cutting into the worktop.

'Well, it wouldn't be a surprise then would it? She works long hours, I wanted to do something nice for her.'

Wilma poked her head around the doorway, grinning. 'Charley, what did that mango do to you to be butchered in such a way?'

'I'm not cutting to be precise, I'm cutting to get the job done,' he said, looking at his mango which was shaped like a football.

'Half of the flesh is stuck on the peel.' She grabbed it, nibbling the leftover fruit.

'Wilma, don't be cheeky, you know Charley isn't the type to cook,' Curtis disciplined as he measured out the saffron powder.

'Evidently,' she said sarcastically.

'You're in for it now,' Charley said as she darted into the hallway, giggling. He chased her up the stairs, grabbing a hold of her. In one strategic lift he flipped her upside down, her tight braids dangling as she laughed uncontrollably.

'What was that, Wilma? Charley is the best cook in the whole of London?' he teased as Curtis walked into the hallway, amusement dancing on his face.

'You're the best cook in London!' Wilma said, her ribs aching from laughter.

'That'll teach ya,' Curtis said as she was gently placed back on her feet.

As the door swung open, Ricky bounded through. Throwing off his scarf, it landed on Wilma's head. She quickly threw it back at him, but he was too pre-occupied with his own thoughts to react as he wandered up the stairs.

'Have you had a good day?' Curtis asked.

Ricky stopped, turning back to them. 'The best day of my life, Albie showed me his record collection, said I could come over and listen to them whenever I wanted,' he said enthusiastically.

The church was decorated to perfection. Francesca had managed to get some white roses to line the centre aisle. Paper snowflakes made by the Sunday school children hung from the ceiling. Purple ribbons tied into delicate bows sat on the end of each pew. The Priest stood at the main altar, waiting patiently for the bride. He wore white robes with gold embroidery, a pleasant change from his usual black robes. Judy had her fingers hovering over the organ, ready for the command. Francesca had her head stuck out the window, anxiously awaiting Charlotte's arrival. Everything was set in place like a military operation.

Harry stood nervously at the front, accompanied by Oliver. He wrung his hands with anticipation as he looked back to meet the full congregation. Wilma and Kerry were nattering the seconds by. Isla and Jack were seated on the back pew, a little unnerved as the odd scowl was sent in their direction. Charlotte's sister sat at the front in a purple taffeta dress accompanied by Harry's brother. She held a picture of her mother tightly, making sure she had a perfect view of the main altar. Albie and Jackie were contemplating life. He wore his finest grey suit with a purple waistcoat, his bright locks of hair combed meticulously. Even Ricky was in attendance dressed in a suit that was a little too big for him, evidently a hand-me-down from Curtis who was much larger. Charley, Curtis and Elaine sat a few rows from the front, also dressed in their finest. Sitting behind them, Susan gripped Colin's hand tightly. He was a little worse for wear and his head was still heavily bandaged, but he smiled widely.

As the car pulled up, Francesca gave the signal, hurrying quickly to her seat. Charlotte stepped onto the frosty pavement, her white dress hovering a few inches from the ground. She wore a delicate pair of kitten heels that peeped out from the bottom of her nylon petticoat. A bouquet of white roses with integrated purple diamantes sat in her hands. Her blonde hair was in tight victory rolls. Kerry and Wilma found a veil down Portobello Road. It looked like one from the 1930s, but paired with the simple, white-lace dress, it matched surprisingly well.

'I can't believe this is actually happening!' she exclaimed as her father led her to the church doors.

'You deserve every happiness in the world,' he said, hugging her.

The Priest nodded at Judy who ran her fingers across the organ, the sound amplifying through the pipes. Harry's face lit up as he met eyes with his bride. She proceeded slowly, smiling at everyone as she walked with her father. Meeting Harry at the top of the aisle, she held his hands.

As a series of hymns played, the congregation sang to the best of their ability. Jackie was a brilliant singer and put everyone to shame with her angelic voice. Albie sniggered as he watched everyone else painfully wade their way through the verses.

The Priest continued the service, directing everyone to the relevant pages. Oliver offered the rings that sat in a little purple box. The two placed a band on each other's finger, swearing their vows at their very own royal wedding.

White roses and snowflakes were placed about the dance hall. A large buffet filled the centre. Cocktail sausages sat next to scotch eggs, cheese and pineapple skewers were placed next to an assortment of sandwiches. Francesca invited everyone from the main congregation to the reception, mixing the old generation with the new. The East End was out on full display from Mile End to Bethnal Green, Limehouse to Whitechapel and Bow. Everyone was in support of the new marriage.

As Charley pushed Colin into the hall, Susan stood loyally at his side with her enormous baby bump. He was met with an array of smiling faces. The christened baby recognised him and extended her hands. He welcomed her into his arms, and she began to play with the crucifix around his neck.

'Sorry little one, but I've got to give that to somebody.' He smiled as he pulled the neckless off, holding it tightly in his palm. Passing the little girl back to her mother he spotted Jack and Isla sitting in the corner.

'You want to talk to them?' Charley asked.

'Please.'

Wheeling him over, Charley left him before them.

'How are you, Jack?' he asked.

'I'm fine,' he answered. 'Sorry about the bullet, I wasn't thinking straight,' Jack apologised as he caught Susan's sinister glance out of the corner of his eye.

'It's fine, I'm gonna have one nifty scar,' Colin said as he watched them both. 'So, I heard you've found some faith.'

'Don't push it, I'm still no Bible basher,' he joked as Isla whacked him on the shoulder, making him reconsider his words. 'I mean it's a work in progress,' he added quickly.

'Then you're going to need this,' Colin said as he gifted the crucifix to him.

'But it's yours,' Jack refused.

'It'll help you more than me, I've already had my fair share of miracles,' he said.

'We'll never be able to repay you for this, Fran.' Harry grinned as he met her side.

'I don't expect you to, it's what friends do for one another. I've got one more surprise for you,' she said as she picked up a large, wrapped parcel hidden under the buffet table. It was fastened with a huge purple bow and lots of glitter. Passing it to Charlotte, her eyes grew wide with excitement. 'Here's your wedding present, to replace that old gramophone,' she said as Charlotte tore at the wrapping paper.

'No, we can't take this.' Her mouth gaped with shock as she picked up the wireless set.

'It's a present from all of us,' she said as the others lifted their glasses in their direction.

Wilma scoffed a plate of cocktail sausages. Kerry watched her with amusement.

'You know if you had a pound for every one of those you've eaten—'

'I'd be a millionaire.' Wilma grinned as she forced a few more into her cheeks.

'I'll be having that,' Albie interrupted as he nicked the last one off her plate, disappearing into the crowd.

'Cheeky git,' she tutted as Kerry looked at her intently.

'I got you a Christmas present.' She rummaged through her pocket.

'But it's not Christmas yet,' Wilma said, confused.

'Well, it's an early present then, close your eyes and put your hands out,' Kerry said nervously as she felt the silver chain between her fingers.

Wilma sat with her arms outstretched. She opened her eyes to see the delicate necklace in her palms, the little heart pendant shining under the dance hall lights. 'You got this for me?' she asked with gleaming eyes.

'I wasn't going to get it for anyone else,' Kerry mumbled. Before she had the chance to scowl, Wilma straddled her lap and kissed her. Kerry's cheeks turned redder than they had ever been, and as Wilma pulled away, she felt her heart thump in her chest. She hoped it wasn't noticeable, but of course Wilma noticed, making her smile.

'Normally people just say thank you. Was it really necessary for you to sit on me?' she questioned, staring up at her.

Wilma smirked. 'Would you like me to get off?'

Kerry shook her head. Gripping her waist, she pulled her close, their lips meeting again.

'I think we need to chat,' Oliver said, standing in front of Jack. Isla was guilt-stricken, the sight of him making her stomach drop. The two proceeded out of the dance hall doors, leaving her on her own. Recognising her discomfort, Francesca sat down beside her.

'I'm sorry about what I said, I didn't mean to call you a whore, I was just upset,' Francesca explained.

'It's understandable. The last thing I wanted to do was hurt you.' Isla frowned.

'I know, it's in the past now, don't beat yourself up about

it.'

'That's the problem, I always beat myself up,' she admitted.

'Somebody once told me that before we can accept anyone else into our hearts, we first need to learn to understand ourselves. You need to accept yourself, flaws and all, that's what I've done. Just how you taught me to be comfortable with my body, you need to be comfortable with your heart, to know it, make it beat for you first.' Francesca grinned.

'I think you're right, thank you,' Isla said, hugging her.

Oliver stared at Jack, feeling himself swell with rage. It was dark outside and he could easily give him a wallop without anyone noticing. He clenched his fists in his trouser pockets, making his decision.

Jack slumped against the wall, gripping his knees like a child. He looked blankly down the cobbled street, Colin's crucifix clutched tightly in his hand, so tightly that his skin went pink.

Oliver recognised it glint under the moonlight. He thought of his weary friend. *Colin's forgiveness was all that mattered.* Pulling out a packed of cigarettes, his hands relaxed.

'I didn't know what I was doing, I know that's no excuse, I'm sorry for the damage I've caused,' Jack apologised as Oliver passed him a cigarette. He lit it with a match, the orange flames glimmering against his sunken eyes. He passed the match up to Oliver whose shadow was towering over him, darkening the red brick wall at his back.

'What you did was unforgivable.' Oliver paused as Jack hung his head with shame. 'But I have also done unforgivable things, I shouldn't have let my temper get the better of me, so I'm sorry too. The main thing is that my sister is smiling again,'

Oliver said as he exhaled smoke into the dark, cool air.

'So, we're good?' Jack asked.

'Yeah, we're good, but if you ever hurt my family—'

'I know, you'll make sure I see a sticky end.'

'This city has enough villains in it, I know you're not one of them,' Oliver said, sitting down beside him.

'I'm going to try and change my ways.'

'I'm going to try too.'

Bright lights were expelled from the dance hall as the band played. Francesca wandered outside, shuddering as the frosty breeze met her cheeks. She pulled at her cardigan as Curtis met her side. They both watched the clear night sky.

'I wonder if humans will ever get up there?' She pondered, staring at the moon and the glistening stars that surrounded it.

'Maybe one day. It's a miracle we can get in the sky at all. You've done a good job today.' He smiled, yet his tone was melancholy.

'What's the matter?' she asked.

'I need to tell you something, and I don't want you to argue.'

'You're making me nervous,' she said as he took her hands.

'I'm sorry, as much as I'd like things to go forward between us, I can't let that happen,' he said gently.

'Why not?' she asked, puzzled by his sudden reluctance.

'You're young and have your whole life to live. We're at different stages in our lives, and I can't justify holding you back because of my own selfishness.'

Francesca stood, watching him with bleak and empty eyes. As she processed his words a little more, she came to the realisation that he was right. 'I understand, Curtis. Whoever I end up with, they will hold no comparison to the kindness you have shown me, you're a true gentleman. It was lovely getting to know you,' she spoke sincerely, trying her best not to cry as she let go of his hands.

'Truthfully, after the war I struggled to let people in, especially women. You are the first woman who has made me feel wanted.' He ran a hand across his chest. 'I want to give you something, because it's Christmas and all.' He passed her a little package with brown paper wrapping and a red bow.

Taking the gift, she looked at him thankfully.

'Goodbye, Francesca,' he said, planting a kiss on her forehead.

As she watched him disappear inside, she felt her heart grow heavy. *The one who got away.*

'Are you alright, Fran?' Kerry asked as she left the hall, pulling out a packet of cigarettes.

Francesca stood still, her eyes glazed over.

'I just wanted to say sorry for what I said about Curtis and the others, I didn't understand. Or didn't want to understand. I just shouldn't have said such horrible things—'

Before she could finish, Francesca hugged her, her arms tight around her waist. Standing awkwardly, Kerry felt her whimper into her shoulder. Letting out an accepting sigh, she hugged her back, stiff but equally heartfelt.

Sitting on her bed, she pulled at the wrapping. Curtis's copy of Jules Verne's *Twenty Thousand Leagues Under the Sea* was tucked safely inside. Tears fell from her eyes and met the delicate pages. Reading the first page, she spied his handwriting at the top, with a smile she followed the black ink: *To help you escape.*

As New Year's Eve began its countdown to 1956, Francesca, Charley and Elaine sat on the edge of the dock. The calm, glistening black water jilted and swayed with the gentle current as midnight approached. Not a word was spoken between them as they waited patiently on the river's edge.

With a sudden burst, fireworks exploded in an array of colours from purple to red, orange to blue and green. Spirals of whizzing light were contrasted by large bangs, and so the display continued. They were mesmerised by the sparks of light reflected in the water in front of them. Distant ship horns sounded, so many that they echoed across every wave, down every street, into every part of London. Francesca rested her head on Elaine's shoulder, her gold locket hanging firmly at the centre of her chest. Charley watched them both, smiling.

'Mr Montgomery, I'm handing in my notice,' Francesca informed, placing a piece of paper in front of him on the old wooden desk.

He seemed far from in the new year's spirit as he looked over her with deprecation. 'Oh, are you now? And where am I going to find someone who meets the likes of you?' he questioned, scraping a hand through his silver hair.

'My friend, Elaine, if I may put her forward, Sir. She's from Mile End like me and would be perfect for the position.' She recommended.

'You've got this all figured out, haven't you?' he said, tending to his paperwork.

'So, you'll take her on?' she persisted, looking around the office for a final time.

'Well, I can't refuse somebody that you so highly recommend, now can I?' Mr Montgomery smiled. 'May I ask what you intend to do with your life now, Francesca?' he asked, fingers tapping on the desk.

'I've joined the Air Force. I don't want to be a pilot or anything like that. It would scare my mum half to death so I promised her that my feet would remain firmly on the ground,' she said proudly.

'Well I never, good luck with your future, I'm sure it will be quite eventful.' His eyes scanned the surface in front of him. 'Here, take this, it'll help you find your way home,' he said as he gifted her the antique compass. As she accepted it into her grasp, she looked at him thankfully. 'Now go on Amelia Earhart, some of us aren't fortunate enough to have our head in the clouds.'

She pulled on her new uniform. It was not what she was used to with a muted blue blazer, skirt and matching cap. Anxiously peering at her brother's portrait, she tucked the intricate gold locket under her blouse. Her hair was in a tight bun and her stomach was in nervous knots. She grabbed hold of her large bag as she bundled down the staircase, leading her to meet eyes with her apprehensive mother. Vera sat, grinning in her armchair as Houdini squawked.

'Now, you be careful, write to me every day,' her mother said, planting a kiss on her cheek.

'Of course. I expect letters from both of you too,' Francesca said as she hugged her grandmother.

'You'll have the time of your life. Now go before you're

late!' Vera exclaimed, her face beaming with pride.

'I'll see you both when I get back.' With a final glance, she left the house.

A dark green bus pulled alongside the pavement. She waited giddily as the driver checked her papers, then let her aboard.

1966

THE SHIFT

A FEW HUNDRED people had lined the streets in anticipation of the pageant. There was a tremendous procession that consisted of dancers wearing brightly coloured outfits. Feathers, diamantes and organza sparkled under the glow of the late-summer sun. Francesca walked along the road, her plain blue uniform an underwhelming comparison to the flamboyant performers. Live singers sang along to the beat of the steel drums, the noise lifting high into the air. The crowds clapped along, wide smiles covering their faces.

Francesca stopped, taking it all in. It reminded her of the first time Elaine dragged her to a dance hall; the rhythm causing goosebumps to form upon both of her arms. She thought of her best friend. They had taken different paths in life, yet always found their way back to each other. Elaine had made quite a name for herself in the finance industry to the point of gaining Mr Montgomery's position after he retired. Francesca had popped in a few times to drop off the occasional Cadbury bar. Nobody was too important for chocolate.

The sun beat down upon her.

As Charley approached, he gave her a tremendous hug, creasing her uniform. 'Your grandmother would be so proud of you,' he said. This was the first time he had seen her in years. Francesca ran a hand across her chest, feeling the delicate gold locket. She opened it, smiling as she met the glances of her brother and grandmother.

'I've missed you, Charley,' she said, looking up at him.

'I've missed you too, kid.'

Catching sight of a few familiar faces, she couldn't help but smile. She recognised Colin dancing with his little girl while Susan clapped along. In a past letter to her, Susan had revealed their daughter's name, Robin. And so little Robin danced with her parents. They'd split their time between Dumfries and London, making sure their daughter experienced the East End just as they had when they were younger.

Francesca continued along the pavement, navigating her way around the crowds of people. Out of the corner of her eye, she spotted Jack who sat with Isla perched on his lap. With the crucifix around his neck and a lemonade in his grasp, it seemed that he had turned a page. Meeting her glance, he toasted in her direction with the half-empty cup.

Nearby, Harry swung Charlotte around in his arms. Their expressions were no different from that of their wedding day. Charlotte became a nurse not long after Francesca left for the first time and worked closely with Jackie who had later acquired the position of Matron, allowing her more power and a better wage. Francesca would often visit them when she returned home, bringing with her one of her mother's homemade cakes. They'd sit for a while and drink tea, putting the world to rights. She recognised Jackie through the crowd. She was dancing with Curtis and had a colourful set of feathers placed in her long hair. The curls swept past her shoulders as she moved with the music. They both stopped, waving at the procession.

Francesca turned to meet the floats and was shocked to see Ricky performing on top of one. She knew he had taken to learning the guitar, Albie had encouraged him to do it many years ago, but she never realised how good he had got. His expression was cheerful and the people waved and clapped as he played.

She thought of Albie, how he'd love to see the pageant with its eye-catching patterns and vibrant costumes. He had left for Paris a year after she joined the military and found success in displaying his works of art. He called them abstract innovations, that made her chuckle. She couldn't bear to think what he'd have to say about her bland blue skirt and blazer, but at least it was better than trousers, she cringed at the thought. Kerry could always pull them off, Francesca much preferred a circle skirt and a cardigan. Her androgynous friend was now a tailor based down Savile Row, of course, this was a result of Wilma's encouragement. Wilma sourced the materials from the Ladies' Market, a place Kerry took her to often when they first got together. Now they lived happily in a flat near Morpeth Street. They were the most unlikely pair, but as Francesca remembered someone told her a long time ago, opposites attract.

Watching, she grinned as London appeared on full display. The pageant distracted from the few ruins that remained within the area, and the children ran alongside the performers, eager to take part, waving ribbons in the air. Feeling a presence that was all too familiar, she looked at the man at her side.

'Hello treacle, long time no see.' Oliver smiled.

ABOUT THE AUTHOR

E.J. Burgess is a social and criminal historian from Essex, England.

Her expertise lies in exploring organised crime and gang culture in the late-nineteenth and twentieth century. Specifically, she focuses on the areas that her family originate from in the East End of London. Growing up with familial stories, she was inspired to write after hearing tales of their bravery, resilience and humour in times of adversity, significantly influencing her characters. She is currently completing her History PhD after gaining a Master of Research and a Bachelor's Degree in that field. 'The Youth of Our Time' is E.J. Burgess's debut novel.

Printed in Great Britain
by Amazon

12011650R00246